Christopher O...

THE HERB

a novel by

Christopher Olson

Roberta,
Thank you for your interest!
Enjoy the book!
Chris
1/03

ISBN: 1-4033-2992-3 (e-book)
ISBN: 1-4033-2993-1 (Paperback)
ISBN: 1-4033-2994-X (Dustjacket)
ISBN: 1-4033-2995-8 (RocketBook)

Library of Congress Control Number: 2002105732

This book is printed on acid free paper.

Printed in the United States of America
Bloomington, IN

1stBooks - rev. 10/22/02

Acknowledgments

Most American medical schools would not allow a medical student to earn credit by writing a fictional novel. But fortunately, the faculty and administration at the University of Connecticut School of Medicine shared my excitement and vision for this manuscript. Their wholehearted support helped to make *The Herb* a reality, and for that I am sincerely grateful. To everyone at UConn who generously read the story and gave me feedback, I thank you. In particular, I give special thanks to an advisor, mentor, and friend, Dr. Tony Voytovich. I also give special thanks to Ms. Judy Lewis.

To all others who reviewed this novel, and to those who advised me on matters such as immigration law and Chinese culture, I thank you. You have made this story a better one.

My biggest supporters, however, have been my family. Thank you to Mom, Dad, Jon, Cindy, Ron, and Shiral for your unwavering enthusiasm for *The Herb*. Ron, thanks for suggesting the title! And to my wife and best friend, Shiron: whenever I questioned or doubted my work, you strongly defended it and recharged my commitment to the novel. Without your love and support, *The Herb* would not have been completed. Thank you.

For Shiron

Prologue:

In the Mongolian Empire, c. 1219

A wave of warriors' cries pierced the cold night air as thunderous hoofbeats rocked the snowy ground. Brilliant orange flames danced from the men's torches, painting a fiery sky in this midnight hour. Two hundred black horses, clad in protective leather and metal, charged forward like a sea of iron locomotives. Seated on each horse was a creature of mammoth size, strength, and stature; these mighty Mongolian warriors easily commanded their reins in one hand while wielding their torches in the other.

Trailing the warriors, about three hundred yards behind, were two black-robed figures on white, decorated horses. They silently rode, side by side, with their eyes fixed on their men.

As they neared their destination, the larger of the robed men grunted. "I still do not understand the meaning of this. Burning villages of the unfaithful I can understand. Burning fortresses of our enemies I can understand. But burning an open field? Especially a field that we have already conquered! It is a waste of..."

"Enough!" The command was sharp and powerful. Its speaker was inconspicuously different from all of the men in his company. He was thin—almost emaciated—and wore a long gray beard that extended to his torso. His weathered face showed deep wrinkles in a leathery tan complexion. He turned to his young companion. "Genghis Khan trusts me on this venture, General. Should I inform him that your wisdom suggests he is wrong?"

"No, no, sir! I...I just mean to say..."

"Then silence! We are almost upon it."

General Lo Hachai swallowed hard. He should know better than to question the wisdom of Yeh-lu Chu-tsai, the most trusted advisor and shaman of Lord Genghis Khan. Besides Chu-tsai's unparalleled powers in healing with oils and herbs, he could navigate the stars with supernatural accuracy, and he could read the future from sacred sheep bones. This magician was a gift to the Mongols from Koeke Moengke Tengre, the almighty Eternal Blue Heaven. Lo Hachai should know, he realized, to dare not upset or question the great mystic.

The group traveled on. Before long, in the firelight, Chu-tsai saw the faint outline of a forest ahead of the warriors.

"Let's go." Chu-tsai swiftly jerked his horse's rein, and the beast retorted with an angry neigh before galloping forward.

With the general at his side, the shaman pressed towards the large body of warriors. When he was almost upon them, he shouted to Lo Hachai, "Tell them to halt!"

With a fierce grimace, the general kicked his heels into his horse's sides, and charged out to the side. His powerful steed encircled the group within several seconds.

"Halt!" he cried, raising his right arm to demand attention.

The members of the well-oiled military machine abruptly stopped their steeds and closed their mouths. Within a moment, the only sound in the open plain was the wild crackling of two hundred fiery torches. With Lo Hachai facing the warriors from the north, Chu-tsai quietly rounded them from the south. He joined the general's side.

Chu-tsai studied the faces of the battle-hardened men as they glowed in the flickering firelight. Matted dark hair covered full, sharply defined faces. In their dark, hungry eyes, the shaman saw strength and righteousness; but upon looking more closely, he also spotted fear and obedience. Amazing, he thought, what Genghis Khan had done with this army!

"Warriors," began Chu-tsai, "you will soon be upon a thick forest. Shortly into those woods, you will come to a wide but shallow river. Cross it. On the other side, there will be a large circular clearing in the forest. That clearing is the target, men. Set it ablaze, and then retreat to this side of the river. We will then return to camp."

A low rumbling overtook the crowd. The mission was to set a field into flames? Where was the honor in that?! But with a quick raising of the general's fist, silence again encompassed the crowd.

Chu-tsai and Lo Hachai moved to the side of the group. The shaman then nodded slightly.

"Now!" yelled the general, and with a deep roar, joined his men in the charge. Battlecries again pierced the night air, and the group plunged towards the forest.

Chu-tsai quietly watched them go. He saw the army of orange light rage forward into the blackness. Their cries gradually softened from where the shaman waited.

As they vanished into the black forest, Chu-tsai closed his eyes. He silently reflected upon the slaying of eighty Mongolian warriors that Genghis had ordered days ago. The warriors had become possessed by demons, according to the great leader. Indeed, the men had acted strangely, deliberately disobeying clear commands and dishonoring the Mongol nation. But Chu-tsai knew that a deeper source was behind those demons. The men, it had been reported, had been smoking a peculiar plant days before their execution. The plant had been described to Chu-tsai as short and stubby with many exotic purple flowers, shaped like six-pronged stars. The shaman had instantly recognized the description of the evil Devil Flower, and had sought out to find its source. After days of searching, he had come upon the forest clearing this morning; it was not far from camp. Around the perimeter of the open clearing, in the shade of the nearby forest trees, grew hundreds of thousands of Devil Flowers. He had found his target, and he had instantly known that each plant had to be destroyed.

The Devil Flower, according to shaman legend, was a life form that contained the souls of countless immortal devils. Legend claimed that fallen angels had planted these flowers to fool the unwary healer who carelessly chose his medicines from nature's array of healing agents. When a man ingested the flower, it was said, the demons flowed into his body and overtook his mind and his spirit. The victim then became a new person—a dark, immoral, evil person. Supposedly, all Devil Flowers had been destroyed in ages past; Chu-tsai now knew that that was untrue.

He opened his eyes to the sounds of hoofbeats and shouting men. Lo Hachai and the warriors were now returning towards him. Chu-tsai gazed upwards, and saw a fiery smoke rise above the treeline. Looking into the forest itself, the shaman could see blazing branches and flames littering the ground. Within moments, the entire forest lit up.

"Sir!" Lo Hachai galloped towards him.

"You only needed to set the clearing ablaze, not the entire forest!" snorted the shaman.

"I cannot blame my men for being aggressive and thorough," remarked the general.

Chu-tsai jerked the reins, and wheeled the horse around. With Lo Hachai at his side, the burning forest behind them, and the warriors all around them, they headed back to camp.

PART ONE

Curious Symptoms

1

Erin Malloy nervously stood before the closed door, holding a pen in one hand and a manila folder in the other. She swallowed hard, and then peered down at the folder. "Camitelli, Helen" read the label. Erin flipped open the cover, and stared at the first page of Ms. Camitelli's medical chart. She bit her lip; how amazing was this! She was about to visit her first real patient of medical school. She gently rebuked herself: Focus, Erin! This isn't the time to gloat. With a sweaty palm, she flipped through the pages of the chart, noting various progress notes and medication lists. There was so much information here! Well, she didn't have time to digest it all now; she might as well dive in head first and meet this patient.

Erin closed the chart. She placed her pen into the front pocket of her new, glistening white medical coat. Of course, this was a student coat; the length ended at the waist, to differentiate medical students from physicians. Erin liked the symbolic distinction; the long coat was something to strive for; it was the goal of the long journey ahead of her.

She nervously brushed back her short red locks, adjusted her glasses, and knocked on the door.

"Come in!"

"Ms. Camitelli?" she sheepishly asked as she entered the room.

"Oh, yes, that's me dear."

Erin put on her wide, toothy grin. Seated before her was a beaming elderly woman with a grandmother's smile. Her white curly hair was cropped short, her thick, blue-rimmed bifocals were taped in the middle, and her pink floral polyester shirt tightly covered an undeniably obese torso.

"My name is Erin Malloy; I'm a first year medical student from the University of Connecticut School of Medicine."

"Oh, I know. Jackie asked me if you could be here. And I said of course, of course dear!"

Erin smiled again. Jackie was...the blond nurse or the brunette nurse? She had just met them both thirty minutes ago; one would think she'd remember their names!

Erin took a seat on the stool at the physician's desk. Wow. She felt so…official!

"So, Ms. Camitelli…"

"*Mrs.* Camitelli, dear," the gentle woman corrected with a smile. "Guiseppe has been gone for sixteen years, but he's still my loving husband."

"Oh, I'm sorry. Well, Mrs. Camitelli, Jackie told you why I'm here?"

"Well, she said that you're a student. Are you studying to be a nurse, dear?"

"Uh, no. Actually, I'm a medical student. So I'm learning to be a doctor."

The elder's eyes lit up. "A *doctor*! Oh, goodness, dear. Good for you! A woman doctor, just like Dr. Evans, eh?"

Erin flushed. Dr. Jade Evans, whom she had only fleetingly met ten minutes ago, would be her preceptor for the next three years. And yes, she was a 'woman doctor'!

"Where do you go to school, dear?"

"At UConn School of Medicine, over in Farmington."

"Oh," she cried. "My grandson Albert is at UConn, too! You must know him. He's studying English, I think."

Erin glanced at her watch. Okay, time to start the business soon. "Well, actually if he's studying English, he's probably in college. I'm in medical school, which is a four-year school *after* college."

"Ohhh." She winced. "So did you go to college?"

"Uh, yes, Mrs. Camitelli. I went to Brown."

Erin swallowed hard again. Dr. Evans had asked her to meet this patient, learn why she's here, and then come out and get her. That should take about four or five minutes. She needed to get going!

"So then," began Erin. "What brings you here today?"

"I come to see Dr. Evans every three months."

"I see." That didn't really help much. "So why do you see her every three months?"

"Oh, you know, the regular stuff." She shifted in her seat. "You are so young to be a doctor, dear! I just can't get over it! You know, my neighbor's grandnephew became a doctor. He works in a pharmacy now. Handsome boy, that Douglas is."

Great. "Well, Mrs. Camitelli, what exactly is 'the regular stuff'? What kinds of health problems do you have?"

"You know." She shook her head, almost in annoyance. "The heart, the knees. The regular stuff."

Erin felt her heart start to pound faster.

"Yes, that Douglas is the pride of my neighbor's family. He's still unmarried dear." Her eyes twinkled at Erin.

Erin was not amused. "So," she said politely. "Does anything bother you today?"

"Oh yes!"

Good! What? Erin nodded for her to go on. She retrieved a pen and notepad from her coat pocket. Clicking on the pen, she prepared to scribble down some notes.

"The milk that I just bought five days ago was sour this morning! So I look at the date on the milk. Sure enough; expired three days ago! Tell me, Erica, why would a store carry milk that's gonna go bad in just a few days!"

"Mrs. Camitelli…"

"A full gallon, too!" She sighed in frustration. "And you know what really got me, dear?"

No, and I don't care, lady! You're going to make me look bad on my first day here!

"No, Mrs. Camitelli. What really got you?"

"What really got me," she paused. She began to lose her train of thought, but instantly recovered it. "What *really* got me was that the same thing happened last year at the same store!"

"Mrs. Camitelli…"

"And oooohhhhh did I complain!"

There was no stopping her now. Erin dropped her pen, plopped her elbow on the desk, and rested her chin in her sweaty palm. Damn it.

Damn it. Damn it. Damn it.

The elderly woman went on to bark about the rudeness of the store manager on that blustery winter day last year. Erin checked her watch. Fifteen minutes had already passed.

Just then, the door swung open. A woman in a long, worn white coat stepped into the room. Her sandy blond hair was thrown back into a bun; a smooth complexion covered her sharply defined facial features.

She smiled warmly. "Hi, Helen."

The older woman's eyes lit up, and her babbling instantly ceased. "Oh hello, Doctor. How are you today?"

"I'm doing great, thank you."

Erin awkwardly shuffled up from the stool, and moved to an open chair alongside an adjacent wall.

"Thanks, Erin," said her preceptor as she took the stool. "So, what is Mrs. Camitelli here for today?"

"Well," the student began. Her cheeks began to redden. "She's here for the regular stuff. You know: heart, knees." Her entire face became lobster-red.

"Ah. I see." Her preceptor winked at Erin and grinned knowingly. "Good job."

"You have such a darling helper, Doctor. She wants to be a woman doctor, just like you. We were talking about some milk I bought that went bad this morning. I couldn't believe it. I bought it…"

"So what can I do for you today, Helen?" The tone was gentle but strong.

"Oh, it's my regular check-up. You know, every three months I see you, just for a check-up. Last time was May. Yep, it was raining that day…"

"Is that right? Tell me, Helen. Any new problems?"

"Who, me? Oh, no…"

"Any chest pain?"

"Not in the last ten years."

"Shortness of breath?"

"Ah, no…"

"Swollen legs or ankles?"

"Um..." she had to think about that one. "Sometimes in the evening, Doctor, I do notice my ankles getting more puffy."

"Are you taking your diuretic?"

"My what?"

"Your water pill?"

"Oh, well, I ran out of it the other day..."

"The other day, Helen?" Her voice was now firm; the smile was gone. "When did you run out of the water pill, Helen?"

The older woman glanced at Erin and grinned like a mischievous schoolgirl. The student swallowed and fixed her eyes on Jade.

"Helen, you need that water pill. Fluid is pooling in your legs, mainly due to your weak heart. As you know, it can also start pooling in your lungs. This is not a laughing matter." Her face was stern, her voice unshaken.

Erin stared at her preceptor. Dr. Evans couldn't be older than her mid-thirties, and yet she commanded a strong, solid presence that betrayed her warm and gentle appearance. The younger woman admired her lean physique and pretty features. She decided that her assignment to Dr. Jade Evans was indeed fortunate; she already seemed to be a terrific role model.

The older woman sighed. She looked down, and her lip began to twitch. "I know, Doctor." Her voice began to break. "But, honestly, I'm having trouble affording those pills."

Oh, you poor thing! thought Erin. Her heart sank as she watched the elderly woman.

"Are you still taking herbal supplements?" Jade's voice remained stern, and was completely unsympathetic.

"Well..." She paused.

"Helen. Which ones?"

"Oh, you know. The common ones. Ginkgo. Ginseng. St. John's Wort."

"Uh-huh. What else?"

"Well, there's hawthorn..."

"Berry, leaf, or flower?"

Helen looked at her quizzically. "Berry, leaf, or flower? How should I know?"

Jade sighed. "What else, Helen?"

"Black cohash."

"Black cohash! Are you still feeling the symptoms of menopause, Helen?"

"Oh, I just think it's good for me."

"I see. Anything else?"

"No." A pause. "Just ginger. Oh, and a daily multivitamin with extra herbs in it. It's better that way."

Erin sat with her mouth open and eyebrows clenched. What herbs *wasn't* this woman taking?

"Okay," said Jade. "So that's easily a hundred bucks a month. Probably double that. You need to stop *all* those herbs, Helen. Take a simple multivitamin. Buy your furosemide diuretic. And still save yourself over fifty bucks a month."

Helen stared at her doctor in disbelief. "But...but, I need those herbs."

"What you need, Helen, is to get rid of your excessive water. None of those herbs will do that. In fact, none of those herbs are shown to give *any* substantial benefit when scrutinized by good, solid scientific tests. They are an absolute waste of your money. Am I clear?"

The patient shifted her weight and adjusted her bifocals. Nearly pouting, she paused to think about Jade's words. She had been using herbal supplements for over fifteen years; she couldn't just drop them on the spot. True, this wasn't the first time her doctor had admonished her about the issue. Yes, these herbs were expensive. Yes, regular doctors thought they didn't work. But regardless, Helen enjoyed going to her local health food store and buying the herbs. It gave her, in some small way, a bit of control over her own health.

Helen sighed. "Okay, Dr. Evans. You're right. I'll buy the water pill, and I'll stop the herbals." Well, she thought, at least I'll cut down on the herbs.

"Good." Jade cracked a wry smile. "Promise, Helen?"

"Yes, I promise I'll buy the water pill today. But, I think I need a prescription for a refill."

"I'll call it in to your pharmacy."

Erin watched the remainder of the interview. Jade smoothly glided from one focused question to the next. She let the patient speak freely, but also steadily kept her on track. After the essentials had been covered, Jade asked about Helen's two rabbits. She called them each by name. Helen's eyes lit up, and she exploded into an enthusiastic diatribe about her precious furry friends. Jade put down her pen, winked at Erin, and listened.

After two-and-a-half minutes of monologue, Jade interrupted her patient. "Well, glad to hear they're doing so well, Helen. Now, Erin and I need to do a physical exam on you. Why don't you change into this gown, and we'll be back in a few minutes."

The white-coated women exited the room as Helen continued to describe Snowball's new food dish. "Let's head to the office," suggested Jade.

Jade led Erin into a small room with an old wooden desk, a tattered gray carpet, and rows of bookcases and cabinets. Sunlight shined through two open windows, set along adjacent walls. Three towering green plants enlivened the otherwise plain office; the beautiful plants were impressively full and blossoming with life.

Jade took her seat behind the desk, and motioned for Erin to sit on one of two cushioned wooden chairs opposite the desk.

"So," the preceptor smiled. "You've seen your first patient. Congratulations."

Erin cocked her head and squinted her eyes. "Yeah, I guess. I didn't really get that much information out of her, though."

"Well, if I had a choice, your first patient wouldn't have been a nonstop chatterbox like Helen Camitelli. It took me years to learn to effectively dodge tangents and get to the point with some patients. Trust me, Erin, you did well."

The student grinned.

"So, as we were discussing earlier, you're doing a three year apprenticeship with me, correct?"

"Yes. Essentially, I'll be coming here every Tuesday afternoon for the next three years. It's part of UConn Med School's core curriculum; they call it the Student Continuity Practice. This is where I learn lots of the practical, 'hands-on' medicine; you know, things like interviewing and doing physical exams."

Jade nodded. "What an incredible opportunity for you guys. I mean, here you are, just starting medical school, and you're already working with patients. When I was a student, I didn't see a real patient until my third year."

Erin smiled. "When did you graduate, Dr. Evans?"

"I finished med school eight years ago. Then I went to a family medicine residency for three years, and so I've been practicing in this group for five years now."

Jade glanced at her watch. "Not to cut short our discussion, but we have a busy schedule today. Let's do Helen's physical."

The pair left Jade's office, and reentered the patient room. Once Helen was sitting on the examining table, the physician placed her stethoscope diaphragm upon her back. She motioned for Erin to do the same. Together, they listened to breath sounds for a minute, repositioning their stethoscopes with each new breath. They then turned to her heart. Jade closed her eyes and listened carefully, concentrating on the intricate details of those soft beats. Next, Jade showed Erin how to feel for a liver, and then for a spleen. Neither organ was palpable under the large layers of fatty tissue in Helen's belly. Jade then moved to the legs. She told Erin to indent her thumb into Helen's ankles. As the student did so, it felt like she was pressing her thumb into soft clay; she made an imprint in the soft tissue that remained there for several minutes. This was due to excessive water in Helen's legs, explained Jade. The diuretic would clear that up.

The physician used various lights and scopes to examine Helen's eyes, ears, nose, and throat. She felt her neck for swollen lymph nodes, felt for her thyroid gland, and completed a thorough breast exam. She finished by checking her neurological function and her musculoskeletal strength and flexibility.

"Okay, Helen," she declared. "You're doing well, except for the swollen ankles. You promised me you'd pick up that water pill today."

"Yes, Doctor."

"Very well. I'll call it in to your pharmacy. And we'll see you again in three months."

Helen exchanged several more pleasantries with both Jade and Erin. She then left.

Erin followed her preceptor back towards her office. As they passed the waiting room, Erin peered in. Nine or ten people—including children, middle-aged adults, and elders—sat there. They looked bored, or sick, or both.

The remainder of the workday proved to be busy, but fascinating for the student nonetheless. For the most part, she shadowed Jade. She admired her easy transition from the man with the junky cough, to the lady with the recurrent headaches, to the child with a sore throat. There was an unmistakable common thread in all of these encounters: each patient glowed when Dr. Jade Evans entered the room. She had a wonderful way with patients; she was very efficient and oftentimes very firm, but she also laughed with her patients. She always asked about their family, their work, and their hobbies. Her patients liked her.

Yes, thought Erin, she was indeed fortunate to be assigned to Dr. Evans for the next three years.

2

The blue-haired woman repeatedly scanned the shelves before her; it had to be here somewhere! Small glass jars of various herbs and oils darted in and out of her view. How could they not have it? She shifted down the aisle a bit, and continued looking. Maybe they just don't carry…

A-ha! She smiled as she spotted the horehound herb. Hmm; there were several varieties. She grabbed a narrow glass jar with a piece of blue-and-white checkered cloth tied on for a lid. 'Dried Horehound' read the handwritten label; there were no other markings on the jar. She peered back at the shelf and spotted a tincture, or alcohol-based, variety of the remedy. She picked up the narrow bottle, unscrewed the cap, and smelled. A pleasant floral odor filled her nares. Aah; this smelled wonderful! A succus, or pressed juice, and another dried preparation were also options on the shelf. Again, the markings on the jars were minimal; they simply identified the active ingredient to be horehound herb.

"Can I help you, ma'am?"

She turned to see a handsome Asian man smiling at her. His clean-shaven face and neatly cropped black hair gave him a youthful appearance. His smile was large and pleasant, and he looked strong beneath his casual light blue button-down shirt and khakis.

"Well, perhaps," answered the older woman. "I've had a bad cold for a couple of weeks, and I wanted some horehound herb to help me cough up some of that junk."

"Okay," beamed the man. His voice carried a thick accent, but he was easy to understand.

"Problem is," she confessed, "I'm not sure the best one to take. I didn't expect to find all these varieties here. I mean, is the tincture better than the dried herb? Or should I get the succus? And how about the difference between the two dried versions?"

He nodded. "To be perfectly honest, I think the dried version works just as well as the tincture and the succus. For the sake of cost, I would buy the less expensive dried herb; the other one is slightly more concentrated in horehound, but it's not really worth the price."

"Well," she sang, somewhat taken aback. "That's awfully honest of you. I do appreciate that." She leaned closer to him. "I hope the owner doesn't hear you talking like that. I'm sure he or she is out to make a profit!"

A wave of innocence flashed across his face. "No, ma'am. I am the owner of this shop. Believe me, I'm out to be an honest shopkeeper—not to take advantage of folks."

She looked stunned. "Well how about that!" She extended her hand. "Sir, my name is Marla Kerabutski and I'm your newest faithful customer."

He graciously accepted the handshake and beamed. "I am delighted to meet you, Ms. Kerabutski. My name is Yu-lan Tang."

"I just moved here to Manchester, Connecticut. My husband recently passed away…"

"I am so sorry to hear that!" His voice was genuinely empathetic and gentle.

"Oh, thank you, dear. We had lived in Florida, but after Theodore died, I decided I wanted to be near family again. So here I am. Haven't been back in Connecticut for twenty-three years. Believe me, dear, Manchester looks incredibly different. All those big stores and that huge mall!" She shook her head. "I don't care for those big chains. Not at all."

Yu-lan nodded in agreement.

"So, Mr. Tang, how long has this shop been here?"

"Oh," he chuckled. "Natural Essentials is brand new; we've only been here a month."

"You're kidding!" Her eyes lit up. "That's fantastic! Look how bustling this little shop is already!"

Yu-lan peered down the aisle; indeed, four customers were in this aisle alone. "Yes," he admitted. "We've been happy with our success thus far."

"Well, the secret is obvious," she replied. "You give people good, honest service like you gave me, and you're gonna get a good name. And even though Manchester is growing, it's still a small town. Believe me, a good name goes real, real far in a small town."

He bowed slightly. "I certainly appreciate your kind words, Mrs. Kerabutski."

"Don't you mention it. Very well, I'll take this jar of dried horehound. Just a teaspoon a day, I guess..."

"Well, do you have a scale, Mrs. Kerabutski?"

"A scale? No."

"I really do recommend one, ma'am. You don't need more than four-and-a-half grams of pure dried horehound per day. That mixture is fifty percent horehound by weight, so you need nine grams per day. Just using a teaspoon is an awfully inaccurate way to measure, ma'am."

She thought about this, and started nodded thoughtfully. "You're right, Yu-lan. You are right. Boy, you are helpful!" She shook her head in admiration. "Now, where can I get a scale?"

"Well, we sell them, fortunately."

"How convenient!"

"Yes. Let me show you where they are."

Jade Evans finished scribbling down her final notes of the day at 6:45 p.m. The medical student had gone home two hours ago; the nurses and the receptionists had likewise left a while ago. Jade closed the manila patient chart, and clicked her pen shut. She got up, removed her white coat, and exchanged it for her casual lightweight jacket. Jade moved toward the door, and shut off her office lights.

She wondered if the other members of the group practice were still here. She walked down a hallway and turned right. Dr. Walter Bartlett's door was closed and his lights were off. She silently chuckled; Walter's gone home early again? What a shocker! Moving on, she came upon Dr. Betsy McGrath's office. The door was open, but the lights were off. Betsy was probably out of here, too. Finally, she turned another corner and heard the ruffling of papers coming from Dr. John Harper's office. The light from his office spilled out into the hallway.

"Hey John," she said cheerfully at his doorway.

"Oh, what's up Jade?" John Harper was a thin, attractive man with long brown hair pulled back in a ponytail. His round, wire-rimmed glasses made him look more like a 60's classic rocker than the soft-spoken family doctor that he was. John had joined the practice one year before Jade had. Of her three partners, she liked him best.

"Working late?" she asked.

He put down his pen and grinned. "Yeah, just catching up on charts. It was really busy today."

"Yeah, me too." Jade had always admired the man. In fact, when she had first joined the practice, the two began having dinners out together. She had thought—and hoped—that a relationship was on the horizon. However, she quickly learned that John had just been through a very difficult divorce; his wife had been secretly dating her boss. Jade instantly recognized that the last thing John needed was a new romance, at least at that point of his life. Fortunately, they had been good friends ever since. Unfortunately, their relationship had never blossomed into anything more than that.

"You wrapping up soon?" asked Jade.

"Actually, I could be done right now. I think I might finish these charts in the morning."

"Well, if you're interested, I thought I'd head to Chip's. I really don't feel like cooking tonight."

John raised his eyebrows and glanced at his watch. "Hmm. That could be a very good idea. Not for the food, mind you." He smiled. "I need a big glass of cold beer."

"It's on me. I owe you like four of them!"

He shrugged. "I'll save the other three. But one sounds perfect for tonight. Meet you there?"

"You got it."

"Give me five minutes, and I'll be on my way."

"All right."

Jade turned and headed for the front door. She stepped out into a cool September night. The evening sky was beginning to deepen into a twilight blue, and the scent of freshly mowed grass filled the air. She approached her car, a brand new red Saab. The freshly waxed paint glowed under the parking lot's overhead lamp; yeah, this was her new baby. No husband, no boyfriend, no children—not yet, anyway. She didn't know why, but somehow that had justified the purchase of this car.

Jade plopped down behind the wheel, and slowly inched out of her parking space. She slid back the sunroof, and shifted into drive. Yes, she thought, no husband or children. Whether or not she liked to admit it, that had been occupying her mind lately. At thirty-three years old, Jade was by no means old, but she had always pictured herself married by now. It was becoming somewhat frustrating to be a family doctor, but to have no family of her own. Then again, she strongly believed that finding a soulmate couldn't be rushed. In time, she believed, it would happen. It would just be nice if it happened soon.

She saw the neon lights of Chip's just ahead on the right. Chip's was a new grill and bar in Manchester; it had become an instant success in this rapidly growing town. As Hartford continued to enjoy an economic boom, the surrounding suburbs like Manchester were clearly reaping some benefits, and the popularity of this new restaurant was just one example. She pulled into the driveway, and parked away from other cars in a secluded corner space. She got out of the car, and pressed her remote lock & alarm key; the car responded with a cheerful 'chirp-chirp'.

As expected, the inside of Chip's was bustling with action. Classic pop songs blared overhead, and the bar was alive with laughing young adults wielding beer mugs and shot glasses. The restaurant section was busy; people of all ages sat, chatted, and ate juicy burgers with greasy fries.

Before long, John entered the restaurant. He wore his faded brown leather jacket over his neatly pressed shirt and tie. He smiled at Jade.

"It's pretty happening tonight."

"Always is."

"Welcome to Chip's, folks," chimed a bleached blond twenty-something with a plunging neckline and extra tight blue jeans. "Smoking or non?"

"Non." The simultaneous answers were loud and clear—almost obnoxiously so.

"Right this way."

Jade and John were soon sitting at a wide booth. John had ordered his seasonal Sam Adams, and Jade asked for a margarita without the salt. They agreed to share a chicken caesar salad and a couple of appetizers.

"So, anything unusual today?" asked Jade.

"Well, do you know Tyrone Williams?"

"Mmm, I don't think so."

John sighed. "Seventy-one year old guy; past medical history of hypertension, diabetes, high cholesterol. Nicest guy in the world, but he doesn't necessarily live the healthiest lifestyle. Smokes half a pack per day, eats lots of crap, and exercises maybe twice a year."

"Sounds like the model of good health."

"Yeah. Anyway, he comes in with some substernal chest pain, not relieved by Nitro. But it doesn't really sound like angina anyway. It's more of a burning sensation, worse when lying down."

"Sounds like reflux."

"Right. And an EKG was normal; so I figure it's just reflux, and I'm ready to send him on his way. You know, give him some H2-blockers."

"Okay."

"But then, as he's heading for the door, he springs a weird one on me. He says that since the chest pain began three weeks ago, he's had these incredible sexual urges that come in spurts. He gets two or three a day, and he doesn't remember ever having urges this strong."

Jade raised her eyebrows. "Odd."

"Yeah. I guess his wife isn't too thrilled about it, either."

She smirked. "Yeah. Three times a day would be a lot for me, too."

"Anyway. I've never heard of that before."

Jade shook her head. "That's a tough one, John. How about ordering a testosterone level?"

He cringed. "Why would he suddenly develop high testosterone levels? His physical last month revealed no testicular masses, and he has no other signs or symptoms of endocrine dysfunction. Besides, does high testosterone make you *that* excited?"

"Couldn't tell ya. Any new meds?"

"Nope. I thought of that one. Also no major life-changing events lately. So I didn't know what to do."

"What did you do?"

"Sent him on his way with the H2-blockers. I said if it doesn't improve in a week or so, call me. In that case, I'll probably put him back on a beta blocker. I might also try methyldopa."

"Both should decrease libido."

"Yeah."

"Poor wife in the meantime."

"I know."

They shook their heads, but they couldn't suppress small smirks. Both doctors grabbed their drinks, and took a couple big gulps.

An overly-cheerful waitress served their appetizers and salad. The pair munched on stuffed mushroom caps, chicken strips, and a chicken caesar salad. They turned their focus of conversation to college football, and then chatted about national politics for some time. At 9:00, they agreed to call it a night.

Jade drove home along winding back roads; she reached her house in about six minutes. Even now, after five years, she loved the sight of her red Colonial. With the stone wall in front and the tall maple trees encircling the property, her home radiated historic New England. Others had told her it was too big for one person, but she didn't care. She liked it.

After shutting her garage door, Jade walked up the cobblestone walkway. She cautiously opened her oak front door, expecting a certain furball to try to zip outside while it was ajar. Sure enough…

"No you don't, Nora." She gently nudged her Birman cat back inside with her foot. She closed the door. Nora poked her nose along the side of the closed entryway. Humph! Foiled again.

Jade picked up her furry white friend, and kissed her charcoal nose. "Have you been a good kitty today?" She carried her to the spacious kitchen, and set her down. After tossing a few cat treats her way, Jade retreated to her bedroom. No phone messages. She stretched out her arms, and yawned. Tomorrow would be another early day; it was time to get ready for bed.

3

"Is that all?" Yu-lan Tang asked the stocky, gray-bearded man.

"I think that should do it."

As Yu-lan rang up the St. John's Wort, the man spotted a colorful display next to the cash register. 'Quazhen: For Balance, Energy, and Harmony' read a handwritten cardboard sign. In front of the sign, two or three dozen brown glass jars were neatly aligned. The small cylindrical jars had purple and green cloth covers; they were less than two inches tall. A handwritten label simply read 'Quazhen'.

"Quazhen?" barked the man. "Never heard of it."

"I'm not surprised," smiled Yu-lan. "It is brand new, and you can only get it here. It is a family secret, you see."

The man snorted. "A family secret? What the hell is it?"

"It is an herb from my homeland in China. Quazhen is very, very scarce. In fact, I do not think it grows anywhere but on my grandmother's plantation. But my family has used it for generations."

The man looked skeptical.

"This special dried herb," continued Yu-lan, "gives one a renewed sense of energy. It also soothes one from the stresses of daily life. Essentially, it's a wonderfully potent tonic."

The man looked at the jars. He then looked up at Yu-lan. Back at the jars. Then, "A wonderfully potent tonic?" He huffed. "Sounds like bullshit to me. How much for the St. John's Wort?"

Yu-lan swallowed and flattened his expression. "Thirteen ninety-two."

"Fourteen bucks," grumbled the man under his breath. "Here."

They completed the transaction, and he left. Yu-lan began wiping the counter with a dry cloth.

"Asshole," said a deep voice.

Yu-lan quickly looked up. An Asian man with sharp facial features and an angry scowl was standing beside him; he was glaring at the store door. The man wore a tight white tee-shirt that displayed his well-sculpted chest; his arms boasted bulging muscles, and his hands were squeezed into fists.

Yu-lan sighed at the sight of his brother. "You scared me. I didn't even see you there."

"What an idiot," the other man grumbled, ignoring the comment. "I should go out and kick his ass."

Yu-lan shrugged. "Whatever. Quazhen's not for everybody, you know?"

His brother was unmoved. "Calling Grandma's herb bullshit. *He's* full of..."

"All right, man," Yu-lan said firmly. "Don't worry about it, Feng. It's one guy, you know?"

Feng slowly turned his gaze to his brother. He stared at him for a moment with heavy black eyes. Then, "Have some respect," he snorted sharply.

Yu-lan picked up his cloth and continued wiping the countertop.

"By the way," Feng growled. "We're running a little low on the Quazhen, don't you think?"

"No," was the defiant response. "We've got three huge boxes in the back. I don't think we're running low at all." He continued to wipe the counter.

"We're running low," he slowly repeated, enunciating each syllable.

Yu-lan threw down his cloth, and turned to face his brother. "C'mon, Feng. We have plenty of the stuff to last us awhile. I'm not going to write to Grandma for more. I just won't do it."

The brothers glared at each other.

"Now," continued Yu-lan, "maybe if someone continues to provide all those big corporations with free samples of the stuff, then yeah, we'll probably run low soon. But since I promised Grandma that selling Quazhen would remain a family business, I don't see why either one of us should be wasting samples on corporate big-whigs. Okay?"

Feng glared at his brother and twisted his lip. He shook his head in disgust. A cold silence hung in the air as Yu-lan reflected the hard stare.

The store door suddenly opened.

"Oh, hello Yu-lan Tang!" sang a chipper voice.

He quickly brightened his face and smiled. "Hi, Mrs. Kerabutski."

The blue-haired woman approached the counter. "I forgot to get echinacea yesterday. Don't know how I forgot..."

She abruptly paused, staring at Feng. "Well, how about that?" She smiled widely. "You two *must* be brothers, right?"

"Yes, ma'am," beamed Feng politely. He extended his hand. "My name is Feng Hou Tang. A friend of my twin brother is a friend of mine."

"Oh," she blushed. "How do you do, Mr. Tang? I am Marla Kerabutski. Twins, eh? I thought so. Yu-lan has shorter hair, obviously, but otherwise you two look absolutely identical!"

Feng chuckled warmly. "Yes, Marla. That's why I wear longer hair. Otherwise, I think we'd have trouble telling ourselves apart!"

She laughed, delighted at the innocent humor. Then, "Now, you've been in America for only a month, too, Feng Hou?"

"Actually," replied Feng, "this *shop's* only been here for a month, but my brother and I have been in America for several months now."

"Boy," she smiled, shaking her head in pleasant surprise. "You two speak impeccable English for being such recent immigrants."

"Well," explained Yu-lan, "we both spent two years in Oregon as high school exchange students. At that age, you can become fluent pretty quickly."

Marla's eyes lit up. "How wonderful!"

"After two years with American teenagers," added Feng, "you do learn correct English grammar, but you unfortunately learn a good deal of slang, too." He smiled warmly. "Ain't it a shame?"

She laughed, but moments later, she became more pensive. "I would think it must be difficult for Chinese students to come to America."

"Actually, no," said Feng. "China rivals Japan as the largest source of foreign exchange students in the U. S." He pleasantly embarked on a diatribe about the ins-and-outs of obtaining student visas from China.

"So," interjected Yu-lan, growing sickened by his brother's obnoxiously charismatic front, "can I get you that echinacea?"

"Yes, please."

Yu-lan escaped around the counter as his brother continued to charm the older woman. He headed to the rightmost aisle, to retrieve her echinacea.

His palms were still sweaty and his temples were still throbbing from the confrontation with Feng. These petty confrontations were happening much too frequently lately. Yu-lan knew that he had every right to kick his brother out of the store, out of the business, and out of his life. When he left China to come to America nine months ago, Yu-lan had never expected that his twin would follow him here. Yu-lan had come to New England to begin his life as an herbalist. He knew that Americans' interest in herbal medicine was exploding, and he believed that he could build a decent savings by opening this shop. He intended to return to China after five or six years here; this stint was simply to have some fun and make some money.

Of course, his H-1B non-immigrant visa would only allow for six years maximum in the U. S.; so even if he wanted to stay longer, he really couldn't. As it was, he was tremendously fortunate that he had the visa. His former exchange student host, Mr. Cameron Steele, had helped him obtain it. Steele, a top executive in a West Coast biotechnology firm, had petitioned the U. S. Immigration and Naturalization Service on Yu-lan's behalf. He had stated that Yu-lan had exceptional talent in the specialty field of herbal medicine, and that America would be lucky to have his services for a few years. Though it was unbeknownst to Yu-lan, Steele was a frequent contributor to various national political campaigns; he had many tight connections in Washington, D. C. It was no surprise, then, when his petition was immediately granted. Yu-lan was issued the visa. To make matters even better, Steele arranged for Yu-lan to receive a discounted rent on a small shop in Manchester, Connecticut; Steele's brother-in-law happened to own and lease several of those Manchester shops.

All Steele wanted in return for all these services was a few boxes of joherbi, a rare Chinese herb that was a cousin of yohimbe. Joherbi was hailed by many herbalists as the most powerful enhancer of sexual energy available; one could only find it in China.

Yu-lan was especially grateful for the opportunity to work in America as an herbalist, primarily because his parents had always talked about coming to America for this same reason. That dream was never realized, however, with their tragic fate three years ago; a fatal car crash had taken both of their lives. After that horrible event, Yu-lan had become much closer to his paternal grandmother, Lu Mian. She had taught him much about herbalism and Chinese medicine, and it was then that she had introduced him to Quazhen.

Quazhen was a peculiar plant; it was short and stubby, and its purple flowers each had six sharp pointed edges that fanned away from the central stalk. It had been named, according to Lu Mian, by an ancient Tang ancestor, and it was only known to grow on the property of the Tang family. The plant's flowers, she had told Yu-lan, contained a powerful medicine that heightened one's energy and soothed one's worries. She said that it had been a family tonic for centuries, but she didn't know why it had been kept a family secret. Lu Mian believed that nature's beautiful Quazhen should be enjoyed by all men and women; it was not meant for one family.

Yu-lan had tried the herb for several months. He had felt slightly more alert, but a bothersome dizziness had accompanied that alertness. He had therefore stopped using it, assuming that he was unusually sensitive to the herb. But his grandmother swore by Quazhen, and he therefore never questioned its efficacy in most people.

Given his grandmother's unselfish attitude towards the herb, it was no major surprise that she suggested he take some to America. She knew he was opening the shop, and she encouraged him to sell it there. She offered to continue shipping as many boxes of Quazhen as he needed, should it become popular.

And so there it was. Yu-lan was coming to America for several years to work as an herbalist and to make some money. He had many catalogs from which he could order a good stock of products, and he had the special Quazhen from his grandmother. He insisted that he would send her some of his profits, and though she adamantly refused, he still intended to do so.

Enter Feng Hou Tang. Feng had abandoned his parents and twin brother twelve years ago, at age seventeen. He and Yu-lan had returned home to China from their American student exchange only six months earlier. Almost immediately upon returning to China, Feng had entered into a life of drugs and crime. Besides robbing homes (including his parents), he privately admitted to murdering "several" people for "personal reasons". Within a year, his father had declared him banished from the family, citing repeated dishonor for which he'd never be forgiven. His parents would have turned him in to the authorities, but they knew they would not be able to bear the shame that would come upon the Tang family. Also, as his grandmother noted, one would not know where to start looking for the wicked son. It was believed that he had fled China shortly after reentering it.

It was a surprise, then, when Feng came to Yu-lan in China eighteen months ago. The twin was looking for money. He had sworn that he was drug-free, and he wanted to begin a new life. At first, Yu-lan angrily dismissed him. He berated his twin for missing their parents' funeral, and for leaving the family in dishonor. But as weeks drew on, Feng was persistent; he repeatedly apologized and asked for forgiveness. Lu Mian, upon hearing of Feng's return, insisted that Yu-lan report him to authorities. She threatened to do so herself if he did not act.

Perhaps it was their brotherly bond, however, that caused Yu-lan to cave in. After countless sleepless nights, he ultimately embraced his twin brother, and agreed to help him financially. Before long, however, Feng learned of Yu-lan's plan to go to America. He begged his brother to let him go with him. He wanted to run the shop with his brother. How grand it would be, Feng said, to live in America together as brothers! Yu-lan openly and strongly opposed the idea. This was *his* dream; it would be *his* business. He expressed his disapproval of his twin in no uncertain terms; he had given him some money; that would be enough. Aware of his tenuous status among family members, Feng backed down. He thanked his brother for the money, and then retreated into hiding.

It was an unpleasant surprise, then, for Yu-lan to find his twin brother at his doorstep four months ago. Feng had come to Connecticut, had rented an apartment several blocks down the road, and was now looking for work. Initially, Yu-lan angrily refused to help him; he was outraged that his brother followed him here. He was also furious to learn *how* Feng got here. Apparently, an American "friend" from his exchange student days had arranged for Feng to be boated to Australia. From there, flawlessly counterfeited documents had given Feng an easy pathway into America. This "friend", Yu-lan understood, had been handsomely rewarded with both cash and illicit drugs.

For several weeks, Yu-lan angrily threatened to turn Feng into American authorities. Over subsequent weeks, however, Yu-lan found himself hearing his brother's desperate pleas, and listening to his endless promises about finally abandoning his life of crime. Then, two months after Feng appeared on his twin's doorstep, Yu-lan reluctantly agreed to let him work at the shop until he found a permanent job.

That was over eight weeks ago, and Feng still hadn't begun looking for a job.

Though Yu-lan regularly corresponded to his grandmother with lengthy letters, he did not tell her that Feng was with him in America. After all, it would be disgraceful to host someone who had dishonored their family. Granted, he was his brother. But to Lu Mian, that simply wouldn't matter. She would probably exile Yu-lan for taking in his brother. And so Yu-lan kept him a secret; at least for the time being.

The store owner carried a small jar of echinacea back to the counter. "Here you are, Mrs. Kerabutski."

"Perfect. I've been chatting with your brother, here. You two are so similar! Such nice young men!"

Yu-lan forced himself to crack a smile. "Thanks. So, anything else today?"

"No, dear...oh, what's this?" Marla picked up a small brown jar of Quazhen. "For balance, energy, and harmony?"

"Ah, yes, Marla," replied Feng proudly. "That wonderful tonic has been a family secret for centuries. Only now is it available to the world."

Her face brightened in delight. "How wonderful! I'll take two!"

Yu-lan smiled. "Perhaps you should start with one, and if you like it, then come back for more? Each jar is thirty dollars, Mrs. Kerabutski. It's a rather expensive product."

Feng chuckled openly. "Oh, my good brother," he said good naturedly, and patted him hard on the back. "Always the cost-conscious businessman. I personally think that buying two jars is a very wise choice, Marla."

"Yes?" she asked.

"Oh yes, ma'am," Feng replied, now more seriously. "We have a very short supply of this wonderful family gem. I would hate for you to come back for more, only to find that we've run out of it."

"Yes, that does make sense," she admitted.

"And trust me," Feng smiled. "This is the most wonderful herb you've ever taken. I take it regularly, and I can't tell you how much it's improved my energy and inner peace."

"Oh?" Her eyes lit up. "Gosh, will two jars be enough?"

Feng raised his eyebrows and began to shake his head. "Well, now that you mention it, you might…"

"Yes, Mrs. Kerabutski," interjected Yu-lan. "Two should be plenty. We won't run out anytime soon." He hurriedly put the product in a small paper bag. "Now then. Anything else?"

"No thank you, dear. You two are so wonderful!" She continued to beam, completely oblivious to any hostility between the brothers.

Yu-lan rang her up, collected the money, and said good-bye. Feng added several more pleasantries, and walked her to the door.

"Please do come again!" he shouted cheerfully as she left the building.

"Oh, I will!" Her voice trailed off in the light breeze.

Feng turned back and strutted toward the counter. "You stupid ass," he snorted.

His brother ignored him.

"When's that chick getting here?" asked Feng.

Yu-lan shook his head. Jennifer, a lovely woman in her mid-twenties, was 'the chick'. She was one of three cashiers that Yu-lan had hired last month. "Jennifer will be here at noon, Feng."

"All right. I'm going out for some smokes." He turned back towards the door. He opened it, and then looked back. "And do me a favor, will ya? Just write to Grandma and get some more Quazhen. Okay?"

"For the last time, it's *not* okay. Picking the flowers, drying the herb, and shipping it here is not an easy process. It's also borderline illegal."

Feng rolled his eyes.

"I'm telling you," continued Yu-lan, "we have plenty of Quazhen for now. I'm not asking her to send more. Period."

The door slammed. Finally, Yu-lan was alone in the store. He wiped his brow, grabbed the broom, and began sweeping the floor.

"Good morning, Charlie." Jade glanced down at her watch as she entered the exam room. "See, I'm two minutes *early* today."

The gray-bearded man laughed good-naturedly. "Well, I should hope so, Doctor. I'm only your second patient of the day."

She took her seat on the small leather stool. "So, how's the theater going?"

He rolled his eyes. "Some of the students are—how shall I say it?—a bit less experienced this time around. Last spring's production of Macbeth was phenomenal…"

"I know. I saw it."

"But we have several novices for Jekyll & Hyde. Their auditions were superb, but now that we're into the thick of rehearsing, their lack of experience is showing."

She grinned. "Charlie, with you in the director's chair, I'm absolutely certain that the production will be a smashing success. Even with amateurs."

He beamed and brushed back his thick gray hair. "Well, thank you for your kind words, Doctor. But I'm not so sure you're right!"

"So, you're here for a yearly physical."

"That's right."

"Any major changes since last visit?"

He paused to think. Then, "No, not really."

"Okay. No health complaints?"

He grinned. "My hair keeps getting grayer. Is that a valid complaint?"

She smiled. "What are you, fifty now?"

"As of nine days ago," he growled.

"Oh, well happy belated birthday." She briefly flipped through a few pages of his chart. Then, "You've never had any intestinal problems, have you Charlie?"

"Well, some gas now and then. Nothing major."

"Hmm. I don't think you've ever had a flex sig, have you?"

"A flex what?"

"Sorry. A flexible sigmoidoscopy. It's a study in which a long, thin camera is used to examine your rectum and lower intestines."

"Now *that* sounds fun!" he cringed. "No, I think I'd remember that, Doc."

She flipped through one more page, and then looked up at him. "You should have one."

He wrinkled his forehead. "Doctor, I have no intestinal problems. Why on earth would I need a big camera up my behind?"

"They recommend it every five years once you reach age fifty."

"They? Who are *they*?"

"The experts."

Charlie glared at her with his eyebrows raised and his mouth open. He slowly digested this information, and then asked, "Who are these experts?"

"The U. S. Preventive Services Task Force." It easily rolled off her tongue. "They're the folks who put out guidelines about preventive medicine. That includes screening for diseases, giving vaccines, and so on. Flex sigs screen for colorectal cancer."

He still had a skeptical eye on her. "How do they come up with these guidelines?"

Deep down, Jade felt a slight twinge of frustration. The most difficult patients always were doctors, followed by other health care workers, and followed in turn by college professors. These patients almost always wanted to examine the clinical reasoning themselves; they seldom would simply trust their doctor. But, she realized, this was good ol' Charlie, one of the nicest people she knew. That being the case, she instantly extinguished her own fire.

"They come up with these guidelines," she explained, "by scrutinizing lots and lots of studies. Many times, several studies that pertain to one topic have conflicting results. You need sophisticated statistical tools to sort out where the truth lies in such situations. So if five studies on colorectal cancer tell you one thing, and if five different studies on the same subject tell you the exact opposite, you can turn to statistical testing to determine what's right."

"I see," he said enthusiastically. He not only seemed to understand the information, but he appeared to be genuinely interested. Charlie was like that; his thirst for new knowledge was unquenchable. Jade decided to go on.

"Those same statistics," she continued, "can also tell you how strong one piece of information is. So in our colorectal cancer example, maybe the statistics say there are distinct benefits to screening for colorectal cancer at age thirty."

"With flexible sigmoidoscopy, you mean?"

"Yes. But perhaps the benefits are quite small. Perhaps you'll catch one cancer per million at age thirty. Sure, catching even one is nice, but there are certain risks to doing any procedure—even a flex sig. And besides the risks to the patient, the more flex sigs you do, the most likely you are to mistakenly call one positive, when it's actually negative. And *that* can cause more harm than good to everybody involved."

"Okay."

"My point," she went on, "is that statistics can tell you if the benefits of a procedure outweigh the risks. Every decision we make in medicine is really based on a risk-benefit profile."

"Uh-huh." He motioned for her to continue.

"So in the case of screening for colorectal cancer with flexible sigmoidoscopies, statistics have been used to analyze many different research trials. And based on those statistical results, the experts on the Preventive Services Task Force have declared that the benefits of screening people every five years, starting at age fifty, definitely outweigh the risks. The benefits also outweigh the costs, but we can save the cost-benefit discussion for another day."

Charlie curled his lip, and nodded thoughtfully. "So the 'flex sig', as you call it, will detect cancer in my bottom?"

"That's the idea. Now, it's not one hundred percent effective. It could miss the cancer in some people. But generally speaking, it's very, very good."

"Hmm. Well, do we do it today?"

"Oh no. We'd make another appointment for you."

He sighed. "Great. Happy birthday to me. Well, if you think so, Doc, I'll do it."

"Yeah, I do think so."

He smirked. "That statistics stuff is fascinating. If theater hadn't mesmerized me as a college student, I might have gone into mathematics. I really enjoy puzzles and numbers."

"It is neat," she agreed. Jade glanced at her watch. She knew that her next patient had canceled, and so she had a little bit of time to spare. It wasn't everyday that a patient wanted to 'talk shop' with her. She allowed herself to press on. "The whole notion of doing rigorous scientific testing on new medical ideas, and then analyzing those tests with statistics, is called evidence-based medicine. It is *the* sacred tool of modern medicine. If an idea hasn't been rigorously tested and analyzed—if it hasn't been subjected to evidence-based medicine—it is absolutely worthless."

"Really?" He shook his head. "I knew you guys did lots of research on new drugs and all, but I've never heard of 'evidence-based medicine'."

"The term is somewhat new, but the idea is old. It's basically common sense: before we give someone a new medicine, or before we do another lab test, we should know that the medicine will probably work, or that the lab test will give us some useful information."

"Makes sense," he agreed.

"Yeah. See, a major problem in the history of medicine was the relative lack of evidence-based medicine. Doctors would prescribe a drug because they had good experience with it in the past. But, you see, that's really dangerous. Maybe a drug *seemed* to cure a patient, but perhaps it really didn't. Maybe that patient just got better on his own. In such a case, a doctor starts praising a drug that really doesn't do squat!"

"Uh-huh." He started to sound bored.

"But in the era of evidence-based medicine, that doesn't happen. At least, it shouldn't. Before a doc uses a drug, he or she should be checking the literature to find good evidence—that is, good scientific tests and analyses—to show that it works."

His interest was fading. "Interesting."

She sensed his dwindling enthusiasm, and smiled. "Anyway, that's enough about evidence-based medicine for now. So. Where were we?"

The topic changed to Charlie's other biological systems. No chest pain, no shortness of breath, no belly pain, no nausea, vomiting, or diarrhea. No urinary problems, no numbness or tingling, no weakness. Jade continued to survey her patient with direct questions, and then allowed him time to ask her questions. He had none. After discussing various social issues, from his family life to his alcohol consumption, she asked him to put on a gown for the physical exam. Before long, she had completed a thorough physical, and he was on his way. He made an appointment to return for the flexible sigmoidoscopy in four weeks.

Jade's next patient was Gunther Petchov, a forty-year-old elementary school teacher. Jade liked him very much; his hearty laugh and warm smile could lift anybody's spirits.

"Good morning, Gunther," she said cheerfully upon entering his room.

"Hi, Doc." He wasn't smiling today, and he spoke in a low, raspy voice. Must feel pretty lousy, thought Jade. Probably a nasty viral infection, or something similar.

"What's up, my friend?" she called out.

The balding man looked at her with glassy eyes and frowned. "Feel like shit."

She was taken aback, but then smiled. "Gee, you *must* feel awful. I've never heard you curse before. I didn't think third-grade teachers were allowed to say bad words!"

He turned his head and stared into her eyes. His gaze was intense and serious. Then, "Well, I guess you're fuckin' wrong then, ain't you?"

Jade's smile quickly dropped into a confused frown. Something very serious was going on here. Gunther Petchov was a very active member of the local church. He was also the guy who always dressed up as Santa Claus and visited kids in the children's hospital each Christmas. This was a gentle, gentle man; what could possibly account for this odd behavior? Several worst case scenarios raced through Jade's mind. Had a family member died? Did someone get a terminal diagnosis? Did his wife leave him?

"Gunther," she said softly, "what on earth has happened?"

He continued to stare at her. His eyebrows now tightened, and his face twisted into an expression of disgust.

"Gunther," she repeated. "Tell me..."

"Fuck you."

Her heart started to pound. What the hell was going on here?

"My appointment was at 9:30," he spit out fiercely. "It ain't 9:30, Doc."

Jade looked at her watch. 9:32. She opened her mouth to speak.

"Don't give me excuses, lady," continued Petchov. "What is with you people? You just shit on your patients, and that's okay with you?" A deep red hue spread across his sweaty face.

Jade swallowed hard. She returned his glare, and then forced herself to take a slow, deep breath. Something was obviously underlying this. She shouldn't take this personally. Gunther had suffered some kind of severe psychological or emotional stress...

"You can pay me for lost work time, Doctor. You bitch."

Okay. This was a brief psychotic reaction to something. Basically, she reasoned, the guy snapped. Who knows why. Make sure he's not immediately dangerous to himself or others, and get him to the hospital.

"Wanna know why I'm here, Doc?"

She raised an eyebrow. She hadn't expected that question. "Yes," she answered coolly. "I do."

He leaned closer to her. "Cause I can't get it up." His lips twisted into a slight smile, and he placed one hand on his crotch and the other on her shoulder. "Can you help me honey?"

She quickly dropped her pen and stood up. Without a word, she spun around and headed for the door. Her heart raced faster as she placed a hand on the doorknob. Suddenly, a strong hand grabbed her left hip from behind.

In a flash of primal instinct, she screamed, jumped to the side, and swung her right fist through the air. It caught Petchov in the jaw; he appeared stunned for a moment, but then recovered. Enraged, he grabbed her right wrist and pinned her against the door. A lightning bolt ripped down her spine as she saw him turn the button on the doorknob to lock the door. Damn those locks! She had told the other group members that they should remove the locks for safety! She shivered as she realized her worst nightmare was coming true.

"I know you can help me." He pressed himself closer to her. His breath reeked of alcohol.

Jade heard screams on the other side of the door as the nurses Jackie and Beth tugged at the doorknob. She could hear Walter's authoritative voice ring in the background, and John was also yelling and coming to the door.

"Come and help me, honey." He slithered closer.

With buckets of adrenaline shredding through her body, Jade screamed out and jutted up her knee. He howled, and with all her weight, she leaned into him. The man tumbled backward, and before she fell to the ground on him, she whipped her right hand back. She broke his grip, and she maintained her balance as he landed on the cold tiled floor.

In a panicked frenzy, she unlocked the door. It violently swung open, knocking her into the corner of the room. John stormed in, followed by Jackie, Walter, and Beth. John leaped onto the assailant and pinned him down. With a swift motion, he whacked him across the chin, and soon Jackie and Beth each held an arm. Patients flooded in from the waiting room, and excited cries filled the room.

"Step aside folks! Now!" An armed police officer charged into the room, with Elaine the receptionist on his tail. "*You* don't move!" he ordered Petchov, placing one hand on his holstered firearm.

Swiftly, the officer cleared the room of patients, ordered Petchov to stand, and pinned him against a wall. As he placed the metal handcuffs, he pronounced him under arrest and recited his rights.

John embraced Jade, huddled in the corner of the room. She assured him that she was okay. He turned his head towards the other group members and staff. "Why don't you guys clear out for now, too. Let me be with her for a few minutes. She says she's okay."

"Wait," commanded the older partner, Walter. "What the hell happened?" He stormed towards Jade.

"I was attacked," Jade retorted, frustrated and outraged and afraid all at once. She suppressed tears, but bit her lip and buried her head into John's chest. John motioned for Walter to back away. She needed her space.

"Elaine," John called. "Cancel the rest of her appointments for the day. Mine too."

"No, John," Jade began. But the rest of the group immediately overrode her protest, making it unmistakably clear that she was done for the day. Betsy McGrath said she'd see Jade's most important patients; Walter chimed in that he'd help, too.

The officer called out to Jade. "Doctor, I will need to talk with you about this."

"Certainly it can wait a couple hours," John barked.

The officer met the questioning stares of all the white-clad professionals. "Yeah," he agreed. "Can you have her down at the station by noon, though?"

"Okay with you, Jade?" asked John.

"Yeah, that's fine," she conceded. "Thank you, Officer..."

"Officer Steve Ryan. I'm sorry this happened, ma'am. We'll talk more at noon." As he roughly shuffled Petchov towards the door, a second officer appeared in the doorway. Ryan assured him that everything was under control. They left with Jade's attacker.

"All right," Walter stated to the others. "Let's leave Jade with John." He turned towards the victim. "When you're ready to discuss things, just let any of us know." The others readily concurred. They then left, and ushered wide-eyed patients out of the hallway, and back into the waiting room.

Jade and John were alone. Tears began to roll down her cheeks. He held her strongly, and placed his chin over her head.

"It's okay," he soothed. "It's okay."

The tears began to flow more freely as Jade reflected upon what had just happened. Never, never in a million years, would she expect this kind of thing to happen to her. Sure, she had seen several rape victims in her years as a resident. But those women were just unlucky victims who were in the wrong place at the wrong time. She wasn't one of them. She was Dr. Jade Evans, good-natured and innocent Jade. Things like this didn't happen to women like her. Especially not here, in her examining room. And especially not with churchgoing teachers like Gunther Petchov! Fear and anger collided as she digested the episode; tears exploded into sobs.

"It's okay, Jade. They got him." John gently patted her back and whispered his support.

They stood there for a few minutes, just embracing. Finally, Jade slowly backed away. She wiped her eyes, and brushed tears off her cheeks. "Man," she swore quietly, shaking her head. "Thank God it only got so far."

After another minute, John spoke. "Do you want to be alone?"

"No," was the instant reply. "Stay with me?"

His heart sank at the plea. "Of course! Jade, I promise I'll stay with you." He smiled as she managed a half grin. "Where do you want to go?" he asked.

She sighed. "Is Chip's open?"

He looked at his watch. "It's ten of ten. I don't know."

"Can we try it?"

"Of course."

They both smiled, and embraced again.

4

Marla Kerabutski sipped her meadowsweet tea and stared at the television screen. She was plopped down in her favorite overstuffed recliner, and her feet were resting on the cluttered coffee table. Her living room reeked of litterboxes that should have been changed weeks ago. Clothes were spread all over the floor, and the cats were sprawled out all over the living room carpet.

She flipped the channel with her remote control. Ah, yes. Her favorite soap opera was back on. Her eyes fixated on the beautiful actors and actresses. But after a minute of watching, her mind was drifting. She was hungry. What would she have for dinner tonight? She didn't feel like cooking. Maybe she'd order pizza again. Well, she'd figure it out later.

She shifted her attention back to the television for a few minutes. But before long, she was drifting off again. She was hot. Were the windows closed? She looked over; no, they were all wide open. Maybe it was her cold that was making her feel hot. She sipped some more tea.

Back to the television. But after a few minutes, she was thinking about her bills and her finances. Marla began to tap her heels on the coffee table. She casually looked around the room, and looked at all her cats. Maintaining those cats was not cheap; even with coupons, feeding seven cats was expensive.

She refocused on the television. Marla began to feel annoyed with herself. She was feeling rambunctious, but she didn't know why. Maybe the soap opera was just too boring. She flipped to another channel. An angry man in a dark suit pointed at the camera, and insisted that you needed to be compensated for your injury, and *he* was the man to get you your money. She sighed, and flipped again. A talk show displayed four young men strutting across the stage barechested. The caption below read, "My Boyfriend is a Male Prostitute". Marla put down the remote.

"Hey, if them boys want to sell their bods for cash, that's their right!" said an audience member into the host's microphone. The crowd erupted into a loud cheer.

"No, no!" exclaimed a black-haired woman seated on stage. She waved her finger back and forth. "Jamie is my man! *My* man! I don't want no girl touching my man!" Boos and hisses radiated from the television.

"It's my life," said one of the shirtless men, standing on the edge of the stage. His bulging chest muscles glistened in the overhead light, and his sculpted abdominal musculature rested like a stone shield on his lower trunk. "I'll do what I wanna do." More cheers filled the room.

Another man spoke. His dark brown skin covered a hulking body; he was a perfect model of physical male beauty. "That's right. If the ladies are gonna pay, they gonna get some of this." The crowd erupted into wild cries as he lowered his trousers. A small red dot censored his private area, but regardless, little was left to the imagination.

A seated woman jumped out of her chair and started barking some spiteful words. Most of her commentary was bleeped out by audio censors. Another male Adonis grinned, turned to the camera, and flexed his powerful biceps.

Marla stared at the screen, entranced by the men. They started dancing. She wiped her brow.

She watched as the men continued strutting on stage. For a fleeting moment, thoughts of her long-deceased husband Theodore entered into her mind. She had always adored him, and after his death, she had never entered into another relationship. She had had no boyfriends, and certainly no sexual relations. She really hadn't thought much about sex after his death…

But now…

The phone suddenly rang.

Marla's trance was broken. Annoyed, she reached to the phone on the coffee table.

"Hello?" she snapped.

"Hello, Mrs. Kerabutski? It's Yu-lan Tang. I found your driver's license outside the store. You must have dropped it on your way out this morning."

She grunted. "How long you guys open?"

Yu-lan sounded somewhat taken aback. "Till six o'clock tonight, ma'am."

Marla looked at the clock. 10 a.m. "Damn," she said. "I wish you had found it earlier. Now I gotta drag myself all the way across town!"

The voice was silent at the other end. Yu-lan was shocked.

"Aw, screw it. Hold onto the license until tomorrow, will ya? I'll pick it up then." She hung up the phone.

She sat back in her chair, and reached over to the endtable. She grabbed a small brown jar; it was open. Without looking, she poured another small pinch of dried herb into her meadowsweet tea. She stirred the contents, and then put down the jar. Marla was fond of mixing different herbs in her teas; she thought each herbal ingredient could contribute a small benefit to the overall concoction.

"There," she said, smelling her now-strengthened tea. "Nothin' like this Quazhen stuff to liven up the meadowsweet." She took another sip, sat back in her chair, and stared at the television.

Only three cars were in the parking lot of Chips, and they likely belonged to employees of the establishment. Still, John parked his silver Volkswagen Passat near the front entrance. He and Jade got out and approached the red double doors of the restaurant. They spotted a small blue sticker on one door that listed the restaurant's hours.

"Eleven till two a.m." read John. It was now ten. "Well, do you want to wait around until they open?"

Jade looked up at the sky. It was a beautiful cloudless blue. The air was unusually warm for September; it must have been about eighty degrees. "Yeah. Why don't we sit on that bench."

The two reclined on a stained wooden bench that faced the parking lot. They took a moment to take in the gorgeous day.

John looked at Jade. She had been quiet on the ride over. She had obviously been deeply wounded; still, he didn't know any details.

"So," he began. "Do you want to talk about it?"

She sighed. "Believe it or not, there's really not too much to say. He was going to rape me. Thank God, I got away before anything happened."

He shook his head. "Man." He squeezed her hand. "You okay?"

She shrugged. "As okay as it gets."

The silence hung for a few moments.

"Do you know Gunther Petchov?" she asked.

"No."

"He's a third-grade teacher at Manchester Grammar School. He's the nicest guy you could possibly know..."

"What?!"

"I mean, he *was* the nicest guy. At least I thought so." She wrinkled her brow. "No," she said adamantly. "He *was* a good man. I've known him for five years—ever since I came to Manchester. He was always a kind and gentle spirit."

"So what the hell happened to him?"

She shrugged. "I have no idea. But the second I entered the room, he wasn't himself. He had this dark and cruel manner to him...I don't know; I can't explain it."

John watched her cringe. "If you don't want to talk..."

"No, I do. I do." She sighed. "He starts cursing right off the bat, for no good reason. Then he tells me off, simply because I was two minutes late. Then, he tells me he came in because he 'can't get it up'. He grabs his crotch, grabs my shoulder, and tells me to help him out; at this point he has this sinister grin and he's breathing in my face."

John sat, motionless and attentive.

"So I figure I gotta get out of there. I assume he had some kind of brief psychotic reaction to something. But regardless, I realize I'm in a very unsafe situation."

John nodded.

"So I go for the door, but he grabs me. You pretty much know the rest. He pins me against the door, locks it—by the way, can we now get rid of those damn locks?!"

John bit his lip, and simply nodded.

"Anyway, he locks the door, and starts coming closer. So I kneed him in the groin and shoved him to the floor. Then I unlocked the door, and you guys came in. That's it."

John let the silence hang for a few moments. His heart sank as he played back the incident in his mind. What a traumatic mess for Jade!

"Well," he said, "do you have any idea what got into him?"

She shook her head. "His breath smelled of alcohol, but I don't think it was all drunkenness. And besides, as far as I know, he never used to drink. It had to be some kind of psychotic reaction."

"Yeah, you said that. But did he mention any hallucinations? Or any delusions?"

She thought about this. "No, he didn't." She got his point. Despite the common usage of the word 'psychotic', in medical terms it described a very precise condition that usually included delusions or hallucinations. As far as she could tell, Petchov had had neither.

"So what else could it be?" she asked.

"Did he have any drug history?"

"Not that I knew of."

He shook his head. "I'd place big money on drugs. For someone to suddenly switch personalities like that, and to do something as ruthless as what he did, it's gotta be drugs."

She considered it. "I guess so." She didn't sound convinced. "But I don't get it, John. The guy's from a wonderful family; he has a great wife and three lovely kids. He loves his job, and he loves his church group and holiday activities. I mean, this is the quintessential family man. He's a family doctor's model patient, you know? So why would he turn to drugs? And besides, what drug turns a decent human being into a rapist?"

John sighed. "Good questions. I don't know."

They both looked out into the air. They were confused and frustrated, but Jade's fear was now subsiding. Her pulse was beginning to slow down towards normal, and she was starting to feel like herself again.

"So," she said sarcastically, "how was your morning?"

He gave a slight laugh. "Pretty uneventful, I guess. Nothing compared to yours…"

"Yeah, but I want to forget about mine for a minute or two. How was your morning?" She looked at him with serious eyes.

He nodded. "Not bad, not bad. I only got through three patients; I was on my fourth. Actually, it was a pretty good morning, considering."

She looked at him. "Considering what?"

"Oh, Frank Davis came in this morning."

"You poor thing! I thought *I* had the rough morning!"

John laughed. Davis had a definite reputation around the office. The ornery sixty-something-year-old had visited each member of the group, and he was highly critical of each one of them. But besides that, he was a highly noncompliant patient who complained about anything and everything. And his nature was absolutely rude and obnoxious. The other group members didn't know why John hadn't dropped him yet.

"Yeah, I saw Frank. But the weirdest thing happened today."

She nodded for him to go on.

"He was nice."

"Yeah right," she began to smile.

"No, seriously. The guy was really, really nice. He was smiling, and laughing, and saying how happy he was to have me as a doctor. It was strange. It was almost as if he had a totally new personality…"

John suddenly cut himself short. His eyes widened, and he slowly looked over at Jade. She was returning a wide-eyed stare.

"Um, okay," said John. "Are we in a Twilight Zone episode? This is really, really odd."

Jade swallowed. "Why would two people have sudden personality changes?"

They shook their heads, and stared at the ground. Three minutes passed before John spoke. "Could just be a coincidence."

Jade cocked her head and wrinkled her forehead. "Yeah. I guess so."

5

Feng Hou Tang dangled a cigarette from one hand and held his whiskey sour in the other. He puffed a cloud of smoke before taking another sip. The clang of pool balls suddenly echoed along the pub's walls; Feng turned to see a scrawny kid clad in denim aiming at the cue ball with his stick. Beside the kid, a busty redhead looked bored. She met Feng's stare, and after sizing up his robust body, shot him a wink and a smile.

Feng turned back to see a scruffy man pumping quarters into the jukebox. Before long, Jimi Hendrix was blasting throughout the small wooden-walled pub. The place was practically empty. Besides Feng, the kid at the pool table, his companion, and ol' Scruffy, the only people in the pub were the bartender and a waitress.

"So dear," said a voice from behind. Feng turned to see a wrinkled face on an attractive body. The waitress got out her pad and pencil. "Have you decided yet?"

"I thought I told you," grumbled Feng. "I'm waiting for someone. I'll order when he arrives."

"Oh, that's right. Sorry." She shuffled away.

Feng took another puff from his cigarette. Just then, the main door opened. The bartender, the waitress, the scruffy man, and the busty redhead all turned. A clean-shaven man with short blond hair, a neatly pressed gray suit, and a leather briefcase walked in. He removed his sunglasses and frowned. He seemed anxious to turn around and leave; he almost did so when he met Feng's eye. The man smirked and walked towards the round wooden table.

"Mr. Tang," he said evenly. "Good to see you again."

Feng smiled and shook his hand. "Likewise, Jimmy."

Jimmy Walters rested his briefcase on one stool, and got up on another. He felt the heat of every eye in the pub resting on him. His gut instinct cried out to leave immediately; this was rough territory, and he didn't belong here. Still, he just smirked.

"So," Jimmy said. "You've brought some samples?"

Feng chuckled. "You get right to the point, eh?" The other man laughed nervously. "Yeah," Feng replied. "I got some Quazhen. I think your company will be very impressed."

"Quazhen. Hmm." Jimmy nodded slowly. He was about to speak when the waitress approached the table.

"What can I get you, dear?" she smiled at the well-dressed man.

"How about a Bud," he replied. "And do you have menus?"

She stared at him. Feng smiled and puffed on his cigarette. Then, "No, they don't have menus." He turned to the waitress. "Two burgers and fries, Susan."

"Two burgers and fries," she repeated, and scribbled it onto her notepad. "Coming right up."

"So," Feng said as she walked away. "You were saying?"

The other man cleared his throat. "Yes. Well, I was just going to mention that nobody at Botanicure has heard of this Quazhen. You say it's been a family secret?"

Feng frowned. "I thought we've been through this, Jimmy."

He gave a weak laugh. "Well, yes. But I thought that maybe I alone hadn't heard of it. But apparently no one in my company has, either. So, ah, it seems to be pretty rare stuff. Yes?"

Feng snorted. "Yes, Jimmy."

The businessman looked down and adjusted his tie. This Feng guy was a jerk; that was obvious. Jimmy was tempted to get up and walk out. After all, in some respects, Feng was lucky that Botanicure was even considering the product. Still, his manager wanted Jimmy to come back with the samples. No matter what.

The waitress placed Jimmy's beer on the table. He quickly took his first gulp. Ah, much better, he thought.

"Quazhen," Jimmy said, reflectively. He said his next words slowly and carefully: "What exactly is it, Mr. Tang?"

The Chinese man sipped his whiskey sour and glared at the man. He watched the blond shift in his seat, wring his hands, and clear his throat. Feng continued to stare at him in silence. Jimmy was about to speak again, when Feng finally answered. "You won't find it in the United States

Pharmacopoeia or the National Formulary, Jimmy. You won't find a Latin name for it. You won't find any mention of it in botanical archives. You want to know why?"

Jimmy nodded, annoyed. "Because it's a family secret."

Feng winked. "That's right."

Jimmy took another gulp of beer and looked Feng in the eye. "But with all due respect, sir, if you give us absolutely no background on this herb, we can hardly make a deal."

Feng raised an eyebrow. "No?"

The other man swallowed hard. "No. I mean, you could be selling us cut-up grass for all we know. If Botanicure is going to mass market this product, we need to know what we're selling!"

Feng puffed his cigarette, and continued to glare at Jimmy. Jimmy finished his beer with a final gulp, and then motioned for Susan to get him another.

"If what I give you works, and if people buy it, what do you care what's in it?" asked Feng. "If it makes you money, you should be happy with it."

Jimmy snorted. "Well, if you fill it with cannabis or another illicit substance, I'm sure people will like it. But we don't want…"

"Aw, come on, Jimmy!" His voice was powerful and commanding. "Trust me a little, will you? Or should I take Quazhen elsewhere?"

"No," he answered quickly. "No sir. I just mean to say…"

"You can do spectrophotometric testing to ensure there's no cannabis, opioids, or other illicit substances. And yes, perhaps when we make a deal, I'll show you the natural product in its unadulterated form."

"The plant itself?"

"Yes, the plant itself."

Jimmy smiled. "Well, that's all we're asking for right now, Mr. Tang. That would be…"

"*Maybe* I'll agree to show you the plant at that time, Jimmy," he repeated forcefully. "But until then, let's cut the crap. You and I both know that when you sell an herb, you're under no obligation whatsoever to disclose anything besides its name. You don't have to prove its safety. You don't have to state the concentration of the product. You basically just have to bottle it up and sell it."

Jimmy began to sip his second beer.

"So," Feng continued, "let's face it. I'm handing you a goldmine. But until we have a deal, I'll be keeping the details of the product confidential. I'd be an idiot not to!"

Jimmy nodded thoughtfully. Then, "Okay. Sorry to get you worked up, Mr. Tang. Just doing my job."

Feng sat back, and glared at him.

"So," continued Jimmy, "I'd be happy to deliver your samples to the company. Then we'll see the wonders of your herb for ourselves."

Feng grinned. "Good. I have a small box of the stuff in my car. After we eat, it's yours."

Jimmy swallowed. "Great."

Jade opened the heavy brass door and entered a small rectangular room with a beige utilitarian carpet and yellow walls. John followed closely behind. They approached a wooden counter that ran the length of the room; a thick glass plate stretched from the countertop to the ceiling. Behind the counter sat a navy clad receptionist with her brown hair in a bun.

"Can I help you?" asked the receptionist through the glass.

"Yes. I'm Jade Evans, here to see Officer Ryan. He's expecting me."

The receptionist nodded and picked up a phone. "Hi. A Jade Evans here to see Steve? Okay." She put down the phone and looked up. "He'll be here in a minute. Please take a seat."

John followed Jade to a row of metal folding chairs lining a wall. He stopped at a water fountain to take a few sips. He had eaten that chicken sandwich at Chip's too quickly; not only was he now thirsty, his stomach felt like it contained a small hunk of iron!

Before John sat down, Officer Steve Ryan opened a door facing the chairs. "Dr. Evans?"

Jade stood. When John started following her towards the door, she turned and smiled. "I'll be all right from here, thanks."

John grimaced sheepishly. "Right." He returned to the chairs and sat.

Jade followed Ryan through a series of narrow hallways and into a small plain office. He motioned for Jade to sit at a circular table; he then took his seat.

"So Doctor," he began. "Why don't you tell me what happened. I'll be tape recording, if you don't mind, and what you say will go down as your official statement."

Jade said that was fine, and then described the incident in detail. She was matter-of-fact; the whole episode seemed so long ago, and so her emotions had now returned to baseline.

As she finished the story, a voice came from the door. "That's all of it, Doctor?"

She turned to see an overweight man with disheveled black hair and a ruddy complexion. He wore an officer's uniform, and from his demeanor, he seemed to hold a high rank.

"This is Sergeant Kolowski," introduced Ryan, as the man entered the room and joined them at the table. Ryan clicked off the tape recorder.

"Well, yes Sergeant," replied Jade, "that's it."

He shifted his weight and squinted his eyes, fixing his stare on Jade. His expression was one of superiority and power; Jade disliked him instantly.

"So, Doctor," Kolowski said, leaning towards her, "You never saw Gunther Petchov acting in this fashion in the past?"

"No."

"I see." He continued to glare at her. "And you've known him for a long time?"

"Yes. Five years."

Kolowski nodded slowly. Then, "Ever know him on a personal level?"

"No. Only in a doctor-patient relationship." She was resenting the questioning. Why was she on trial here?

Kolowski sat back, still staring at her with squinty eyes. Ryan glanced at his boss, and then shot a small smile at Jade. He seemed to acknowledge Jade's distaste for the other man's attitude. Jade concluded that this behavior was not new for Sergeant Kolowski.

"I'm confused, Doctor," said Kolowski, in an accusatory tone. Jade felt her heart start to pound. Police officer or not, he was a jerk. "Why would a good man like Gunther Petchov do something this horrible?"

"A good man?" she shot back.

"Yes. A good man." His voice was firm and unmistakably condescending. "I know Gunther from church, Doctor. And I'm really having trouble believing your…"

"You're having trouble believing my what?" Jade met his hard stare with fiery eyes.

"Folks…" began Ryan.

"I'm having trouble," repeated the sergeant, louder, "believing your story, Doctor. I think some important facts may be missing."

Ryan turned to him with a perplexed expression. "Sarge…"

"I talked to Gunther myself," continued Kolowski. "He tells a different story."

Jade did all she could to remain seated and somewhat civil. "Please go on," she spat out.

Kolowski cocked his head and raised his eyebrows, like a father silently expressing disapproval towards his child. "I will, thank you. My friend Gunther Petchov says that he came to see you with a sensitive male problem." He paused and lowered his voice. "Impotence." He paused, looking for signs of sympathy. Then, "And he says for no good reason, you suddenly went ballistic on him. You started screaming, and ran to the door. You then locked the two of you in, and started striking him."

Jade rammed the palm of her hand on the table. "And you believe that?!"

"Calm down, Dr. Evans!" ordered the sergeant.

"Sarge," barked Ryan, forcefully. He then lowered his voice and leaned towards his boss. "What's up, Sarge? I was there, remember? What's going on here?"

The older man turned to him. "You were in the room at the time of the alleged incident, Steven?"

"Well, no, but…"

"You saw him assault her?"

"No. But I heard her screaming..."

"Why don't you wait outside, Steven."

"But..."

"*Now*, Steven." Kolowski had his ruddy face two inches from Ryan's nose.

"Yes sir." Ryan and Jade exchanged confused glances, but he then swiftly left.

"I don't get it," said Jade, angrily. "You honestly think Gunther Petchov is the victim here?"

Kolowski sat back, put his hands behind his head, and lowered his voice. "Not really, no."

"Well, then why..."

"But I don't see him trying to rape his doc. I just don't see it."

"What the hell, man! I was there! You weren't!"

Kolowski put both hands up and closed his eyes. "Doctor, I heard your story. I'm no lawyer, and I'm certainly no judge. Yes, I think Petchov's story is far-fetched. But I also think your story is, well, unlikely."

She slowly shook her head in disgust. "Thanks." They exchanged glares for a few moments. Then, "So am I done here?"

"Well, we do need to know if you're going to press charges."

She continued to glare at him. "I assume the state will be prosecuting, or are you gonna pat him on the back and give him a lollipop on his way out of this place?"

"Watch it, Doctor. Yes, the state will be prosecuting."

"Fine. That's enough for me. I'm sure you guys will let me know when you need my testimony."

He nodded.

"Anything else?"

"No."

"Good. Just so you know, I'll be speaking with your captain, or chief, or whatever. You are the rudest officer I have ever met, and your badge should absolutely be revoked. I cannot believe you call yourself a law enforcement officer, and I have no idea how you rose to the position of sergeant. I was sexually assaulted, and not only do you have no empathy, but you side with my would-be rapist." She vehemently shook her head and stood up. "Unbelievable."

Jade spun on her heel and walked out the door.

"Doctor," called Kolowski behind her. But she stormed out to the lobby and slammed the door.

John was startled. "Jade, what…"

"Let's go," she huffed. She threw open the brass door and walked out, with a very confused John following close behind.

6

Jade steered her Saab into her driveway, and drove it into the garage. She sighed. What a long, crazy day! It was now 5 p.m.; she had gone to John's house for several hours before coming home. John had been outraged when he learned about Sergeant Kolowski's behavior, and he had insisted that Jade call the police chief from his phone. As it was, she had gotten the chief's voice mail. She had left a long, irate message, and then had tried to forget about the whole episode.

Now exhausted, she cracked open her front door, pushed back Nora, and went in. After playing with her cat for a few minutes, she went to her bedroom. The answering machine beeped and flashed rhythmically. She pushed the playback button.

"Message one," stated the digital voice. Then a woman spoke hurriedly from the machine. "Oh, hi Dr. Evans. This is Liz Goldstein. Sorry to call you at home..." No you're not, thought Jade, annoyed. "...I tried you at the office, but Elaine said you're out for the day. Anyway, I have a small emergency." That's why we have a group practice, thought Jade. Let whoever's covering know about your 'small emergency'. And how did you get my home number, anyway? "Mitchell has been acting real funny lately. He's...well, he's scaring me a bit. Just seems kinda...I dunno...different."

Jade started listening more carefully.

"He seems really angry lately, and you know Mitchell. He doesn't get angry. So, anyway, I was hoping to get you to talk with him. Just to make sure his mind's okay, you know? Thanks, Dr. Evans. Our number is 555-9247."

"End of messages," said the digital voice.

Jade reached into her back pocket for her calendar. She opened it to find out who in the call group was on call tonight. It was Walter. She was about to give him a call, when she suddenly stopped herself.

Mitchell Goldstein wasn't himself.

He was really angry lately.

And that's just not him.

With a new surge of energy, she picked up the receiver and punched in seven digits.

Two rings, and then, "Hello?"

"Hi, Mitchell?"

"Yeah, who's this?"

"It's Dr. Evans. How are you?"

"What do you mean, how am I?"

She bit her lip. "Just asking how you are, Mitchell."

There was a pause at the other end. Then, "What do you want?"

This was definitely not the well-mannered Mitchell Goldstein whom she had known since she began practicing five years ago.

"Mitchell," she asked, "is Liz there?"

"Why?" He was short, and obviously annoyed.

"It's between her and me, Mitchell."

Another pause, and then, "She's grocery shopping. Okay, lady?"

She swallowed. "Mitchell, you sound very upset. Is something wrong?"

"Yeah. Why the hell you calling here? You're making me miss the game!"

"I'm sorry. Mitchell, when Liz gets home, have her call me, okay?"

"Yeah, sure." He hung up with a slam.

Jade stood with the receiver in her hand, staring out a bedroom window. Gunther Petchov, Frank Davis, and now Mitchell Goldstein had all recently had marked personality shifts. All were sudden; all were out of the blue.

She called John.

"Hello?"

"Hey John, it's me." She related the episode with Goldstein. "What do you make of it?"

He sighed. "Something weird's going on, Jade. I have no idea what, but something's going on."

"What do we do?"

He paused, and sighed again. "I don't know. Let's get more info on those three men."

"I certainly don't intend to call Petchov's family. I'm washing my hands of that episode."

"Of course, of course. We'll forget calling him. I'll look into Frank Davis. You find out more about Goldstein. And tomorrow, let's ask Walter and Betsy if they've noticed any strange behavior in their patients."

"Sounds good."

Unsettled, they said their good-byes, and hung up. Jade plopped herself down upon her bed. She closed her eyes, and before long, she was fast asleep.

Jade arrived at her office early the next morning. She reassured the office staff and her partners that she was okay, and she thanked Walter and Betsy for covering her more serious patients yesterday.

She was sipping coffee at her desk when Elaine entered the room.

"Doctor," she said, "Mrs. Liz Goldstein just walked in. She's asked to speak with you." Elaine's voice carried an unusual sense of urgency.

Right, thought Jade. Liz hadn't called back the night before; she wondered if she had even received the message. Jade glanced at her watch. 8:17 a.m. Her first patient wasn't scheduled until 8:30.

"Thanks Elaine. Please send her in."

A tall woman in her mid-forties entered the room. Jade's jaw dropped as she saw the businesswoman's unkempt hair, pale face, and bruised cheek: her left eye was swollen shut amidst puffy magenta skin. Jade immediately stood up, and moved towards the woman.

"Liz," she whispered, and outstretched her arms.

The other woman's face melted into wrinkled anguish, and tears began to flow down her cheeks. She embraced the doctor, and began sobbing into her shoulder.

Jade, still stunned, gently patted her back. "You'll be safe now, Liz. You're safe now."

The doctor held her for a few minutes, just patting her and reassuring her. The taller woman then loosened her grip, and gently backed away.

"I'm sorry," she sobbed.

"No, no," Jade said empathetically. "You have nothing to be sorry about. Here, please sit."

Liz took a seat as Jade softly closed the office door. She then sat next to Liz in an adjacent chair.

Silence filled the room for a moment. Then Liz spoke. "He…he's never done this before." She stared at Jade's plain desk, looking into nothingness.

Jade nodded, and listened.

"I mean," Liz continued slowly, "this just isn't Mitchell." She shook her head in disbelief.

After a minute of silence, Jade spoke. "What did he do, Liz?"

She clenched her eyelids closed. "He hit me. Eleven times."

Jade nodded. "Why?"

She faced the doctor and shrugged helplessly. "I have no idea. He was fine yesterday morning. Totally fine, totally himself."

"And he's never been violent before?"

She snorted. "Never violent, never aggressive. Only a good, loving husband and a good father."

Jacob and Carol Goldstein flashed into Jade's mind. Both kids were in college; both were out of the house. Good.

"So," continued Jade, "have you two been arguing about anything? Have things been strained at home?"

A tear fell down her cheek. "No, Doctor. That's what's so frustrating. Everything has been great recently. We even celebrated our anniversary last week!" She shook her head. "I mean, there was one trivial difference in opinion yesterday, but nothing major."

Jade leaned closer. "Tell me."

"It's stupid really…"

"Please, Liz. Tell me."

She looked at the ceiling, and wiped a tear. "We were out shopping yesterday afternoon. I had gotten home early, and Mitchell had the day off. We went to some new health food store down on Main Street." She paused to think. "Natural Essentials, or something like that. Heard of it?"

"Is that the brand new one across from Jack's Guitars?"

"Yes, that's it."

"I know of it, but I've never been inside."

"Well, anyway, we were in there because Mitchell had run out of creatine."

Jade rolled her eyes. "He's still using that?"

"Yes," she replied, almost apologetically. "So we're in there, ready to check out. And Mitchell sees this new herbal concoction. It's called Quazhen, or something?"

Jade shrugged.

"Anyway, the ad says it's for energy and harmony, or some garbage like that. I really didn't think he needed it; it cost thirty dollars for a tiny bottle! But Mitchell got all excited, and said he wanted to just try something new. So we bickered for all of ten or fifteen seconds, and then I gave in."

Jade listened attentively.

"And that's it," continued Liz.

Jade reflected on this for a few moments. Then, "I don't know. I wouldn't expect that tiny argument to cause that behavior."

"I know."

"Well," Jade said softly, "you're not going home, Liz. Who do you have to stay with?"

She nodded in agreement. "My sister lives over in West Hartford. I went there last night, and that's where I'll be until I have some answers."

"Good. Did you call the police?"

"I didn't yet, but I still might."

Jade stood up. "I want you to see a wonderful woman who specializes in domestic violence crises. Her name is Tabitha Brown, and she's an absolute angel. Her office is down on Center Street. Can you go now?"

Liz nodded.

"I'll call her for you. Let me give you directions."

Jade scribbled down directions, expressed her sincere support, and walked her to the door. Before she left, Jade asked, "Liz, are you sure there's nothing you can think of that could account for that nasty change in Mitchell's personality?"

She shook her head. "Nothing."

"Okay."

Jade hugged her, and watched her leave. She returned to her desk, and phoned Tabitha Brown. Tabitha, in her strong and nurturing way, promised Jade that she'd take good care of Liz. Jade hung up, confident that Liz would be in good hands.

As she hung up, John walked in.

"Was that Liz Goldstein I passed on the way in?"

"Yeah. Her husband beat her up. No history of domestic abuse. No recent fights." She sighed. "No clues whatsoever. The only slight bickering prior to the attack yesterday was regarding some new herbal crap. Quazhen, I think she called it."

"Quazhen," John repeated, reflectively. "I've heard of that one." He dropped his head in concentration. Then, "Oh yeah. Tyrone Williams. He was using it."

"Williams, Williams…Oh, wasn't he the one with the turbo sex drive? We discussed him at Chip's."

"Yes. That's him."

They exchanged quizzical looks for a moment.

"I don't know," said John. "Let's keep our antennae up for any other wild personality fluxes today."

"Yeah."

He left.

Feng awoke to the shrieking cries of his alarm clock. With a heavy fist, he rammed down the snooze button and rolled over. He sighed. It was too late; he was awake. Annoyed, he turned back to the alarm clock, shut it off, and got up.

With sleepy eyes, he stumbled over to his window and looked out. The sky was gray, and puddles on the asphalt below told him that a shower had occurred overnight. Feng winced; with this kind of weather, he just wanted to crawl back into bed. He yawned, stretched, and glanced back at the clock. 9:00 a.m. He was supposed to be at the shop from noon to six; he'd probably get there by one or so. There were some important errands to do first.

Feng tossed on a tee-shirt and jeans, and then sat down on his bed. He picked up the phone, and dialed.

After a few rings, a voice answered. "Hello?"

"Hey. It's me," replied Feng.

"Where are you, man?" The deep voice was clearly annoyed.

"I'm in my house, Jay. I told you I'd be there at nine or ten."

"You said eight."

Feng huffed. "Whatever. So what've you got?"

The other man sighed. He knew he should expect this from Feng. "I got eight hundred…"

"That's it?"

"Yeah," he snapped. "Come on, man. Hittin' up a diner isn't exactly robbing Fort Knox, you know?"

Feng grunted.

"So I got eight hundred bucks and change. Brett said he nailed some old hag in an alley for a decent ring and earrings. Should be worth a grand, he said."

"Bullshit. Ten bucks if he's lucky."

"No way! Look, they're nice earrings…"

"I ain't taking no ring and earrings, Jay."

"Come on, Feng! I'm the guy who got you to American soil, remember?"

"How many times do you intend to pull that line? I compensated you well for those services. That deal has long been done."

The other man sighed. "Look, forget about the ring and earrings. We'll hand over a G; you hand us two bags. Oh, and Brett needs some more syringes. And will ya toss in some of that Quazhen crap? I like that stuff."

"First of all," Feng snapped, "the syringes are an extra fifty. Secondly, the Quazhen is my grandmother's special plant; it's not crap, Jay."

"An extra fifty bucks, dude? Come on!"

"One thousand fifty. I'll be there in half an hour." He slammed down the phone.

Feng sauntered to his kitchen, got himself a bowl of Frosted Flakes, and sat down with the morning paper. Yep, he thought. It would be another typical day.

*   *   *

Jade finished with her final patient of the morning at noon. She walked back towards her office, but she spotted John having an intense conversation with Jackie in the hallway. Out of curiosity, she approached them both.

"...for energy and harmony," said the blond nurse. "I've been using it for three weeks. I definitely think it helps."

"How?" demanded John.

"I don't know. I just have more energy, and I'm less stressed than usual."

John looked at her with cynical eyes. "It couldn't be that week-long vacation you just had? Couldn't that ease your stress and invigorate you?"

She met his stare. "No," she answered firmly. "The Quazhen works, John. For me, it just works."

Jade nudged closer to the couple, making her presence more obvious. "Sounds like we're discussing that Quazhen herb?"

"Yes," answered Jackie. "Our dear Doctor Harper here thinks it's snake oil. He says it doesn't work. Which of course isn't surprising, since all you doctors are close-minded to complementary medicine."

"Whoa," said Jade. Jackie often treaded the line between playfulness and rudeness rather unsteadily. "That's quite a generalization, don't you think?"

She shrugged and smiled. "Not really."

"We're not opposed to alternative medicine," defended Jade. "We just prefer therapies that have been shown to work. We want good, solid evidence-based medicine to show the efficacy of our medications. If a drug hasn't undergone rigorous testing in randomized, double-blind, placebo-controlled trials, then we can't be sure it really works."

"Wawa wawa wa," laughed Jackie. "There you go with your close-minded lingo again. You're just proving my point, Jade."

The doctors exchanged helpless glances.

"What's so big about this Quazhen herb, anyway?" asked Jackie.

"Well," began John, "we're a bit concerned about it."

We are? thought Jade.

"Jackie, this may be very personal," continued John.

She looked offended. "Come on, guys," she said more seriously. "I think we have a pretty good relationship. Nothing's too personal."

"Okay. Then tell me. Since you began using this herb, have you felt any…well, different?"

She looked at him like he was the village idiot. "Yes, John. I told you, I have more energy…"

"No," he interrupted. "I mean, have you—or has anyone around you—noticed a personality change?"

She balked, and looked at Jade for support. "I certainly don't think so," she laughed. "Are you saying I'm a changed person?"

"No," he quickly admitted. "No, I haven't noticed any changes. How about this one, though: have you had any change in your libido? Or in your sex life in general?"

A palpable silence filled the air. Jade winced; even among friends, some questions were just too personal. And why, she wondered, was John asking Jackie this anyway?

"Well," Jackie said with an increasingly pink face, "no. Not really. Please tell me John, why on earth are you asking me that?"

"I'm worried about side effects of the herb," he stated plainly.

She shook her head. "Well, no. I'm still me. And my sex life is still my pathetic sex life. No changes." She grinned. "I think I need to go now."

He smiled. "Yeah. Thanks, Jackie."

The nurse walked away, leaving John and Jade looking at each other.

"Let's go into my office," offered Jade.

He agreed, and followed her into her small room. She shut the door, and sat down next to him.

"What's up?" she asked.

"Frank Davis, one of our personality-shifters, has been using Quazhen. I also took the liberty to call Vanessa Petchov, Gunther's wife."

"John!" Jade exclaimed.

"I know, I know. I shouldn't have. But I did." He looked her in the eye. "He was using the same herb for a week before his appointment with you yesterday."

She sat back, with her mouth open. She looked down, and pondered the situation for a moment. Then, "So. Tyrone Williams, Gunther Petchov, Frank Davis, and Mitchell Goldstein have all had personality changes, libido changes, or both. And they've all used this Quazhen."

He nodded.

"Well, that sounds pretty damn convincing," she said. "Where can we learn about the herb's side effects? Let's look it up in the PDR."

"I tried. It's not there."

"Are you sure you spelled it correctly?"

He shrugged. "I tried 'C-w-a', 'K-w-a', 'Q-u-a', and about ten other possible spellings."

"Okay. Then let's try the German Commission E Monographs."

"Tried there too. Nothing."

She wrinkled an eyebrow. "We have an herbal index in the conference room..."

"I know. Nothing on Quazhen. And there's absolutely nothing on the Internet, either."

She looked at him in disbelief. "That makes no sense, John. If we can't find that herb anywhere, what the hell is it?"

He shook his head grimly.

She looked at him for a moment. "Well," she then stated. "There's one place where I know I'll get some answers."

"Where?"

"I'll swing by that Natural Essentials store after work tonight."

He nodded. "I'd go with you, but I'm picking my niece up from soccer practice."

"No problem. I'll tell you what I find tomorrow."

7

Jade parked her car along the side of the road, and got out. It was now 4:55 p.m.; she hoped the store didn't close at five. She crossed Main Street, and approached the row of small shops lining the opposite sidewalk. Directly ahead of her stood a small shingled storefront nestled between a coffee shop and a bakery. Above the double glass doors was a rustic wooden sign with the name 'Natural Essentials' deeply engraved. The wooden shingles that covered the storefront were weathered, giving an ironic sense of age and stability to this brand new shop. A cardboard sign was set into the side of a glass door; it read the store hours to be 9 to 6, Monday through Saturday.

Jade opened a door, and the warm sound of chimes greeted her. She walked into a lovely cloud of a spicy aroma. She looked down to her sides, and saw a dozen thick aromatherapy candles burning on brown wicker shelves; the candles gave a peaceful glow to the store's entryway. Ahead of her was a tall pile of smooth stones; the stones spiraled three feet upwards, and a hidden faucet atop the creation allowed water to gently trickle down. The soothing sounds of an acoustic guitar amidst crashing waves and tropical rain emerged from several speakers overhead, and beautiful exotic plants lined the soft tan walls. Without noticing, Jade began to breathe more deeply, and her shoulders slightly dropped as the warm surroundings subconsciously eased her tension.

She turned left, and slowly strolled down the outermost aisle. To her right, five shelves that ran the length of the store were fully stocked with bottles, jars, and plastic bags. Simple handwritten labels identified various herbs and oils, and pieces of cloth served as the lids of the jars. Walking further down the aisle, Jade came upon more familiar packaging. Plastic bottles of brand-name vitamins and supplements filled the shelves, and small cardboard displays advertised new herbal products amidst the inventory.

"Can I help you?" asked a friendly voice from behind.

Jade turned to see a smiling Asian man wearing a yellow button-down shirt and khakis. He was roughly her height, and his well-toned musculature was apparent beneath his shirt. His black hair was cropped short.

"Yes," she smiled. "I understand you have something called Quazhen at this store."

His smile widened, and he slightly bowed. "Word does spread fast in this town, doesn't it?" he remarked.

"Yes," she replied, with a hint of sarcasm that went unnoticed.

"Quazhen is brand new, and you can only get it here," he said proudly. "That's because it's a unique plant that only grows in one specific part of China. That one spot happens to be my grandmother's plantation!" He softly stepped around her. "Please. Follow me."

He led her to the front of the store, towards the check-out counter. Jade saw another man behind the counter; he was sitting down and reading a magazine. He looked strikingly similar to the yellow-shirted man; they must be twins, she thought. The sitting man, however, wore a white tee-shirt and had long, straight black hair that rested on his shoulders. As Jade approached the counter, the sitting man glanced up briefly, and then went back to reading.

"By the way," said the yellow-shirted man cheerfully, "my name is Yu-lan Tang; I'm the owner of this store. I'm still pretty new in town. Came from China nine months ago." He extended his hand, and Jade politely shook it.

"Welcome to Manchester, Mr. Tang. I'm Dr. Jade Evans. I'm a family doctor in town."

The sitting man glanced up again, but then continued to read.

"A family doctor?" Yu-lan said as he walked behind the counter. "Terrific! Do you prescribe herbs?"

Jade felt her stomach begin to knot. "Well, no. I'm an allopathic doctor—you know, the kind with an M.D. after my name. In this country, naturopathic doctors tend to prescribe more herbs; they have N.D. after their names. M.D.'s as-a-whole are more traditional."

"More traditional, Doctor?" grinned Yu-lan. "Many herbs have been around for centuries, even millennia. I wouldn't call synthetic pharmaceutical chemicals used by Western medicine practitioners more traditional!"

She continued to smile politely. He was a nice-enough guy, she thought. Don't rip him apart. Not yet, anyway.

"So I'm fascinated," continued Yu-lan good-naturedly. "Why is an allopathic medical doctor—who doesn't prescribe herbs—interested in Quazhen?"

"Some of my patients are using it."

Yu-lan's face glowed. "Wonderful! I like that very much! You don't know anything about an herb, but your patients use it. So you make yourself learn more about it. Very good, Doctor!"

She nodded in agreement. "It's always been my way."

Yu-lan motioned towards the small jars of Quazhen, ignoring his silent brother. "Well, this is it. It does wonders for people. It is one of our biggest selling products."

Great, thought Jade. She picked up a small, narrow cylindrical jar with a green and purple checkered cloth lid, and brought it up to her nose. She could smell the herb's robust aroma even through the cloth lid; it was cross between basil and licorice. Jade eyed the handwritten label on the jar; it simply said 'Quazhen'. But a cardboard sign next to the jars said 'For Balance, Energy, and Harmony'. She involuntarily snorted. Feng looked up.

"So," she began. "What exactly is it?"

Yu-lan shrugged. "It's essentially the entire flower ground up. We've found the same health benefits throughout the whole flower."

Jade cracked a wry smile. "*We've* found benefits, Mr. Tang? Who are *we*?"

"My family," he answered more seriously. "Generations and generations have found the same benefits. It's a wonderful tonic. It gives you more energy, alleviates your stress, and cloaks you in a wonderful sense of well-being."

"Ah," she retorted. "Sounds like this should be in America's drinking water."

Feng closed the magazine and looked at Jade.

"So, you never really said," continued the doctor. "What is it? What's the Latin name of Quazhen? I couldn't find it in any books. It's also not on the Internet."

"It's a family herb," said a frowning Feng with a distinct edge.

"Ah," smiled Yu-lan, now obviously uncomfortable. "This is my brother, Feng Hou Tang."

"How do you do?" She extended her hand, and after a rude pause, Feng shook it.

"You won't find a Latin name for Quazhen," said Feng. "It's an exceedingly rare Chinese plant. As my brother told you, it only grows on our grandmother's plantation."

Jade sensed his antagonism very clearly. "Well," she responded, putting down the jar, "are you sure that selling it here is even legal?"

The sudden accusatory question cut through any soft pleasantries that remained lingering; it jostled Yu-lan and angered Feng. They looked at each other, and then turned to Jade.

Feng stood up. "Yes," he snapped, his bulging muscles evident beneath his shirt. "We've reported Quazhen to the FDA; they're fully aware of it."

"Really?" Her obvious surprise was probably rude, but she didn't care. "They allow you to sell it?"

Yu-lan shrugged. "It's just a dietary supplement."

"*Just* a dietary supplement?" she barked.

"Our family has used it as a spice for years; it goes on the dinner table with salt and pepper." Feng said this slowly and coldly.

Jade wrinkled her forehead. "Anyway," she continued, "what do you mean by 'just a dietary supplement'?"

Yu-lan frowned. He disliked confrontations. He also felt particularly vulnerable arguing this topic with an American allopathic physician; he knew that many American doctors resented the rise of herbalism in their country. "I mean," he answered, "that it's not like we're selling hardcore medicines here…"

Wrong answer! thought Jade with a fiery grin. "Oh no! No, no, no, fellows! Look, let me tell you why I'm here."

"Please do," snarled Feng, inching closer to her across the counter.

"I will!" Her face was red; her heart was pounding. She was ready to fight. "A co-worker and I think we've found some pretty severe side effects of this Quazhen herb," she spat out harshly. "Four of our patients who use it have had significant changes in their personalities and/or sexual behaviors. For the most part, they become much more aggressive and much more sexual..."

"Bullshit, bitch," snarled Feng.

She fell silent and stared at him in disbelief. This complete stranger had just called her a bitch! Never, never in her life had someone been so rude! Yu-lan shot his brother a disapproving glare, but Feng's eyes were fixed on Jade.

"Look," she hissed softly but with a razor-sharp edge. "If you ever call me that again, I will have the Better Business Bureau on your ass faster than you can say 'quackery', you big-headed asshole. I was sexually assaulted yesterday by a patient who took your Quazhen crap..."

"Oh my..." Feng cried, throwing his hands up. "So that's why you're here lady?" He raised his voice two octaves and waved his hands sarcastically. "Miss pristine innocent white doctor was traumatized yesterday. She was sexually assaulted. What on earth would make someone attack Little Miss Innocent? Oh, it must have been an evil herb." He instantly changed his voice to a sinister rasp. "That makes a lot a fuckin' sense, bitch. Come on, lady!"

She glared at him with hard, unbelieving eyes. Adrenaline gushed through her veins as her heart raced and her hands quivered. A thick tension filled the store as Feng returned the stone stare.

Yu-lan looked down, placed both hands on the counter, and shook his head. After several steaming silent moments passed, he spoke. "Doctor Evans," he said calmly and softly. "I am terribly sorry to hear of that tragedy yesterday. Are you okay?"

It took her a few seconds to turn away from Feng and face his brother. She was taken aback by the kind words. "Yes," she answered in a measured, calm voice. "Thank you for asking. I'm okay. He was stopped before anything really happened."

Yu-lan closed his eyes and nodded. "Good. Good."

Feng continued to glare at her.

"Look," offered Yu-lan. "If you have genuine concerns about the side effects of Quazhen, we certainly want to hear about them. Maybe we can arrange a time to discuss it tomorrow."

"I don't…" began Feng, loudly.

"Enough!" Yu-lan slammed his fist upon the counter and fired a menacing stare at his brother. Feng looked at him, not showing his surprise at his brother's assertiveness. After a tense moment, he huffed, shook his head, and turned around. Feng walked towards a door at the far end of the counter.

Before he could leave, Jade spoke. "You are one lucky bastard," she spat out at him. "If it weren't for your brother, I would have the Better Business Bureau all over this place in a heartbeat." She turned back towards Yu-lan, but spoke loudly enough for both to clearly hear her. "There's an FDA program called MedWatch which allows doctors to call in concerns about herbs, vitamins, and other dietary supplements. I'll be calling them to report my concerns about your grandmother's drug."

Feng turned towards her and shot her a look of unparalleled disgust.

"But," she continued, "I accept your offer, Yu-lan, to meet to discuss the herb. I'll call you tomorrow with some times that would be good for me. But I don't want your brother there." She turned to Feng. "In fact, I never want to see your face again, as long as I live."

With that, she spun around, headed for the double glass doors, and left.

8

"So are you going to call the Better Business Bureau?" asked John as he closed the microwave door. He punched the keypad and pressed start. He and Jade were alone in the office conference room, which nicely converted to a lunchroom around noon each day. They were discussing yesterday's events.

"Not yet. If I call at all, it will probably be tomorrow," replied Jade, before chomping down on her turkey sandwich.

"Tomorrow's Saturday," he reminded her. "I doubt they're open on weekends."

She shrugged and swallowed. "Oh yeah. I don't know. I'll probably drop it. But I'm certainly not dropping the MedWatch issue; it's my responsibility to contact the FDA about this. I mean, I'm really worried."

He nodded in agreement. The microwave beeped, and he removed his reheated spaghetti.

"I talked to Walter and Betsy," he said, joining Jade at the large rectangular table. "They don't know of anyone on Quazhen."

"Not surprising," she answered dryly. "Fifty bucks says they never ask their patients about herbal medicines."

"You're probably right." He took a bite of his lunch. Then, "You know what's bothering me most right now?"

She shook her head.

"I've been losing sleep over one key question. If this Quazhen stuff really causes aggression, altered libido, and even personality changes, how can we possibly explain that physiologically?"

She raised her eyebrows and nodded vigorously. "I know. I've been contemplating that one, too. How does it produce those side effects?"

"If it caused dry mouth or blurry vision, that would be easy to explain."

"Sure," she agreed. "In that case, we'd assume it inhibited the parasympathetic nervous system, like many drugs out there today."

"And if it caused nausea and vomiting, we might assume that it activated the brainstem chemoreceptors."

"Or the receptors in the gut," she added.

"Right. But how on earth could one drug cause personality changes, and cause heightened sexuality?"

She slowly shook her head. "I don't know."

The two pondered this mystery for a few minutes. They then changed the topic to the merits and dangers of a new anti-asthma drug which a pharmaceutical representative had been pushing. Before long, 12:45 had rolled around.

"I should get to my office," said Jade. "My first afternoon patient is at one."

They parted, and Jade returned to her small room to find the typical pile of envelopes on her desk. As usual, mail had been picked up and delivered during the lunch hour. She plopped down at her desk, and began flipping through the envelopes. Advertisement from Pfizer, advertisement from Eli Lilly, advertisement from GlaxoSmithKline, notice from New England Journal of Medicine—her subscription was about to run out, invitation to another pharmaceutical dinner. Come on, she thought. Where's the mail? Package from the University of Connecticut School of Medicine.

Finally. That could be interesting. She tore open the thick white envelope, and found a cover sheet attached to a schedule of some sort. She read the letter:

Dear Dr. Evans,

Thank you again for agreeing to participate in our Student Continuity Program (SCP). By now, you should have met your student, Erin Malloy, who is scheduled to spend each Tuesday afternoon with you during her first three years of medical school (with the exception of school vacations).

As we discussed at our summer retreat, one important objective of SCP is to correlate your teaching of history-taking and physical exam skills with Erin's didactic and conference schedule. For example, during a week in which Erin learns about cardiac anatomy and physiology, you would ideally focus upon the cardiac history and how to properly listen to the heart. It is our belief that such coordination of the various teaching arenas will maximize our students' learning.

With this in mind, we have attached a copy of Erin's syllabus for the entire first year. At your convenience, please peruse it, so that you may be better informed of the subjects that Erin is learning in any given week.

Please do not hesitate to contact me with any questions or concerns. Thank you again for contributing to the education of UConn's medical students!

Sincerely,

Luis Gonzalez

Director of Student Continuity Program

Jade smiled. She hadn't seen a medical school syllabus in eight years. She wondered if they had changed much.

She sifted through the contents of the syllabus. Let's see, she thought. Whew! In the opening week-and-a-half, Erin had been taught all of biochemistry, including protein structure, bioenergetics, and metabolism—both aerobic and anaerobic. She then had gone on to cell biology, and learned all about membranes, DNA replication, and DNA transcription and translation. Wow; she was already done with that.

They then launched her into the various organ systems, starting with the nervous system. Jade grinned in a mixture of jealousy and sympathy for Erin; she had always found the nervous system to be challenging but fascinating. The four-week nervous system curriculum had begun last week, when Erin had learned about neuronal transmission, which included action potentials, neurotransmitters, and synaptic clefts. Earlier this week, she began an introduction to various components of the nervous system. Monday was about the peripheral nervous system, which included dermatomes (areas of skin innervated by a common nerve root) and reflexes. On Tuesday, she was introduced to autonomics, which involved the crucial sympathetic and parasympathetic nervous systems. Wednesday was a broad introduction to the brainstem and cranial nerves. Yesterday, Erin began her education in the cerebral cortex and the cerebellum; these huge topics included discussions on the primary sensory and motor regions of the brain, higher intellectual functions, and the coordination of movement, which included posture and balance. Today, Erin would be exposed to cerebral circulation; there would also be a section on the hypothalamus and limbic system…

The limbic system.

Wait a second, thought Jade.

The limbic system!

"John!" she cried, as she jumped out of her chair and tore out of her office. "John, I think I've got it!"

Erin Malloy sat between her friends Sarah and Jennifer in the crowded lecture hall. Amidst the loud chatter of the class, they enthusiastically made weekend plans, starting with tonight. They would meet at Wild Sam's at eight, have a couple drinks, and then go to Teddy and Ron's party; Sarah agreed to drive. Jennifer began discussing what to wear when Dr. Klaus Tolshwin attached the portable microphone to his coat lapel, and moved to the front of the 125-seat lecture hall. He cleared his throat, adjusted his bow tie, and smiled. As always, Tolshwin's navy suit was perfectly pressed, and his black shoes sparkled under the fluorescent lights; his proper attire nicely matched the beautiful wood-paneled walls of the lecture hall. As the chattering class quieted down, Erin opened her notebook to a blank page, and clicked open her pen.

"Good morning, my friends," began the well-liked professor in a mild German accent. Tolshwin had bushy gray hair and a thick mustache; he could easily pass for a younger Albert Einstein, or perhaps a German Mark Twain.

The soft roar muffled to complete silence, and the students attentively listened to the professor.

"Today, my friends, we begin our exploration of a wonderful part of the brain: the limbic system. Let me begin with a story."

He clicked a button on a handheld remote control. A black-and-white photograph appeared on the large white screen that covered most of the front wall. It showed a rugged man wearing a white tee-shirt and dark pants. He carried a shovel over his shoulder, and he grinned into the camera.

"This is Phineas Gage, a New England railroad construction foreman in the mid-1800's," began Tolshwin. "Gage had a reputation of being the best at what he did. Contractors eagerly employed this foreman because he was so conscientious and capable; he also had a business sense which made him more efficient and in-tune with his contractors' timelines.

"Gage was well-liked by his co-workers. He had many friends, and he was known as strong and smart, but also compassionate and easygoing. Everyone knew that this guy was going places; he had 'success' written all over him.

"That all changed on September 13, 1848." Tolshwin clicked his remote button, and the picture on the screen changed. A disturbing sight filled the screen: a human skull was pierced by a thick metal rod; the rod went into the left cheek bone and out the top of the head. "That's a computer-generated image," admitted the professor. "But it illustrates exactly what happened.

"Gage and his men were working on the Rutland-Burlington Railroad, north of here in Vermont. In a freak accident, a charge accidentally exploded, and it drove an iron rod through Gage's head. The three-and-a-half foot rod had a sharp point that entered Gage's left cheek bone, exited the roof of his skull, and landed about twenty-five meters behind him."

Several rumbles and gasps filled the auditorium.

"Strangely," continued Tolshwin, "Gage never lost consciousness. Fortunately, he was quickly treated by this young physician, Dr. Harlow." A facial shot of a young, serious man with a ponytail and a stern look filled the screen. "Harlow quickly realized that most of Gage's left frontal brain must have been destroyed. Despite that, Harlow skillfully treated his wounds as best he could, and in less than three months, Gage was actually sent home to New Hampshire."

The image on the screen flipped back to the skull and iron bar. "So there he was: a survivor of massive, massive brain injury." Tolshwin sighed. "It's what happened next that is most tragic. Gage wanted to return to work. But his contractors wouldn't hire him because, to their shock and dismay, he was a completely changed man. Phineas Gage, who had always been a smart, gentle, and likable man, was now angry, fitful, and grossly profane. He would disrespectfully bark obscenities at his fellows, and would enter fits of rage at the drop of a hat. His motivation to succeed in life had also changed; he carelessly ignored any future plans which he had once held so dear. In essence, my friends, he had a completely changed personality.

"From there, the story gets blurrier, but gloomier nonetheless." Tolshwin clicked on a picture of a dilapidated wooden barn in a barren field. "Reportedly, Gage never worked as a foreman again. He worked at a museum, then at this stable, and then driving coaches and caring for horses in Chile. Some reports—and mind you, these reports may be fanciful—claim that Gage also worked in a circus, fell victim to severe alcoholism, and lost all sexual inhibitions. Regardless, he died under his mother's care in San Francisco in 1860."

Tolshwin slowly strutted around the front of the auditorium, watching the disturbed expressions on his students' faces. "I do not mean to disturb you with this story," he said. "I do mean to allow Mr. Gage to introduce you to a primitive part of the brain that influences emotions, including anger, rage, placidity, and social attraction: the limbic system.

"You see, researchers believe that when the iron rod speared Gage's brain, his frontal lobe—which as we said yesterday, offers many inhibitory signals to other parts of the brain—disconnected from his underlying limbic system. Therefore, many primitive emotional expressions, such as rage and possibly sexual aggressiveness, were disinhibited. They were unleashed, if you will. So in essence, the separation of Gage's frontal lobe from his limbic system gave us a unique window into the limbic system, which is usually masked by our more-evolved higher inhibitions."

Tolshwin paused, cleared his throat, and clicked on a cross-sectional drawing of a human brain. "So then. What exactly is this limbic system? What does it do? The limbic system is a collection of neural structures that are interspersed throughout the brain; it includes the cingulate gyrus, the amygdala, and the hippocampus. For the most part, the limbic system forms a ring around the brainstem." Tolshwin shined a small red laser light on the screen; he circled the brainstem as he spoke.

He then clicked onto a portrait of a serious white man. "This is James Papez. In 1937, he suggested that the limbic system forms a neural circuit which is the anatomic basis of emotion." He clicked again, and showed two more portraits of white men. "Also in 1937, Heinrich Kluver and Paul Bucy reported that the destruction of both temporal lobes in monkeys—which include the amygdala, hippocampus, and several other limbic structures—causes dramatic changes in the monkeys' emotional and sexual behavior. Together, Papez, Kluver, and Bucy are really the pioneers of studying the neurobiology of emotions."

Tolshwin clicked the brain drawing back on. "So then, the limbic system is involved in emotions and in certain primitive behaviors. But how?" His red light started dancing over the brain drawing. "Parts of the limbic system, such as the amygdala and the hippocampus, provide input to this brain structure—the hypothalamus. The hypothalamus in turn coordinates this input with input from other parts of the brain to influence various body functions and certain behaviors. For example, the amygdala may 'tell' the hypothalamus that it wants to increase sexual behavior. The hypothalamus will 'weigh' that request against whatever inhibitory signals come from the cerebral cortex. If the limbic signals 'outweigh' the inhibitory signals, so to speak, the hypothalamus will prepare the organism's body for sexual activity."

Tolshwin paused. "That, of course, is quite simplified. But I hope it gives you a general sense of what the limbic system can do."

Erin Malloy scribbled down a few notes. Her brow was wrinkled, and her attention to Tolshwin was beginning to fade. The story of Phineas Gage bothered her, but she couldn't completely figure out why. According to Tolshwin, it made sense that his personality had changed; after all, his limbic system was unleashed to release 'primitive' emotions and behavior. Sure, that should make sense.

But, Erin asked herself, did that mean that personality was simply a web of nerve cells?

She frowned, and continued to scribble down notes for the remainder of the lecture.

Jade Evans sat at her office desk, picked up the phone, and punched in the 1-800 number.

A recorded female voice answered. "Welcome to MedWatch, the medical products reporting system of the Food and Drug Administration. If you are reporting an adverse experience with a medical product, press one. If not, press two."

She pressed one.

"If you would like to report an adverse experience with a medicine, press one. If you would like to report an adverse experience with a medical device, press two. To report an adverse experience with a vaccine, press three. To report an adverse experience with an animal medicine, press four."

She pressed one again.

"Please hold, while I transfer you to a representative."

Jade listened to soft classical music as she held the line. She glanced at her clock. 3:40. Her next patient's appointment was in five minutes.

"Welcome to MedWatch," said a friendly female voice. "This is Janet. How can I help?"

"Hi," she replied. "This is Dr. Jade Evans. I'd like to report a worrisome side effect of an herbal medicine."

"Okay, Doctor. You've encountered this side effect in your patients?"

"Yes I have."

"Okay." Jade heard the tapping of computer keys. "Please continue," said the representative.

"The herb in question is called Quazhen," began Jade. "I hadn't heard of it before, but it recently appeared in a local health food store."

The tapping on the computer keys got louder and faster. "Hmm," said the other woman. "How do you spell it?"

Jade strained hard to remember the jars she had seen at Natural Essentials. Indeed, the labels' single word, 'Quazhen', came back to her. She relayed the correct spelling.

"I don't have that name here. Could it be under a different name?"

Jade's face reddened. "I was told that it had been reported to you under the name Quazhen. I don't think there is any other name."

The other woman kept typing. "No," she said, quite nonchalantly. "It's not here."

"How could that be?" asked Jade, getting irritated at the woman's cavalier demeanor.

"Well, to be honest, lots of supplements are marketed under crazy names; it's anybody's guess what's in many of them. I'm not terribly surprised that we have no file on this Quazhen."

"Really?" She was stunned.

"Yes. Really. Now then, let me start a file on it. Okay. What would you like to report?"

"Well," said Jade, unsettled. "A colleague and I have had several patients who have experienced behavioral changes with the herb."

"Oh, your colleague will need to report his own patients."

Jade sighed. "Fine. Well, then I've had two patients who suffered heightened aggression, and in one case, increased sexual behavior after using Quazhen."

She heard the typing. "Aggression and increased sexual behavior," the woman repeated. "Okay. Do you know for how long they were using it?"

"In one case, a day. In the other case, I don't know."

She typed that in. "Okay. Do you know the manufacturer of this product?"

"I think so." She gave her the name Natural Essentials, and said it was in Manchester, Connecticut.

"Okay," said the woman. "Anything else?"

Jade was taken aback. "That's it?"

"Yes, Doctor. That's it. Unless you have any other adverse experience reports to offer."

Jade raised her eyebrows. "No. No, that's it." She paused to think, and then asked, "Tell me, what happens with that information?"

"Well, it goes to the FDA Center for Food Safety and Applied Nutrition. A panel there will review the report, and they'll then take one of several possible routes. They may ask the manufacturer for a sample of the herb, to study it themselves. Of course, it's then up to the manufacturer whether or not to comply with their request. Alternatively, the panel may choose to alert the public in a safety alert. But that would be a pretty sudden and severe move. More than likely, they'll accept the information, and then store it until other complaints come in with similar concerns about the product."

Jade wrinkled her brow. "So you're telling me that since this is the first complaint against Quazhen, probably nothing will be done?"

"Well, to be truthful, yes. Now, if lots of incriminating reports come in, the panel could take stronger action. They could ask the manufacturer to remove the product from the market, or in severe cases, they could bring the manufacturer to court, to try to force it off the shelves."

"Wait a second," said Jade, her frustration beginning to climb. "So if an herb comes out that causes obvious and severe damage to consumers, the FDA requires a court process to get it off the market?!"

"Yes. The FDA cannot just pull an herb off the market. Of course, the Secretary of Health and Human Services *can* immediately stop the sales of any herb; but that only happens if there's an extremely high suspicion of immediate danger from that herb. And a trial must then occur to permanently remove that product from the market. Frankly, it would be rare for the Secretary to unilaterally halt an herb's commerce, even if such an action is temporary until a court process occurs. That power is for extreme cases. With all due respect, Doctor, the Secretary's not going to yank this Quazhen because you say it causes 'aggression and increased sexual behavior'. That's a little soft, you know?"

Jade closed her eyes and took a deep breath. A little soft? Her heart started to pound.

"Okay," surrendered Jade. "Fine. But could you write in the report that this Quazhen stuff is, to the best of my knowledge, only sold in one store? It's supposedly a rare Chinese herb that's only available in a small Connecticut town. So I doubt other complaints will be pouring in about it. And I'm really, really concerned."

"Yes, I'll report that. Would you like me to include your name and phone number in the report."

"Please." She gave her phone number and email address. She then thanked her and got off the phone.

"Unbelievable," she muttered to herself. Jade couldn't help but believe that some of that information had been wrong. At the very least, some important details about the regulation of herbs must have been left out. After all, the FDA was a strong organization; surely it had stronger control over herbs than the MedWatch woman had disclosed.

Frustrated by the phone call, she left to see her next patient.

At the end of the day, John walked into Jade's office.

"I was reading up on the limbic system. I think you've nailed this one," he remarked. "Quazhen must affect the limbic system."

"Yeah. Unfortunately, I don't think anything's going to be done about it, though."

"What do you mean?"

"I called MedWatch, the FDA reporting system. Essentially, they need multiple complaints to really do anything about it. And even then, the guys at Natural Essentials could drag it through a long court battle." She sighed. "By the way, you need to call MedWatch yourself about your own patients."

John frowned. "That's ridiculous. This herb almost definitely has a really serious side effect. You were sexually assaulted because of it."

"Well, can we prove that?"

"Why the hell should we have to?! We're doing society a favor by warning them about a bad drug—I mean herb!"

"Drug is the right word. Yeah, I obviously agree with you. But apparently the laws are set up such that it's hard to get an herb off the market."

"So nobody's reported any problems with Quazhen in the past?"

"Oh, the stuff wasn't even on file. They've never heard of it before."

"And yet they can sell it?!" John's eyes were wide and his face was red. He seldom got this worked-up.

"I guess so." She shook her head. "You know, I have a lawyer friend down in New Haven. I think he used to work at the FDA, before he went to law school. His name's Phil Santiago. Maybe it would be worth it to give him a call; he might know more about the legislation that affects how these herbs are regulated."

"Sounds like a good idea. But in the meantime, what do we do?"

"Well, we start by telling our patients not to use the stuff." Her face suddenly lit up. "You know, I suppose we could contact the media."

His eyes twinkled. "Yes. Yes, Jade, that's a very good idea." He thought about it. "Let's write an editorial to the Hartford Courant."

"And we'll spread the word around the office, and to the other practices."

"Good."

They stared at each other, satisfied about that first step.

"You know, though," said Jade, "I wonder if the Natural Essentials owner might voluntarily help our cause."

"Huh? I thought you said he was a major jerk."

"No. His brother was. But the owner seemed like a decent guy. And he did say he wanted to talk more about possible side effects…uh-oh."

"What?"

"I told him I'd call him today to arrange a time to meet. He wanted to know more about these side effects."

John looked at her skeptically. "You think he'll voluntarily yank Quazhen off his shelves? Not too likely, Jade."

"Well, here. Give me that phone book." She took the yellow pages from him. "Let's see…here they are." She punched in some numbers. "You want to meet with them, too?"

"If I'm free, yeah."

The phone rang.

"Natural Essentials. Can I help you?" said a pleasant female voice.

"Hi. Dr. Jade Evans here. May I speak with the owner of the store? He's expecting me."

"Sure. One minute please." Jade heard her call over to Yu-lan. She cringed as she heard Feng's voice in the background grumbling some unintelligible comment.

"Hi Doctor. Yu-lan Tang here."

"Yes. Hello, Yu-lan. How are you?"

"Fine, thank you. And yourself?"

"Okay. Yu-lan, I called the FDA's MedWatch program today. They've never heard of Quazhen; yet your brother said they had been informed about it."

"Hmm." He spoke to Feng to the side. "Dr. Evans called the FDA today. They said they've never heard of Quazhen. I thought you contacted them about it."

Jade heard the brother's disgusted tone. "She called the damn FDA?"

The brothers' conversation became muffled; Yu-lan was obviously covering the mouthpiece with a hand. Regardless, Jade clearly heard Feng's angry tone in the background. She caught a few cuss words, surely aimed at her.

Yu-lan addressed her again. "I'm sorry, Doctor. Perhaps there was some confusion; my brother insists he had contacted them months ago."

"Whatever," she said. "Anyway, I was hoping we could still meet to discuss the side effects of the herb."

"Yes, yes. I would like that. Is tomorrow okay?"

She looked at John. "Tomorrow okay?" He quickly nodded. "Yes; tomorrow's fine. I'd like to bring a colleague of mine. We could be there at ten."

"Very well. Ten it is. I'll be expecting you both. Thank you, Dr. Evans." He hung up.

The doctors agreed that Jade would pick up John at quarter-to-ten. After discussing the herb for another minute, they said their goodnights, and then left.

Jade spent over an hour at the supermarket before returning home. It was eight o'clock by the time all the groceries were put away. She threw a couple of low-fat hot dogs into the microwave, and then made herself a simple salad.

"Excuse me, Miss Nora," she said, stepping over her cat and moving to the living room. Jade set her dinner down on the coffee table, plopped herself down on the sofa, and grabbed the remote control.

She munched on a hot dog, and flipped through channels. Nothing was on. She glanced at her small video collection; maybe tonight would be a good night for a movie…

Through an open window adjacent to the television, she saw a dark figure flash by. It had moved from one side of the window to the other.

She froze. Her wide eyes stared at the open window.

There was nothing more to see. Just the gray night air.

She clicked off the television, and slowly rose. Her heart racing, she slowly and cautiously took measured steps toward the window.

A twig snapped outside.

She stopped in her tracks, two feet from the window. Her head began to throb as she strained her ears.

Silence.

She began to move closer…

Squeeeal! She jumped at the sudden sound of a vehicle tearing down the road. It was moving away from her house.

Within seconds, the sound of the vehicle was gone.

Jade shuddered.

It had come from her driveway.

Her heart pounding and her palms drenched, she turned and ran towards her front door. She flipped on the outside lights, and then looked out a front window. She saw nothing. In a moment of frenzy, she unlocked the front door and swung it open.

Nothing.

Nothing but the cool, refreshing night air.

She froze, staring outside for a few minutes. Her eyes could barely make out the gentle swaying of trees in the darkness. With a chill bolting down her spine, she opened the screen door, and stepped outside.

She felt her heart furiously whack against her chest wall as she moved towards her garage. Her walkway was well lit from the outdoor lights. She got to the closed garage door, and stared at it.

Maybe this wasn't a good idea. Maybe she should turn and bolt towards the house. And lock herself in.

She closed her eyes, and took in a deep breath. In a swift motion, she punched the garage door opener, and crouched down to look inside.

Thank God. Her car was still there.

Breathing hard and fast, she stood up, and closed the garage door. She turned and faced her yard. She was still for a few minutes.

Nothing.

Finally, Jade slowly walked back up the walkway. She opened the screen door, and entered her house. She quickly locked the front door and fastened the deadbolt.

Something pressed into her ankle.

"Aaaraugh!" She screamed and jumped to the side. She raised both fists in front of her face, and stared.

Nora stared back, confused at her startled owner.

Jade stood, shaking. She slowly dropped her hands, and allowed herself to gradually calm down. "Bad kitty," she whispered.

When her breathing rate was closer to normal, she walked around her house. She closed all the windows and locked them. She checked to make sure the back door was locked. She then turned on every light in her house.

And then, she sat down, and shivered.

Jade grabbed a phone.

"Hi, John? Yeah, it's me. Hey, would you come over?"

PART TWO

THE DEVIL'S PRICE

9

Like the previous few days, Saturday morning was unusually warm in Manchester. The yellow sun was shining in a cloudless blue sky. But despite the pleasant weather, a large flock of dark birds was silently moving overhead. Situated in their characteristic V-shaped pattern, the birds were heading south in an effort to flee the upcoming New England chill.

Wearing a green short-sleeve polo shirt, John followed Jade into Natural Essentials. He admired the stone fountain, spicy scent, and soft music; but upon seeing the shelves of herbs, he became enveloped in cynicism.

Jade approached the front counter. An attractive young woman with short sandy-blond hair greeted her. "Can I help you?"

"Yes," Jade smiled. "We're here to see Yu-lan. He's expecting us."

A faceless voice called out to her from the far aisle. "I'm here, Doctor. Just a minute."

Yu-lan appeared from around the corner, carrying a large cardboard box full of jars. "Jennifer," he asked the cashier, "when you get a minute, would you finish stocking these?"

"Of course," she replied, and immediately took the box from him.

Yu-lan faced his guests. He was in an orange button-down shirt. "Now then. Hello." He then turned to John and extended his hand. "I'm Yu-lan Tang. Welcome to my store."

John graciously accepted the handshake. "John Harper. Nice to meet you."

"You're a friend of Dr. Evans?"

"A friend and fellow family physician, yes."

"Great. Shall we go to the back room?" proposed the Asian man.

The doctors shrugged good-naturedly, and followed him through a side door behind the counter.

"Can I get you some tea? Or coffee?"

"None for me, thanks," replied Jade. John also politely declined.

Yu-lan led them to a square wooden table in a small, sparse room. The plain white walls strikingly contrasted the beautifully decorated main store.

Rows of cardboard boxes lined three walls, and a narrow wooden counter was pushed against the fourth wall. Atop the counter was a microwave, a coffee maker, and a brown compact refrigerator. In the far left corner of the room, an open door led to a bathroom. The only part of this room with some character was the slick, tiled floor, which extended into here from the main store.

They all sat around the table.

"Well," smiled Yu-lan, clearly uncomfortable. "Let me start by apologizing to you, Dr. Evans, for my brother's behavior the other night. He can be quite moody, but that's no excuse. He was rude, and it was unacceptable."

Jade nodded. Good, she thought. That was appropriate. "Thank you. Out of curiosity, is he a co-owner of this store?"

Yu-lan folded his hands on the table, and began rubbing his thumbs together. "No. Actually, he's a temporary employee. We both came from China recently, and he's just working here until he finds another job."

Very telling, thought Jade.

"So," continued Yu-lan. "About the Quazhen. My family has been using it for centuries; we've never noticed any aggressive or sexual side effects. I'm very interested to hear your stories."

"Yes," began Jade. "John and I have identified four patients in the past week alone who have suddenly started acting oddly. They have essentially changed personalities. Two of them changed from pleasant men to aggressive monsters; one of those two also sexually assaulted me, like I had mentioned. Another one of the four patients is a gentle elderly man who suddenly became extremely sexual. The final of the four has always been terribly aggressive, but he now suddenly became unusually placid and friendly. There is one common link among all four men: they have recently been using Quazhen."

Yu-lan nodded slowly. "Hmm. That is unusual. Tell me, do you know of anyone else using Quazhen?"

"An office nurse uses it," chimed in John. "Besides that, no."

"Well, has your office nurse changed personalities?"

“No,” replied John. “But of course, medication side effects don’t occur in everybody. In our small sampling, four of five people did get the side effect from Quazhen; that’s pretty substantial.”

“Well,” Yu-lan smiled, “with all due respect, Doctor, that’s a big statement. We don’t know for sure if Quazhen has anything to do with these strange happenings. Correct?”

Jade frowned. “It would be a pretty darn big coincidence, don’t you think, Yu-lan?”

He shrugged and shook his head. “Honestly, no. Not really. Because add this into your calculation: I’ve sold about two hundred bottles of Quazhen to about one hundred people since we opened. I’ve heard of no such ‘side effects’ from any of those people. So really, you’re finding a side effect in four of about one hundred people.”

“Wait a sec,” said John, a bit louder. “You can’t possibly know who develops this side effect and who doesn’t. If they become more aggressive or sexual, why would they report it to you? The fact is, eighty of those one hundred people could have changes in their personalities.”

Yu-lan shook his head. “How do you possibly think that Quazhen affects someone’s personality?”

Jade spoke up. “We think it may affect the limbic system, which is the part of the brain that deals with emotions and behavior, including sexual behavior.”

Yu-lan looked unconvinced. “With all due respect, Doctors, I’m having trouble believing your evidence.”

John shook his head. “What exactly is Quazhen, anyway? How do we know it’s not a known toxic plant?”

“Quazhen is a very rare flower found in China. For generations, it has been known that it only grows on my family’s plantation. Please trust me, sir, it has never been sold in America before now.” His eyes showed his sincerity. “I swear, if I knew that Quazhen was unsafe, I would never sell it. I swear.”

John twisted his lip. “How do you get it here?”

“My grandmother mails it. Simple as that.”

"You can just mail plants from one country to the next? What about customs?"

"Oh, sure. It has to pass through customs. I'm not sure about the details, but I think they take some and test it for parasites and other critters. I know you also need the proper permits to send plants into the U. S. But all in all, the process works. From the time she sends a shipment, it takes about three months to get here. She's only made two shipments so far."

"I think we're getting off the topic," interjected Jade. "Look, Yu-lan. We're concerned about the herb. I'm sorry if you flat out don't believe us, but I think we have good evidence that Quazhen could be a very dangerous product. Now, we've contacted the FDA already, as we mentioned. Unfortunately, we found that it's a long, drawn-out process to get them to take any action. The quickest way to immediately protect *your* customers and *our* patients is to pull Quazhen from the shelves."

Yu-lan gave a startled expression. "Doctor, that's awfully extreme..."

The door suddenly opened. With wet hair and a white tank-top, Feng entered the room. He looked surprised to see everyone there.

"Feng," said Yu-lan firmly. "We're in a meeting."

"Sorry," he replied flatly. "Mind if I grab some coffee?"

Yu-lan looked at Jade. She looked at John. He looked at the table.

"Quickly, okay?" said his brother.

Feng strutted over to the coffee pot. Seeing that it was empty, he strolled to the bathroom to fill it with water. He carefully avoided eye contact with Jade.

"We don't think pulling Quazhen is extreme at all," said John to Yu-lan. "It doesn't have to be permanent. Just until we all do some more investigation on the matter."

From the bathroom, Feng silently shot him a glare. Nobody noticed.

"Until who investigates?" asked Yu-lan. "Who is 'we'?"

"Well," continued John, "I for one would like to ask more of our patients about it. I know Jade would want to do the same. You yourself could ask your customers about these side effects."

"And," said Jade, getting excited, "perhaps you could call the FDA yourself."

Yu-lan wrinkled his brow.

"Perhaps the FDA would voluntarily investigate the herb, if its distributor requested it out of good conscience."

Feng walked back towards the coffee maker. He literally bit his tongue to prevent himself from talking. Last night, Yu-lan had made it very clear that he didn't want Feng to be a part of this discussion. And though it disturbed him to admit it, this was still Yu-lan's store. And he was still, supposedly, a temporary employee.

"I don't know," said Yu-lan, sitting back in his chair. He shook his head and sighed. "Yes, I want my customers to be safe. That's obvious. But again, I just don't know if I believe your…"

"Yu-lan," said John, more forcefully. "I know we can't prove that Quazhen is dangerous. But you can't prove that it's safe, either. What harm does it do to hold the Quazhen until everybody is more certain about its safety?"

Feng watched the coffee dribble into the pot, silently fuming.

"I don't know…"

Jade helped apply the pressure. "Really, Yu-lan. Let's work together as responsible adults, here. Like John said, what harm does it do to hold the herb for a little while?"

"Only hundreds of dollars in lost sales," spat out Feng, his back to them. "Maybe thousands."

"Feng!" barked Yu-lan. "You're not in this conversation!"

Feng spun around. "Come on, Yu-lan. I can't listen to this anymore!" He looked at the doctors. "What you guys are doing is illegal."

"What?!" retorted John.

"Seriously," continued Feng, over his brother's commands. "You have no proof whatsoever that Quazhen is dangerous."

"Right," shot Jade. "We have no absolute proof. But we have some pretty good evidence, nonetheless. Are you really going to put your business profits over people's health?!"

"Hey," replied Feng. "It's not our job to prove Quazhen's safety. That's a fact, lady. That is a fact."

Irate, Jade stared at Yu-lan, wondering why he was suddenly silent. "Yu-lan," she pleaded.

He shook his head. "I'm sorry. I think my brother's right on this one. Remember, Doctors, Quazhen has been a family tonic for *centuries*. There have never been any adverse effects in all that time."

Jade and John exchanged frustrated stares. They had lost.

"Well," snapped John. "Just so you know, we'll be writing editorials, contacting the media, and doing whatever else we can to educate the public about Quazhen. Even if you refuse to do your moral duty, we'll still certainly do ours."

Feng glared at him coldly.

"Quazhen *will* be off your shelves," fired Jade, standing up. "I promise you that."

Feng turned to glare at her, even more coldly.

Yu-lan frowned. "Folks, I'm sorry. Sometimes good people can disagree on things, you know?"

John stood up. "Whatever."

The two doctors abruptly turned and left, slamming the back room door behind them. Yu-lan heard them muttering angrily through the store. The chimes sounded as they left through the main doors.

Feng joined his brother at the table. He watched his brother silently berate himself and question his own actions. "Yu-lan," he said.

His brother looked over.

"They're wrong. We're right. Period."

He cocked his head. "But what if they're right? What if Quazhen does cause those bad side effects? Maybe it's simply in our genes not to be affected."

"Yu-lan, no." He was firm. "Quazhen is a good herb. A very good herb. You hear me?"

He shook his head. "I don't need bad press, either, Feng." He sighed. "Maybe I should pull it. Just for awhile."

"Yu-lan." He was raising his voice.

His brother turned. "Well, at the very least, now I'm definitely not asking Grandma for more. Not yet, anyway. I want to see where this all goes first."

Feng stared at him with wide eyes. He curled his lip.

He needed that shipment.

Feng looked at the empty seats where Jade and John had been sitting.

"It won't go far, Yu-lan. I promise you. It won't go far."

10

Jade hummed along to the catchy pop song, blaring out of her car speakers. She had just dropped off John, and after spending an hour at his house, was now heading home. During her short stay at his house, John had reminded her to call Phil Santiago, her lawyer friend in New Haven. She called him from John's place, but only got his answering machine. Jade had left a long message, asking him to call her back; she said she had some questions regarding the regulation of herbs by the U. S. government.

Delighted with the beautiful day, she tried to clear her mind. She wanted to forget about the frustrations at Natural Essentials. Now that a beautiful weekend was here, she just wanted some time to relax. She slid back her sunroof, and put on her sunglasses.

She approached the local carwash. Should she swing in? Too late to decide, she thought as she drove by; maybe she'd go later today. The pop song ended; Jade flipped through stations to find another upbeat tune.

Her road was coming up. She slowed down, flicked on her blinker, and turned right. She slowly accelerated up a gently sloped hill. As she rounded an ascending corner, she glanced down at her radio, wondering where she was on the frequency spectrum. She was about to hit the 'seek' button when something caught her eye.

Up the hill, about a hundred yards ahead, was a large black pick-up truck. It was parked on the side of the road, and it faced ahead, away from Jade.

It was parked in front of her house.

Jade clicked off her radio, and slowed down. She needed to make a decision. Should she pull into her driveway, or keep going straight?

She neared the truck. It was mammoth. Its body boasted shiny black paint that glimmered in the sunlight, and bright rays also glistened off its chrome bumper. The windows were tinted jet black.

She quickly thought about the Gunther Petchov episode. Then she thought about the shadowy figure last night.

She accelerated, intent on going straight past the truck. As she drove around it, she looked over at her house.

A man in a black leather jacket and black pants stood in her driveway. He was tall, had brown hair and a brown beard, and wore dark sunglasses.

He looked right at her.

Her heart pounding again, she slammed down on the gas. The police station was about ten minutes away—maybe less with shortcuts. She sped forward, rounding corners too fast and braking too little. As she moved forward, the road became more and more deserted. A thick forest lined both sides of the road, and no other cars were in sight. She swallowed hard. The road would be this way for another two or three minutes. Eventually, it would open up onto another main road.

She cursed as she approached a stop sign. There was absolutely no need for a stop sign on this road; apparently, someone just wanted to slow down traffic.

She slowed down, not intending to fully stop. She glanced up at her rearview mirror.

The black truck was flying towards her.

"Shit!"

She punched the gas again, and sped forward. She tingled with alertness, and stiffly sat up in her seat. Every other second, her eyes darted to the rearview mirror.

He was gaining.

She cried out in a fearful frustration as she continued to accelerate. She whipped around corners and sped up and down hills.

He was still gaining.

Terrified, she watched as his front bumper came within inches from her rear bumper. The colossal chrome grill stretched across her rear window. Then…

"Asshole!" she shrieked as he nudged her Saab with his truck. The impact jolted her forward; her seatbelt snapped her back. She stayed steady on the road, and held the gas pedal to the floor.

"Hey!" Another nudge jostled her again, and she momentarily skipped to the left side of the road. With chills in her spine, she regained control of her car.

Who was this?! What did someone want with her?!

Suddenly, the truck veered left, and began to pass her.

Horrified, she glanced left, out her driver's side window. She watched as the truck came within an inch of her car. Then…

"Bastard!" she screamed as it grazed against the Saab. Like nails on a chalkboard, the rubbing metal emitted a screeching cry. Jade was shoved to the right, and watched in terror as a tree quickly approached her.

She slammed on the brakes and whipped the wheel to the left. Her tail flung to the right as the brakes screeched in protest; she skidded harshly forward. Out of the corner of her eye, she saw the black truck speed ahead. She spun ninety degrees, and continued to skid forward.

Then suddenly, she stopped. She was in the middle of the road, facing left.

She looked right. Further up the road, the truck was stopped. Its brake lights were on.

He was waiting.

"A car phone would be good," she grumbled to herself. "A cell phone would be even better." She cursed herself as she stared at her phoneless center console.

She looked right again. He was still waiting.

With a hard, swift motion, she shifted into reverse and spun the wheel right. The car jarred back and to the right. She then ripped the shift into drive, straightened the wheel, and plunged forward, back towards her house.

As she expected, he turned around, and started following her again.

She had a head start on him; she slammed down on the gas and crossed her fingers. Hopefully, she could make it to the main road before he caught her.

She sped around corners, praying that nobody was coming the other way. Her house was now approaching on the left. As she whizzed by, she shot a hurried glance at it. It looked okay in that fraction of a second.

Her eyes darted back to her rearview mirror.

He was gone.

She whipped her head to her left; was he in her blind spot?

No.

Her heart pounding and lungs burning, Jade gradually slowed down. Where was he? Where could he possibly have gone? He easily could have caught her by now. She shook her head. He must have stopped, turned around again, and continued up the road.

She released a long sigh. She was safe. For now, anyway.

Her sheer fright gradually yielded to anger. What was going on here? Who was this bearded man in the black truck? What on earth did he want?

Frustrated, she sped forward, towards the Manchester Police Department.

Jade arrived at the police department, parked her car, and went in. The same receptionist from a few days ago sat behind the long, wooden counter.

"Can I help you?"

"I hope so," Jade replied, her voice shaking. "Someone's after me. I don't know who. I don't know why..."

"Okay, ma'am, okay." The woman was matter-of-fact, which in these circumstances seemed rude. "Wait here. I'll get an officer."

Jade turned as the receptionist picked up her phone. Within half a minute, the side door opened.

Sergeant Kolowski stood there. He looked at her for a moment, and then he rolled his eyes.

Great, thought Jade. She turned back to the receptionist, but she was already on the phone with somebody else.

"Well, well," huffed the sergeant. "The good doctor is back."

With painstaking effort, she faced him. "Look, I'm scared. Someone is after me."

He was unmoved. "My chief chewed out my ass the other day," he said, clearly annoyed. "Apparently, you called him and said lots of wonderful things about me."

Her adrenaline started shooting again. "Someone," she spat out, "is after me, Sergeant. Did you not hear me?"

The receptionist briefly looked up, and then returned her attention to the phone call.

He stared at her with accusatory eyes. "Get in here," he snapped, and abruptly turned.

She caught the door before it slammed shut, and she reluctantly followed him to the same small room. He plopped himself down on a chair, and rested his hands behind his head.

She remained standing. "Maybe I should meet with someone else," she suggested. "Maybe that's in both of our best interests."

He closed his eyes and shook his head. "Nobody else here, Doc." He flipped his eyes open and smiled wryly. "You're stuck with me."

She silently cursed, and sat down.

"All right," he sighed, dramatically. "What happened?"

She took a deep breath. Then, "It started last night. I saw a shadow move across the window. A few seconds later, I heard a vehicle speed off from my driveway." She then told him about today's events, doing her best to describe the bearded man and the black truck, and then reemphasized that she had no idea who would do this.

He shrugged. "I don't know, Doc. I can't imagine a nice person like you having any enemies."

She almost cursed him out right there. But she bit her lip.

"Well, Doc, why don't you put everything down on an official record. I'll get you a pen and paper."

"Fine. What are you going to do in the meantime."

"Well, that depends. Did you get his license plate number?"

"No. Things went too fast."

"Right. Well, I'll alert my patrolmen to a big black truck with tinted windows. If they find one that looks suspicious, they'll pull him over and question him."

"What do you mean, 'one that looks suspicious'?"

He shrugged. "I can't have every black pick-up in the town searched, Doc."

They stared at each other, barely maintaining civility.

"Okay," she said. "What else can you do?"

"What do you want me to do?"

She bit her lip again. Harder. Then, "Can you have a patrolman swing by my place every so often?"

He cracked another wry smile. "Sure. Every so often. Sure."

"Sergeant Kolowski, I'm concerned here."

He dropped his smile. "So am I, Dr. Evans."

She looked at his ruddy face and overweight body, and decided she had had more than enough. She was done here. "Fine. Then I'll be going."

He stood up. "Wait. You need to fill out that incident report, remember?"

He got her a blank form and a black pen. She scribbled down exactly what she had told him, and then handed it back to him. Without a word, he took it, and left the room.

Disgusted, she decided that if she didn't see a patrol car drive by her house by dinnertime, she'd call back here. And ask for a different officer.

Jade stood up, and began to walk out.

Suddenly, several chirping beeps rang out from her right hip. She looked down, and silenced her beeper. Odd, she thought. Who was paging her on a Saturday?

555-2000.

Hmm. Wasn't that Hartford?

Jade exited into the waiting room, and approached the receptionist.

"Hi. I'm a local physician, and I just got a page. Would you have a phone I could use?"

The receptionist handed her a phone receiver through a small hole in the counter's glass. She asked for the number, and then dialed it for Jade.

A few rings, and then, "St. Francis operator."

Jade wrinkled her brow. St. Francis was one of two large hospitals in Hartford. "Hi. This is Dr. Evans. I was paged to this number."

"Yes, Doctor. I'll connect you to the other party."

A moment later, she heard the nervous voice of Tammy Harper, John's sister.

"Hi, Jade?"

"Yeah, Tam, it's me. What's up?" Her heart started to race.

"John's here in the intensive care unit," she said in a broken voice. "He was in an accident."

11

Jade exited the elevator and hurriedly approached the receptionist. A well-dressed Hispanic woman with straight black hair smiled at her.

"Welcome to St. Francis Intensive Care Unit. May I help you?"

"Yeah, hi. I'm Dr. Jade Evans, a family physician in Manchester. Can you buzz me through to the ICU?"

"Do you have your badge, Doctor?"

"Actually, I don't admit to this hospital. But a doctor in my practice is in there. His name is John Harper."

The receptionist looked sympathetic, but started shaking her head. "I'm sorry. Dr. Harper just got here. He's not allowed to have visitors, not yet anyway. I know his sister was around here, somewhere. Maybe she went down to the cafeteria, if you'd like to try to find her."

Jade's blood instantly started to boil. "Look, could you call in to Dr. Van Martin for me?"

"Sure." The receptionist picked up her phone and pressed a single button.

Dr. Pierre Van Martin was a nationally renowned intensivist who had worked for over forty-five years at St. Francis. Jade had been taught by him back at UConn Medical School. He had been one of her very best teachers; besides knowing virtually everything about intensive care medicine, he was the nicest guy you could ever know.

"Dr. Van Martin?" said the receptionist. "A Dr. Evans is here for you." A pause. Then, "Yes. Dr. Jade Evans. Okay."

She turned to Jade. "He'll be right out."

Within moments, a set of wooden double doors opened to her left. A tall man with wrinkled tan skin, thinning gray hair, and a long white coat greeted her. His mouth turned into a warm, wide smile.

"Jade Evans," he said, approaching her with outstretched arms. "There's a name from the past! How are you, dear?"

She grinned for a moment, embraced him, and then looked up. "Actually, not too well, Pierre. John Harper is a partner in my practice."

His expression instantly began grim. Frowning, his closed his eyes and shook his head. Then, "Come, come."

He led her through the double doors. They entered a long, bright corridor with stretches of wooden desks on the right, and many patient rooms on the left. There were three walls per patient room; the fourth side—the one that faced the corridor—consisted of a large glass door and a curtain.

Jade followed Pierre past a flurry of white-coated residents and blue-scrubbed nurses. People were busy; one resident quickly flipped through a patient chart; two others stared at a computer monitor and read lab results. A nurse hurriedly entered a patient room with a bundle of green cloth; another one exited a different room with three empty syringes. Jade ducked out of the way of a lab tech wheeling a portable x-ray machine towards her; she almost walked directly into a bright red 'code cart', which resembled a four-foot toolbox on wheels.

Pierre rounded a corner, and then stopped ten feet short of a very busy room. Jade joined his side, and they watched as twelve people wearing yellow paper gowns, white latex gloves, and blue masks hovered around a single patient bed.

"As you know," stated the intensivist, "trauma patients go to the surgical team. I only care for medical patients."

"So that's Surgery in there, with John?"

"Yes."

They both looked on in silence.

"What do you want the vent settings to be?" barked a woman in dark blue scrubs.

"I want assist-controlled with a rate of twelve, tidal volume of seven hundred, PEEP of five, and an FiO_2 of fifty," said a yellow-gowned man. "Edward, is that subclavian line in?"

"Yep, I just got it."

An African-American woman spoke under her blue mask. "The new ABG back yet?"

"Yeah," someone replied. "PCO_2 of thirty-seven; PO_2 of one seventy-one; pH of seven point three six; bicarb of twenty-five. That's on FiO_2 of sixty."

"All right," she replied. "Get another one after that vent setting change. How about the DPL cytology?"

"Still pending."

"You sent it stat, right?"

"Oh definitely."

She looked up at a colorful monitor displaying several fluctuating numbers and a few dancing waves. "Why's that blood pressure eighty over fifty? Let's go people. We've sent blood for type and crossmatch?"

"Yes, ma'am. And we've got two liters of normal saline going wide open right now."

An Asian doctor spoke. "That chest tube's putting out some serious drainage. This guy's actively bleeding into his pleural cavity."

"That blood could've been there," replied the woman. "I'm not convinced he has an active bleeder. Okay, folks. Be on top of that DPL cytology. I'll warn the OR just in case this thing goes south."

She ripped off her paper gown and removed her gloves. As she exited the room, Pierre approached her.

"How does it look, Sandra?"

The dark-skinned woman shrugged. "I think he'll make it. I was worried about liver or spleen lacs, but the diagnostic peritoneal lavage was pretty clear when we drew it; now we're just waiting on its cytology. He had a hemopneumothorax, but the chest tube is draining out blood from his thorax well."

"Pulmonary contusions?" asked Jade.

"Likely, yes. But nothing he needs the OR for. Not yet anyway."

Pierre motioned to Jade. "This is Dr. Jade Evans, a family physician in Manchester, Sandra. Sandra Jackson, Jade, is the finest surgical attending I've seen in years."

"How do you do?" They shook hands.

"So," Jade said, still shocked. "What happened, anyway?"

"Car accident," she replied. "The guy hit a phone pole on some back road. I think it was in Manchester. We're doing a blood alcohol level and a u-tox to screen for drugs."

"Negative," snapped Jade. Realizing her harsh tone, she quickly softened her voice. "Sorry. I'm sure they'll be negative. John Harper is another family doctor; we practice together in Manchester. He's a wonderful guy."

"Oh my." Sandra gently touched Jade's shoulder. "I didn't know that. I'm very sorry." She shook her head. "Gee. Then it probably was some freak accident." She looked back into the room. "Man. Poor guy."

Jade curled her lip and nodded slowly. "Yeah. A freak accident."

"Well," said Pierre. "It sounds like he'll come through this. I know he'll be in excellent hands."

Sandra grinned. "Thanks. I gotta move. I have a lap chole waiting in the day hospital. Nice to meet you, Jade. I promise I'll take good care of John."

"Thanks." She managed a weak smile. "Nice to meet you, too."

Pierre turned to her. "He's out, right now, Jade. As you know, when patients are put on ventilators for respiratory support, we sedate them. You might want to come back another time."

Staring at John, she slowly nodded. "Yeah. You're right."

"You're welcome here anytime." He gently patted her back. "I'm sorry, Jade." He then left.

Alone, Jade simply stared at the horde of doctors, nurses, and technicians still swarming around John. She approached the open glass door, and looked more closely at her friend. Large purple blotches and streaks of maroon covered his face, arms, and legs. A thick blue tube ran from John's mouth to the large, digital ventilator, adjacent to his bed. Intravenous tubes and intraarterial catheters dangled from his limbs, and a narrow, plastic nasogastric tube fed out of his left nostril.

A tear fell down Jade's cheek. At the same time, a storm of rage began building inside her. This was certainly no accident. She thought about asking for the police report, but she knew there wouldn't be anything useful there. She would call the police department, and make her case for this being a hit-and-run.

But who hit and ran? Who wanted to hurt both John and her?

Suddenly, her stomach sank.

She turned, and quickly walked to the double doors.

Tammy was still not in the waiting area. That was fine, Jade thought; she'd call her later today.

She hit the down button, and impatiently waited for the elevator to arrive.

It was time to pay another visit to the Tang brothers.

She whipped open the door to Natural Essentials, and stormed towards the counter. She was actually delighted to see Feng Hou Tang there.

"I have some questions for you," she fired.

He wrinkled his brow. "Excuse me," he growled. "There are customers in this store. Wanna keep your voice down?"

"No. I don't." She was yelling.

"Then I'll call the police," he snorted sharply.

She silently stared at him for a minute, her anger rising steadily. He quietly returned the hard glare.

"John was in an accident today," she said. Feng continued to stare at her, unmoved. "But I don't think it really was an accident. I think it was a hit-and-run. Someone drove him off the road and into a phone pole."

He continued to stare at her, expressionless.

"Thanks for your sympathy, asshole," she snorted. "Anyway, I think it was a hit-and-run because somebody tried to run me off the road today, too."

He shrugged nonchalantly. "And?"

She shook her head in disgust. "And I wonder who would be angry at both John and me. Who would be angry enough to try to hurt us both? Who would be capable of that?" Her fiery eyes shot into his.

His eyes widened, and he leaned closer. "Are you accusing me of doing this?"

She leaned in. "I think it's pretty damn possible, yes."

He started breathing heavier. Sweat beads started to accumulate on his face.

Suddenly, the attractive young blonde emerged from the back room.

"Jennifer," shot Feng, still looking at Jade.

"Yes?" she asked, alarmed.

"Have I left this store all day?"

"No," she replied innocently.

He raised his eyebrows at Jade.

"I'm not saying *you* did it yourself, Feng," charged Jade.

Suddenly, a twinge of dread overcame her. She could be barking up the wrong tree all together. Maybe he wasn't behind it...

"No? You think it was Yu-lan?"

"No." She was quite sure of that.

"Well, then. So you *are* accusing me of somehow landing your friend in the intensive care unit..."

"How do you know he's in the ICU?!" She stepped back, eyeing him like a hawk eyeing a rat.

Without missing a beat, he snorted. "That's where people usually go after an accident, isn't it Doctor?"

"No. Not at all. It completely depends upon the accident." She stared at him in disbelief. "You did do it, didn't you? You mother..."

"No!" he shouted, his fiery rage beginning to explode.

A thin woman suddenly approached the counter. She walked cautiously, aware of the loud voices. Jennifer quickly went to the register, and cheerfully rang her up.

Jade and Feng continued to glare at each other, each one's heart thudding hard and fast.

"I'm done here," Jade abruptly stated. She turned to walk out.

Without saying a word, Feng watched her go.

When she had left the store, he slapped a rag down onto the countertop. He retreated to the back room, and grabbed a phone. He dialed. It only rang once.

"Jay, you fuckin' idiot. You need to try again, *now*. She left the store two seconds ago. And Jay, you mess this up again, and it's your ass. Am I clear?"

12

Jade waited at the stop light, bursting with anger and frustration. She punched off the radio; the happy pop song was annoying her. She thought about the best way to get back to the police station.

She shook her head. No matter what, she thought, she would not speak with Kolowski. She would simply sit and wait for somebody else, preferably the chief.

The light turned green, and she drove forward.

Suddenly, a blue Ford Escort pulled out in front of her, forcing her to slam on the brakes.

"Hey!" she yelled, blaring the horn. Idiot, she thought. Cutting her off like that could have caused an accident.

The old blue Ford began to accelerate, but it then slowed down. Soon, it was going twenty-five miles per hour.

"Oh, come on!" Jade yelled, slamming her fist on the steering wheel. She looked in her rearview mirror; nobody was there. Why couldn't this guy have waited until after she had passed!

She threw both hands up in desperation as the car slowly turned right. She, too, needed to go right. The other way to the police station would take an extra five or ten minutes; she wanted to get there as soon as possible.

Hoping the car would soon turn off, she followed it onto the new road. It was a back road with occasional houses interspersed between thick trees.

The car slowed down to twenty miles per hour. It then gently moved left, towards the middle of the road. It was now impossible for Jade to pass.

"What the hell!" She wondered if traffic was starting to pile up behind her. She glanced into her rearview mirror.

The monstrous chrome grill of the big black truck filled the mirror.

Suddenly, the Ford stopped short. Jade slammed down on her brakes, but she gently nudged the car regardless. Her back jostled forward as the truck banged into her rear bumper.

A mixed sense of terror and rage enveloped Jade. This was it, she thought. Something big was going to happen.

The door of the blue Ford swung open. A scruffy man with long blond hair stepped out. He was wearing a gray sweatshirt and jeans. He slammed his door and started walking towards Jade. Behind her, she watched as the bearded, brown-haired man in sunglasses also got out and approached her driver's side door.

Jade quickly locked her doors and rolled up the windows. She closed the sunroof. She couldn't drive away, she realized. She was wedged between their vehicles.

Both men reached her door at the same time. They stared down at her with angry scowls.

The bearded man tried to open the door. He seemed surprised that it was locked.

Stupid thug.

"Who are you?!" Jade called out through the window.

The blond man punched her window. It didn't break.

Okay, she thought. This was not good. She impatiently waited for a car to drive by. Surely, somebody had to be on this road!

The blond punched her window again. The slam was louder, but the glass still didn't crack.

Terrified, she slammed down on her horn. It wailed in a long, unbroken cry.

The window suddenly crashed as a bloody fist powered through. The glass shattered into thousands of cubic pieces. Jade screamed. As the blond man grabbed the lock and yanked it upwards, Jade hopped over to the passenger seat. She quickly unlocked the other door, and flung it open.

Unintentionally, Jade kicked down on the blond man's bloody hand as she jumped out of the car. He yelled out, and then barked at his partner.

Jade got out the passenger side door, and quickly stood up as the bearded man started hopping over her hood, towards her side of the car.

Suddenly, a red van appeared from farther up the road. The driver, a rugged older man, stuck his head out the window.

"What the hell's going on there!" he shouted.

"Help!" cried Jade.

But in a split second, the bearded man was on her side of the car. In a panic, she bolted back towards his truck. She ran past the truck, and narrowly missed the outstretched hand of the blond. Together, the two men chased her down the street, back towards the main road.

Behind them all, a door slammed. The van driver shouted as he darted towards them.

"Stop, you fellas! You stop right now!"

"Shit!" one of the men grumbled. They cried some unintelligible words to each other, and then suddenly turned around. Not looking back, Jade kept running forward.

The two men quickly ran towards the van driver. With tremendous force, they knocked him to the ground. He yelped as his head met the hard pavement.

Another car rounded the corner near the main road. Jade bolted towards it and waved her hands.

The men quickly got into their vehicles. The Ford sped off, and the black truck backed up, and then charged forward, around Jade's Saab.

They were gone.

Jade stopped a white Honda Accord with a teenage girl in it. The girl jumped out, and together, they ran up the road to the van driver.

Shaking violently, Jade did her best to stay in control.

"Sir!" she yelled, rattling his clothes. "Sir!" She looked at the girl. "Get help! We need an ambulance!"

The girl nodded, and sprinted back towards her car. She picked up her car phone, and dialed 911.

Jade pressed her cheek against the man's mouth. She felt his breath, and she watched as his chest rose with each inspiration. She checked his carotid pulses; they were weak, but there.

Sirens cut through the afternoon air as an ambulance, a fire truck, and three police cars blazed toward the scene.

A police car arrived first. A young officer jumped out, and ran to Jade's side.

"What happened?"

"I was attacked by two unknown men," she said hurriedly. "This driver of that red van stopped to help, but the men turned on him. I didn't see it, but I think they hit him hard."

"Where are they now?"

"They both took off in separate vehicles. They went straight up this road."

"Can you identify those vehicles?"

"Yes sir." Jade described them, and the officer repeated her words into his radio.

"We'll get some patrolmen after them. Did you get their license plates?"

"No."

They were then joined by two paramedics and two more police officers. The first officer told the story.

Jade interrupted. "I'm a doctor," she told the paramedics. "His ABC's are okay, but I'd collar and board him; he could have c-spine injury."

"All righty, Doc."

After an efficient minute-and-a-half, the ambulance sirens were wailing, and the man was off to Manchester Hospital. The fire truck left, and Jade was left with the three officers.

"You okay, ma'am?" asked one of them.

She felt tears starting to well up. She forcefully held them back. "Physically, yes. But I'm scared as hell."

"That's your car?"

"The Saab, yeah." She looked over at the shattered driver's side window and the dented bumper. Her heart sank.

"The van belongs to the patient," remarked the first officer. He then turned back to Jade. "Why don't you let me bring you to the station. We'll get your car there for you."

"Okay."

He turned to the other two. "Take care of the van, too, all right?"

"You got it."

As Jade rode in the patrol car, the young officer introduced himself as Officer Ted LeChatlier. He questioned her more fully, and she gave him the entire story, starting with the shadowy figure last night. She mentioned that she had seen Sergeant Kolowski this morning, and that the sergeant had promised to alert the officers about the black truck. LeChatlier shook his head; he hadn't heard from Kolowski all day. Jade also mentioned John, her suspicion of a hit-and-run, and her suspicion of Feng Hou Tang.

As they entered the police station, the receptionist shot a frown at Jade. Back again? she seemed to say.

LeChatlier brought Jade through the side door, further down the main corridor than she had been before, and into a larger conference room. He asked her to wait there for a moment. He left, but then returned with a bearded man in a shirt and tie, an Asian woman in street clothes, and to Jade's great dismay, Sergeant Kolowski.

"My goodness, Doctor," smiled Kolowski. "You must like it around here."

She turned her attention to the others.

"Dr. Evans," said the woman, "I'm Detective Wu. This is Detective Michaels. And I see that you know Sergeant Kolowski."

"Yes. Nice to meet you, Detectives."

Wu and Michaels got out notepads and pens. "Please," said Michaels, "tell us the whole story."

Jade sighed, and repeated the whole thing, one more time. When she finished the details of the two thugs, she mentioned her suspicion of Feng being involved in John's 'accident'.

"Hmm." Wu looked up at her. "Why would you suspect that?"

She related his comment about the intensive care unit.

Kolowski shifted his weight. "I wouldn't call that hard incriminating evidence. People in accidents do often wind up in the ICU. Why did you accuse Mr. Tang in the first place, Doctor?"

"Because," she replied, sounding defensive. "This is a really shady guy who was clearly upset at both of us this morning." She briefly described the confrontation over Quazhen.

"Quazhen?" said Wu, taken aback. "I started using that stuff two weeks ago. What do you mean it's unsafe?"

"You should stop using it, Detective," Jade admonished her. "John and I think it may affect one's personality. Some people become more passive, but more commonly, they become more aggressive and more sexual."

Wu stared at her, and wrinkled her brow. She then cracked a smile. "No really, why do you think it's unsafe?"

"I'm serious, Detective."

The officers exchanged quizzical glances.

"Wait a sec," muttered Kolowski. "This herb wouldn't have anything to do with Gunther Petchov assaulting you, would it?"

"What?" exclaimed Michaels.

"As a matter of fact, yes. I think so," replied Jade.

Kolowski threw his hands up. "Oh, come on, Doctor!" He then started chuckling, and looked at Wu, Michaels, and LeChatlier in obvious amusement. Michaels and LeChatlier each cracked a slight smile.

"Who is Gunther Petchov?" asked Wu.

Kolowski related the story in an exasperated tone. Jade watched and listened in disgust; her role was quickly shifting from victim to crazy yahoo.

"So," continued Wu, trying to conceal her skepticism. "You were saying that you accused Mr. Tang this afternoon of intentionally causing Dr. Harper's accident. And you did so because he was mad at you two for attacking his Quazhen?"

"Yes." She was firm. She tried to hide her growing frustration for this crowd. "He was mad at us for attacking Quazhen, and threatening to expose its side effects to the media."

"Hey Doctor," smirked Kolowski. "Any thoughts on who killed JFK? I mean, who *really* killed JFK?"

LeChatlier lowered his chin and smiled. The detectives simply let the comment go.

"You guys think I'm full of shit, don't you?" Jade asked.

"Excuse me, Doctor?" Wu acted shocked. "No. No. Something clearly happened to you today. We have a teenage girl who witnessed it. We certainly don't mean to make light of it."

"Okay." Jade looked around the table. Kolowski, Michaels, and LeChatlier darted skeptical eyes back and forth.

"But," continued Wu, "I think you'll agree that your situation...er...*situations* are a bit complex, when taken as a whole. We'll need to do some serious investigation."

Jade stared at her. "Do you people think *I* did something wrong?"

An uncomfortable silence filled the room.

"It's too early to know what to think, Doctor," said Wu. "We need to do some serious investigation."

Jade nodded slowly. She eyed everyone there, but nobody met her stare for more than a fleeting moment.

"So what about John?" Jade asked.

"What about him?"

"Will his so-called accident be in your 'serious investigation'?"

"Um," Wu looked around the table. "Yes. Yes, Doctor. It will be."

Jade nodded. "Fine. And what about my safety?"

"Do you have someone you could stay with for a few nights?" asked Michaels.

"My family's in Rhode Island. I suppose I could stay with John's sister, Tammy Harper. I'd have to call her first."

Michaels nodded. "Why don't you do that. When you know for sure where you'll be, let us know. We'll send a patrol car by the house every couple hours."

Jade nodded. She looked around. The police officers glanced at one another. She felt very, very alone.

And unprotected.

"Anything else?" she asked them.

"That's all." Wu looked at her. "For now."

Jade left the building in disgust. Officer LeChatlier ran out behind her.

"Dr. Evans," he called.

She turned.

"We left your car at a garage for now. I can drive you there, if you want to pick it up. Or, if you'd like, leave it there until they repair the window and bumper. For the time being, they gave you a rental."

He pointed to a 1984 green Subaru. Patches of rust covered the roof and side panels.

"You know, you might be safer driving a different car for the time being," he suggested.

She shook her head. "Fine."

He handed her the keys and some papers. "Just call your auto insurance; they'll need to cover the rental."

"Right."

With that, she turned, got into the green car, and left.

Jade turned up her road at 4:10 p.m. She decided to go home first, feed Nora, and then call Tammy Harper. She agreed with the idea of not staying home alone tonight, and perhaps Tammy could use the company. Of course, she intended to spend much of the evening with her at St. Francis, visiting John and following his progress.

As she turned into her driveway, she considered calling her parents in Rhode Island. Rather quickly, she decided against it. They would panic—with good reason—if she informed them of this nightmare. No, she thought. Wait a couple days for things to cool down; then give them a call.

She reached up for her electric garage opener. Of course, it was in the Saab. Annoyed, Jade parked in the driveway, locked the Subaru, and headed for her front door.

She walked in, cuddled Nora, and checked her machine for messages. There was a message.

Maybe it was Phil Santiago, her lawyer friend, returning her call. Then again, maybe it was someone else…

With a slight hesitation, she pressed play.

"Hello Dr. Evans. It's Yu-lan Tang." He sounded hurried, and his voice was barely above a whisper. "Please call me at 555-5970. Please call me immediately. It's about your safety."

That was all.

She closed her eyes and took a deep breath. A tear rolled down her cheek. This little adventure had to stop, she thought. The events of the past few days flashed through her mind. Another tear rolled down. Okay, she thought. I want to wake up now.

Jade took a deep breath, composed herself, and picked up the phone.

A few rings, and then, "Good afternoon. Natural Essentials."

Was that Yu-lan or Feng?

"Yu-lan?" she asked nervously.

"Ah, Dr. Evans. Thank you for returning my call."

Good, she thought. "Yes. What's so urgent?" She thought she already knew the answer. Feng probably had told his brother about her accusation; Yu-lan was probably calling to defend him.

"I want to meet with you, Dr. Evans."

A sea of red flags went up before her eyes. "You do? Well, why?"

"For one thing, I want to discuss Quazhen."

She sighed. "Look, Yu-lan, I'll be away for some time…"

"I believe you, Dr. Evans." He sounded worried. And desperate.

She paused. "You believe me?"

"Yes. I believe you. I'm going to pull Quazhen from the shelves."

Hmm. Either he had seen the light, she thought, or this was a trap. "Is that right?" she asked.

"Yes," he said quietly but urgently. "And there's another thing."

"Uh-huh."

"I know about Dr. Harper. Dr. Evans, please believe me. I am truly, truly sorry."

She was silent.

"I know my brother was behind it."

She clenched her fist.

"And Dr. Evans, he wants to hurt you, too." He sounded worried. And sincere.

"Go on," she said.

"Dr. Evans, we need to meet. When can you be here?"

Her radar was screaming. "I won't meet at your store, Yu-lan. Let's go to an open, public place."

"Fair enough. How about the coffee shop in the mall?" he suggested.

She considered it. Yes, that would do. "Fine. I'll be there in twenty minutes."

"Good. I'll see you there." He hung up.

Jade sat down. What did she do to deserve this? But quickly, she shoved her fear far aside, stood back up, and picked up the phone again.

"Tammy," she said when the other woman picked up.

"Oh, hi Jade. I just got home. I needed to feed the dogs."

Jade told her that she had been down to St. Francis, but that they missed each other. She mentioned that she had seen John, and that the surgeons were optimistic.

She didn't mention the truth behind the accident. Tammy had enough on her plate right now.

Tammy sounded strong and optimistic. Excellent, thought Jade. She then popped the question: would she mind if she stayed over tonight? Tammy enthusiastically welcomed her, and asked if she was okay. Jade reassured her that she was, 'for the most part'. They agreed to meet at the hospital at seven, and then hung up.

Jade sat with Nora for a few minutes. She stroked her long white hair, and kissed her wet nose. The cat purred, and immediately rested her head upon Jade's lap.

"At least one of us can relax," she whispered.

Jade arrived at George's Coffee House, in the Manchester Mall, just before 4:30. Two couples sat in the small shop, sipping coffee and chatting away. Yu-lan was not there. Jade walked across the yellow and green tiled floor to the front counter, and ordered an iced cappuccino and a large chocolate chip cookie. While she waited, she tapped her fingers to the pop music playing overhead.

As she sat down in a secluded corner with her cappuccino and cookie, Yu-lan walked in. He spotted her and smiled.

"You want coffee or anything?" she asked as he approached her.

"No," he smiled. He wore the same orange shirt that he had been wearing that morning. He sat down across from her.

"Okay," she said seriously. "What's up?"

"Well, where should we start?"

"How about with John. And Feng."

He nodded. "Well, first of all, have you seen Dr. Harper?"

"Yes. He's stable. For now, anyway."

He nodded. "Thank God. I will pray for him." He paused, and then, "Now listen. I was in the shop bathroom when Feng entered the back room. This was, oh, two hours ago. I'm certain that he didn't know I was there. Anyway, he picked up the phone, and he called a druggy friend of his."

"A druggy friend?"

He nodded. "Yeah. Anyway, he basically started screaming about how only one of you are in the hospital, when he specifically wanted you both there. He just went off on this friend of his, and the more he yelled, the more he revealed."

She sipped her cappuccino and stared at him with wide eyes.

"Apparently, there are two people—this friend and another one—who Feng had ordered to cause 'an accident' with you and John."

She shook her head and shrugged her shoulders. "Yu-lan, why? Is it simply about the Quazhen? I mean, what the hell?"

"I know, I know. Sounds pretty drastic, eh? But here's the truth, Doctor." He sighed, and he looked into her eyes. He caught her off guard. For a split second, she noticed his handsome face and his rich, dark eyes. "You see, Doctor, Feng needs the Quazhen to sell well. Whether or not I like it, he needs it to sell well."

"What do you mean?"

He sighed. "Feng is in the middle of a deal to sell our herb to a major dietary supplement industry. He thinks I don't know as much as I do, but he underestimates my sharp eyes and good ears. I know that he's weeks away from making a big sale. At least, he thinks he is."

"And you're going along with this?"

"No. Not at all. I've made it very clear that I won't sell out on Grandma's herb. It's a family plant; its profits will stay in the family. But, Feng always laughs at my protests. He says 'I'll come around' when he shows me the final deal." Yu-lan sighed and shook his head. "Anyway, in his warped mind, he's close to making a sale. The last thing he needs, Doctor, is for two American family doctors to raise a big stink about the safety of the herb. When you guys threatened to tell the media, I think you scared him half to death. If the media started questioning Quazhen's safety,

Feng's deal would go into major jeopardy. And as you can imagine, there are big, big bucks in this kind of deal."

"So he wanted to silence us until after the deal's made," she concluded.

He snorted. "Apparently so." He looked her in the eye again. "I swear, Doctor—I *swear*—if I had the slightest clue that he would go this far, I'd have kicked him out for good. Again, I had no idea that he was sinking this low until I overheard his conversation with his idiot buddy."

She nodded. She wasn't sure why, but she knew she could trust Yu-lan. He was for real. "What do you mean, you'd have kicked him out for good?"

"Feng shouldn't be at the store. He shouldn't be in my life. First of all, he's in this country illegally. And secondly, my brother is a lying, cheating, stealing, murdering bastard whom my family ostracized years ago." He explained the family history to Jade, who listened very attentively. Yu-lan described his brother's rebellious youth and his life of crime. He remorsefully talked about the secret shame that he had brought to the Tang family. He told her about their grandmother, Lu Mian, and how she despised Feng with a vengeance. How she would never forgive Yu-lan if she knew Feng was here with him in America.

"So why did you take him in?" asked Jade.

He sighed. "Because he's my brother." He looked at her with soft, caring eyes. "I wanted to give him one more chance."

Jade digested this. Her gut feelings were being confirmed. The two twins were polar opposites. Feng was an absolute devil; there was no question about that. But Yu-lan—the handsome man across from her now—Yu-lan was looking more and more like an angel.

"So when you say that your grandmother sends you shipments of Quazhen," said Jade, "you really mean that she sends *you* shipments. Not Feng."

"Exactly. Oh, if she knew his dirty hands were on her plant!" He gave a mock shiver. "I would not want to be there that day."

She softly smiled.

"Now," he continued, "since you brought up Quazhen. Let's move on to that topic."

She nodded, and sipped more cappuccino.

"After you and John left this morning, I started reflecting more and more on what you had said. It really bothered me. So I called some customers on my own. And I asked about it."

"And?"

"Of the six people I called, three of them have noticed a real negative energy; I guess you could call it aggression. And two of those three admitted to strange sexual urges."

"All since using Quazhen?"

He nodded. "Yes. So I extend my apology. I think you're right. I have no idea why it affects Americans, because it has never affected my family..."

"Does Feng use it?"

He stopped, completely off-guard. "Well, yeah." He thought about it. Feng was certainly one of the most aggressive people he knew. He curled his lip. "Yeah. Maybe you have a point.

"Regardless," he continued. "I offer you my deepest apology, and perhaps more importantly, I offer you my promise. I will pull Quazhen from the shelves, at least until we get some studies done on the herb."

She grinned. "Well," she remarked softly, "I'm delighted to hear that. But what about Feng and his deal?"

"Oh, I guess I never really mentioned that. Feng will be behind bars, Doctor. After we're done here, I'm turning him into the police. And his druggy friends, too. What they did to Dr. Harper, and what they're trying to do to you, is evil. Pure evil. They're out of my life. Forever."

A three ton weight suddenly floated off her shoulders. She looked into his eyes and smiled. "Thank you, Yu-lan," she whispered.

He reached over and placed his hand on hers. For a minute, they simply sat in silence.

"Also," he continued, "I'm going to have my grandmother stop shipping the Quazhen. Knowing her, she's boxing some up right now, just waiting for my request for more shipments."

"You'll call her?" Jade asked.

"No," he replied. "I made it a policy with her to not ask for shipments over the phone. She never questioned why, but simply agreed to it."

Jade wrinkled her brow. "That's an odd policy."

"Not when you realize that Feng and I sound identical over the phone. I certainly don't want him calling her, pretending he's me."

"Ah," she said. "Very smart. So, how do you correspond?"

He smiled, and reached into the left front pocket of his orange button-down. He pulled out a tan paper, folded into quarters. He unfolded it, and placed it in front of Jade.

Before her was a blank parchment paper, shaped into an oval, and decorated with beautiful Chinese letters along the entire outer edge. The letters were in two colors, black and red. Below the letters, a beautiful gold pattern swirled along the inner edge of the margin.

"Wow," said Jade, taking the parchment into her hands. "This paper is beautiful. Wait a second...are those letters hand drawn?"

He beamed. "Yes. Before I left China, my grandmother handmade one hundred individual pieces of stationery for me. Each paper is a work of art; each one is slightly different from all the others."

Yu-lan watched her examine the parchment in great detail. Her wide eyes and glowing smile proved her genuine interest in this precious gift from his grandmother. He stared at her, and felt a sense of peacefulness within.

After a few special moments had passed, Yu-lan spoke. "It became our agreement, that whenever I ask for more shipments of Quazhen, I would make the request on this special paper."

She grinned, and handed the paper back to him. "How sweet." She meant it.

"Yes. So I've already written her about the Quazhen side effects on this paper. In my letter, I tell her that I'm stopping its sales, at least until we learn more about its safety profile. I haven't sent it yet; it's at the store."

Jade smiled. Then, "One question, though," she said. "If you avoid the phone because Feng could impersonate you, aren't you worried about Feng forfeiting a request from you on your stationery?"

He shook his head. "No. First of all, he doesn't know where I keep my papers. Secondly, I always sign my letters to Grandma with a special handwritten seal; she taught me how to draw it when I was eleven. Feng has no idea how to draw it. And it's too complex to copy."

She smiled. "You and your grandmother have a pretty stealth coding system in place, don't you?"

He laughed. "Well, there's a lot of love in that stealth coding system. We started doing it because it's fun. The fact that it keeps Feng at bay is just a nice little extra."

She smiled. Yu-lan Tang, she thought. Hmm. What an interesting man.

"The *only* annoying thing about the stealth system," continued Yu-lan with childlike contentment with the conversation, "is that the mailing system in China stinks."

She chuckled. "Really?"

"Yeah." He shook his head in mock anger. "I write to Grandma once or twice a month. Writing for Quazhen shipments is really a rare event; I usually just write to say hello. Anyway, for some unknown reason, only half of my letters make it to her. If that."

She raised her eyebrows. "Really?"

"Uh-huh. We don't know why. The problem could lie anywhere from her local postman to the Chinese government." He shrugged. "It's too bad, because I always write on her beautiful stationery. I can't stand to think about it getting lost."

Jade nodded. "Yeah. That would be too bad. So what if she doesn't get this important letter about the Quazhen that you'll be sending her?"

He shrugged. "I'll call her in a week or two. If she never got it, I'll just write her another letter, and try again."

"No chance of just telling her on the phone?"

He waved his finger back and forth, smiling. "Weren't you listening, Dr. Evans? The phone's a no-no. To be authentic, she must get information on Quazhen through the mail." His smile grew wider. "It's just our quirky little thing. Loving, but quirky."

She smiled. "Yu-lan, please call me Jade."

"Very well, Jade."

She finished her cappuccino. "Well," she said. "I, for one, am ready and willing to accompany you to the police station. I can take you to the two detectives on the case."

He wrinkled his brow. "What do you mean, 'detectives on the case'?"

"Yu-lan, your brother's druggy friends have already tried to knock me off. Twice. And I had put two and two together on my own, and had a major hunch that Feng was behind John's accident. In fact, I confronted Feng at your store this afternoon. Didn't he tell you?"

"No."

"Well, I did. Anyway, I've contacted the police. And they've started investigating the case."

He shrugged. "Well, good. Were they receptive to you?"

"Not really," she admitted. "Which is why you have made my day—no, my year! The truth you have will tie this whole thing together for them. It's a pretty twisted story, but it makes sense."

"The truth can be that way. Well," he said, standing up. "Let's go, then."

"Gladly." She glanced at her watch. 5:00 p.m. She had two hours to meet Tammy in Hartford. That should be plenty of time.

"You know," Yu-lan suddenly said. "Jennifer's at the store right now with Andrea. I don't think you've met Andrea yet."

She shook her head.

"She's a sweetheart. Anyway, do you mind quickly swinging by the store? I'm going to close early and send the girls home. We could be at the police station for a while, and I'd hate for them to be stuck at the store after six. They don't have the key to close up, and I promised I'd be back before closing."

Jade shrugged. "That's fine."

"Thanks. It should only take five minutes."

They walked out together. By chance, they had only parked one row away from each other.

"Yu-lan," Jade said, outside in the parking lot.

He looked at her.

"You really don't mind turning in your brother? I mean, he is your brother."

He scoffed. "I don't mind at all, Jade. My grandmother is right. My family is right. He is evil, and he belongs in jail. Simple as that."

She nodded. She admired his courage and righteousness.

They reached their cars. "Meet you at the store?" asked Yu-lan.

"Sounds good," agreed Jade.

She followed him there.

13

Jade parked the green Subaru behind Yu-lan's red Nissan Altima, alongside the Main Street curb. He got out, and approached the doors of Natural Essentials. Jade stayed in the car for a moment, flipping through radio stations; to her dismay, the rental car's reception was awful. Annoyed, she decided to get out, and follow him in.

Yu-lan had already moved into the store. She barely caught the closing door, and walked in thirty feet behind him. She immediately noticed that the lights were dimmed; also, the familiar soft music that usually played overhead was turned off. To her left, the front windows of the store were covered by ornate red and gold Chinese shades.

Odd, thought Jade. The place already looked closed up.

Jade realized that Yu-lan didn't know she was behind him; he thought she had waited in the car. As he neared the front counter, she was about to call out to him…

"Feng," said Yu-lan, surprised. Yu-lan continued walking to the middle of the front counter, out of Jade's view. Jade stopped in her tracks, in the leftmost aisle of the store.

She bit her lip. Feng wasn't supposed to be here now, was he?

Yu-lan echoed her sentiments. "I thought you were off now. I thought Jennifer and Andrea were working."

Still out of their view, Jade listened.

"I sent them home early," Feng growled. "I decided to close up early. If you didn't notice, the store sign says 'closed', and I started turning everything off."

Jade glanced back at the double doors. Sure enough, the 'open' side of the cardboard sign faced into the store.

Yu-lan sounded annoyed. "What are you doing, man? Why are you sending home my workers and closing my store early?"

"We're gonna have a little talk, Yu-lan."

There was a thick, awful silence. Jade felt moisture accumulate on her palms. Her eyes were wide open, and she started breathing more rapidly.

"Yu-lan," Feng sang out, in a clearly accusatory and condescending tone, "what are your plans for the Quazhen?"

A brief silence. Then, "What do you mean?"

His voice became deeper and firmer. "What are your plans for the Quazhen?"

Thick silence. Jade's heart began to race.

"I'm going to keep selling it. Business as usual. I'm not sure what you're getting at." His voice was even, unshaken.

"What I'm getting at," Feng said calmly, "is this."

Jade heard the soft ruffling of a paper being exchanged between the brothers. Uh-oh, she thought. Feng had found Yu-lan's letter to his grandmother. Yu-lan had said he had written it, but not yet mailed it; and it was in the store.

"What the hell is that, Yu-lan?" Feng's voice was louder, and more menacing.

There was no answer.

Suddenly, like a deafening clap of thunder, Feng bellowed. "What is that you bastard?! Tell me, asshole! Tell me what the hell you are up to!"

A cold chill rushed through Jade's body. She froze in terror.

"Feng, I…I…"

"You *what*, you piece of shit? You were gonna go behind my back and pull Quazhen from the shelves? You were gonna send this fuckin' letter to Grandma and tell her to end all shipments?" Jade could actually feel Feng's reverberating roar in her bones. "What the hell are you doing?!"

"Look," Yu-lan shouted, with a force that paled in comparison to Feng's verbal beating. "I called some of our customers today. Half of them had these side effects…"

"And?!" he demanded in a deafening scream.

There was no answer.

"So there are side effects," bellowed Feng. "What the hell do we care?! If you're too stupid to realize it, Yu-lan, I'm about to make a very big business transaction with the Quazhen. And like I told you, you'd be entitled to some of my profits…"

"First of all," barked Yu-lan, "for the last time, you're not selling out on the family herb! Second of all, your sense of entitlement to this store and to that herb has really got to end! You…"

"My sense of entitlement?" cried Feng, hammering a fist onto the countertop. "My sense of entitlement?"

There was another thick momentary silence. Jade looked at the door behind her. Maybe she should bolt. Maybe it was time to get help.

"Get out of my store!" fired Yu-lan.

"What?!"

"Get out of my store, Feng!"

Jade had never heard Yu-lan this angry. His voice was strong and powerful.

"I never want to see you again," Yu-lan continued. "You're fired, Feng!"

Another thick silence.

Yu-lan pressed on. "Not only are you fired, but you'll be spending some time behind bars."

No! thought Jade. Bad idea! Bad idea! Just let the cops come and arrest him!

"I know that you put one of the doctors in the hospital."

"And how do you know that?" hissed Feng. "You been sleeping with the blond doctor? That whore!"

"Shut up, Feng! She's a good person…"

The thunder struck again. "She's a good person?!! Don't even tell me! Oh my…! You *are* sleeping with that slut, aren't you?!"

Jade looked at the door again. Okay. Time to go…

Suddenly a hard smack was heard ahead. Feng had rammed his fist into Yu-lan's jaw. Yu-lan yelped out as he went crashing down to the floor.

"Bastard!"

"No!"

The two fought furiously on the ground. Jade heard the loud cracks of punches and the shuffling sounds of struggling. Suddenly, Yu-lan slid across the floor towards the left.

Right into her view.

He turned and looked at her.

She was a deer in headlights. Her heart pounded furiously, and her muscles tingled with alertness. Maroon blood dribbled down Yu-lan's cheek; a thick chunk of skin was ripped open under his right eye.

Yu-lan quickly looked away from her, without saying a word. But inconspicuously, he shook his right hand at her. He was telling her to get the hell out of there.

Immediately, she turned back and sprinted.

Shit! Where was the door?!

Her heart sank. In her furious dash, she realized, she had passed the door!

Needing to make a split second decision, she kept bolting forward, toward the back of the store. She quickly slid left, and hid behind the narrow end of the leftmost rows of shelves.

"You're gonna put me behind bars, Yu-lan?" spat his brother. "You're gonna turn in ol' Feng? Why?" He hissed, "So you can sleep with the doctor?"

"How can you be so dense, Feng? No, I'm not sleeping with her, you idiot! I just know that she's right! Quazhen has some serious side effects, especially in this American population!"

"That doesn't matter…"

"It does matter!" screamed Yu-lan at the top of his lungs. "It does matter, Feng! Sure, we can sell Quazhen in this country, knowing that it's unsafe! Sure, the laws will pretty much allow us to get away with it! But come on, Feng, that's morally incorrect! Don't you understand that?! It's morally incorrect!"

Another hard punch, and Yu-lan bellowed out in pain.

Jade turned to look at the door. She quickly snapped her head back; both brothers were now at the front of the leftmost aisle. She would certainly be seen if she ran.

And if Feng saw her, he would pummel her.

Or worse.

Another hard smack from the front of the store. Another cry from Yu-lan. Then a series of thuds. Shrieks of pain from Yu-lan.

Shit! she thought. Maybe it was time to make the mad dash to the door, regardless of Feng seeing her. Yu-lan needed help…

"What are you doing, Feng?" His terrified, pleading voice suddenly chilled Jade.

Feng was silent.

"Feng, what are you doing? Come on, man!" His voice became weak and shaky.

What was going on?

"Feng, I'm sorry. I'm sorry; you're right. I'll tear up the letter. That letter to Grandma—the one on the counter over there—I'll tear it up."

What the hell, thought Jade.

"Please Feng, we can get through this. You can have the Quazhen. You can have it, man!"

Jade's eyes suddenly widened. Her stomach sank. Yu-lan was pleading for his…

Bang! Bang! Bang!

Three staccato shots reverberated off the walls. Less than a second later, three more shots rang out.

Bang! Bang! Bang!

"No!!!" Jade screeched wildly in terror, and rolled left to face Feng. He was holding a smoking pistol in the air. Lying at his feet was the bullet-ridden body of Yu-lan, motionless and drenched in blood, from his forehead to his abdomen.

Feng turned to face Jade. His lips were curled in a snarl.

He reached into his pocket, retrieved some small bullets, and started walking towards her.

"Aaraugh!" She cried and ran right, towards the far right wall of the store. Feng's heavy footsteps thudded towards the back of the store.

Her head pounding, heart racing, and soul screaming, Jade sprinted up the far right aisle.

A shot rang out. Bang!

Jade screamed and dived to the tile floor. A second later, she realized she was fine. She scrambled up, and ran towards the front of the store.

"I'm gonna kill you, bitch." He was loud and matter-of-fact. He was somewhere in the middle of the store.

She reached the front counter. She looked left, at the motionless body of Yu-lan.

Another shot rang out. Bang!

Jade jumped as a glass vase on the counter shattered. It was two feet in front of her.

This kind of thing didn't happen to normal people! This was the stuff of the movies!

Bang! Bang!

Several dozen glass jars behind her exploded, sending a blizzard of ginseng onto the floor.

Jade cried out, and dashed behind the counter.

"Goodnight, Doctor." He was at the front of the middle aisle.

Crouching down behind the counter, she cringed and braced herself. Images of her childhood, her parents, her colleagues, and her patients flashed into her mind.

There was silence.

Be strong, she told herself. This was her *life*, here!

In a moment of herculean courage, Jade stood up and scrambled to the side door that led to the back room.

As she moved towards the door, she saw an oval-shaped piece of paper on the ground. Inked Chinese letters formed the border, and many words were written in the middle.

It was Yu-lan's letter to his grandmother. It must have fallen off the counter at some point, and landed near the side door.

Jade grabbed it, and burst through the side door. She quickly folded the paper and shoved it into the right front pocket of her trousers.

Bang! A bullet pierced the door and whizzed by her head.

In a millisecond, she looked around. Shit! No doors!

In a frenzied attempt to save herself, she bolted towards the bathroom. She got in, slammed the door, and locked it.

She heard the door to the back room slam open.

"Where are you bitch?" A pause. "Hmm. Golly gee. Could you be in the bathroom?"

Bang! The porcelain lid of the toilet exploded, and several shards of porcelain ripped into her cheek. "Aaaraugh!"

She had one chance, she realized. Before her was a two-foot by two-foot window. Unfortunately, it was made of thick glass; she knew she couldn't break it.

Maybe she could lift it.

She gripped the top ledge of the window and pushed up. It was heavy. She strained, putting all of her weight into it. Come on! she thought. Push harder! Harder!

It didn't budge.

Shit!

She cried out, and tried again. She used all her energy, everything she could possibly muster.

Nothing. It stayed put.

As Jade continued to try to force up the window, an eerie silence emanated from the back room. She paused. Where was Feng?

She stopped struggling with the window, and listened. She strained to hear beyond the loud drumroll of her heartbeat.

She heard the door of the back room swing open again. Listening carefully, she heard the sound of someone dragging a heavy object across the tiled floor. There was a sudden thud.

"There you are, good brother," spat Feng. "You should be comfy in the corner there. But don't get too comfortable; you won't be there for long." He suddenly raised his voice. "Don't worry, Doctor," he called out. "I haven't forgotten about you. I'm just doing a little cleaning, here." He chuckled. "I'll kill you in a minute or two, okay?"

Sick bastard. She turned back to the window. Push! Push!

"Yu-lan!" called Feng from the side of the back room. "Where do we keep the mop? You trailed blood all over the place, you messy, messy little boy."

Jade's muscles tensed. She had never hated anyone in her life. Until now.

"Oh, I found it, Yu-lan," he yelled. "No help from you, though."

Jade listened to the murderer whistle as he exited the back room.

She waited for three or four minutes. She heard nothing.

Now was her chance.

She unlocked the bathroom door, and quietly pried it open. Looking through a small crack, she could barely make out Yu-lan's body in the corner of the room. It was covered by several old, tattered blankets. Jade slowly opened the bathroom door more widely.

She paused. Feng was speaking to someone in the main store.

She listened carefully. He was on the phone. But she couldn't make out any words.

Jade heard him slam down the phone.

She started to inch forward.

The door to the back room suddenly flung open. She yelped as she saw Feng lift his gun and aim at her. In a raging effort, she dived back into the bathroom and slammed the door. She pressed her back against the door.

There were no shots fired.

Quickly, she darted forward to the window. Come on, damn it! she thought as she strained once again to crack it open.

There was a knock on the bathroom door.

Her heart sank. She had forgotten to lock it.

"Hey Doctor," snarled Feng, through the closed door, "the window tends to get stuck. We meant to get it fixed."

In a split second, she dropped to her back, and rammed her feet against the door, hoping to hold it closed. But the thud of her feet against the door went unheard; Feng was firing more shots.

Bang! Bang! Bang! Bang! Bang! Bang!

A piercing crash rocked the room, and tiny sharp shards of glass pelted Jade's face; she quickly covered her face with her hands.

Suddenly, she felt short of breath; she fought for air. Oh God, she was dying. Oh God, this was how it ended. Help...Help...

Wait a second.

She was alive.

She spat out a couple of glass shards, and looked up at the window.

It was completely busted open.

And he had fired six shots, so he needed a second to reload.

The doorknob started to turn.

With a sudden surge of adrenaline, she jumped up and rammed her body into the door. The jolt must have startled Feng; the doorknob stopped turning. She quickly turned the lock...

There was silence.

He must be reloading the gun.

In a frenzied fury, she dived towards the shattered window. She slammed her hands down onto the bottom ledge, where broken glass violently tore into her skin. With her adrenaline in overdrive, she ignored the pain, and hoisted herself up. Her knees landed on the sharp ledge, and a thick blade of glass ripped into her left knee. She cringed for a millisecond in pain, and then reached to the outside ledge. In a swift motion, she thrust herself out of the window, and landed on the hard asphalt, in a sea of broken glass.

Bang! Bang! Bang!

She got up, and sprinted down a back alley. She furiously swung right, and bolted for the road.

In the distance, she heard sirens blaring. They were coming this way.

There was her car.

A few passersby looked at her bloody face, bloody hands, and tattered clothes, which had all been ripped apart by broken glass. They stopped in their tracks, gasped, and started muttering amongst themselves.

With her eyes fixed on the front door of the store, she dashed towards her car. She scrambled in, got out her key, and turned it on.

She continued to look at the front door of the store. Would Feng come bursting out at any moment? Would he actually shoot her out in the open, in broad daylight?

She didn't stay around to find out. She thrust the Subaru into drive, whipped the wheel left, and slammed on the gas. Jade sped off down Main Street.

14

Jade was not sitting behind the rental car's wheel; it was her survival instinct who was most certainly driving. Still fueled by pure adrenaline, she veered left into a supermarket parking lot and whipped around to face the road. She pulled into a parking space, and slammed down on the brake.

Now what?

Jade rolled down her windows. Yes, the sirens were definitely getting closer to the store. Somebody must have heard the gunshots, and then called the police.

Feng would be caught red-handed.

Jade closed her eyes. Oh God, she thought. What had just happened? This couldn't be real. In fact, the whole fantastic experience did seem very surreal, like a strange cross between Salvador Dali and James Bond. Again she thought, this just doesn't happen to real people. The sexual assault, the thugs running her off the road, the attack on John, and now a cold-blooded murder and her narrow escape from death…wake me up! she silently screamed. Please!

Suddenly, a sharp, throbbing pain emanated from her left knee. She looked down, and saw a thick, one-inch piece of jagged glass sticking through her trousers. Surrounding the glass was a large, wet, sticky patch that colored her trousers dark brown instead of the usual tan. She gently swiped the moisture, and fresh blood covered her fingertips.

No, she thought. It was real. All of it.

Jade forced herself to step outside of her present being. That wasn't a difficult task for her; years of medical training had taught her how to occasionally depersonalize herself in order to be more objective with her patients. Since the days of gross anatomy in medical school, she knew how to compartmentalize her emotions and let objectivity take over.

Be logical, she told herself. What should she do next? She had to get to a hospital at some point. That much was clear. But should she tell the police first? She could easily swing by the store, be present for Feng's arrest, and tell the whole story to the authorities. And, she thought, she could show them Yu-lan's body; after all, maybe there was a chance that he was still alive!

That was clearly the way to go.

She shifted into reverse, turned, and then sped forward. She headed back to Natural Essentials.

As she approached the store, she saw a terrific scene of flashing blue lights and black-clad officers. Seven or eight police cars were gathered outside of the storefront, and a hulking red fire truck was sitting alongside the curb. The police cars blocked three-quarters of the road, and a growing cluster of curious onlookers stood on the sidewalk across the street. Several officers were entering the store, some were waiting outside, and a few were talking with the passersby she had seen earlier. One officer was unwrapping yellow crime scene tape, and two others were stopping traffic. She slowed down, and an officer with short brown hair approached her. He held his hand up, motioning for her to stop. It was Officer Steve Ryan.

She slowed to a stop as he approached her window.

"Sorry, ma'am, road's closed. Please take Center Street around…" Then he looked at her. "Oh my God."

She glanced at her face in the rearview mirror. Wow. Caked blood was cemented to both cheeks, and a few shards of glass and broken porcelain hung freely from her forehead. Her hair was ratty and full of the glass shards. She glanced down. Her hands were also punctured with glass and covered in caked blood.

"Hi, Officer Ryan," she said matter-of-factly. "I think I can help you guys out. I was here."

Silent but wide-eyed, he swallowed hard. He then turned to face the others. "Hey! Dave! Juan! I got something big!"

Four officers turned and started running over. Jade didn't recognize any of them.

"I know her," Ryan shouted to them. "This is Doctor Evans, the one I was mentioning to you, Dave."

Great, she thought.

"She says she was here at the time of the incident!"

The others looked at her and dropped their mouths open. A tall, dark-skinned officer approached her window. "Ma'am, why don't you park over there? We'll have plenty of questions."

"Did you get him yet?" asked Jade.

"Get who, ma'am?"

Uh-oh. "Listen!" Jade yelled fiercely. "There is a man in that store with a gun! He shot his brother, and he tried to kill me! He's probably still in there!"

The officers exchanged panicked glances.

"Quick!" ordered the dark-skinned one to all the others. "Run!"

The others sprinted towards the store, and began yelling towards their colleagues.

Following the officer's orders, Jade parked alongside another police car, and got out. Hurriedly, she joined the officer and moved into the thick of the crowd.

"What's going on?" barked a familiar voice above the roaring crowd. Sergeant Kolowski shuffled towards her and then stopped abruptly. "Dr. Evans…what on earth?! What happened to you?!"

Several other dumbfounded stares turned towards Jade, and a circle of police officers quickly formed around her.

"Evans?" Detective Wu joined Kolowski's side.

"Listen!" cried Jade. "There could be an armed man…"

"They know, they know," said Ryan from behind her. He gently tapped her shoulder. "We told them. Our officers are checking it out."

"So?" barked Kolowski. "What's going on?"

"Here's the whole deal," said Jade loudly, so that the dozen people around her could all hear. "I was in that store with the owner, Yu-lan Tang, about twenty minutes ago. I was accompanying him to close up for the night. We got here, and to our surprise, Yu-lan's brother Feng was here. The two brothers got into a major argument, and then a fight, and then Feng shot Yu-lan six times!"

Officers and detectives muttered loudly amongst themselves. Most of them had never seen anything this spectacular in all their years of service.

"Feng then came after me," Jade continued, getting out-of-breath from her nervous excitement. "I barely escaped through a back window, got to my car, and blew out of here. I stayed away until I knew you guys were here…"

"That's her!" yelled an elderly woman.

Jade turned, and a white-haired woman in a red sweatshirt pointed at her, shaking. The woman was standing next to two officers.

"She's the one who came running out of the alley!"

"That *is* her!" agreed an older man in a faded Boston Red Sox tee-shirt.

Jade recognized them both as two of the passersby whom she had flown by earlier. "Yes," she called out. "It's me. They're right. I got out of that back window, and booked down the side alley to get here."

The woman began shaking more fiercely. "That woman almost ran into me!" she screamed. "She's the one, officers! I betcha she robbed that store!"

"I know she did!" agreed the man.

"What?!" exclaimed Jade. "Go away, people! You have no idea what you're talking about!"

The woman pressed on. "You robbed that…"

"I was almost killed in that store, lady!" Jade shot a fiery stare at her. "Were you there, lady? Were you there?!"

"Okay, okay." Two strong police officers held her back.

A man in the crowd stepped forward. He had thin, gray hair pushed to one side, and his thin face wore a frustrated scowl. He was dressed in a white shirt and blue tie.

"Dr. Evans, I'm Chief Preston. You say a man was shot in there?"

"Yes!"

He frowned, and then held up his radio. "I was just speaking with my men inside the store. They didn't find any dead body."

"I can show you where it is…"

"They didn't find any blood, either."

"He mopped it up."

There was more muttering in the crowd. Preston shot a glance at Kolowski.

"Dr. Evans," asked Detective Wu, "you said you were in there with Mr. Yu-lan Tang?"

"Yes! He was the one who was shot. Look, folks, he could still be alive in there. Can I show you where he is?!"

"I thought you said Mr. Tang had caused your friend's accident. And tried to run you off the road, too."

Jade looked at her. "No. His brother, the murderer Feng, did all that…"

Kolowski spoke up. "But weren't you upset at both brothers due to that herb, Quizzoo?"

"Quazhen," corrected Wu.

Jade's temper quickly began to flare. What the hell were they getting at? "Look, folks, that's all true. But it really doesn't change the fact that Feng killed his brother, then tried to kill me, and could still be hiding in that store right now!"

"Chief! Sarge!" yelled a voice from up the road. Officer Ted LeChatlier was waving his hands up in the air.

"What is it, Ted?" yelled the police chief.

"I got the store owner, here! Can I bring him over?"

The entire crowd gasped, and frantic stares darted from one person to the next. Jade's stomach sunk, and an icy chill flooded her body.

"*Who* do you have there?" barked Preston.

"His name's Yu-lan Tang. He owns this place."

"Oh my God!" A new gallon of adrenaline poured into Jade's veins. Could he be alive?! How did he get out?! "Get him to a hospital!" she cried out. "He needs to be in a hospital!"

The bewildered crowd of officers shuffled to the right, to view the oncoming man. In the chaotic excitement, someone stepped into Jade's view, and she couldn't see. Flustered, she skirted around him, trying to see poor Yu-lan…

She froze in terror. She literally could not move for a moment as she watched the man approach the crowd.

A tall Asian man in a button-down red shirt and khakis walked towards the crowd. His strong musculature was apparent underneath his clothes. His face was twisted into an expression of fear and confusion. With innocent eyes, he looked around at the police cars, the mass of people, and the store.

There were no blood stains on his face or his clothes.

There were no cuts, bruises, or abrasions on his face; there was no chunk of skin missing under his right eye.

His black hair was cropped short.

"Mr. Tang," shouted Preston. "Do you know what's going on, here?"

The man appeared dumbfounded. He innocently stared at the police chief, and shrugged. "No sir. I was just on my way home from the supermarket." His eyes darted to Jade, but then he immediately looked away. "Did somebody rob my store?"

Jade was too terrified to speak.

"Shots were fired inside your store, Mr..." Preston cocked his head. "What's your name, again? Your whole name?"

"Tang. Yu-lan Tang."

The crowd roared. A hand touched Jade's shoulder.

"You bastard!" she screamed out. "That's not Yu-lan!" She turned to the crowd with desperate, pleading eyes. "That is Feng Hou Tang, everybody! That's your murderer! I saw him kill his brother in cold blood, just twenty minutes ago!"

The crowd roared louder. General excitement subsided to near-pandemonium as confused officers started pointing at both Jade and the other man. Eager voices began speaking above one another, and the loudness on the street quickly increased.

"Quiet!" barked Preston. Nothing. With a bigger scowl, he snapped. "Hey! Quiet! I mean it!"

The crowd quickly hushed down. The only remaining sounds were the static of people's radios, the loud talking of officers inside the store, and the excited onlookers. Blue lights continued to dance above the police cars, giving more intensity to the situation.

Feng broke the silence. "Aren't you Dr. Evans?" he asked.

Her face fixed in hate, she lowered her voice. "You son of a bitch..."

"What...what happened to you?" he asked, appearing genuinely concerned. "And, I'm sorry, why are you so upset?"

She shuddered and turned towards Preston. "Listen. This is Feng Hou Tang. He is the murderer. I can show you Yu-lan's body inside the store. It's in the back room. I swear, you've got to believe me..."

"*Yu-lan's* body?" Feng cracked a smile. "Uh, I'm Yu-lan, folks."

All eyes fell to Preston. He nodded, adjusted his tie, and then slowly approached Feng. "Mr. Tang. Would you mind showing me some identification?"

He shrugged, reached into his back pocket, and pulled out a wallet. Feng opened it, and handed a license to the chief.

Preston took the license, and stared at it. He glanced back at Jade, and then looked again at the short-haired Asian man.

Sighing, he walked over to Jade, and showed her the license.

She shook her head, repulsed. Of course, it looked just like Yu-lan. In fact, it probably was Yu-lan. Yes, this was almost certainly Yu-lan's real license.

"They're twins," she pleaded, handing the card back to Preston. "This isn't really him. Chief, please, you've got to believe me!"

He gave the card back to Feng, and twisted his lip. He gave a very skeptical look to Jade.

Kolowski started approaching Jade, his weight shifting with each step. Preston shot him a disapproving glance. Not yet, he seemed to say.

"Mr. Tang," said Preston. "Dr. Evans says that you are really Feng Hou Tang, and that you killed your brother in that store. She claims that you then tried to kill her, but she barely escaped out of some back window."

Feng quickly shook his head and cracked a hesitant smile. "You're kidding, right?"

Preston shrugged. "Apparently not."

"I can show you Yu-lan's body," muttered Jade through her clenched teeth.

Preston raised his eyebrows. Then, "Very well. Please do that."

A few surprised voices ruffled through the crowd.

"Fine. Come on."

Jade turned towards the store entrance. Following very closely behind her, Preston, Feng, Kolowski, and another seven or eight officers approached the main doors. With Jade at the lead, they passed the aromatherapy candles at the entrance, and turned left to go up the outermost aisle. Jade paused at the front of the aisle.

"This is where he shot him," she said, pointing down at the floor." She swallowed. Damn, Feng had done a good job cleaning. Apparently, blood could easily wash off the shiny tiled floor.

She knelt down. No, there was no trace of blood whatsoever.

Frowning, she stood up and led the crowd to the back room. Along the way, they stepped over the shattered glass vase and the dusting of ginseng on the ground.

"My gosh," said Feng. "What happened to my store?!"

The officers that had already been in the store joined the crowd as they entered the back room.

Jade stormed towards the far corner.

And then froze.

Yu-lan's body was gone.

There was no body, no blankets, and no blood. Her heart pounding, she looked back at the crowd. They just stared at her, expectantly. Feng, for a split second, grinned at her. He then put on a straight face.

Jade carefully looked around the room. Her eyes moved from each corner to the center, and back to the corners.

She spotted the mop closet.

Hurriedly, she walked to the closet and flung open the narrow door.

It was empty.

The crowd continued to silently watch her.

Her head began to throb as she moved into the bathroom. A few officers quickly followed her, making sure she was only an arm's length away. The bathroom was empty. She stared out the broken window, and looked down. Only shattered glass covered the back alley; there was no sign of a body, or of blood, anywhere.

Shocked, she slowly turned around, and walked out to the back room.

"Well?" asked Preston, softly.

She nervously looked down. Her hands began to shake. "It's not here."

He tightened his lips together, and placed his hands in his pockets. "I see."

"So, excuse me," said Feng, sounding a bit flustered. "But what happened to my store?"

"Mr. Tang," said Preston. "Do you know Dr. Evans?"

He looked at her. "Yes. She has been by the store a few times. She has made it abundantly clear that she dislikes my business, and has actually been quite rude to me and my workers."

She glared at him.

"Go on," said Preston.

"Well, Dr. Evans stopped by this morning, sir. And she said something about doing whatever it takes to pull a certain herb from my shelves."

"Quazhen?" asked Detective Wu.

"Yes, ma'am. Quazhen." Suddenly, Feng's expression changed; he put on a look of sudden shock. "Oh my goodness…Now I understand. That explains why she's all bloody, and has glass all over her." He put his hand to his open mouth. "Oh my goodness."

"You son of a bitch, Feng. You little…"

"That will be enough, Doctor," retorted Preston. He nodded to a nearby officer. "You're under arrest."

"What?!" She instantly became lightheaded and nauseous. She felt physically beaten. "Chief Preston, what are you doing?!"

Two strong officers approached her. "Please move to the wall, ma'am."

"One thing I don't get," said Feng. "I understand that she broke in, but didn't someone say there was gunfire?"

The officers pressed Jade against a wall. One began reading her the Miranda rights; the other began to handcuff her. They ignored her desperate protests.

"That's a good question," agreed Kolowski. Then, "Oh, wait a second…Mr. Tang, were there any employees in the store when this happened?"

"Hmm," he replied. "When did it happen?"

"Say half an hour ago."

Feng bit his lip. Deceitful thoughts raced through his mind; *quickly*, he thought to himself. What's the best option? What makes the most sense?

Then, "No. The store was definitely closed."

An officer spoke from the back of the room. "The front door was locked when we got here, sir."

Preston nodded. "No. I don't think she shot anyone. She was here to sabotage; just look at the broken glass in that main store."

"Hey!" yelled Jade, helplessly.

"I know she really wanted Quazhen off the shelves," remarked Wu, staring at her. "I didn't know she wanted it this bad."

"Sirens scared you out of here, Doctor?" asked Kolowski.

She shook her head and stared at the ground. This was no longer Dali meets Bond. This was hell on earth.

The officers shuffled Jade out of the store in handcuffs. As she left, she heard Feng profusely thanking the officers for their amazing work. She was pushed harshly outside, and taken to a police car. The onlookers gasped and gabbed as they watched her being shoved into the car.

"Good for you, officers!" howled the elderly lady in the red sweatshirt.

With Jade in the back seat, the car's sirens began wailing, and they took off down the road.

15

Jade stared out the window as the police car pulled up to the Manchester Hospital Emergency Room.

"What are we doing here?" she asked.

"We need to get your wounds looked at, Doc."

She cringed. "Guys, can we please go to a different hospital? Come on, this is where I work. If they see me coming in from a cop car..."

"No. It's here or nowhere."

She looked at her left knee. The glass shard was still protruding out, but her pain was somehow lessened. In a swift move fueled by anger and frustration, Jade grabbed the shard and yanked it out.

"Shit!" she yelled, wincing in pain.

"Doc..."

"Just wait a sec, will ya?"

The two officers exchanged glances, and looked back at her.

Jade lifted her left leg onto the vinyl back seat of the car. She pulled up her pant leg. Thick maroon-brown blood was plastered against most of the entire outer leg. Also, criss-crossed scratches and shining pink skin appeared on the inner aspect of the lower leg. Fresh red blood slowly dripped out of fresh wound beneath her lateral knee cap. She looked at the wound more carefully. It was actually quite small; apparently, only the tip of the sharp shard penetrated through her skin.

Jade wiped away the fresh blood with her shirtsleeve, and inspected the knee more closely. Actually, the shard had inserted an inch below the knee, and it pointed down, towards her feet. Her joint space was really in no danger; it had definitely been untouched. She slowly bent the knee, and then straightened it. She then grabbed her lower thigh with her left hand, and placed her right hand over her lower leg. Straining, Jade pulled and twisted her leg in various directions.

She nodded with confidence. "I'm fine. Take me to the station."

"I don't know, ma'am..."

"I'm a doctor!" she snapped. "I'm telling you, I'm fine."

The officers exchanged questioning looks.

"Look, I'll be out on bail tonight, and I'll get myself checked out tomorrow. For now, I do not want to go to this hospital. In fact, if you make me go, I'll refuse care, and I'll sign out against medical advice. Okay?" She bit her lip. Of course, if she did go in, the E. R. physician would probably get a psychiatric evaluation on her, after hearing her wild story. And the psychiatrist would probably hold her in the hospital, making it illegal for her to leave against medical advice. But she didn't tell them that.

"Well," said the driver. "If she refuses, she refuses." He stepped on the gas. "She's the doctor."

Relieved, Jade watched the hospital disappear behind her.

Jade picked up the phone at the police station. It rang a few times.

"Hi, this is Dr. Jade Evans. I need Tammy Harper paged to this number. And if you get no response in a minute, please page Dr. Van Martin stat to this number. This is an emergency."

Thirty seconds later, Tammy picked up.

"Hey Jade, what's up? We still meeting in twenty minutes?"

She grunted. "Maybe. But not at the hospital. Tam, I'm in jail."

The other woman was silent for a second, and then began laughing. "Yeah, sure. What, are you stuck at the office or something?"

"No, really, I'm in jail. In Manchester."

"Um, you're not serious are you, Jade?" She sounded more concerned.

"Yes, Tammy, I am." She paused. The other woman was speechless. "Tam, can you bail me out?"

She sounded confused. "Yeah, sure...Jade, what on earth happened?"

"Please let me explain later. It's a huge, huge mix-up. Anyway, my bail is ten thousand dollars. If you can't do it, Tam, please just tell me. I know it's an incredible sum of money..."

"Don't be silly." She was now serious. "Manchester Police Department? I'll be there as soon as I can. Probably half an hour or so, okay?"

"That's great. Thanks, Tam." She hung up.

Steve Ryan led her to an open cell, and gently closed the door. He looked at her with sorrowful eyes, trying to make sense of the whole episode.

"Officer Ryan," she said, sitting down on a thin, rock-hard mattress, "when did you say my court date was?"

"Two weeks from today, Doctor."

She nodded. "Does it usually take that long?"

"Usually longer. Two weeks is pretty good."

"Right." She shook her head.

"Do you have a lawyer?"

She hadn't given that much thought. "Yeah. I have a friend down in New Haven."

He smirked. "Good." Ryan then turned, and walked towards a metal desk, thirty feet away.

Jade brushed back her wet hair. She wondered if Steve Ryan was supposed to have let her wash up. As it was, he had let her use an employee bathroom, and had brought her extra paper towels. She looked down at her hands. Her palms had small, scattered punctate lesions that had been washed thoroughly; the back of her hands had a few scratches, but nothing major.

Jade leaned back, and laid down on the thin, hard mattress. She closed her eyes.

The sound of a metal door sliding across metal rollers awoke Jade. She sat up quickly, and saw Tammy Harper standing next to Officer Ryan. Tammy's face was pale under her long, curly black hair; she wore an expression of disbelief.

"Are you okay?" she asked softly.

Jade stood up. "Yeah, I guess so." She rubbed her knee. "Tam, thank you for coming. Really."

She frowned. "Don't be silly. I just can't believe this happened to you."

"Well," said Ryan, placing a key into the heavy cell lock, "you're free, Doctor."

He shoved aside the iron bars, and she walked out. Tammy embraced her, and the two quietly exited the cell block. Before they left the station, an officer provided Jade with a handful of papers. She signed several documents, promising to return on her court date, and promising to not leave the state before that time.

Then, they left.

"Before I explain everything," Jade said, walking towards the green Subaru in the station's parking lot, "how's John?"

Tammy sighed. "I don't know, Jade. The doctors say he'll be okay, but he looks so awful right now. He's hooked up to a breathing machine, he can't talk, he has all these wires hooked up to him." She shuddered. "I'm really scared."

"I know you are," Jade said, empathetically. "But you know, I'm actually reassured. If the folks down there say he'll be okay, then I bet he'll be just fine. I know he looks scary, Tam. But the ventilator is really to ease his work of breathing, so he doesn't tire out. And he can't talk because he has the endotracheal…I mean the breathing tube…in his throat. The wires are just there to monitor his vital signs, just in case something unexpectedly goes wrong."

"Yeah." She smiled weakly, and then approached her tan Pontiac. "By the way, where are we going? You want to stay with me tonight?"

"Actually, that would be great. But I need to swing by my place first, just so I can get some things and feed my cat."

"Of course. I'll follow you there." She then stood between the two cars, and looked at Jade expectantly.

Jade smiled. "You must be pretty confused, huh?" The other woman nodded. Jade leaned against her car. "Where should I start?"

Tammy said at the beginning, and so she did. She told her everything, from the assault by Gunther Petchov, to the murder of Yu-lan Tang. Tammy listened carefully, with wide eyes and frequent gasps. Jade also mentioned her belief that Feng had caused John's 'accident'. Tammy simply listened.

"I know it all sounds crazy," admitted Jade, when she finished the story. "It sounds absolutely crazy. But I swear, Tam, it's all true."

"No, no," said Tammy, quickly and defensively. "I believe you." But her tone suggested some uncertainty about Jade's tale. Still, her concern and support for her friend seemed rock solid.

Jade bit her lip. Even her friends were doubting her. "All right. Let's meet at my place."

She led the way to her home. They parked in the driveway, and Tammy then followed Jade inside. She immediately started playing with Nora.

"If you don't mind keeping her entertained, I'll just get my things."

"You talking to me or the cat?"

Jade smiled, and retreated to her bedroom. Her answering machine was beeping. Jade pressed the playback button.

"Hey there, stranger," said the friendly voice of her lawyer friend. "It's Phil. Long time, no see. Hope all is well with you, Jade. Anyway, I'd be happy to chat with you about legislation affecting herbs and other dietary supplements. I don't know if you knew, but I spent some time at the FDA's Center for Food Safety and Nutrition back in '95. Dietary supplements were a pretty hot topic back then, since the '94 Dietary Supplements Health and Education Act had just been passed. So hopefully I can be a decent resource for you. Well, anyway, sorry I missed you. Give me a call when you get a chance."

Oh, don't worry, she thought. I'll certainly be calling you, Phil.

She pressed the 'next' button.

"You little bitch," spat out a deep, unfamiliar voice. "I swear I'm gonna kill you. You screwed with the wrong person, lady. Oh, and don't worry about making your court date. You'll be six feet under well before that time arrives!" Slam!

One week ago, hearing that message would have been the most terrifying experience of her life. Now, it just made her angrier.

"Oh Jade…"

She spun around to see Tammy, shaking in her doorway. She had heard the message.

"Oh my…" She looked at her with desperate eyes.

"I wasn't lying to you, Tam. This is for real."

Tammy shook her head. "You've gotta tell the police. You need protection…"

"Won't do any good, Tam. They are certain that I'm the liar. Besides, how does that message incriminate Feng? It's not his voice."

"Whoa." She became more forceful. "They're wrong, Jade. The police are wrong. I'll go with you. I mean, this is ridiculous..."

"They won't listen!" She couldn't help her angry tone. "Trust me, they won't! In fact, I'll only hurt myself more if I go back. It already looks like I'm crazy; in fact, I can't believe I haven't been evaluated by a shrink! If I go back to the station to report more bizarre crap, they'll lock me up in a psych ward! And they should; if I were them, I would!"

"Oh, come on, Jade! You're being stupid, here! You just got a death threat; the police need to know that! That will only help your case, not hurt it. I mean, what else are you going to do?!"

"I'm going to talk to my lawyer. And I'm gonna eventually get Feng's ass imprisoned..."

"And in the meantime, you have someone trying to kill you!"

The women stared at each other, fuming. Jade had to admit, she was probably right. She looked down and shook her head.

"He committed the perfect crime," she said softly. "How the hell can he be found guilty?"

Tammy stepped closer. "Well," she said, more softly, "what about the other employees? Surely they'll realize he's Feng..."

"No they won't," she replied confidently. "I'm telling you, it's impossible to tell those brothers apart."

"So you think he'll just lead the life of Yu-lan?"

She shrugged.

"I mean, how can he do that? At some point, people will want to know where Feng is. At some point, people will want to see them together."

Jade thought about this. "Will they?" she asked doubtfully. "Why couldn't Feng supposedly have quit the store? Or better yet, have left the state? Or the country? Maybe he'll say he went back to China."

"No way!" shot Tammy. "Not when your lawyer demands to see them together in court. If they can't show up together—and have the employees recognize them in the courtroom—then your story starts sounding a whole lot more credible."

Jade looked at her. She thought about this.

Maybe she had a point.

A slight grin crept onto her face. She nodded. "Did you start law school without telling me, Tam?"

Tammy smiled.

"You're right," Jade realized aloud. "I'm sure that's what Phil will do."

"Yeah. And not to bring up a terrifying topic, but that's why Feng wants you dead."

"What do you mean?"

"Right now, nobody would believe your story. Hell, Jade, I almost didn't. But if you push your story in court, you'll win. No doubt about it, you'll win. Your lawyer will ask the court to subpoena both Yu-lan and Feng. But obviously, Feng can't show up as both himself and his brother." She paused. "Trouble is, he knows that."

"So if he kills me before the court date, my lawyer can't demand to see both him and Yu-lan. Because there will be no trial. I'll be dead."

"Probably in some accident," Tammy sneered.

"Yeah. So, what do I do now?"

"Like I said, you've got to get yourself safe. I think you should bring the tape to the police, and let them give you protection."

Jade sighed. "Let me call Phil first. I want his input. I really think the cops won't believe most of what I say. Even with the tape."

"Fine. Then call him from my house. But right now, I think we'd both better get out of here."

Jade agreed. She quickly stuffed several articles of clothing into an old gym bag. She gathered some toiletries, and then followed Tammy to the living room. At Tammy's insistence, she opened a living room closet, and retrieved Nora's cat carrier. She was going with them.

Both feeling uneasy about being in Jade's house, the two women hurried to their cars. Tammy lived in East Hartford, about ten minutes away. They agreed that they would see John in the morning; for now, they wanted to go directly to East Hartford.

Literally fearing for their lives, they quickly got into their cars and left.

Tammy Harper lived in a modest white ranch that lined a busy suburban street. The area was well lit, and people were outside walking along the sidewalks. Jade instantly felt safer than she had at home. Yes, she thought, this would now be home for a little while.

Inside, Tammy showed her to the guest bedroom, and brought Nora to the den. She had brought Nora's litter box and a few toys; Tammy lovingly placed the cat and her belongings in her small den. Bothered by the drastic change in surroundings, the Birman simply cowered under a chair and angrily thumped her tail on the hardwood floor.

After she had settled in, Jade picked up the kitchen phone. She dialed Phil Santiago's number.

"Hello?"

"Hey stranger," she smiled.

"Well, if it isn't the family doctor from Manchester! How are you?"

"Actually, I've been a lot better."

"Sorry to hear that. What's up? Got a legal problem with an herbal medicine?"

"Oh, the herb's the least of my problems right now." Here it comes, she thought. "I was arrested today, Phil. And I have a court date in two weeks."

He was momentarily silent. Then, "You serious, Jade?"

"Yeah. Essentially, the cops thought I broke into a local health food store. But, on the contrary, I actually had witnessed a murder in that store, and had barely gotten out of the place alive."

"Okay, now you're joking."

"No, Phil, I'm not."

There was a long pause.

Then, "Well, okay. So what about the murder? Do they think you did it?"

"Nobody's aware of any murder, because the guy covered himself extremely well."

"Jade," he said, exasperated, "this is really, really wild…"

"Phil," she pleaded, "so help me God, I am telling you the truth. *Please*, please believe me. I need you right now."

Another pause. Then, "Man, Jade. I've only been a defense lawyer for two years now. Couldn't you have gotten yourself into this mess when I still did corporate law?"

She grinned. "So you gonna help me?"

"Okay, now you're being dumb. Of course I'm going to help you!"

"There's more, Phil."

"I'm listening."

"Well, the whole story would take too long; I'd rather be face-to-face for that. But for now, let me just say that the murderer wants me dead. I got a threatening phone call on my machine."

"You called the police?"

"No. They haven't been too helpful..."

"I don't want to hear it, Jade. Call the cops. I'm serious. And I hope you're not at home right now."

"No. I'm at a friend's house."

"All right." He sighed. "Why don't I swing by tomorrow afternoon? How about two-thirty?"

"Sounds good."

"Should I even bother with the herbal stuff? I have lots of papers for you."

"Yeah, bring it, if you don't mind."

"Sure." He paused. "Jade," he said, more solemnly, "are you okay?"

"As okay as I'll get. Thanks."

He offered some words of support, and Jade then gave him directions to Tammy's house. She assured him that she would call the police as soon as she hung up, and they then said their good-byes.

Tammy patiently sat as Jade phoned the Manchester Police.

"Hi, Chief Preston, please. It's an emergency. Thank you."

A few moments passed.

"Preston here."

"Hi, it's Jade Evans."

She explained the threatening phone call, and expressed her concern about her safety and her life. Preston calmly listened. He then ascertained that she was in a safe place. Finally, he told her that he would contact the East Hartford Police, and that he would request a patrol car to sit by Tammy's house overnight. He said he'd also have the Manchester Police check Jade's house every few hours.

Impressed by his apparent willingness to believe her, she expressed her gratitude, and hung up.

"All right," she told Tammy. "They'll have a patrol car outside here tonight."

"Great," smiled John's sister. "The neighbors will be up-in-arms over that one."

They stayed up until midnight, just rehashing Jade's awful story. By the end of the evening, Tammy was convinced that Feng would be imprisoned. She also predicted that Phil would want to push up the court date, for Jade's safety.

After the long discussion, both women went to bed.

Jade laid in bed with eyes wide open. Maybe, she thought, tomorrow would be better.

16

Jade watched Tammy's frightened expression as she stood over her brother, holding his hand. Teary-eyed, she stroked his palm with her thumb. She looked at the rhythmic expansion of his chest as the mechanically-delivered oxygen entered his lungs. John's eyes were closed, and he still was unresponsive to vocal stimuli. Despite Jade's reassurance that his unresponsiveness was simply due to sedating medications, which were necessary to prevent him from fighting the ventilator to breathe, it still troubled Tammy.

Jade moved to the other side of John's bed. She glanced up at the monitor in the corner of the room. His vital signs were good and his rhythm strip showed a strong heart. She looked down at a transparent plastic box attached to his bed; a clear tube ran from John's inner chest wall to the box. Minimal maroon fluid was visible inside the tube; the box contained less than ten milliliters of the same fluid. Looks good, thought Jade. The chest tube could come out soon.

Jade faced her bedridden friend. A shiny purple bruise surrounded his right eye, and several healing cuts ran across his chin.

"John," Tammy called out. He did not flinch. "Hey you. It's me, Tam."

Still nothing.

"I'm here with Jade. You were in some kind of accident, John. But the doctors say you're doing better. Jade says you're doing better." She glanced at the other woman, who nodded in support.

Tammy bit her lip. "Can he hear me?" she softly asked.

Not an easy question, thought Jade. "It's hard to tell, Tam. I don't know how much sedation he's had. But yes, I think there's a good chance that he can hear you."

She leaned closer to her colleague and friend. "Hey there! What's with all this lying around? You're scaring your sister. But you can't fool me, John; I know you're doing well!" She grinned, knowing that if he heard her, he was grinning back deep inside.

The women spent another hour in his room, just being there. A respiratory therapist came in during that time. He informed Jade that the surgeons wanted to try intermittent mechanical ventilation today, which meant that John would be partially breathing on his own. That was good news, Jade told Tammy. It was a first step towards weaning him off the ventilator completely.

At 11:00, they decided to leave.

"Do you know if they have an ATM here?" asked Tammy, in the elevator.

"Yeah. There's one on the first floor, by the information desk."

"Good. I need to swing by. Tell you what, I need to run to the supermarket before I go home. Since we brought separate cars, you want to just meet me at my house?"

"Sure. That's fine."

The women parted ways at the bank machine, and Jade proceeded to the hospital parking garage. She looked beyond the concrete walls to the blue sky; it was another beautiful day out there. But she was still trapped inside her gut-wrenching episode of terror. She shook her head. How again did all this happen to her? Wasn't last week just a normal, run-of-the-mill week for Jade Evans? She sighed; she just wasn't accustomed to witnessing murders, getting shot at, being arrested, and getting death threats!

Jade stepped up several metal steps to the upper level of the garage. Her feet clanged on the metal. She then turned left and proceeded towards the Subaru. Maybe it was time to swing by that automotive body shop and check on the Saab, she thought. It would be nice to have her…

A strong hand grabbed her neck and yanked her to the ground. She fell with a hard thud, and pain seared down her leg.

"Aaraugh! What the…"

A gloved hand smacked against her mouth to silence her. Then she was shoved against the side of a black van. Jade whipped her head around and faced her attacker.

Feng stared through her with devil's eyes. Kneeling over her, he wore a black leather jacket over a plain white tee-shirt.

In a fury, she bit down on the gloved hand.

"Bitch!" He yanked his arm back.

"Help!!" screamed Jade. She didn't recall seeing anybody in the garage.

"Shut your mouth!" He slapped her hard, and then knocked her head against the van. He pulled back his fist, and prepared to fire a hard punch.

She cowered. "Feng! Please!"

"Then shut your mouth! I mean it! You open that mouth again, and I'll kill you!" He knelt over her, his fist posed to strike in any second.

Watching her shudder in fear, he allowed a smile to slither across his wicked face. "How's your buddy in the hospital?" He shook his head. "You're too damn predictable, lady. You get a death threat, and you still come to the most obvious place!" He spat on her forehead. "Stupid, stupid woman."

Trembling, she closed her eyes. This was it, she thought. This was how it ended. There was no escaping this one.

"If you're gonna kill me, Feng," she muttered softly, "just do it." She couldn't believe those were her words. Her survival instinct screamed in bloody protest.

He simply chuckled. "Stupid, stupid woman." He shook his head and leaned closer. "If I killed you here, don't you think it would look a little suspicious?" His breath reeked of alcohol.

Abruptly, Feng stood up, and violently swung open the black van's passenger door. "Get in."

"No way in hell am I…"

"GET IN!" he roared. He whipped out a gun from inside his jacket, and pointed it at her forehead.

Jade stared at the barrel. Maybe she should scream, she thought. Then she would be shot and killed, but like Feng himself said, the murder would look very suspicious. He wouldn't be able to hide this one; blood wouldn't easily come off the concrete, like it came off the store's tiled floor. If she got in the van, he'd probably drive her to a secluded place, and then she'd be quietly killed. And she'd probably never be found.

Looking down the barrel of the familiar pistol, Jade's heart sank. It wasn't the time for reason. Her survival instinct demanded that she continued to live. At least for now.

Feeling defeated, she slowly rose to her feet. In a last attempt of reason, she thought about bolting away. No, a bullet was faster than she was! She was sure that Feng preferred not to kill her here, but if he had to, he would.

She reluctantly approached the van, and got in the passenger's seat. Feng slammed the door closed. Quickly, Jade looked to the driver's side. Damn. No keys. She looked behind her, into the back of the van. Only a few tattered blankets were shoved to one side.

Feng got into the driver's seat, and locked all doors from his door panel. She tried to press her lock button; it didn't work. He shot her a disapproving glance.

Silently, Feng pulled out of the parking space, and slowly drove towards the garage exit. Jade noticed that the gun was between his legs, completely out of her reach.

She fastened her seat belt, closed her eyes, and began to pray.

The van rolled to a stop, and Feng rolled down his window.

"Good morning, sir," said a young Hispanic woman. "That will be six dollars and sixty cents."

Jade shot her a terrified stare, but the woman wasn't looking. Feng caught Jade's signal, and quickly sat forward in his seat, blocking the women's views of each other.

Jade thought about screaming. No. Knowing Feng's evil, there would probably be two murders then. There was no way that she would jeopardize the life of the young cashier.

Feng pleasantly thanked the woman, rolled up his window, and pulled forward. Grinning, he entered the Hartford streets.

A black silence hung in the van's stale air for a few minutes. Feng navigated through the streets, which were rather deserted on this Sunday morning.

When they were on a highway, he turned to Jade. "I want to thank you, Doctor."

She looked at him in disgust. "What?"

"I said I want to thank you." He was strangely jovial. She had never heard this tone from him.

"I still need to kill you, obviously," he said, matter-of-factly. "But I really, really do appreciate what you did for me."

She was silent. Curious, but silent.

"If it weren't for you," he continued, "my idiot brother would still be alive." He chuckled. "Good ol' Yu-lan. Yeah, that little bastard would still be here."

She turned to him with icy eyes. "What are you talking about?"

"Isn't it obvious? I'm too nice of a guy to kill my brother. I like my family. As much as Yu-lan deserved to die, I really didn't have the heart to do it."

She cringed in hate.

"But then you went and meddled in our affairs, you slept with him..."

"We never slept together, Feng!"

"Whatever. Anyway, you ultimately convinced him to pull the Quazhen from the shelves." He grimaced, mocking hurt feelings. "Can you believe that? He was going to tell Grandma to stop shipping it here. And behind my back, too."

She continued to glare at him.

"So, naturally, I had no choice but to kill him." He shook his head. "I mean, I had a business deal on the cusp of being done." He turned to her. "We're talking hours away from being done."

She frowned. "I thought you were a few weeks away..."

"Oh, so Yu-lan was following me closer than I had thought." He sneered, bringing back his normal self. "Idiot. No, no Doctor. At the time of his death, the deal was hours away from being done. In fact, it was completed last night, at midnight."

"What deal, Feng?"

He leaned over her, and opened the glove compartment. He retrieved a single piece of paper, folded into thirds. He handed it to her. "This deal."

She opened the paper, and stared at a copy of a contract of some sort. Her eyes scanned the legal mumbo-jumbo, but ultimately, she got the gist. Feng had signed with a company called Botanicure to sell the Quazhen for...

"Eleven million dollars!" she exclaimed.

He grinned. "That's right, lady. Eleven million bucks for the rights to Quazhen. And Feng's a rich, rich man!" He sighed in happy satisfaction. "See, that's why I thanked you. Yu-lan never would have agreed to this."

"I know, Feng," she spat. "He respected his grandmother…"

He suddenly slapped her cheek hard. "*Don't* mention my grandmother!" he hissed. "And don't you dare talk about my respect for her! Got it?"

She nodded, feeling her burning cheek.

After a few heavy moments, he spoke again. "Anyway, like I was saying, Yu-lan wouldn't have agreed to this. So with me in the driver's seat now, things will be all good. All good, Doctor."

She shook her head. "How are you going to get the Quazhen?" Sure, it was an indirect question about his grandmother. She didn't care.

He smirked. "You think those stupid papers that Yu-lan had couldn't be copied? And their special symbol thing! Yeah, as if that's hard to copy!"

"So you'll just keep contacting her by mail, pretending you're Yu-lan, and forging requests for more Quazhen?"

"No," he replied. "*I* won't. Two of my…" He struggled for a word. "…'friends' will. I'll be sitting my butt on a beach in Fiji, baby! That money is headed for an offshore account." He grinned widely. "Beautiful, eh? My buddies get the Quazhen from Grandma, supply it to Botanicure, and I just enjoy my piña coladas out on a tropical island!"

Her soul screamed in protest. "Eleven million dollars."

He raised his eyebrows. "Well," he said sorrowfully, "actually I'll only see seven million. Four million goes to the two guys I mentioned, the ones back here supplying the Quazhen. They get two million each."

She shook her head. "And your store?"

"Shucks," he said sarcastically. "Poor sales; gotta shut it down. Of course, Yu-lan will do that." He mockingly fluffed his short hair.

She shook her head. "What did you do with his body, anyway?"

He smiled. "Pretty impressive, eh? You should have seen your expression when he wasn't in the back room!"

"Listen, asshole…"

"Excuse me?!" he shouted, grabbing his gun handle.

"Sorry, sorry."

He put the gun down, and snorted. "Anyway, if I may answer your question." He obviously enjoyed sharing his evil genius with his next victim. "I called a couple of friends while you were hiding in the bathroom. I simply told them that there would be two bodies and a bloody mop outside the bathroom window, waiting to be picked up." He spoke with excitement, as if he was sharing his winning strategy after finishing a family board game. "I told them to be there in two minutes, tops." He leaned over to her. "You gotta understand. My guys are good.

"Anyway," he continued. "When you left, I quickly heaved Yu-lan outside. In about forty-five seconds, I mopped up the back room—isn't that tile great?—and then wrapped the mop in a few dry towels; I then tossed it out the window. Like clockwork, my boys were there to pick up Yu-lan and the mop."

"And the second body?" Jade asked.

"Oh, that was supposed to be you. Yeah, you ruined my plan, Doc. Anyway, I quickly followed them out, and I went to Yu-lan's place. I went in, chopped my hair, put on his clothes, and came back to the store. I believe that's when we met again." He smiled, delighted with himself. "Pretty ingenious, eh?"

She just turned to the window, sickened.

Feng slowed down the van, and veered towards the right lane. He approached a Manchester exit.

"Where are we going?" she asked.

"Oh, I thought you knew. I'm so sorry." He grinned wryly. "We're going to your house. You see, the only thing between me and Fiji, Doctor, is you. Not only do you have a court date which I'd have to attend, but you know that I killed Yu-lan. And we just can't have that, can we?

"So I could just shoot you in cold blood, right?" he continued. "Ah, but not so fast. You've already instilled a kernel of doubt into the minds of the stupid police; that kernel pegs me as a murderer of Yu-lan. You also said that I tried to kill you." He looked at her. "I didn't appreciate that, by the way.

"Anyway. If you were murdered, I'd be a suspect. No doubt about it. But," he continued, his face lighting up, "right now, everyone thinks you're crazy. As it is, I don't know how the hell you're not in a psychiatry ward. I mean, you've got to admit that your story sounds crazy."

"Go on," she muttered through clenched teeth.

"So, what do crazy people do? What's the number one thing that psychiatrists worry that their crazy patients will do?"

She was silent. She knew the answer.

"You know it, Doc." He leaned closer, and put on a sinister smile. "Suicide."

She closed her eyes. Damn it.

"We'll just give you a little suicide at your house. That will perfectly fit in with your crazy character, and nobody will be really surprised." He paused, thoughtfully. "You know, I couldn't really decide what the method should be; I was between slashing your wrists and hanging you in your garage. Do you have a preference?"

She was silent.

He became louder and less jovial. "Doctor, do you have a preference?"

She looked at him. She was looking at a devil. "I do."

"Really? Good. What is it?"

"I prefer that you die the most painful death imaginable, after endless torture and suffering, and that you then burn in hell for all of eternity." She smiled. "That's my preference."

He was expressionless for a moment. He then grinned thinly. "Charming. Just charming."

He turned up her street. "Okay. Hanging it is."

17

Feng turned into Jade's driveway, and parked the van. She stared at her beautiful red Colonial with desperate eyes and a nauseous stomach. Her end was almost certainly near.

Feng got out of the van, and came around to her side.

Okay, she thought. I need a plan.

He opened her door, and motioned for her to get out. His gun was not in sight; it was presumably inside his jacket.

Jade stepped out of the van, and onto her driveway. "Feng," she said carefully. "Maybe we can work something out..."

"Save it," he snapped. "I don't want to hear it."

"Is there *anything* I can do to change your mind?" Though she almost vomited in doing so, she put on her best seductive voice. With all her effort, she smiled and licked her lips.

He looked at her long, blond hair. Loosely thrown back in a bun, it shined radiantly in the sunlight. She was certainly pretty; he couldn't deny that.

Feng drew closer to her. He gently placed a hand on her cheek. He leaned towards her, and put his mouth inches from her ear...

"No!" he barked.

Startled, she jumped back.

Damn.

"Open the garage," he ordered. He then moved to the back of his van, and opened a rear door. He leaned in, dug beneath the blankets, and emerged with two leather gloves. He put them on, and then dug out a large, thick rope.

Terrified, she just stood there. Now what?

She turned to face the road. 11:30 on a Sunday. Surely, some cars must be traveling on that road.

"I said, open the garage...Hey!"

Feng slammed the van door and sprinted after Jade. She was furiously running towards the road. He retrieved his gun from an inside pocket, and fired into the air.

Jade stiffened and stumbled at the sound of the gunshot. Still, she managed to stay on her feet, and kept running. She had no real plan, but anything would be better than slowly allowing her murder to transpire.

"Stop!" he roared, and fired another bullet into the air.

Jade reached the road, and quickly bolted left. It was now, she thought, that closer neighbors would certainly be nice! As it was, the next house was two hundred meters away. She dashed towards it.

Another gunshot cracked the Sunday air. She glanced back. To her horror, he was only twenty feet away!

"Help!" she screamed, as she scurried forward. His footsteps were sounding closer, and closer, and…

"Bitch!"

"Ugh!" She met the hard pavement with an excruciating thud. His arms were wrapped around her ankles; his tackle was strong and solid. Her head throbbed in agonizing pain, and old wounds in her outstretched hands reopened.

He climbed up her back and grabbed her hair. Pulling hard, he yanked her head up. She screamed out in pain.

"You don't get it, do you bitch?" He slammed her head back down onto the ground. "A hanging is a very quick way to go. Your neck snaps, and bam, it's all over. The pain would have been very short."

He grabbed her hair again. "But now…"

"Feng," she mumbled weakly. "Please…"

He violently rolled her over, and punched her left cheek. She cried out. He swung again.

Oh please, God, she prayed. Send an angel. Oh please. Oh please.

He swung again.

And again.

Fading towards a blurry semi-consciousness, she suddenly heard the sound of a car.

It was coming this way.

In his blind rage, Feng didn't hear the approaching car. At least he didn't appear to. He kept swinging at her face.

"Screw the suicide!" he bellowed. He reached into his pocket, and retrieved his gun. "Think of me on the beaches of Fiji, bitch!"

She half-opened her eyes, and stared down the barrel of his pistol.

In a surreal moment of slow motion, Jade watched Feng suddenly look up. A car had appeared from around the bend, and by the sound of it, the car was speeding directly towards them. Jade watched as Feng's expression dropped into an angry look of shock and confusion. He lifted his gun, and aimed it at the car.

The car screeched as the driver slammed on the brakes. Feng jumped off Jade, and positioned himself in front of the car. He pointed his pistol at the driver.

And fired.

Bang!

Bang!

Bang!

With a lingering dose of adrenaline, Jade rolled over, and got to her knees.

"NO!!" she cried, watching Feng fire into the windshield a police car. Frozen in horror, Jade watched him blast the driver mercilessly.

It was Officer Steve Ryan.

Ryan's car skidded into a tree, and it abruptly crashed to a halt. Shooting demonic eyes at the bullet-torn officer, Feng approached the driver's side window, and reloaded his pistol.

Fully loaded, he stood squarely at the side of the window, aimed at the officer, and started shooting again.

Bang! Bang!

Jade's heart practically stopped as she watched another car whip around the corner.

It was another police car.

In slow motion, Jade watched Feng turn to face the oncoming car. He was still pointing his gun at Ryan. Feng's eyes widened and his sneer twisted into a pathetic expression of fearful surprise.

Blast! Blast! Blast!

Jade watched Feng fly through the air, and land hard on the ground. Like a smashed tomato, his chest spurted blood as bullets ripped into him.

The second police car skidded to a stop. Officer LeChatlier jumped out of the driver's side and ran to Ryan's car. Detective Wu thrust open the passenger side door and dashed forward towards Feng.

Squirming at the door of death, Feng rolled to his side, and got to his knees. He snagged his nearby pistol. With glazed, helpless eyes and a dropped jaw, he started to raise it.

Blast! Blast! Blast!

Standing four feet away from him, Wu fired her firearm into his skull.

Through blurry eyes, Jade watched Feng drop his gun and sway for a couple seconds. He slowly turned his lifeless eyes to Jade. Then, with blood gushing out of his forehead and spurting from his chest, his empty body slammed to the ground with a heavy thunk.

Thank you, God, thought Jade.

She then collapsed.

PART THREE

DOUBLE STANDARD

18

"Can she hear us?"

"I don't know. The doctor couldn't say."

"I just don't get it. Why didn't she tell us?"

"That's Jade for you. She probably didn't want us to worry."

"Oh, my little dear. My precious, precious little dear."

"The doctor said her cat…cat thing was okay, right?"

"Cat scan, George. Yes, it was perfectly normal."

"Well, that's good, at least. By the way, where did Tammy go?"

"I think she went down to the intensive care unit. Apparently her brother is coming off the breathing machine tonight."

"Oh."

Where was she? What happened to her?

Why were her parents here?

Jade tried to raise her arm to scratch her forehead. Ouch! A sharp pain ripped down her arm. Wincing in her mind, she relaxed.

But the itch persisted. She tried to move her arm again. Pain—sharp pain! But she wanted to scratch her forehead. Try. Try harder!

"George! She's moving!"

"Jade! Jade, honey! Can you hear us?"

What was going on?

Slowly, with great effort, she lifted her eyelids.

The tender faces of her parents stared down at her. Their countenances, pressed very close to hers, were aflame with loving concern.

"Jade," said her mother, touching her right hand, "you're okay, sweetie. You're okay." A tear rolled down her mother's rosy cheek.

Her father gently brushed her hair back. "We know everything, Jade. The police called and told us everything."

The police? Everything?

Wait a second.

Feng Hou Tang. The murder. The death threat. Her kidnapping. Running; running down the street. The tackle. The beating. The pain; the awful pain. Officer Ryan…

Oh God. Officer Ryan.

The second police car. Officer LeChatlier. Detective Wu. Feng's bloody chest. His bloody head. His lifeless eyes.

Oh God.

It was all real.

"Jade, dear," said her mother lovingly, "it's all over. Your awful, awful nightmare is all over."

Jade closed her eyes, and breathed slowly and deeply. Yes. It was indeed all over.

She opened her eyes again, and concentrated hard. "Mom, Dad…"

"Oh!" Her mother grabbed Jade's palm between both hands, and allowed her tears to freely flow. The tears fell onto Jade's chin. Her father gently wiped them off.

In her inner mind, Jade cried out in delight. She shouted with joy, and embraced her parents. It was over! The nightmare was over! On her outer surface, however, Jade barely managed a small smile. It hurt too much to move her face much more than that.

"We love you, Jade. We love you so much." Her father leaned over her and hugged her. He held tightly, and squeezed. She heard him softly whimper.

Jade felt the first tear dribble down her own cheek. "I love you guys, too," she whispered.

The next day was a cool, rainy Monday. Sitting up in her hospital bed, Jade looked out her large window. Yikes; it looked rotten out there. She chomped on her turkey sandwich, and slurped down her orange juice. Thank goodness for that morphine, she thought; she could barely feel any pain at all.

Jade didn't notice as a visitor entered the room.

"Am I interrupting?"

She turned to see Detective Wu cautiously enter her room.

Jade smiled, and swallowed her last bite. "No, not at all."

Wu pressed her lips together into a grin, and approached her bedside. She tried not to stare at the large purple bruises surrounding each of Jade's eyes. "How are you doing?"

She shrugged. "I'm feeling better. They say I'll be going home this afternoon. So I guess that's good. But you know hospitals these days. I could have one foot in the coffin, but if my managed care group can find a way to kick me out, then it's my tough luck!"

Wu smiled. "Well, I'm glad you're feeling better." Her voice was soft; it showed genuine concern. "Listen, Dr. Evans, we…we…" She broke off, and shook her head shamefully.

"Hey." Jade touched her hand on the bed railing. "You guys didn't know."

"But we should have. I mean, you were right there telling us the whole story." Wu lowered her head in heavy guilt. "I…I'm really not sure how to apologize. So, let me just say I'm sorry. Dr. Evans, on behalf of all of us at the station, I am so sorry."

"Look, Detective…"

"Please, call me Arlene."

"Okay. Look, Arlene, I hold no ill will towards you whatsoever. I know that my story seemed fanciful at best. It's like that old expression: the truth can be stranger than fiction. Believe me, you and I are not at fault here. We shouldn't be feeling guilty or shameful about any of this."

She nodded, and smiled weakly.

"Of course," grinned Jade, "that Kolowski guy does need an attitude adjustment."

"Oh, Sergeant Kolowski is a grade A jerk," proclaimed Arlene, quite matter-of-factly. "That's nothing new."

Jade smiled. The women enjoyed a moment of quietness.

Then, "Arlene, about Officer Ryan…"

The weight of the world returned to the detective's shoulders. She closed her eyes and shook her head in disbelief.

"I don't suppose he somehow survived?"

"Steve died. Hopefully, it was pretty much instantly." She swallowed hard. Her voice lifted an octave. "There's a funeral service for him this Thursday." She wiped her eye, and shook her head. "Wonderful guy. Absolutely wonderful. A wife and two little kids."

Jade rammed her fist onto the bed sheets. Damn, she thought. She stared at the ceiling, and allowed a solemn moment of silence to envelope the room.

A minute later, Jade broke the silence. "By the way, how did you guys know to come by my home?"

She shrugged. "We didn't. Steve was driving by because Chief Preston told him to swing by your house every three or four hours. Apparently, you had gotten a death threat the previous night?"

She nodded.

"So Steve was just doing a standard check. But he must have seen you struggling with Feng, and then gotten right on his radio. In a very rushed call, he called for emergency back-up at your house. As luck would have it, we were headed down Pine Road, ten seconds from your place."

Jade nodded. "As luck would have it, all right."

Arlene tightened her lips. "Let me ask you a question. Do you have any idea what happened to the real Yu-lan Tang?"

"Yes. Feng actually kidnapped me from this hospital yesterday morning, and on the ride over to my house, he told me all about it."

"The ride over to your house?"

"Oh sure," she said, in a tone of sick sarcasm. "He was going to help me commit suicide."

Arlene slowly shook her head in horror.

"Anyway," continued Jade, "like I had originally said, Feng shot him in his store; that part I saw. But apparently, after I escaped, Feng threw Yu-lan's body out the window, and two 'friends' of his carted him away. I have no idea who those friends are. However, I do know of two hoodlums who tried to run me off the road and chase me. They're the ones I had told you about when we first met. I'm not positive that those are the same guys, but I would place a small wager on it."

"Wow. So Yu-lan's definitely dead?"

"No question about it."

Arlene sighed. "This whole episode is absolutely incredible. This is the stuff of fiction, you know?"

"Oh, believe me. I know."

"Sorry. Of course you do. By the way, this may not be a tactful time to say this, but we'll certainly need a very detailed report on everything that happened to you over these recent days. We'll also want to know exactly what Feng said to you yesterday. And if two so-called friends of his are still on the loose, we'll want any leads that you can give us."

A sudden chill overcame Jade. That was true, wasn't it? At least two of Feng's friends still were on the loose. Of course, this time the cops would be actively hunting them down.

"I'll help in any way I can," assured Jade. "By the way, have you reached Yu-lan's family about this?"

"Family?" She obviously had given that little thought.

"Yeah. I know he and Feng had a grandmother back in China. That's the only living relative that I know of."

She nodded. "You know her name or address?"

Jade winced. "I think he told me her name once, but I forgot it. And I have no idea about an address."

Arlene nodded. "We'll see what we can do."

"Okay."

"I should get going, Doctor…"

"Jade. Just call me Jade, Arlene."

The other woman smiled. "Very well. I need to go, Jade. At your convenience, whenever you're feeling up to it, please swing by the station. Just to fill out that report, okay?"

"You got it. I promise I will."

They shook hands, but that quickly became a strong hug. After one more apology and a wish for a speedy recovery, the detective left.

Ten minutes had not passed when several familiar voices drew closer to Jade's room. She turned as her parents, Tammy, and her colleague Walter all entered the room. Walter was carrying a large bouquet of colorful carnations and several cards.

"Wow!" smiled Jade. "I'm getting quite the audience!"

"Tammy, your father and I met Dr. Bartlett in the elevator," explained her mother. "Quite a coincidence, isn't it?"

Jade grinned at all of them. She found it somewhat amusing to see how friendly Tammy and her parents had become; they had only met once before at a holiday party. It made some sense, though. Tammy was thoughtful enough to call her parents when she learned that Jade was in the hospital; her parents' appreciation had been beyond words.

Walter approached her. "How ya doing, kid?" He placed the bouquet and cards on a long side table.

"Physically, I'm a little better. But emotionally, I'm split. I mean, on the one hand, imagine a cold-blooded murderer who desperately wants to kill you; and now imagine him dead!" She grinned. "In that sense, I've never felt this good in my life. But on the other hand, I'm falling apart inside." She shook her head. "Talk about a traumatic experience, you know?"

He nodded, and openly stared at her facial bruises. "You went through hell and back. All in a weekend." He shook his head in disbelief.

"Well, her hell started before the weekend, Doctor," mentioned her mother.

"Yes," he added quickly. "That's true. I was there when the assault happened in the office. Let's see, that was…"

"Wednesday," said Jade flatly.

"Right."

Jade looked at the flowers. "Thank you, Walter. They're beautiful."

"They're from all of us at the office. There were two bouquets; I had just delivered one to John." He smiled. "The cards are from the folks at the office, too."

"Thank you." She glanced at the clock. "Are you on your lunch break?"

"I am."

"I assume my patients were canceled for today?"

"Of course, honey," said her father. "Don't you worry about that, now."

"That's right," agreed Walter. "Your appointments are canceled for the week; so are John's. And by all means, Jade, if you need more time, you just let us know."

Her mother approached her. "Sweetie, your father and I want you to take more than a week off. You need time for yourself."

"And that would certainly be fine with us," promised Walter. "In fact, I would like you to see a counselor with whom you can discuss the whole experience."

Jade nodded. "Well, to be honest, I agree with you. I do need to digest things, and try to make sense of it all. Actually, I was thinking that I'd take two weeks for now, and maybe more after that time."

Walter nodded. "Consider it done. I'll tell everybody back at the office. Of course, I'm sure they'll be in to see you later today, too."

"Thanks, Walter." She turned to Tammy. "Hey, how's John?"

She smiled. "He's doing really well. He's a little weak, and he has no appetite. But otherwise, he's looking good."

"You didn't tell him about me?"

"Not yet. I thought I'd break it to him this afternoon."

"Good. He needs to heal himself before he starts worrying about me."

The group chatted for a few more minutes; Walter then left. Before long, Tammy also left. Jade's parents remained with her.

They spent some time in the quiet peacefulness of each other's company. Jade glowed as she looked at her parents. Her mom, with her short, curly salt-and-pepper hair, and her dad, with his gray, receding hairline, brought her tranquillity. She had been blessed to have a childhood filled with love and respect, and their mere presence blanketed her with security.

"Jade," said her mom, "we think you should stay with us for a little while. Let us care for you back in Rhode Island."

She smiled. "Mom, I'm thirty-three."

"So?" replied her father. "Doesn't matter how old you are; you've been through the most traumatic experience imaginable."

"You're a family doctor," reminded her mom. "You know the healing power of families."

Jade looked down, and grinned. Somehow, staying alone in her big red Colonial didn't sound too enticing right now—especially when the tragedy climaxed in front of the place. Yes, she thought, staying with them could be therapeutic.

"Well, if you guys don't mind..."

Her mother shot her a guilt-laying look of insult.

"I'd love to. Thank you guys." She smiled. "But there are some things I need to take care of, first. I need to meet with my lawyer. Actually, I was supposed to meet with him yesterday afternoon. Anyway, I also need to fill out a police report. I definitely want to see John. And I'd really like to get my car back. *My* car, not the rental."

"You got it," promised her father. "Leave that part to me."

Jade frowned. "And I definitely need to go to Officer Ryan's funeral." She shook her head.

"We're all going to that," said her mother softly.

The three of them agreed on a plan of attack. Jade would call Phil then and there. Her father would go to the automotive shop to get her Saab, whether or not it was ready. And her mom would sit in the room and just be with her child.

With that, her dad left, her mom sat, and Jade picked up the phone. After a few rings, Phil answered. He practically jumped out of his seat when he learned it was Jade.

"It's so good to hear your voice," he said, emotionally. "You probably didn't know it, but I was with you in the hospital yesterday afternoon. You were completely out."

"Sorry, I didn't know that. But I am doing a lot better now. Listen, Phil, I need to give a report down at the police station; I know they'll also have lots of questions for me. Just for my own comfort, would you mind accompanying me there?"

"Of course I wouldn't mind. When are you going?"

"Well, I'm actually getting discharged this afternoon. I might just swing over later today, and then be done with this whole thing."

"Why don't we say 4:00? I'll meet you there. Just call me on my cell if you're running late."

She agreed and thanked him. Then they hung up.

Jade's mother was quietly reading a magazine. Jade glanced at the clock; it was only noon. She sighed. "Mind if I turn on the television?"

"Of course not."

Jade pressed the power button on her remote control. An advertisement for St. Francis Hospital played on the introductory screen. She clicked 'channel up'. A college football game was on; Boston College was taking on Notre Dame. Maybe, thought Jade. She pressed 'channel up' again. A beautiful redheaded actress in a wedding dress was screaming at a drop-dead-gorgeous actor in a tuxedo; apparently he had slept with her maid-of-honor last night. No soap operas, thank you, she thought. Channel up. A rowdy audience cheered on two sisters on stage; they were fighting over some scrawny guy wearing a backwards baseball cap, an offensive tee-shirt, and size 52 blue jeans. She sighed. Definitely not. Channel up. A suited reporter stared into the camera.

He was in front of her house.

"...Officer Ryan was shot to death here, on Middle Valley Lane in Manchester, less than twenty-four hours ago. Reports say that as the murderer brutally shot the officer, a second police car arrived on scene. The murderer was then shot to death by another Manchester police officer. The identity of the murderer has still not been released, and no other details of the episode are available at this time. When we learn more, we will certainly let you know. Back to you, Carmen."

The words 'Murder of a Connecticut Police Officer' were boldly printed at the bottom of the screen. A Hispanic woman looked into the camera from her news room in Hartford.

"There will be funeral services for Officer Steve Ryan this Thursday, September 23, at St. Joseph's Church in Manchester. Cards and flowers may be sent to his family via the address on your screen. And like Simon said, when we know more details, we'll be sure to let you know. Now, back to our regularly scheduled programming."

'Channel 7 Special Report: Murder of a Connecticut Police Officer' covered the screen as a musical jingle played in the background.

"My goodness," said her mother softly, shaking her head and staring at the screen.

"I bet it's in all the papers, too," said Jade.

Suddenly, the phone rang.

"Hmm. Who could that be?" asked her mother.

"I don't know." She reached over to the phone. "Hello?"

"You are one lucky bitch!" snapped a deep voice. It was the one who had left a death threat on her answering machine. "Your ass should be dead, not Feng's!"

Jade froze, speechless.

"I bet you think this whole thing is over, don't you?"

She became nauseous, and started shaking.

"Tell you what, honey. If you even hint to the cops that Feng had help, I swear I'll kill you. Do you understand that, bitch? If you want to lead your normal life, you put this whole thing behind you. You forget about the fact that *I* buried Yu-lan's body. You forget about the fact that *I* put your friend in the hospital. And you forget about the fact that *I* tried to land you in the hospital, too. Is that clear?"

Her mother ran over to her and tried to grab the phone, but Jade angrily pushed her arm away.

"And don't you dare mention our involvement in the Quazhen deal. You remember what I told you, Dr. Jade Evans. We'll be watching you." He slammed down the phone.

19

"You are calling the police, Jade! That's final!"

"Mom, stop it! This is my life here—quite literally, I might add!"

The two women stared at each other with stubborn eyes. The daughter reflected the mother's headstrong nature.

A nurse appeared at the door. "Um, everything all right here?"

Jade glanced at her. "Yes, yes thank you. We're fine." She glared at her mother.

"Okay. Just tell us if you need us." The nurse left.

Her mother stormed back to her chair, and sat down. "For Heaven's sake, Jade, you just got another death threat! Why on earth would you not report that?!"

"Because like I told you, he said that if I keep quiet, he won't hurt me. And you know, call me crazy, but I'm really ready for the end of this thing!"

Her mother stamped her foot in frustration and turned to the window. Jade stepped out of bed, and moved into the bathroom. She closed the door, and her mother heard her lift the toilet seat. Her mother closed her eyes as Jade wretched into the bowl.

Her father entered the room, smiling. "Good news, folks. I got the car…" He looked around. "Where's Jade?"

"Vomiting in the bathroom," was the dry reply.

The tension was clear as glass. "What happened?"

"Oh, she got another death threat. Right here in her hospital room. The bastard called and said if she tells the police about Feng's help, he'll kill her." Her mother shrugged. "But she doesn't want to tell the police about the call."

Jade emerged from the bathroom. "Look, I'll talk to Phil about it. Okay?"

"A death threat, Jade?" Her father was just beginning to digest the news.

Her mother lightened her tone. "Talking to Phil would be a very good idea." She turned, and spoke under her breath. "He'll talk some sense into you."

"I heard that, Mother."

"So," said her dad, trying to regain some peacefulness, "that's the plan. You talk to Phil, and we'll stay out of it." He shot his wife a stare.

The three of them tried to change the subject. The conversation turned to politics, but that became a lukewarm subject after two minutes.

"You know what," offered Jade, "I think I'm going to visit John for a little while. I definitely want to see him before I leave here."

"Good idea," agreed her father. "Your mom and I will get some lunch."

"But we already ate..."

"Then we'll eat some more. Let's go."

With tension still hanging in the room, her parents left.

Jade threw on a pair of jeans and a pullover shirt that her parents had brought for her. She quickly fixed her hair in the mirror, and brushed her teeth. Frowning, she realized there was nothing she could do about her bruised and swollen face. So be it, she thought.

She left her room, and swung by the nurse's desk. She told her nurse that she was going to another patient's room for a little while, and then asked where exactly he was. By coincidence, John was only one floor below her.

Jade took the stairs, and then walked towards his room. As she drew near, she saw him sitting up in bed, watching television.

"Well look who's here," he smiled as she entered. His cut chin was healing nicely, and his bruised cheek was beginning to turn yellow.

"Hey there." She threw her arms around him, and squeezed.

"Tammy told me everything."

She loosened her grip, and stood back. "It's been quite a week."

He shook his head. "I really don't know where to begin. What you've been through is so unbelievable. Are you okay?"

"You know, I don't know anymore." She plopped herself down on the side of his bed. "There's a new development."

"Oh yeah?"

"Tammy mentioned that I had received a death threat a couple days ago?"

He nodded.

"Well, I got a call in my hospital room about fifteen minutes ago. It was him again. He threatened to kill me if I told the police anything about Feng's help."

"Oh God." He shook his head. "What do you know about his help?"

She shrugged. "There's a guy with brown hair and a brown beard who owns a big, black truck. There's another blond guy with a small beat-up blue car; I forget the make of it. They tried to run me off the road and then chase me down on foot. Actually, I already told the cops about them after our last encounter.

"Anyway, according to the guy who called me, he was one of those two men. He says he also buried Yu-lan, and he was involved in the Quazhen deal."

"The Quazhen deal?"

"Oh, when Feng kidnapped me, he said that he had just signed some multimillion dollar deal with an herbal supplement company. He sold the Quazhen to the company. He was going to go to Fiji to live off of the profits, and these henchmen of his were going to supply the company with the Quazhen. They were each going to make a couple million bucks off the deal."

"I don't get it. How would they get the Quazhen? I thought Yu-lan was in control of that."

"Yeah, but with Yu-lan dead, they were going to impersonate him, and just tell the grandmother to continue shipping the stuff."

John sighed. "Wow. That's so sick." He shook his head. "You're going to tell the police all this?"

"Well, I don't know. My caller implied that if I kept quiet, he'd leave me alone. Before I do anything, I want to speak with Phil Santiago, you know, my lawyer friend. I want his advice."

"You're going to need help, Jade. You'll need a counselor at the very least."

"Yeah, maybe."

He reflected upon everything for a few moments. Then, "So what happens to this Quazhen deal, now that Feng's dead?"

"It's off," she said, quite confidently. "I mean, nobody ever told me that, but it would have to be off, right?"

"I would think so. If Feng is gone, how would the company go ahead with the deal? Their contact guy is dead."

"Their contact guy was shot to death by the police after murdering two people. Yeah, I would think that a reputable company would wash their hands of the entire situation."

"But you said they signed some contract?"

She shrugged. "What good is a contract if one party is dead? Besides, I'm sure they can pull back out of the deal. That's a lot of money to sign an absolute agreement to."

He nodded. "So we've seen the last of Quazhen."

"Yes."

They sat there, heads spinning from the incredible episode.

"By the way, John, what ever happened to you? Do you remember the details of the accident?"

"Not at all. I'm completely amnesic about the whole thing."

She nodded.

She sat with him for an hour, just reliving the whole horror over and over again. Just sharing her emotions with him was tremendously therapeutic. His gentle and supportive nature helped her to realize that she would need a lot of time for psychological healing. He was sure that two weeks off from work would be much too short. He was advocating several months, if not a year or more. And he strongly supported her going to Rhode Island during that time.

After the hour, she decided to go back to her room. They embraced, and she gently kissed his cheek. Knowing that he would still be hospitalized for another day, she promised to call or visit before his discharge.

Jade returned to her room to find her parents there.

"Hi, sweetie," her mom said, much more calmly.

She smiled. "Hi."

"The nurse was looking for you. Apparently, the doctor said you can go when you're ready."

"Good. I think I'm ready to get out of here. Do you guys want to swing by the house? I'll need to pack lots of things if I'm going to your place for awhile. Also, we should pick up Nora from Tammy's."

"Whatever you want, dear."

"Okay. Let's do that. Then I'll meet Phil at the police station at four."

"Sounds good."

They gathered their belongings, and left.

Jade arrived at the police station at quarter-past four; her parents stayed behind at her house. She walked in to find Sergeant Kolowski chatting with Phil in the waiting room. Upon seeing her, Kolowski immediately shuffled towards her.

"Doctor, looks like we owe you an apology…"

"Looks like you do," she snapped back. "I need to be alone with my lawyer for a few minutes."

He wiped his brow. "Who would have thought that one maniac could do all that…"

She shot him a cold stare. "Get out of my sight, Sergeant."

His face reddened and he wrinkled his forehead. He opened his mouth, as if to reprimand her. But upon seeing her hard gaze, he backed down.

"You have something to say to me, Sergeant?"

"Uh, no. Just, uh, sorry."

She watched as the pathetic Kolowski tramped out of the waiting room. The familiar receptionist discreetly shook her head as he left.

Seated in a metal chair, Phil smiled at her. He was a handsome man, with short, curly black hair and a five o'clock shadow. His tan skin showed his mother's Hispanic heritage, and his wire-rimmed glasses gave his appearance a distinguished flair. He was wearing a neatly pressed brown suit. "You treat every officer that way?"

"Not at all. I have tremendous respect for most of them. But that guy's the biggest blockhead you've ever met!"

He grinned.

She glanced at the receptionist. "Maybe we should take a quick stroll outside, just for privacy."

As they walked along Center Street, Jade told him all about her kidnapping by Feng. She then brought up today's menacing phone call. She expressed her reluctance to tell the police about the call, since her safety would be in jeopardy.

"You've gotta tell them," he replied. "There's no question." He sighed in frustration. "I thought we had closure on this thing."

"Me too."

"Well, the only way to get complete closure is to get those thugs behind bars." He thought for a moment. Then, "Hey, didn't you say you saw Feng's contract in his van?"

"Yeah."

"Well, if those two thugs were supposed to be part of the deal, were their names mentioned?"

She thought about it. "That's a really good point. But no, I don't recall seeing their names."

"Hmm. I wonder if there was a separate contract for them. Maybe the cops can contact the company, and try to get their names that way."

She frowned. "Phil, I don't know if I want to do this. I'm really, really scared for my safety here. Why can't I just drop it?"

He shrugged. "What does your conscience say?"

She thought about it. She thought about the black truck and the blue car. She thought about John in the hospital. And she thought about Yu-lan. Poor, innocent Yu-lan. With sheer disgust, she thought about the men who buried him.

Phil was right.

"My conscience says you're right. Damn it."

"Hey, the police can provide you with very good protection. They'll get you an alternate identity, if you want..."

"No, I don't want that. I want to be me. I want my life back." She groaned. "I do plan to live with my parents in Rhode Island for awhile."

His face lit up. "Well, there you go. That's a perfect idea. Leave the state for awhile, let the police find these creeps, and then come back when it's safe."

She nodded. "I guess so."

He stopped and turned to her. He put his hands on her shoulders. "Jade, I know how scared you are. Nobody should ever have to go through a hundredth of the suffering that you've gone through in the past few days. But people want to help you now. Believe me, people want to help."

He looked at her with tender eyes and a compassionate expression. He stroked her arms with his strong hands. She looked at him, and flung herself forward into his embrace.

The tears started to flow. He held her tight, on the middle of a Manchester sidewalk, as she cried. He whispered words of support, and continued to hold her.

After minutes had passed, she slowly backed out of his grasp. He wiped her cheeks, and she rubbed her eyes.

"I'm sorry," she said.

"No, don't you even think of apologizing."

They walked back to the police station.

"This is what we're going to do," said Phil. "We're going in there, and we're going to tell the whole story. Everything. We'll explain today's phone call, and we'll get special protection for you. We'll get the police to help you clean your house out, to get rid of any evidence of your parents living in Rhode Island. We'll also have them tell your office that you'll be away indefinitely. Your patients will just have to understand."

"The job will be fine," she agreed. "They can get a temp physician in the meantime. It will probably be someone right out of residency."

"Good. Then you move to Rhode Island, and you stay there until the those bastards are behind bars. That's pretty much it."

She nodded.

"You'll have to deal with lost wages," he reminded her.

"No problem. I don't think my parents will charge me rent." She grinned. "One other thing, Phil. What about John? What about his safety?"

He thought about it. "Well, that's not a bad point. Tell you what, I absolutely don't want you worrying about it. You need to get your mind off this whole thing. I'll contact your friend John. I'll ask him what he wants to do. Actually, I think I will encourage him to get police protection, too."

"And his sister, Tammy? I don't know if they know how much she knows."

He smiled. "Leave it to me, Jade. I'll contact her. Please, you don't worry about a thing."

She turned to him. "Phil, thank you so much."

He winked at her. "Don't mention it. That's what friends are for."

They entered the police station. "By the way," he said, "I have all that literature on the regulation of herbs and other dietary supplements. It's in my car. Do you still want it?"

She shook her head. "Thanks for bringing it, but I want nothing to do with herbs for awhile! No, you can take it back home."

He smiled. "You got it."

They approached the receptionist, and asked for Detective Wu. Everything then went exactly as Phil said it would. Jade documented the entire story in a lengthy written testimony; the testimony included a detailed description of today's phone call. She then answered many questions from various officers. Phil pitched in at that point, and requested special protection for her. Wu and the others quickly agreed, and two officers were assigned then and there to conceal evidence of her parent's address. They were ordered to accompany her home to eliminate such evidence, and Wu said she would take additional measures, such as calling the phone company to make her parents' phone number unlisted. By the end of the encounter, the police had the best description of the two thugs that Jade could remember. They also were reminded to try to contact the Tangs' grandmother to inform her about the tragic deaths, but Jade regretfully couldn't offer them any leads on how to contact her.

Before Jade and Phil left, Wu said that Jade should not attend Officer Ryan's funeral. It would be in her interest of safety, she said, for her to remain in Rhode Island until they found Feng's accomplices. Jade began to protest, but Phil adamantly agreed with the detective. Realizing that her safety was at stake, Jade backed down. But she asked for his family's address, and insisted that she would at the very least write a long letter and express her sentiments. She would also explain why she had to miss the funeral. That would be fine, they agreed.

Jade, Phil, and two officers then left for Jade's house. When they got there, they joined her parents in carefully removing possible signs of the Rhode Island address. The officers then explained to Jade's parents that their phone number would become unlisted, and other actions might be necessary to protect them and their daughter. Of course, her parents were extremely cooperative.

Before leaving, the officers obtained a spare house key from Jade. They assured her that they would check on her house three times a week while she was away. They also promised to collect her mail, and to forward it to her via a secure carrier from the police station. They then reminded her and her parents of the special password that Wu had discussed; if someone called their house claiming to be the police, that person had to know the word 'barnyard'. If not, they told them, it was not the police.

The Evans family heartily thanked the officers, and they then left. Phil then helped the family pack her up. Jade changed her answering machine message to say that she was vacationing in Hawaii, and that she did not know when she would return.

Jade then called Tammy, and vaguely told her that she was going away; she also said she was coming by to pick up Nora. Tammy quickly offered to take care of the lovely Birman during her absence, but Jade politely insisted; after all, Nora was family!

Jade strongly hugged Phil in her driveway. He told her to call anytime, and he promised to offer legal advice and protection to John and Tammy. They agreed to give Phil her parents' phone number, just in case of an emergency. Phil also insisted upon taking Jade's pager. He said he'd arrange for a colleague—perhaps Walter—to take her professional calls. She shouldn't be answering pages from unknown numbers, he advised.

With that, Phil left. Jade and her parents drove separate cars to Tammy's house. From there, Jade called John's hospital room. She told him that she was leaving for awhile; from their previous conversation, he knew where she was going, but he did not say anything over the phone. John insisted that she get psychological counseling, and she insisted that he work with Phil to get police protection. They then offered each other kind words and good wishes, and hung up.

Jade then profusely thanked Tammy for her help. She delicately mentioned that police protection may be a good idea for her, too, and that Phil would be contacting her. Tammy was receptive. They then said their good-byes, and Jade left.

With the caged-in Nora in her back seat, and with her parents following closely behind her, Jade then left for Rhode Island.

20

Like an ocean of diamonds, the gentle blue waves sparkled in the bright sunlight. Several seagulls soared across the cloudless blue sky, and a dozen small sandpipers scurried along the sandy water's edge. The repetitive crashing of waves emitted an entrancing rhythm, and the periodic squawking of birds provided the chorus to this natural maritime song.

Jade sauntered along the sandy Rhode Island beach, wearing her blue UConn sweatshirt and an old pair of denim shorts. Alone, she stared out to the horizon, silently reflecting upon her extraordinary adventure.

It had been two weeks since she had left Connecticut, but the whole episode seemed like yesterday. In a way, it did happen yesterday—and the day before that, and the day before that. Jade's recurrent nightmares had imprisoned her inside of her own hideous memories. Each night since leaving Manchester, she had awoken in a cold sweat. The dreams always took one of two forms. The first took place inside Natural Essentials; it portrayed Feng shooting his brother to death, and then looking over at Jade. She would freeze at that point, and he would then slowly walk over to her. Like a deer in headlights, she would watch him come closer, and closer, and closer. Finally, he would be in front of her. He would raise his gun, snarl, and then—boom—she'd wake up. The second form involved Feng beating her in front of her house. After a long and severe battering, he would raise his gun, aim it at her forehead, and then—boom—again, she'd wake up.

She shuddered at the thought of her dreams. Fortunately, she had known enough to see a fellow physician, a local family doctor whom she had known in medical school. Dr. Guy Zimmerman, who practiced out of Providence, had a wonderfully gentle manner. In his empathetic way, Zimmerman had listened to her story with shock and concern; he then told her that her symptoms sounded a lot like posttraumatic stress disorder, though that diagnosis technically couldn't be made until her symptoms had been present for at least a month. The two doctors agreed that the drug fluoxetine would be a good choice for her, and she agreed to see a local therapist whom he recommended. Zimmerman had assured her that half of all patients with posttraumatic stress disorder recover completely within three months; with her strong premorbid functioning—or pre-incident functioning—he expected her to be in that quickly-recovering half.

Still, the nightmares were dreadful. She hated going to sleep, and she would often stay up until two or three a.m. just to avoid the dreams. At times, she was finding herself to be irritable and hyperarousable. Indeed, it was beginning to interfere with her daily life.

Jade took a deep breath of the cool, October air. She allowed herself to crack a small smile. If anything would heal her, spending time on the tranquil Rhode Island beaches would.

She kicked off her shoes, picked them up, and approached the water's edge. The soft, dry grains gave way to wet, cold, clumpy sand. Her bare feet sunk into the cold ground, leaving shallow imprints. The foot-shaped divots formed small puddles as the rising tide stretched its tentacles across the sandy shore. Jade strolled along, allowing the cold water to tickle her toes as the crashing waves spread onto the sand.

She looked up at the sky. The sun was beginning its descent into the West; the afternoon had already stolen the morning. Realizing that she had been gone for several hours, she decided to turn around. It was time to return to her parent's house.

In no hurry, Jade turned around, and walked along the beach towards her car. She had a good twenty minutes to reach the small parking lot. Feeling at peace, she slowly made the walk.

After twenty-plus minutes, she arrived at her Saab. She wiped her wet feet on the asphalt, got in, and pulled out of the parking lot.

It took her nearly fifty minutes to reach her parents' town of Smithfield, Rhode Island. She always felt refreshed to be back in her hometown. Even now, after two weeks, it still felt great to be here.

Driving down the main street of Smithfield, Jade glanced down at her gas gauge; her tank was below one-quarter full. Seeing a few gas stations on both sides of the road, she turned left into a Shell station. She parked her Saab beside a shiny white dispenser, got out, and began fueling. As she fueled, a small color monitor embedded into the dispenser began showing various advertisements. Amused, she grinned. Televisions while you pump your gas, she thought. What would they think of next?

As Jade watched the advertisements, she heard another vehicle pull up behind her. Paying no attention to it, she continued to pump her gas. Finally, the dispenser nozzle clicked off; her tank was full. She turned to pull out the nozzle…

And she froze.

A big, black truck had parked behind her at an adjacent dispenser. The windows were tinted black. The grill was a shiny chrome. The license plate was a Connecticut plate.

Her heart raced. She quickly jammed the dispenser's nozzle back into its holder, grabbed her receipt, and opened her car door.

The driver's side door of the black truck opened.

Her palms beginning to sweat, Jade put one foot into her car.

The driver began to step out of the truck.

Jade froze in terror, waiting for the driver to appear.

And then, she did.

"Hi there!" said a cheerful young woman in a business suit. Her straight blond hair was neatly cropped to her shoulders, and a bright smile illuminated her pretty face. "Quite the Indian summer we're having, isn't it?"

Jade blushed. "Yeah," she smiled. "It…it sure is."

The other woman pushed her credit card into the dispenser, and lifted the nozzle. She began fueling. Seeing Jade eye her awkwardly, she gave a half smile. "You okay?"

"Um, yeah." Her face continued to redden. Embarrassed, she got into her car. "Have a good day."

"Okay. You too," replied the woman.

Jade sped off.

It goes away in three months, she thought. For at least half of the people, it goes away in three months.

Jade pulled into her parents' driveway. They lived in a white raised ranch with black shutters. The yard was kept pristinely manicured by her father, who found relaxation in gardening and lawn care. The blacktop driveway ended in a two-car garage, and in the side turnaround, her childhood basketball hoop was still towering ten feet into the air.

She parked under the hoop, and got out. She walked up the cobblestone walkway to the front door, a classic red wooden door with brass accents. She opened it, and walked in.

"Is that you, dear?" asked her mother.

"Yeah, it's me." She stepped into the tantalizing aroma of freshly baked chocolate chip cookies. Her face lit up. "All right!" She smiled like a ten-year-old child, which was exactly why her mother had baked the cookies in the first place.

"They just came out of the oven," smiled her mom. "Your father bought a new gallon of milk last night; it's in the fridge."

She opened the refrigerator door, retrieved the cold plastic jug, and poured herself a glass. "Want any?"

"Sure. I'll take some."

She poured another glass, and then put away the milk. "Where's Dad?"

"He's working at Hank's. They asked him to fill in for a sick employee."

Hank's Greenhouses was a small home and garden store in the nearby town of Cumberland. Her father worked part-time there; he said it kept him out of trouble. Since he and her mother had entered retirement two years ago, he had been focusing much of his time on his hobbies, like gardening.

Jade carried two large, gooey cookies to the kitchen table, grabbed a napkin, and sat down. Her mother joined her.

"So," said her mother. "How was the beach?"

She nodded and smiled; her mouth was already full of cookie. She swallowed some milk, and then replied. "Good. It always is. You should go down more often."

She smiled. "I know. But you know your father and me. We don't like to drive all that way."

"Mom, it's under an hour."

"Oh, I know. But you know how it is."

Jade smiled, and took another bite.

"By the way," her mother said, speaking somewhat slowly and deliberately, "your friend Phil called..."

"Phil? Are you serious? What'd he want?"

She put her hand up. "Whoa. Slow down, dear. He didn't have good news, and he didn't have bad news..."

"What's that mean?"

"Jade, if you allow me to speak, I'll tell you. He was just letting us know that the police are still searching for those two men. They tried contacting that company that was dealing with Feng."

"Uh-huh," she said, very attentively.

"But the company couldn't help them. I guess they didn't know of any other party involved in the deal besides Feng."

Jade wrinkled her brow. "That's odd. Why would Feng lie about them? He had nothing to lose by telling me the whole truth; as far as he was concerned, he was going to kill me."

Her mother shrugged. "Phil thought it was peculiar, too."

"And," Jade continued, "the guy himself told me that he had a part in the Quazhen deal. Remember? When he threatened me in the hospital?"

"Yes, I remember. But I don't know what to tell you, dear. Anyway, that road was a dead end. So, there wasn't really anything else he had to say. He just wanted to keep us informed."

"So basically, the police have gotten nowhere?"

"Well, that's a glass-is-half-empty way of putting it."

"No, that's the point-blank truth, isn't it?" Jade put down her milk, and crossed her arms.

"Honey, they'll find those men. I know they'll find them. It's not just the Manchester Police looking, you know. They have agents all over the country looking for them. Killing a police officer is no small crime; any possible affiliation with it is a very big deal."

Jade shook her head. "Anything else new?"

"No." Then she looked up, rather mischievously. "Except, of course, that I beat your high score in Ms. Pac-Man."

Jade allowed a smile to gradually spread across her face. She dropped her arms. "You did not!"

"I did too!"

Jade slapped her hand onto the table, and glared at her mother in mock disgust. Ms. Pac-Man, of course, was a twenty-year-old video game; regardless, the friendly family competition over its top scores was very much alive and well.

Jade smirked at her mom. Then, in a sudden flash, she bolted for the family room.

"Hey, no fair! I'm not a kid, you know! I can't run that fast!"

From the next room, Jade shouted, "I'm not a kid anymore, either, Mom! That excuse doesn't work now!"

Laughing gleefully, the two women plopped down on the sofa, startling poor Nora, who had been peacefully sprawled out on an armrest. They then flipped on the video game console, and continued the twenty-year-old competition.

21

"Any more nightmares last week?" Geeta Sayed looked at Jade with her inquisitive brown eyes. Jade had been seeing the psychologist weekly since Dr. Guy Zimmerman had recommended her to his fellow doctor. This was week number twelve; by now it had been three full months since Jade had left Connecticut.

Jade smiled in response. "Not a single one."

Sayed's face lit up. "Jade, that's wonderful! How about your anxiety level? Do you still get very anxious?"

She paused to consider this. "Tough to say. I think I've always had some baseline generalized anxiety, so it's tough to tease out the overlying stuff. But I'm definitely less irritable and hyperarousable than I was twelve weeks ago."

"Terrific. Jade, that is terrific."

Sayed continued to ask various questions, and Jade continued to give encouraging answers. Jade liked the psychologist. She had a gentle and patient nature, but she also gave solid advice when the situation allowed for it. Jade also liked her office. The small room was wallpapered in a soft, solid brown. Many green plants lined the walls, and two oversized windows allowed plenty of sunlight to stream in. The Indian carpets added an additional sense of elegance to the room.

"So," said Sayed after they had spent half an hour together, "this could be our final session. It's up to you. But I'm very happy with the progress that you have made."

"Well, you've been a great support. I've definitely gotten a lot out of these sessions."

After some more words, the women decided that this was indeed the last session. They said their good-byes, and Jade left with a carefree sense of liberation mixed with success.

Driving home from Providence, Jade reflected upon the past three months. Staying in Rhode Island had certainly been therapeutic. Besides having comfort and security in her parents' house, her months of free time had provided mental restoration. Yes, the nightmares had been horrible, but they had peaked over two months ago; her last one had been twelve days ago. Time, she thought, was certainly a powerful healer.

There were, however, two things that she missed sorely; the first was practicing medicine. Her medical journals were being forwarded to her in the police's bulk mailings. She found herself avidly pouring over the latest research and newest developments. She often thought of specific patients when reading an article, and she wished she could see them to offer some new advice or try some new medication. She hoped that the covering temp physician was aware of the new immunization guidelines, and that he knew about the new class of asthma drugs. After all, he was taking care of her patients. She thought about contacting him to discuss these new developments, but she realized that that would be insulting. He's probably a competent physician, she told herself; at least give him the benefit of the doubt.

The second thing she sorely missed was her dear friend John. She regularly thought about him, but she had only talked to him twice during her time here. He had taken two weeks off after the accident, and he and Tammy had both agreed to police protection. A few weeks ago, he did admit that he thought somebody had been following him home one day. He insisted, however, that he had been wrong. So really, there was not a single episode of a threat or violence against either of the Harper siblings since the whole Tang episode. In general, he assured her, he and Tammy were doing just fine.

The most frustrating news in the past three months was the sheer lack of news. Both Phil Santiago and Arlene Wu called on multiple occasions to keep her informed. But there was not a single lead that would bring them to Feng's helpers. The police checked Jade's answering machine regularly, but there was never a threatening message. In fact, in the past month, there had been no messages at all. In all of her forwarded mail, there was nothing from the men.

Knowing all of that, Jade told everyone that she intended to go home last month. At that time, however, her nightmares were still occurring weekly. Geeta Sayed had strongly advised her to spend more time in Rhode

Island, and her parents also wanted her to stay. Phil frowned upon the idea of her returning home that soon, and the police expressed their concern, as well. The clinching factor, however, was the time of year. Christmas was Jade's favorite time of year, and it was certainly a time to be with family. Her parents wanted her to spend the holidays with them; then, they said, she could consider returning to Connecticut.

It was her mom's Christmas cookies that really decided things.

So here she was, on January 7, and she was finally feeling back to her old self. Even the occasional nightmares that she did have were now truncated; she seemed to be able to writhe out of those horrific situations, and either awaken or change her dream. Yes, thought Jade, it was time for her to return to her life. Time and loving support had healed her. Now it was time to go.

Jade exited the highway in Smithfield, and made her way down the main street. Last week's snowfall had mostly melted away, but the edges of the street were still lined with mounds of brownish-gray sludge. Large trucks had shoveled the newly-fallen snow over to the curbs last week, but since then the sand on the road had been kicked up onto it. The resulting mixture looked like big chunks of muddy ice lining the streets; it was terribly ugly. Oh well, thought Jade. In New England, you take the good with the bad.

She glanced down at her gas gauge. It was low again. She slowed down, and pulled into the familiar Shell station. While she was fueling, she remembered that her mother had asked her to pick up some cough drops. She had developed a minor tickle in her throat a few days ago; Jade had looked in her mouth and told her it was post-nasal drip. She was probably just getting over a cold.

She finished fueling, moved her car to an open parking space, and then walked to the station's convenience store. She entered the store, and proceeded down the middle aisle. They did sell cough drops here, didn't they? Looking around at the huge store, she realized that was a silly question. In today's age of everybody getting into everybody else's business, this gas station probably sold fourteen varieties of cough drops!

She turned down a new aisle, and spotted the cold remedies clustered in one section. She approached them. Let's see, she thought. Ibuprofen, naprosyn, acetaminophen…no, that's not it. Okay, there were the cough syrups; no, her mom wanted drops. Hmm…there were the cure-all wonder pills: decongestant, antihistamine, expectorant, analgesic, and sedative all in one—now with muscle relaxants and skin softeners thrown in as well. She smirked. And there was a cure-all with vitamins C and E plus St. John's Wort; she didn't know that an antidepressant was indicated for a cold! She rolled her eyes as she spotted a few more herbal remedies. Incredible, she thought. Buy your magical plants right here in a gas station!

She finally found the cough drops. There were only five flavors. She grabbed a bag of cherry drops, and turned for the counter.

Then she saw them.

She wrinkled her brow, and then slowly stooped down to see them more closely. Next to the bottles of multivitamins were dozens of small white boxes. The boxes were roughly four inches high by six inches wide by one inch thick. In the bottom right-hand corner of each box, a small picture showed a silhouette of a couple embracing under a palm tree; behind them, the sun was setting over an ocean. Above the picture, in the middle of the box, were flowing cursive words printed in a rich, earthy green.

And above those green words, printed in black block letters, was the name of the product: 'Quazhen'.

22

Jade grabbed a box off the shelf, and stared in disbelief at the words on the front.

'For Energy, Harmony, and Balance. This Gentle Gift from Mother Nature Bathes Your Mind and Spirit in a Wholesome and Relaxing Splendor. Let Nature Awaken Your Life.'

Below, in smaller green letters, it read, 'Intended for Individuals Who Suffer from Stress'.

Unable to help herself, Jade squeezed the small box in her hand until the thin carton crunched down into a wrinkled package. Fuming, she read the tiny black print under the green lettering: 'This statement has not been evaluated by the Food and Drug Administration. This product is not intended to diagnose, treat, cure, or prevent any disease.'

With a beet red face, she flipped the carton around, and stared at its back. The ingredients list was short; the pills apparently consisted of Quazhen and corn syrup. Great. The dosage said, 'Each pill contains 1 mg active product.' Whatever that meant. And the directions advised users to take two pills twice a day.

At the very bottom of the package's back side, she found the following statement: 'Distributed by Botanicure Supplements, Inc.; Foxboro, MA'.

"Unbelievable!" She stood there dumbfounded, just staring at the product.

An elderly man walked by her, cautiously keeping some distance from the strange lady yelling at a carton of pills.

"Uh!" Frustrated, she stormed up to the cashier. She slapped the bag of cough drops onto the counter.

The thin teenager behind the counter itched his acne-laden face and scratched his buzzed, hairless head. "You want that too, ma'am?" He was looking at the carton of Quazhen, which she was inadvertently choking to death in her fist.

She looked at the carton. As much as it would pain her to buy this stuff, she wanted to be able to accurately describe it to John and Phil. "Yeah, I want it," she mumbled, slamming it down on the counter.

The cashier picked up the badly battered box. He tried to scan it through his register, but the bar code was torn.

"Hmm," he said, and he manually punched the price into his cash register.

"Twenty-three dollars!" she exclaimed. "You have got to be kidding me!"

He sighed. "No, that's the price. Do you still want it ma'am, or not?" The poor kid started shying away from this maniacal customer.

She huffed. "Yeah. Yeah, I want it."

"Okay. With the cough drops, your total is twenty-six twenty-five."

Shaking her head furiously, she gave him the cash. "Thanks."

He nodded nervously. "Next in line?"

Jade stomped into her parents home, and flung the cough drops down onto the kitchen table.

"Well, hello Jade," said her mother, very quizzically.

"They're selling it," she retorted.

"Selling what, dear?"

She grunted, and handed her mother the Quazhen carton. Her father emerged from the den, and joined his wife's side. They both read the package's wording.

"What a load of crap," mumbled her father.

"No kidding!" Jade agreed. "Do you guys realize what this means?"

Her mother touched her hand. "Honey, it's not the end of the world..."

"Yes, Mom, it is! This means two things. First, this crap is officially on the market, so that *lots* of people can enjoy brand new personalities and criminal sex drives! Yippee, right? But secondly, it means that this Botanicure company got the product from somewhere. Do you guys realize that? Someone had to supply them with this product!"

"Oh, Jade," soothed her mother, "try to calm..."

"Come on, Terry!" snapped her father to his wife. "Don't poo-poo this. Jade's right. This is a big deal, here."

Her mother threw up her hands. "Well, what are you going to do about it? Yes, it's unfortunate. But I wouldn't jump to conclusions, here. Even if those evil men are involved in the mass marketing of this herb, it doesn't mean they're coming after you, Jade. For three months now, there hasn't been a single threat back in Connecticut. The police are checking your messages, remember? I don't see any connection between this product and your safety. I just don't see it."

"That's not the point, Mom. This product is dangerous. Very, very dangerous. It should never be on the shelves; it causes serious side effects." She shook her head. "There's no way this made it through the FDA. No way."

"And," her father added, "what Jade said is true. Someone is supplying the herb to this Botanicure company. Almost certainly, that means that those men are still out there."

"Of course they're still out there, George. We would know if they had been caught." Her mother sighed. "Look, maybe this could be good news. If you two are right, and those thugs are supplying Botanicure with Quazhen, then the police have a new lead as to where to find them."

Jade thought about this. "But the cops already tried contacting Botanicure. They said they'd never heard of those two guys."

"Well, *somebody's* supplying the stuff to that company."

Jade thought some more. She then looked at her mother, and her face began to lighten. "Yeah. You're right. And they'd better be able to say who that supplier is. If not, the whole damn company should be under an investigation."

Her father nodded. "You gonna call the cops?"

"Oh yeah. But let me call Phil first."

"All right. We'll give you some privacy." He looked at his wife, and together, they moved to the family room.

* * *

"Are you serious?" asked Phil, astonished at Jade's news.

"Yeah. Can you believe it?"

"Hmm," he thought aloud. "Who would be supplying Botanicure with the Quazhen, though?"

"That's my number one question, too. I mean, I would think our two thugs are behind it. Right?"

"Maybe. Then again, if Botanicure signed a deal with Feng before his death, then they would be entitled to the plant. I presume they could just go to China and get it."

"Not a chance," she replied. "Remember, it supposedly only grows on the Tangs' grandmother's plantation. She would only send it to Yu-lan; that was made clear to me."

"But if Feng sold the rights to it..."

"It wasn't his to sell. That's the thing. The fact that Botanicure even has this herb is unlawful in itself. The grandmother owns the herb; she would never sell it to a large American corporation."

He thought about this. "Are we sure it's the same herb? It's not just cut-up grass? They could do that, you know."

She smiled. "I thought of that. No, Quazhen has a distinct smell. It's cross between basil and licorice; I remember smelling it back in Yu-lan's store. I just chopped up a Botanicure pill and smelled inside; it's the same stuff."

He groaned. "Well, I'm sure the police will contact Botanicure again. But if they deny knowing the two thugs, we may be out of luck."

She was taken aback. "What do you mean?"

"I don't think we can force them to identify their supplier. Maybe I'm wrong; corporate law is no longer my specialty. But I think they have various legal protections, you know?"

"But, Phil..."

"Don't get me wrong. I have the same hunch that you do. And I know Detective Wu will think it stinks, too. But I'm just being honest. We may only be able to go so far."

Frustrated, she thought about it. Then, "Fine. Say we can't prove Botanicure's connection to those guys. We can still get Quazhen off the shelves, which actually is more important to me. Two thugs running loose can do damage to society, but a poison on the nationwide market can wreak a lot more havoc than just two people."

"You lost me. How can we get Quazhen off the shelves?"

She wrinkled her brow. "Isn't it obvious? Phil, there's no way that product made it through the FDA. It's too damn unsafe. Botanicure obviously put the product on the market without running it by the FDA. That's illegal, Phil. Even I know that."

He chuckled nervously. "Ah, you're not going to like hearing this."

She was confused. "What?"

"Jade, herbs get onto the market all the time without FDA approval. By and large, they don't need FDA approval. They're just herbs."

She listened with skepticism. "Just herbs? Wait a second. Maybe small herbal boutiques like Natural Essentials can just bottle up grass and sell it. But Botanicure is a major corporation, Phil. I had actually heard of them well before this Quazhen story began. There's no way that a large, mass-marketing corporation doesn't have to run their drugs by the FDA!"

He sighed. "Wrong, Jade. Herbs are considered dietary supplements. Even big corporations don't have to run them by the FDA before marketing them."

"Phil," she contested, getting angry, "that makes no sense. Who checks for the safety of these herbs?"

"Nobody, Jade," he replied flatly. "I mean, supposedly the manufacturer or distributor checks a safety profile before selling it. But who knows if that really happens. Even if a company did find its product to have questionable safety, do you think they'd share that information? Not when the product is on the verge of making them big profits."

She started shouting. "So you're telling me that Botanicure can just package up Quazhen and sell it, with no approval from the FDA or any other official review agency?"

"Hey, calm down a bit. I'm telling you that's *probably* true, yes. I must admit, however, there may be a clause that does obligate them to notify the FDA?"

"Go on."

"I forget the details—it's been awhile since I've worked with this stuff—but I think there's a clause about 'new dietary ingredients'. Basically, if I remember correctly, any *new* herbal product in this country does have to be checked out by the FDA. 'New' means it was first marketed after 1994, I think."

"Well," Jade said, feeling victory approach, "Quazhen would clearly fit under that clause, right?"

"Presumably so. But Jade, there's a lot more to it. I need to review all that stuff before I have an intelligent answer."

"Look, I just cannot believe that Quazhen could be on the market without FDA approval. It *has* to fit under that clause."

He sighed. "Why don't we do this. I'm free today and tomorrow. I'll review my facts about herbs and other dietary supplements today and tonight. Then why don't I meet you at your parents' place tomorrow morning? I'll bring lots of long, boring legal documents, and we'll go over everything then." He paused. "You may have a point about FDA requirements Jade, but honestly, I doubt it."

She huffed.

"Also," he continued, "I'll call Wu to tell her about Botanicure's Quazhen. I'm sure she'll want to look into that company again. All signs really do point to our two thugs being their suppliers."

Jade softened her tone. "Phil, that sounds great. But are you up to this? I mean, you have work to do…"

"You're being silly again, Jade. Trust me, I want to do this. Justice hasn't been done yet. And whether or not I asked for it, I'm involved now."

She smiled. "All right. Thanks. Should I expect you around ten?"

"Ten it is."

"You have directions here? I think I gave them to you a few weeks ago."

"Yeah. I have them written down somewhere. But if I get lost, I have your phone number."

"Okay. See you tomorrow."

Jade called John's house, but as she expected, he wasn't home. It was during the day, and he would be at work. She left a brief message. She considered calling him at the office, but she immediately decided against it. She would end up talking to everyone at work, and that just didn't sound fun right now. Besides, the police still wanted her to minimize her phone calls into Connecticut.

She entered the family room, and found her parents sitting on the sofa, stroking Nora, and watching a courtroom drama on the television.

"How did it go?" asked her father.

She shrugged. "Phil was very interested. But he was awfully pessimistic about demonstrating Botanicure's connection to the thugs. Also, he thought the marketing of Quazhen might be legal, even though it would never pass basic safety trials."

"That doesn't sound right," observed her mother.

"No, it doesn't." She sat down on a comfortable blue recliner. "He's coming over here tomorrow at ten. We're going to go over various pieces of legislation about herbs. I'm convinced that we'll find that Botanicure put Quazhen on the market illegally. As soon as I know for sure, the FDA will be getting a phone call."

"Wait, dear," said her mother, cautiously. "I'm not so sure you want to be getting involved in this."

"I agree," added her father. "Let's assume that those thugs are supplying the Quazhen. If they found out you're trying to ban the stuff, your nightmare could start all over."

"No," Jade replied defiantly. "This will be different. First of all, the police are on my side. Frustrating as it is, that just wasn't the case during the Feng episode. Secondly, this issue is way too important; I can't look away." She leaned forward, and fixed her eyes upon her parents. "The mere fact that Quazhen is on those shelves is a disgrace to Yu-lan Tang. Add that to the fact that his grandmother is being suckered into shipping the herb, and you've got an unforgivable situation." She sat back. "And thirdly, the nightmare can't start all over, Dad. Feng, the monster, is dead. These little minions of his talked big, but after three months of nothing from them, I'm convinced that they're just little punks."

She shook her head. "No. For the sake of Yu-lan, I will get Quazhen off the shelves. The injustice against him will end here."

Phil arrived at 10:20 the next day. He said he didn't realize that no major highway ran from central Connecticut to central Rhode Island.

"Excuses, excuses," smiled Jade.

They went to the kitchen table, and Phil plopped a stack of papers down upon it. After sampling her mother's just-baked banana bread, they sat at the table, and got down to business.

"Okay, let me bring you up to date," he started. "I called Wu, and told her about Botanicure's Quazhen."

"You did? I did too."

"I know. She told me. Anyway, she's convinced that our thugs are involved, and she's going to push Botanicure's buttons to get them to cooperate. She'll pull some legal threats; it should work pretty nicely."

"Good. So ideally, the police will find the thugs, who will be supplying the herb. Once Botanicure's suppliers are behind bars, then Quazhen should disappear from the market pretty fast."

"That would be ideal, yes. But like I said last night, if Botanicure denies knowing those two criminals, then our hands may be tied."

She thought about it. "Okay. No problem. That's why we're going to prove that they're selling the herb illegally. I'm telling you, they never went through the FDA. It never would have passed. We simply notify the FDA of the unlawful herb, and then Botanicure is in major legal trouble. And Quazhen is off the shelves."

"Well, hold your horses. You won't like what I have to say."

"What do you mean?"

He grabbed some papers. "Are you ready for a lesson in the regulation of dietary supplements in this country?"

She shrugged. "Bring it on."

"All right. Have you heard of the 1938 Federal Food, Drug, and Cosmetic Act?"

"Sure," she replied. "I've read it five times. It's really engaging, action-packed stuff." She smirked. "No, Phil. I've never heard of it."

He sighed. "Please try to hold the sarcasm. Anyway, the 'Act'—as FDA officials often call it—was passed in 1938 after over a hundred patients died from drinking a poisonous medicine. Apparently, nobody had tested the safety of the medicine..."

"Whoa, whoa," she interrupted, much more seriously. "Was that the elixir of sulfanilamide? I've heard of that tragedy. The stuff caused acute kidney failure, and it killed a whole bunch of innocent people."

"That's the one. Anyway, the tragedy led to strict regulations on drugs. For the first time ever, manufacturers and distributors of drugs had to prove the safety of their products *before* those products reached the market."

"Good," she commented.

"Yes. And do you remember thalidomide? It was the German sedative that caused nasty, nasty birth defects?"

"Yes," she said regretfully. "Women gave birth to physically deformed babies. That happened in the early 1960's, right?"

"Right. Well, that tragedy precipitated more legislation. The so-called Kefauver-Harris Drug Amendments required manufacturers to prove the effectiveness of their products before they could market them in this country."

"That's good, too. So by the '60's, drug manufacturers and distributors had to prove the safety and effectiveness of their products before they could sell them in the U.S."

"Correct. *But*, before long, a question arose. The FDA had these strict regulations on drugs, but how did that pertain to vitamins, minerals, and other supplements?"

Jade shrugged. "I would assume that they'd be held to the same standards as any other drug."

"But they're not drugs."

"Sure they are. Drugs are chemicals that affect one's physiology. Vitamins and minerals certainly affect one's physiology. Therefore, they're drugs."

"Are they? Doesn't food affect your physiology? It's not a drug."

She sat back, and looked at the ceiling. "Well," she thought aloud, "no. Food is more involved in your biochemistry; it affects metabolism, not intrinsic functional pathways."

"Well, doesn't food contain vitamins?"

"Yeah..."

"Then shouldn't food be regulated as drugs? After all, food contains vitamins, which you said are drugs. Shouldn't manufacturers of food be required to prove the safety and effectiveness of that food?"

"No; you can't subject food to that level of regulation. That would be ridiculous..." She thought about what she was saying. Hmm. He had trapped her.

"You see the problem?" he said. "It's really tough to define a vitamin or mineral. It acts like a drug, but it's ubiquitously in food. So what do you do?"

She shrugged. "I don't know. What do you do? And by the way, how does this pertain to herbs?"

"Patience," he sighed. "We're getting there. Well, if you're the FDA, you decide that the best way to regulate vitamins, minerals, and other dietary supplements is to regulate their labels. That's why in 1991, they established the Dietary Supplement Task Force. They basically wanted to get some ideas for label regulations onto the table."

"Sounds reasonable."

"You would think so, wouldn't you? But the dietary supplement industry wasn't too pleased. As far as they were concerned, their products were headed for extensive government regulation. Some folks in their camp feared that their products would be yanked off the shelves unfairly."

"Okay."

"So, they did something about it. Leaders of the supplement industry started a major campaign to get Congress to protect dietary supplements. They put all kinds of propaganda in health food stores and other venues. They urged health food vendors and consumers to write to their representatives. The industry also used scare tactics to encourage a public outcry. They told retailers that the government regulation of dietary supplements could put them out of business, and they warned consumers that the FDA might strip them of their right to buy their vitamins."

"Those are pretty big exaggerations, aren't they?"

Phil shrugged. "That's what they told them. Anyway, as a result, Congressional legislators received more protest mail on the topic of supplement regulation than on any other issue since the Vietnam War."

"Wow."

"Yeah. Ultimately, the protests ended in the passage of the Dietary Supplement Health and Education Act of 1994. FDA folks commonly call it DSHEA for short. This important piece of legislation finally defined dietary supplements, provided guidelines for their labeling, mandated the establishment of good manufacturing practices, and did a host of other things." Phil flipped through some papers, and retrieved a thick packet from the pile. "Here's a copy of that act."

Jade took the packet. "Interesting. So the protests didn't really work. It sounds like the supplement industry got pretty regulated after all."

He smiled. "I suppose it depends upon your point of view. One of the most important parts of DSHEA is found in Section 2. Here, go to that section."

Jade flipped through the packet. "Hmm. Here it is. 'Section 2: Findings'. Okay; what about it?"

"Go to number fourteen."

She scanned down. "Let's see. 'Congress finds that dietary supplements are safe within a broad range of intake, and safety problems with the supplements are relatively rare.' Huh. I'm not sure that I agree with that. It sounds like a blanket statement that dietary supplements are safe. But at certain doses, pretty much any supplement becomes unsafe."

He shrugged. "You're not alone in your sentiments. But that's one major thing that DSHEA does; it presumes that dietary supplements are safe."

"Wait," she said. "How do they define dietary supplements again?"

"Go on to section 3."

She flipped ahead. Phil watched her eyes bulge. "Wait. It says here that 'the term dietary supplement means a product (other than tobacco) intended to supplement the diet that bears or contains one or more of the following dietary ingredients: a) a vitamin, b) a mineral, c) an herb or other botanical, d) an amino acid…'. And it goes on." She looked at him. "You're not telling me that this federal act presumes herbal medicines to be completely safe?"

He nodded. "That's what I'm telling you. That's the law."

Her head was spinning. "Wait a second. We just discussed that 1938 act that requires drug manufacturers to prove their products safe before marketing them. But if our government presumes herbs to be safe…"

"Then herbal drug manufacturers do *not* have to prove their products to be safe before marketing them." He sighed. "Some would call it a double standard. An herbal medicine just doesn't have the safety requirements that a non-herbal medicine has."

She stared at him in disbelief.

"Furthermore," he added, "check out section four. It directly addresses the safety of supplements."

She turned to that section.

"As you can see," he continued, "there are a bunch of conditions in which the government does say that a supplement may be unsafe."

"Well, that contradicts what you…"

"Let me finish. Yes, DSHEA acknowledges that situations exist in which the presumption of safety regarding herbs and other supplements is wrong. *But*, read this." He pointed to a certain paragraph.

She read it. "Whoa. What's this about the United States bearing the burden of proof to show that a supplement is unsafe?"

"It means just that. Although all pharmaceutical manufacturers must prove the safety of their drugs before marketing them, supplement manufacturers do *not* have to prove the safety of their products before marketing them. And as you've just read, if an unsafe supplement does get onto the market, the only real way to get it off is for the FDA to prove it unsafe!"

She looked at him. "So Botanicure never had to prove that Quazhen was safe. And if we want it off the market, the FDA must prove it unsafe!"

He smirked.

"What kind of bullshit law is that?!"

He continued. "I should mention that one possible exception exists. If a supplement is so blatantly dangerous that it poses an 'imminent hazard' to public health and safety, then the Secretary of Health and Human Services may halt its sales. But even then, a proceeding must occur to determine whether or not the supplement stays off the shelves. And frankly, increased libido and increased aggression aren't exactly emergency hazards, you know? I can guarantee you that the Secretary wouldn't yank a supplement without strong evidence of an immediate major danger posed by that product; we're talking strong evidence of a life-and-death situation."

Jade shook her head in frustration.

"Now," continued Phil, "remember we mentioned 'new dietary ingredients' last night?"

"That's right. What's the deal with those?"

"Go to section 8."

She flipped ahead. It was a short section; she skimmed it quickly. "Okay. So what I get out of this is that a 'new dietary ingredient' is any dietary ingredient—I guess that means anything you can eat—that was not marketed in the U. S. before October 15, 1994." She reread a line. "It's also defined as something that does not contain any dietary ingredient marketed in the U. S. before that same date." She looked up. "That's confusing. Is Quazhen a new dietary ingredient, or isn't it? The Botanicure form contains corn syrup, and that was marketed in the U. S before October 15, 1994. Does that exclude Quazhen from the 'new dietary ingredient' definition?"

Phil wrinkled his brow. "Hmm. I didn't even think of that one. That would be an interesting point to discuss in court. Anyway, let's say that Quazhen is a new dietary ingredient; we'll use a worst-case scenario. I say 'worst-case scenario' because these so-called new dietary ingredients are actually pretty regulated. I mean, relative to other supplements, they are."

"Okay."

Phil continued. "As you read in section 8, a new dietary ingredient is actually presumed *unsafe*—unlike every other supplement—unless it meets one of two criteria. Either it had to be present in the general food supply before its use as a supplement, or its manufacturer or distributor must submit to the Secretary of Health and Human Services *why* they think the supplement is safe."

"Okay. Well, Quazhen was never in the 'food supply', was it?" She thought about it. "Wait! Feng did say once say that his family used the herb as a spice back in China!"

"No," said Phil. "It has to be the United States food supply."

"But that's never explicitly said in the act."

He thought about this. "Still. Feng would be on thin ice with that claim." He thought more about it. "Maybe you found another loophole, but I think the courts would say this means U. S. food supply."

"Fine," she said skeptically. "So that leaves us with the second condition."

"Right. For a new dietary ingredient to *not* be presumed unsafe under the second condition, the manufacturer or distributor must tell the Secretary of Health and Human Services how they concluded that the supplement 'will reasonably be expected to be safe'. That's in section 8."

Jade's head was spinning again. "That's a stupid way to write it. In other words, they have to prove the supplement to be safe, right? Just like the pharmaceutical companies with their drugs?"

"Wrong. They just have to say why they think it will be safe. Their conclusion can be based upon published scientific articles, but it can also simply be based upon a long history of use, or even based upon skewed studies that the manufacturer themselves conducted. You follow?"

"So it's another bullshit clause."

He grinned. "That's kind of strong. But yes, the evidence of safety required to allow a new dietary ingredient onto the market is pretty weak compared to what a pharmaceutical company needs to prove. Furthermore, listen to this: distributors of these new herbal products need to notify the FDA at least 75 days before their product is marketed. *But*, after those seventy-five days, they're free to market the product—whether or not the FDA has notified them of their approval!"

She shook her head. "So the bottom line is that herbs and other supplements are horribly unregulated in this country."

He nodded. "Pretty much, yeah. And we didn't even get into issues of supplement labeling, which is another nightmare in and of itself." He sighed. "You've followed everything then?"

She nodded. "Yeah."

"Well, then you'll understand my bad news."

She shot him a questioning look.

"I called the FDA last night. I asked about this Quazhen stuff. Apparently, Botanicure *did* register it with the FDA. Although most herbs are never registered with the FDA, Botanicure took no chances. They considered Quazhen to be a new dietary ingredient, and they registered it."

She stared at him. "No..."

"Yes, Jade. They approved it. Like we just discussed, even getting a new dietary ingredient onto the market isn't too hard. They probably submitted their own biased studies. Or perhaps they claimed a long history of use in China. Whatever they did, it worked. The FDA approved it."

She shook her head in disbelief. "How could they?"

"Don't blame the FDA. They were just following the law. The law simply doesn't require the manufacturer or distributor to prove a 'new' herb safe. They just need to say why they expect it to be safe. Apparently, Botanicure had that weak evidence."

She stared at him helplessly.

"So," he continued, "that explains why we haven't seen the mass-marketed version of Quazhen on the market until now. Like I said, the law requires that, from the time the distributor registers with the FDA, they must wait at least 75 days before they put their product on the market. These three months were simply the mandatory waiting period."

She continued to stare.

"And like we discussed," he continued, "now that Quazhen is on the market, the FDA has to actually prove it unsafe before it comes off."

Jade digested this. It was unfair. It was dangerous. It was absolutely, positively moronic. And she could do nothing about it.

"Well," she said, "so I guess we're screwed. Quazhen stays on the market. People suffer massive side effects. Maybe eventually, the FDA proves it unsafe, but in the meantime, how many people get hurt?" She threw her hands up in disgust.

He frowned. "I'm frustrated, too. But remember, there is hope that the police will arrest Quazhen's suppliers. Without them, they'll run out of Quazhen, and they'll be forced to pull it from the shelves."

She shrugged.

Suddenly, a high-pitched phone rang. It was Phil's cell phone.

"Hello." He shot a smile at Jade. "Hey Arlene." He whispered to Jade that it was Detective Wu. "Guess where I am? Nope. I'm with Jade Evans. Yes. Yep, that's right. Oh, she's doing great. Much, much better. Yes, I'll be sure to tell her for you. So anyway, what's up?"

Jade watched his cheery expression suddenly drop. He glanced at Jade, but then quickly looked down at the floor. "Uh-huh." He slouched back in his chair. "I see." He began to frown. "Yeah."

What was going on?

"Okay. Well, hey, you did what you could. Right. Uh-huh. Right. Okay. Well, hey, thanks for the call, Arlene. Yep. Okay. Bye."

He clicked off his phone and looked at Jade. He sighed. "Botanicure denied knowing our two thugs. They openly said that their supplier was a family-owned company in China."

She looked at him with doubting eyes. "They're lying."

He shrugged. "Jade, how can we prove that?"

"I want the name of that family-owned company."

"Arlene had it. Chu-tao, or something like that. Botanicure openly offered to give her their address." He shook his head. "They're being more than cooperative, Jade. There's only so far the cops can push."

Jade slapped the table. "I'm telling you, Phil, that's a blatant lie. Yu-lan's grandmother is sending the herb to a Connecticut address, and then our criminals are supplying Botanicure with it. They're getting big bucks in the meantime."

He looked at the ground.

She stared out the window.

Infuriated, she began to conclude that getting Quazhen off the shelves anytime soon would be impossible.

It wasn't fair, she thought…

And then, finally, the obvious struck her.

23

"Phil," she said, her facing beginning to lighten up.

"Yeah?" He looked up at her.

"Why are we trying to intercept the middleman? Why don't we cut off Quazhen at the source? Why don't we contact Yu-lan's grandmother?"

She didn't expect his fast reply. "Because we have no idea where she lives."

She wrinkled her brow. "How do you know?"

He sighed. "Jade, I've been in very close contact with Wu. You know that. She's told me that they've made every possible effort to find the Tangs' grandmother. They searched Yu-lan's apartment. They searched Feng's apartment. They searched the shop."

"How could the shop not have her address? Isn't her return address on the boxes of Quazhen?"

"There are no more boxes of Quazhen in that store. Apparently, they had run out." He raised an eyebrow. "Or else someone took them. The point is, nobody has her address. It's a shame. Wu really, really wanted to contact her to notify her about Yu-lan's death. And Feng's, too."

She shook her head. "No. No, Phil, this is too perfect. Come on. We contact the grandmother, tell her that Yu-lan is dead, tell her to stop shipping the herb, and we're done with it!" Her face suddenly enlivened even more. "*And*, Phil, the grandmother knows where she's shipping the Quazhen! Clearly, Yu-lan's impostor has told her to ship it to a new address; after all, Natural Essentials is closed down. If she tells us to where she's shipping the stuff, then the police can intercept the sketchy middleman right then and there at that address!" She beamed. "It's perfect!"

He shook his head. "Jade, please try to understand this." He spoke slowly and deliberately. "We don't know where she lives. We have no idea how to find her."

She looked into his firm eyes. No, she thought. No, something that trivial couldn't stand in the way of her perfect plan. But as she looked at him, and as she evaluated the situation, she realized his point. He was right.

She slumped back in her chair. The two of them let the silence hang in the air.

"Oh my God!" She sprung up to her feet. "Wait here!"

Confused, Phil watched Jade sprint out of the kitchen. She bolted down her parent's hallway, and dashed into her old bedroom—now a guest bedroom. Curious, Phil got up and followed her.

"Where are they? Where are they?" She madly rummaged through her bureau drawers.

Phil appeared at the same time her mother did.

"What on earth are you doing, dear?" asked her mother.

"Mom," she shot, "where are my old khakis?" She turned. "The ones I had on when I saw the murder? You know, the left knee was torn open by a glass shard. There were blood stains."

"Oh," said her mother, stepping into the room. "You didn't want those, honey."

"Mom," she said fiercely, "where are they?"

Her mother turned to Phil with desperate eyes. She then turned back to Jade. "I threw them out, dear. I threw them out months ago, when you first got here. You don't need those memories."

"Mom!" she bellowed. "You did not!"

Her mother put her hand to her own chest. "Jade, dear, I'm sorry." She looked at Phil for reassurance. He shrugged at her; he was also in the dark.

Jade slammed a bureau drawer shut. "I needed something in those pants, Mom."

Her mother's face brightened. "Well why didn't you just say so, dear? You know I always check pant pockets before I wash them—or in this case—throw them away. I put everything in the top right sock drawer."

Jade's heart sank, and she gave her mother a disapproving stare. She never used the sock drawers.

Jade whipped open the drawer.

"Yes!" She pulled out a crumpled up piece of paper. She opened it, and smoothed it out.

With a wide grin, she held up the oval-shaped piece of paper with the Chinese border.

She couldn't read Yu-lan's letter to his grandmother; it was mostly in Chinese. But strangely, in the upper right corner of the letter, a few English words were written.

It was the grandmother's address.

24

Jade's father opened the front door of his house, and quickly shut it. "Man," he complained to nobody in particular, "it's cold out there!"

He stomped his shoes on the slate foyer to remove some slushy snow, and then kicked them off. He took off his coat, and proceeded into the house.

He found his wife, daughter, and Phil all sitting around the kitchen table. None of them were talking, and they all wore nervous expressions. Jade was fidgeting with her fingers; Phil was staring outside; his wife was gulping her coffee.

"Hello," he said, somewhat concerned. "Everything okay?"

Jade smiled. "Hi Dad. Yeah, everything is more than okay."

"Oh." He was relieved, but now confused. "Then what's with the long faces?"

His wife looked at him. "We're waiting for a phone call, dear. Detective Wu is using the address of Yu-lan's grandmother to find her phone number. When she has the number, she's going to call here and give it to us."

"Ah," he said, slowly nodding. "Everything's so clear now." He smiled wryly.

Phil smiled back. "Your daughter found a way to *quickly* get Quazhen off the shelves, and to very possibly locate those two men who buried Yu-lan's body."

He looked proudly at his daughter. That's my girl, he thought. "Go on," he said, taking the fourth seat around the circular table.

"The police haven't been able to contact Yu-lan's grandmother," explained Jade. "They didn't know her name, address, or phone number. But I remembered that I had a letter from Yu-lan to his grandmother; her name and address was on the letter."

"Okay. So how exactly does that information help you?"

"When we finally contact the grandmother, we'll tell her that Yu-lan and Feng are both dead. We'll tell her that whoever is requesting shipments of the Quazhen is a phony; it's not Yu-lan. Then, she'll be able to do two things for us: 1) tell us where she's been shipping the recent boxes of Quazhen; that will help us locate Botanicure's phony suppliers..."

"Who we suspect are those two thugs," added Phil.

"Right. And 2) she'll obviously stop shipping the Quazhen. Without shipments, Botanicure will run out of it pretty quickly, and it will come off the shelves much, much faster than if we asked the FDA to try to prove it unsafe."

"*If* the FDA even agreed to look into it," added Phil, "that process could take months or years."

"A lot of people would be hurt in the meantime," said Jade.

The father nodded thoughtfully. Then, "I have a question. How do you know that Botanicure isn't planting their own Quazhen? Maybe Yu-lan's impersonator requested seeds from the grandmother to get them started. If that's the case, your whole plan falls apart."

Phil started to drop his mouth.

Her mother suddenly widened her eyes.

Jade simply smiled. "Nope. Not a chance. Yu-lan was very clear that this strange plant only grows in a specific small region. I don't know if it's the soil, the climate, or what; but for whatever reason, Quazhen would only grow on his grandmother's plantation. It certainly wouldn't grow in snowy New England."

"Can't they put it in a special greenhouse?"

She shook her head. "I strongly doubt it. If this plant is so stubborn that it only grows on one family's plantation, I really don't think you could make it grow in a greenhouse! And besides, how would the impersonator word that one? 'Hey Grandma, I just bought a million dollar special greenhouse to grow our exotic plant. No reason, or anything.' Remember, she didn't want it mass-marketed."

He pressed on. "I'm sure he could lie about why he bought the greenhouse. He could say he wants to lift the burden off her from shipping the herb all the time."

"No, it was no burden. The grandmother enjoyed picking the plant and shipping it. And how would Yu-lan—the real Yu-lan—have the money to buy a fancy greenhouse?" She shook her head. "Good thought, Dad. But I'm sure that my plan would solve *all* our problems. Just contact the grandmother. Simple as that."

He grinned. "Okay. Guess I can't outsmart the fox in this family."

Phil's cell phone rang. Jade and her mother jumped.

"Hello, Phil Santiago here. Yes, hi Arlene. Doing well. We've just been waiting for your call. Yeah. Uh-huh. Really?" He started to frown.

"Come on!" whispered Jade.

"Hold on a sec, Arlene." He turned to Jade. "They found her number, but it's been disconnected."

Jade wrinkled her brow. How trivial! "Well, call her phone company!"

"They've tried that; it didn't help. So basically, they're still working on getting a hold of her. Arlene's just letting us know."

Jade groaned.

"Yeah," said Phil to the detective. "We know. Uh-huh. Let me ask her." He turned back to Jade. "Why not just mail her our message? We can put Yu-lan's letter in the mail."

She shook her head. "Yu-lan once told me that half of his mail never makes it to her. I'll hand deliver this letter before I let it get lost in the mail."

"Jade, I'm sure we can send it securely with a special carrier."

She shook her head. "I don't want to be sitting here wondering if she got it, and waiting for a reply. Come on; it's the twenty-first century. We can make a simple phone call!"

He relayed this to Wu. The detective assured him that they would keep trying. After a few more words, they hung up.

Jade crossed her arms and grimaced in frustration. She pictured Yu-lan's grandmother living on hundreds of acres of open Chinese fields. Although she was a few centuries off, she pictured the stereotype of a traditional Chinese woman wearing brightly colored flowing garments, and carrying stone jugs of water to her house. She imagined the grandmother not bothering with "modern" annoyances like telephones, and totally immersing herself in her small cultural world. She visualized the grandmother receiving the phony requests for Quazhen, and then without question, shipping out bulk quantities of her herb.

Jade stomped her foot in frustration.

Her father turned to her. "I wouldn't be upset. They'll get a hold of her; don't worry."

But they didn't get a hold of her. The day fell to night, and they had no word from Wu. Phil left, promising to check in the next morning. He did, but he had no good news. That day came and went, and the following day came and went. On several occasions, Jade called the detective herself. Wu complimented her on a clever plan, but she expressed her own frustration that they couldn't contact the grandmother.

"Jade," she said over the phone, on the third day of searching for the number. "Did Yu-lan ever mention phoning his grandmother?"

She thought about it. "Yes. He said that he would follow-up his final letter with a phone call, to be sure she received his message. So until recently, the grandmother had a working phone."

The detective sighed. "Presumably."

Jade began to protest. "Arlene..."

"Listen," the detective interrupted. "maybe it's been disconnected for months. You know, Jade, many folks in China do not have telephones. In many parts of that country, phones are real luxuries. My great aunt lived in China for many years, and I visited her there once. You wouldn't believe how old-fashioned she was! Granted, she lived in the middle of nowhere; the closest city was a day away. But she had no phones, no running water, and no electricity!"

Jade shook her head. Maybe her stereotype wasn't far off. "I don't know, Arlene. The woman is able to ship large boxes of her herb to another country; I would think she has some level of technological sophistication!"

"That's true. But regardless, Jade, I think we're going to try to contact her by mail. That seems like the best way to go."

"No, Arlene..."

"Jade, this is getting silly. We've contacted various officials in her town; they've been of no help. As frustrating as it is, we just can't reach her by phone. We're going to use the mail. I know Yu-lan told you that the mail system is unreliable, but we'll use a very reliable parcel carrier. Trust me, it won't get lost in the mail."

Jade still disliked the idea. "So what are you going to do? Just write a letter in Chinese that says her grandchildren are dead, and an impostor is asking her for the Quazhen shipments?"

"You have a better idea?"

She sighed. "Can you imagine how devastating that would be? To open up an American package saying your grandson is dead, your other exiled grandson is also dead, and an evil impostor is writing to you? I mean, would she even believe that, Arlene?"

"Well, how would a phone call be better?"

Jade's training in family medicine quickly flowed into the conversation. "Oh, Arlene, a human voice is much more convincing than a piece of paper. And if she does believe the horrible news, you want a person available to provide some support and counseling. I mean, think about the psychological trauma that such news will bring her."

"That certainly sounds ideal, Doctor, but like I said, the phone really isn't an option anymore. And you're forgetting something. We'll put Yu-lan's letter to her in our mailing. That will erase any doubt from her mind as to whether or not we're being truthful."

Jade grunted. "I don't know, Arlene. I don't care how secure you say your parcel service will be; I will not lose that letter."

Wu was becoming more and more frustrated. "Jade, you're being unreasonable. Look, we have to somehow contact the grandmother. And it would certainly be nice to get Yu-lan's letter to her. If you really want those thugs caught, and if you really insist that Quazhen should be off the shelves, you need to realize that I'm right here. We can't contact the grandmother via phone. That's that. I really doubt she has email; actually, I have someone checking that out, but you and I both know it's a futile measure. The officials in her town haven't been very cooperative; one said he's never even heard of her street address. Look, the only other way to contact her, Jade, is to send a mailing." She sighed. "I mean, unless we want to deliver the information in person."

Jade was silent. Wu could practically hear her thinking.

"Jade, I was joking. We're not sending a messenger to China..."

"I'll go." Her voice was strong and firm.

Wu released a small chuckle. "You'll go? You want to fly to China, find this woman, and deliver the news?"

Jade's adrenaline started running. "Yes. Yes, Arlene. That's a perfect idea! If I go, I won't have to sit around, waiting to hear her response. Think about it. We won't have to wonder if she got our mail, wonder if she believes us, and wonder when we'll hear from her—if we hear from her at all!"

"I don't know, Jade..."

"No. There's no question, Arlene. I'm going. For Yu-lan, I'm going."

The other woman considered it. "It wouldn't be unprecedented," she thought aloud, "to send a messenger across the world to give important news. I mean, we are trying to find two suspected criminals."

"Exactly. And hey, my Chinese isn't that good, but I can buy a dictionary..."

The other woman laughed aloud. "I forgot about that! You can't go, Jade. You don't know the language!"

"So? Yu-lan's letter is in Chinese..."

"Oh, I see. And when the grandmother starts firing questions to you about it?"

She struggled for a reply. "Well, maybe she speaks English."

"Uh-huh. Look, sending someone in person is a decent idea. I think it's within our scope to do that. But it won't be you, Jade. Our government has people that do that kind of thing for a living..."

"No, Arlene!" she snapped resolutely. "I want to go. If anyone is to deliver the news about Yu-lan's death, I want it to be me. For the sake of Yu-lan, I want it to be me!"

Wu thought about this. She nodded into the phone, and bit her lip. The idea was firmly in Jade's head; she realized. There would be no getting it out. And besides, Jade had a point. There were still two thugs on the loose; those thugs were accomplices in a murder by a very sick man who also killed her fellow police officer. Arlene Wu had to admit, she desperately wanted those thugs behind bars. And the surest and fastest way to do so was, as Jade was saying, to visit the grandmother in person.

"Jade," she said softly. "You can't survive just using a Chinese dictionary."

"But..."

"No buts, Jade." She sighed. "I'm going with you."

25

Despite her parents' protests, Jade stubbornly insisted that she and Arlene Wu were going to China. In person, they would give the grandmother the news about Yu-lan's death, Feng's murders and his own death, and the wrongful selling of her herb to an American corporation. They would also give her Yu-lan's final letter. In addition, they would tell the grandmother that an impersonator was asking for the shipments of Quazhen, and they would determine the location to which she shipped her herb.

Phil and John were both reluctantly receptive to the idea. But as long as Wu was going with her, they said, they were okay with it. When Jade told John her concern about missing more work, he quickly dismissed it. He pointed out to her that she wouldn't be able to concentrate until this whole episode was finally behind her. So coming back to work now, he claimed, would actually be a disservice to her patients.

Jade allowed Arlene to make the travel plans. The two women would fly to Shanghai from Providence in two days. Arlene was arranging for hotels, as well as for transportation to the grandmother's plantation. She asked if Jade had her passport; indeed, she did.

The day before their travel began with a beautiful January morning. The air was brisk, but not overly chilling. The sky was a rich blue, and a thin layer of newly-fallen snow was blanketing the region in pure whiteness. It was the perfect day, in Jade's opinion, to bundle up and head to the beach. Nobody would be there; she would have a long stretch of shoreline to walk and enjoy.

Jade drove down in the morning, and began her long waterside stroll before 10 a.m. She was preoccupied with tomorrow's flight. In one sense, she was looking forward to the adventure. She had never been to China; that in and of itself would be exciting. But more importantly, this would be the crucial step in getting Quazhen off the shelves, *and* in bringing the men who buried Yu-lan to justice. And of course, she realized, this would close the door on those disturbing death threats. Yes, she thought, this trip was the start of her really getting back to her old life.

But at the same time, she was apprehensive. She had to tell a woman that her grandson had been murdered by another grandson. And she had to tell her that she has been tricked into providing a major supplement industry with her family's herb. Jade was used to giving bad news to patients with terminal illnesses, and to loved ones of deceased patients. But all the same, giving bad news never became easy for her.

Another disturbing thought was haunting Jade, as she walked along the snowy shore. What if the grandmother wasn't shipping Quazhen anymore? What if Botanicure was actually being truthful, and another source was providing them with the herb? It was very unlikely, she thought, especially since the Tang family owned the name 'Quazhen'. But still, the remote possibility was there.

Jade strained to remember the name of the Chinese company which Botanicure claimed supplied their product. Was it Chi-too? Chu-tse? She grimaced. No, she couldn't remember.

Jade bit her lip as she stepped around a beached hermit crab. It could be very useful to have the name and address of that company. Then, if the grandmother surprised them by denying any recent shipments of Quazhen, they could contact this new company. Wu would have the company's name, she thought. But did she have their address?

If that company really did exist, reasoned Jade, they couldn't be located far from the grandmother. After all, Quazhen supposedly only grows in a very tiny and very specific area within China. If Wu and she were over in the area anyway, maybe it would be useful to have that address. Then, if the grandmother was not helpful, they would have a back-up plan: they could go directly to Botanicure's supposed supplier, and see for themselves if 1) the company really existed, and 2) they were really supplying Quazhen to Botanicure.

It was a good idea, thought Jade. But how would they get that supposed company's address?

Wait. Didn't Phil say that Botanicure was being 'more than cooperative'? Why didn't she just ask them for the address of this Chu-tse, or Chi-too, or whatever?

It couldn't hurt, reasoned Jade. She turned around, and headed for her Saab. Botanicure's headquarters, in Foxboro, Massachusetts, was just over an hour away. It was practically on the way back to her parents. Jade considered running her idea by Arlene before knocking on Botanicure's door. But her request for the address was so innocent and harmless, she really didn't need to check with the detective. It would be more trouble to stop and find a pay phone than it would be to just swing by the corporate building.

With that in mind, Jade left the beach. She made good time; she was in Foxboro in only an hour. Now, she thought, where were they located? She remembered seeing their building after a New England Patriots game a few years back. She thought it was down this road…

Yes! Directly before her was an elaborate office park. Towering above the other brick buildings was a ten story concrete edifice. In large green letters, attached to the top of the structure, was the name 'Botanicure'. She drove towards the corporate headquarters, and pulled into a giant parking lot. Wow, she thought. How many people did this place employ? The lot was easily five acres, and most parking spaces were full.

She found a spot, parked, and approached the main entrance. She looked down at herself. She wasn't looking her best; after all, coming here had been an impulsive decision. She wore a white turtleneck and faded blue jeans beneath her wool winter coat. Her hair was straight down, falling to her upper back. Oh well, she thought. She wasn't exactly meeting the CEO of the company.

Jade entered the large double doors. She was impressed by the spaciousness of the elegant lobby. Four green, marble pillars lined each wall, and a beautiful crystal chandelier hung down in the center of the room. The tiled floor was a checkerboard of green and yellow marble, and gold trim lined several doorways.

Gee, she thought. I guess the herbal supplement industry is doing just fine.

She approached a large, mahogany desk at the far end of the room. A young, pretty woman with dark brown skin and straight black hair sat behind it. She was looking at her computer monitor and rapidly clicking her mouse. As Jade approached, she saw two cameras attached to the wall behind the woman's desk; they were aimed at the desk. Apparently, someone wanted to watch this receptionist work.

Jade walked up to the desk. She was within the field of view of the cameras.

"Hi," said the receptionist cheerfully. "May I help you?"

"Yes, hello. My name is Dr. Jade Evans. I was hoping you could answer a question for me."

"I'd be happy to try," she smiled.

"I'm interested in your product, Quazhen."

Her smile widened. "Isn't it marvelous? It's been our hottest product since the Ginkgo-infused suntan lotion."

Jade forced a smile. "Is that right? Well, anyway, I understand that your supplier for that product is a small company in China. Chi-too, or something?"

The woman twisted her lip. "Hmm. I'm not sure."

Great. "Well, I was just hoping to get the address of that supplier."

The woman tilted her head. "Gee, that's not an everyday request." She smiled. "May I ask why you're requesting that information?"

This could be harder than she thought. "Oh, I just wanted to write to them for some facts and figures." Ouch, she thought. That didn't sound too good.

"Well, what facts and figures? Perhaps we can provide them to you."

"Ah, well…"

The receptionist's phone rang. "Oh, sorry. One minute, please," she smiled. She answered the phone.

Jade smiled back. Phew! she thought. Saved by the phone! Now, she told herself, think of something! Think of a better reason…

"…she's looking for facts and figures from our supplier of Quazhen."

Jade shot her a startled look. How did she get into the conversation? And who was that on the other end of the phone?

"Really?" asked the receptionist, obviously taken aback. "Well, sir, I don't think I'll use those exact words. Right." She laughed and blushed. "Yes sir. Okay. Yes. Yes. Okay, I'll tell her. Thank you, sir. Good-bye."

The receptionist looked up at Jade. "Um, Dr. Evans," she began, obviously uncomfortable. "That was our vice president of Marketing."

Jade smiled politely.

"He, uh, wanted to know if he could help you."

Jade wrinkled her brow. "What? What do you mean? How did he know I was here?"

With an innocent grin, the receptionist pointed to the two cameras on the wall.

Jade shook her head. "Okay. So your vice president just sits in his office, watching your desk? And he calls down every time someone approaches your desk?"

"Well," she said, embarrassed. She then lowered her voice and leaned forward. "He's a little odd. He's new here; he only came on board a couple months ago. He really likes to micromanage. I don't think he trusts many people yet."

Jade leaned forward and smiled wryly. She whispered. "Kinda sounds like a jerk."

The woman was taken aback. But she immediately smiled widely, and put her index finger to her mouth. "Shhh. I think he can read lips."

Okay, thought Jade. This was childish. And it was getting to be annoying. "Fine. So your new VP called down. Does he want to give me that address himself?"

"Uh, no. When I told him your request, he uh, said we can't provide that information."

Jade glared at her. Then she looked up, and glared at one of the cameras. Then at the other camera. Then back at the receptionist.

"What do you mean, you can't provide that information?"

"That's what he said. I guess it's company policy." She shrugged, clearly uncomfortable. "Sorry."

Jade frowned. "What's going on here?"

"I'm sorry, Doctor?"

Jade raised her voice and dropped her pleasant expression. "What's going on here? Why can't you give me that information?"

"Well, I, uh, you see…"

"Let me speak to your vice president."

"Well…"

Jade leaned closer. "Let me speak with…"

The phone rang again.

"Yes sir," said the receptionist. "No, she really wants that info…"

"Let me have the phone."

The receptionist pulled back. "The police? Right. I'll tell her."

In a moment of frustration, Jade whipped the phone out of the receptionist's hand. "Excuse me," she spat into the phone. "Hello Mr. Vice President? Jade Evans here. Could it be that the reason you won't give me the name of Quazhen's supplier is because you're hiding the real supplier? Could it be that you're aware of the shady background of Quazhen's real supplier? Could it be that you know that even selling Quazhen is illegal?"

There was silence at the other end.

"Let me tell you something," she continued, losing control of her emotions. "I know that you guys are illegally getting Quazhen from an innocent woman in China. I'll have you know, sir, that I'm flying to see that woman tomorrow. I will be disclosing your little operation to her, and Quazhen, mister, will be off these shelves…"

Click.

Jade looked at the receiver in disbelief. "He hung up on me." She slammed the phone down. The receptionist nervously stared at her.

Suddenly, a side door burst open. A large security guard stomped in. The big, Hispanic man quickly walked towards her. "Please leave this establishment, ma'am," he ordered.

She nodded. "Fine." She started backing away from the desk.

The guard approached her, placed a hand on her shoulder, and roughly moved her along towards the door.

"Get your hands off me! I can walk by myself!"

He let her go. "Good. Get out of here. If I see you here again, ma'am, you'll be arrested."

"What is with you people..."

"That's my orders, ma'am," he fired. "That's final."

Infuriated, Jade tramped out of the building, and slammed the door behind her. Without a doubt, she thought, Botanicure was getting Quazhen from those thugs. And what's worse, they knew that they were getting the herb illegally. They knew that Yu-lan's grandmother was being tricked into shipping it.

Enraged, she got into her car, and pulled out of her parking spot. Wait until I tell Arlene, thought Jade. Even after the grandmother stops shipping Quazhen, and even after those two criminals are behind bars, she would want a criminal investigation into Botanicure. How dare they be so crooked!

Jade realized that the entrance to the parking lot had been a one-way entrance. Frustrated, she turned around, and headed through the parking lot to a distant exit. On the way, she passed the front of the building again.

It was probably her angry preoccupation with this recent episode that made her oblivious to her surroundings. She just sped forward towards the exit, paying attention only to the frustrated thoughts in her own mind.

Had she been more alert to her surroundings, she would have noticed that she was passing the reserved parking spaces for the senior executives of Botanicure.

Had she been paying more attention, she would have realized that, in particular, she was passing the spot reserved for Botanicure's new vice president of Marketing.

Had she been more observant, she would have seen the big, shiny black truck with tinted black windows that was parked in that vice president's spot.

PART FOUR

LESSONS FROM CHINA

26

Several dozen people gathered their belongings and headed for the terminal gate as the departure of Flight 3289 was announced. Sitting across from the gate, Jade quietly watched as the passengers anxiously waited for their row numbers to be called. She glanced at the digital display above the gate counter; the plane was headed for Orlando. Ah, she thought. Sunny Florida! Now there's a destination for which she would trade her flight to Beijing! Orlando was only three hours away, and it was full of sun, palm trees, and eighty degree weather. Beijing, on the other hand, was thirty-two hours away, and temperatures averaged twenty degrees this time of year.

Of course, twenty degrees would be warm, relative to her ultimate destination. Lu Mian Tang, the important grandmother, lived in the northern part of China, in Inner Mongolia. Its bitter cold winters didn't exactly make it the ideal vacation destination in the middle of January.

She glanced at her watch. It was eleven a.m. In ten minutes, she and Arlene would board a flight headed for Newark, New Jersey. From there, they had a direct flight to Beijing Capital International Airport. Arlene had arranged for hotel accommodations in Beijing for the first night; they would then travel by railroad on the following day to Hohhot, the capital of Inner Mongolia. Supposedly, they could rent a jeep from there; Lu Mian was less than an hour outside the capital. The plan was to contact the grandmother that first full day, and return to Hohhot in the evening. Arlene had a hotel for them there. The following day, they would return to Beijing, and they would stay in one more hotel that night. Their return flight was scheduled for the next day.

Jade glanced at Arlene, who quietly sat across from her, reading a novel. She was thrilled to have her company on this trip. After all, Arlene was fluent in Mandarin Chinese, and she also spoke some broken Mongolian. Although she was born and raised in Pittsburgh, she had a thorough knowledge of China. Indeed, her grandparents had both lived there when they were children.

Jade reflected upon yesterday's hectic events. After leaving Rhode Island at noon, she had met Arlene in Hartford. Due to her position as a detective on assignment, Arlene had obtained their visas in less than an hour. And due to Jade's influence as a fellow physician, they had both received their vaccinations for Hepatitis A, Japanese encephalitis, rabies, typhoid, and cholera within hours from a Hartford Hospital clinic. During all that running around, Jade informed Arlene about the episode at Botanicure. After subtly expressing her disapproval of Jade going in the first place, she admitted that it was suspicious. She notified another detective about the incident, and told Jade she'd look into it herself upon their return from China.

"So are you ready for this trip?" asked Arlene.

She grinned. "It should be quite the vacation. How cold did you say Inner Mongolia gets? Zero?"

"I hope it's that warm."

Jade rolled her eyes. "I just home Lu Mian is home, you know?"

The other woman shrugged nonchalantly. "Like we discussed yesterday, if she's not home right away, then we'll just extend our stay. That's easy to do. We'll just wait for her; simple as that."

Before long, Flight 23 to Newark was announced. The companions gathered their small carry-on bags, and boarded the plane.

Watching them disappear down the flight deck, a man in a long, black wool coat put down his newspaper. He nudged a blond man in a black ski jacket, seated beside him.

"There she goes."

"Who's she with?"

"Fifty bucks says it's the detective. Her name is Wu, or something like that. She's been pestering the company left and right."

The blond man scratched his scruffy face. "So Evans just went ahead and told you she's flying to China. What an idiot."

The first man shook his clean-shaven face. His brown hair was now cropped very short, and his brown beard was shaven off. "Yeah. But then again, how would she know that we stepped up the deal with Botanicure?

You got your stocks; I got my position as VP. The point is, she had no idea who she was talking to when she blurted out her little plan to me."

The blond shook his head. "Still, she's an idiot." He sighed. "But she did make our lives much easier. I was getting tired of waiting for her to return home."

The other man smiled.

"Jay," continued the blond, "we are brilliant. Really, we're brilliant. Yulan's dead. Feng's out of the picture. Now we have just one loose end to tie up. And then guess who will be on the beaches of Fiji?"

Jay grinned. "I know it, Brett. Let's just tie up that loose end quickly and swiftly. Before they leave Beijing, I want them dead. Both of them. I have to attend a board of directors meeting in three days; I don't have time to waste here."

"You got it."

Row numbers nine through fourteen were finally called.

"Come on," said Jay, standing up. "That's us."

With that, they boarded the plane.

Jade settled into her aisle seat in row twenty-five. Arlene was seated next to her, and against the window was a quiet teenager wearing headphones and staring outside. A female flight attendant with short black hair slowly walked down the aisle, checking all rows to ensure seat belts were fastened and luggage was properly stowed. Jade reached into the seat pocket in front of her, and retrieved the in-flight magazine. After placing a pillow behind her head, she opened the front cover, and began to read.

Thirty meters ahead of her, the two men entered the plane.

"Is she back there?" asked Brett to his partner. He removed his ski jacket, and placed it in an overhead bin.

"I don't see her, but we know she is." He looked at the blond. "Don't stare! We don't need them seeing us. Not yet, anyway."

The men settled into row nine. Jay called a flight attendant, and ordered two beers in cans. He then stretched out, and prepared for the take-off.

The flight to Newark was smooth and uneventful. The men quietly reviewed their plans with each other. Jade and Arlene silently read, completely oblivious to the life-threatening danger sitting sixteen rows ahead of them.

Upon their arrival at Newark International Airport, the two men quickly exited the plane, and inconspicuously hid by a terminal window. They faced outside.

"Well, the easy part's done," said Arlene as they walked onto the airport terminal. "Now for the thirty hour stretch."

"I know. What gate is our flight?"

"I think they said B12. Let's check the monitor."

After confirming the correct gate, the women walked down the terminal corridor.

Jay turned to Brett. "All right. Let's go."

Staying a hundred feet behind their prey, the men quietly moved through the busy corridor. On several occasions, they dodged flailing suitcases and skirted speeding taxi carts. Before long, they approached a very crowded intersection. Several neighboring gates all had flights arriving, and hundreds of people overflowed in the corridor, blocking the steady flow of traffic.

"What the hell," mumbled Jay, as he lost sight of the women.

"I don't see them; do you?"

"No," he replied, annoyed. "No big deal, though. We know where our gate is. Just make sure they don't see us, okay?"

"Right. Hey, why don't we hang back for a second? I gotta use the men's room, anyway."

Jay sighed. "Fine. Hurry up." Both men moved through the thick crowd to the side of the corridor. Jay waited by some water fountains as Brett made his way into the men's room. Staring ahead down the corridor, he strained to see the women. But he didn't see them.

Suddenly, he lost his balance as someone in the thick crowd pushed into him from behind.

"I'm so sorry, sir! You okay?"

He turned to see an apologetic face showing her genuine concern.

It was Jade.

His heart racing, Jay forced himself to maintain composure. Maybe, just maybe, she wouldn't recognize him with short hair and no beard. He quickly waved his hand, as if to say 'no problem', and then turned away. He shuffled towards a water fountain, and took a long sip of warm, stale water. Then, he slowly turned around.

She was gone.

Shit. Did she recognize him, or not?

Jay angrily slapped his hand on his outer thigh. As Brett emerged from the men's room, he scowled softly. "She saw me! Damn it, she saw me!"

"What do you mean?"

"Evans! She accidentally bumped into me, and then she looked me in the eye."

"She recognize you?"

"I have no idea. I turned away, and when I looked back, she was gone."

Brett tightened his lips. "Why would she be back here? They were both a hundred feet ahead of us."

He shrugged. "Probably had to use the ladies' room." He cursed again under his breath. Then, "Let's keep going."

Ahead of them, at gate B12, Jade caught up with Arlene. "Man," she said. "The ladies' room was a nightmare!"

"I thought it would be. The whole area was pretty crowded back there."

Jade sat down next to her. She glanced at her watch, and then at the digital display over the ticket counter. They would board in twenty minutes.

"I was trying to make my way through the crowd back there, and I bumped into this guy by accident."

"Was he cute?" smiled Arlene.

"Actually, no. But I swear I know him." She shook her head. "That ever happen to you? When you see someone, and you're positive you know him, but you just can't place him?"

"I think that happens to everybody once in awhile."

True, thought Jade. But that didn't help. "Well, maybe it will come to me."

Jay and Brett slowly approached gate B12. Seeing the women sitting with their backs to them, they sighed some relief, and moved to the waiting area of neighboring gate B11.

"She doesn't look too upset," noted Brett. "If she recognized you, she'd be jumping off the walls."

"Yeah. You're probably right."

Before long, both parties were boarding Flight 547 to Beijing, China. This time, Jay and Brett were seated in the back, and the women were in the front. Unfortunately, realized the stalkers, this meant they had to walk by their targets and board first. The men agreed to switch coats, to help prevent Jade from noticing Jay again. They then boarded separately, with their backs to the women. Brett put on a baseball cap and regular glasses, to create a small disguise. It worked. Jade and Arlene were completely oblivious to them as they boarded the large jet aircraft.

Once seated in row thirty-six, the men watched as the other two took their seats, about fifteen rows ahead of them. They then smirked at each other. Yes, things were going exactly as planned, with the small exception of Detective Wu accompanying Jade for the trip. No matter, thought the men. Four of them were going to China. Only two of them, however, would be coming back.

27

Jade had difficulty sleeping on the overnight flight. Thoughts of her upcoming encounter with Lu Mian kept her awake. What would the grandmother be like? Would she be a nomadic Mongolian huntress, like many of the inhabitants of the region? Unlikely, she realized. Besides the fact that hunters were usually young men, Yu-lan often referred to his grandmother's plantation; a nomad probably wouldn't have a plantation. Would she be an industrial Chinese citizen, perhaps someone who worked in the city of Hohhot, but who enjoyed gardening on the side? No, thought Jade. That just didn't fit her image of this older woman. Most likely, she predicted, Lu Mian Tang would be a gentle, grandmotherly woman who farmed for a living. She did live an hour south of Hohhot, and the southern part of Inner Mongolia, according to Arlene, was vastly agricultural.

The flight was long and difficult. After managing to catch a few hours of sleep, Jade restlessly read a book. She tried listening to music via the airplane's entertainment system, but she quickly became bored. Jade was thrilled when Arlene finally woke up; she could now talk with someone.

"So how many provinces did you say China has?" she asked the groggy detective, trying to stir her into conversation.

"Twenty-two." She yawned. "Twenty-two provinces, five autonomous regions, and lots of disputed territories."

"Hmm. So Inner Mongolia is one of the provinces?

"No." Arlene smiled. She knew Jade wanted company, and she actually didn't mind starting a conversation. "It's technically an autonomous region. Inner Mongolia is still under the control of the Chinese government, but the politics and administration are slightly different than they are for provinces."

"I always thought Mongolia was its own country. I mean, I knew that Genghis Khan and his armies conquered China centuries ago. But I thought China took it back, and Mongolia then remained as a separate country."

"Actually," explained Wu, "there are two Mongolias, if you will. The Mongolian People's Republic, or Outer Mongolia, is an independent nation. Inner Mongolia belongs to China. But it wasn't always that way; in fact,

Outer Mongolia was also under Chinese rule until the early 1900's. That's when the former Soviet Union helped them separate from China, and for years, that northern portion of Mongolia was technically under Soviet rule. Of course, with the break-up of the Soviet Union, Outer Mongolia has been its own republic for many years now.

"Regarding Genghis Khan," continued the detective, "it is true that his armies conquered Central Asia in the early 13th century. But it was really his grandson, Kublai Khan, who led Mongolian forces into China later in that century. They ended up conquering all of China, and they then went on to found the Yuan Dynasty within its borders. Actually, the winter capital of that dynasty was where Beijing now stands; it used to be called Dadu, or Khanbaliq, depending upon who you ask."

"I've heard of that name." She stretched back to an old college history class. "Didn't Marco Polo visit Khanbaliq?"

"He sure did. Though his Venetian contemporaries didn't believe him at the time, his stories about 13th century China were right on the money."

"Neat stuff," grinned Jade. She glanced out the window. "Oh wow, Arlene. Look!"

The women peered through the small porthole of a window. Far away, along the distant horizon, bands of white, yellow, and orange slowly widened into view. The white band bled upwards into a bluish hue; then the blue became purple, and that in turn faded into the blackness of the night sky.

Arlene grinned. "Looks like the sun's about to come up. Only ten more hours, Jade."

Jade rolled her eyes good-naturedly. She then picked up a magazine, and flipped through the pages for the fifth time this flight.

Due to changing time zones, Flight 547 arrived in Beijing at ten p.m. Thrilled to be there, but exhausted from the trip, Jade stood and stretched. She and Arlene grabbed their bags, and marched off the plane. Not far behind them, Jay and Brett followed.

The international gateway was flooded with chatting people. Jade instantly felt vulnerable and dependent upon Arlene; she could not understand a word of the harsh, Mandarin dialect. Overhead voices rattled off incomprehensible announcements, and a sea of Chinese people crowded the large room.

Arlene led her to a customs station. Two lines were formed; a blinking light was positioned at the front of each. Jade started wandering towards the red light line, but Arlene quickly steered her towards the green light line.

"The red channel is for people who have something to declare," she told her. "Ours is the green channel."

The line moved quickly, and Jade was soon showing her visa to a friendly customs officer. She smiled brightly, hoping to just hurry through the gate. Indeed, he passed her through without any problem. She quickly found Arlene, and stuck to her side.

"I thought you could just get by with a Chinese dictionary," smiled the detective.

"Yeah, yeah. All right. We didn't check any bags, so I guess we can just head for a taxi."

Arlene started walking to a small kiosk. "Let's exchange some money first, don't you think?"

"Oh, right." She quickly followed her to the Bank of China window. Yes, thought Jade. Having Arlene here was a very good thing, indeed.

Before long, the women were sitting in the back seat of a red taxi cab. Arlene told the driver their destination in fluent Chinese, and the cab took off.

Less than ten meters behind them, Jay hurriedly flagged down another cab. In perfect Mandarin, he said to follow the women's cab. Brett grinned as they got into the cab. Jay had spent much of his life illegally shuttling foreign immigrants into America; he therefore had an impressive command of several languages. His knowledge of several Chinese dialects had made him the perfect choice to correspond with Lu Mian; after all, as Feng had once pointed out, all of Yu-lan's letters were in Chinese.

Jade looked out the window. At first, she saw rows of white and gray buildings with red tiled roofs. They looked residential, but she could not tell for sure. After ten minutes, however, the plain and quiet landscape gave way to the bustling streets of Beijing. Even from the car, she was impressed with the nightlife of this capital city. Young men and women casually roamed through the crowded streets in large packs, laughing and joking with one another as they walked. Many of them wore thick, trendy winter coats made of glittering fabric. Beneath their coats, they commonly wore stylish sweaters over colorful turtlenecks. Even their hairstyles were fashionable; several of them had long, curly hair that was dyed red or brown. Jade grinned as she watched many young people strut down the street in their dark twilight-blue blue jeans which America had popularized decades ago. This was a pretty happening place for a communist city!

The streets were lined with bustling clubs and restaurants. Pink neon lights pulsated above the clubs' entryways, and sounds of eighty's-style rock bands boomed from the establishments. As they rounded a corner, Jade saw several kids hanging out outside a disco bar. Through a dark window, she could barely see the spinning lights cast by a twirling disco ball. Wow, she thought, reflecting upon her own childhood. This city actually seemed pretty fun!

The taxi proceeded away from the bustling street, and approached a more governmental section of the city. Arlene leaned over, and pointed down a wide street. That, she said, led to the Forbidden City and Tiananmen Square. Visions of the bloodshed during the 1989 democratic protest wiped Jade's smile away from her face. Amazing, she thought. It had happened right down there.

Jade sat back, and continued to take in the sights of downtown Beijing. She admired the mammoth bronze sculptures of powerful dragons and mythological creatures. She viewed the incredibly ornate edifices that lined the busy streets. Many of them had huge red walls lined with golden baroque trimmings. Some of them towered high into the night air, while others were squat and long. The roofs of the buildings were constructed of colorful tiles that often curved upward at their pointed ends. Plastered to many of them, magnificent Chinese letters identified the names of the establishments. But Jade, of course, couldn't read any of them.

Ten minutes later, the taxi pulled up to a tall, blue and white tower that rose into the night sky. Jade smiled as she finally saw some English words displayed underneath a larger Chinese sign. 'Hyatt Resort Beijing' it read. Perfect! she thought selfishly. An American hotel! The taxi meter read 'RMB24'. Arlene promptly dug out some money, and paid in the Chinese currency.

A cheerful bellhop helped the women out of the car. He insisted upon taking their two carry-on bags; after the tiring flight, Jade was happy to let him have them. She followed Arlene inside the hotel, and patiently waited to the side as the detective checked them in.

"Okay," Arlene said, leaving the front desk. "We're in 410. Let's take that elevator."

They entered the small elevator. As the doors closed, Brett lowered his newspaper. He rose from his wooden bench, tossed his paper onto the bench, and looked at his partner. Jay quickly approached him from the front desk.

"Were you able to overhear them?" asked the blond, scruffy man.

"Yeah," smiled Jay. "They're in 410. Let's go."

Jade slid her keycard into the metallic door slot, and swung open the door. She walked in, and flicked on the lights. Before her was a small room with two full beds. The wallpaper had a yellow floral pattern, and the carpet was an olive green. Two white wicker chairs were placed in the corner of the room, and a wooden television set rested upon a white wicker bureau, across from the two beds.

"Hmm," she said.

Arlene walked in and smiled. "Could be worse."

Jade took off her short, black wool coat. She hung it up in the closet, and then moved into the bathroom. A few minutes later, she emerged with an empty ice bucket.

"Any idea where the ice machine is?" she asked Arlene.

"Yeah. I saw a sign that said ice and vending machines were down the hall. Just go straight down, away from the elevator. It's down there somewhere."

"Okay. I'm gonna get some ice. They have boiled drinking water for us in the bathroom, but it's pretty warm. You want anything from the vending machines?"

"No thanks."

Jade left the room, and walked down a long, narrow corridor. A white sign, written in both Mandarin and English, indicated that ice and vending machines were to the left. She followed its direction, and proceeded down another long corridor. At its end, a new sign pointed her to the right.

"Come on," she groaned, and turned again down another corridor. It was another long walk, and finally she reached the machines in a small room on the left.

Meanwhile, Arlene was removing some jewelry and placing it in an endtable drawer. A knock suddenly sounded at the door. Ah, she thought; the bellhop. She reached into her pocket, and retrieved a couple of yuan bills. Though tipping was not expected in China, she still liked to do it.

Arlene went to the door, and opened it.

Nobody was there.

"Huh," she said aloud. She stuck her head out, to look down the hallway.

In a flash instant of terror, a gloved hand covered her mouth and strong arms forced her inside the room. The door slammed shut behind her, and Arlene was thrown to the floor.

"What the…!"

Brett dived on top of her, and sealed her mouth with his greasy leather glove. He put his nose an inch from hers. "You're the cop bitch who killed Feng, aren't you?"

Jay circled them both, and quickly scanned the room for Jade. When he didn't see her, he scurried into the bathroom.

"Where is she?!" he barked in his deep growl.

With wide, horrified eyes, Arlene stared at the scruffy blond man. Her heart racing, she strained to push up against his weight. But her effort was useless; she was pinned down. She tried to scream, but his strong hand squeezed her lips together.

"You heard the man," hissed Brett. "Where's the good doctor?"

Arlene started kicking her feet onto the ground, just to make some noise. How thick could these hotel walls be, anyway?

Jay swiftly kicked her left leg with a strong, booted foot. "Quit it!" he snapped. She winced in excruciating pain. She quickly became nauseous as she realized what was happening. She had killed these minions' master. As far as they were concerned, revenge would most certainly be theirs.

"Move your hand," ordered Jay to the other man. "Let her answer."

Brett pulled his gloved hand back, and slightly moved his face away from hers. She laid there, panting. She stared at Brett, and then at Jay.

"Answer me, damn it!" growled Jay. "Where is she?!"

That was it, wasn't it? thought Arlene. More than anything, they wanted Jade. Sure, they probably wanted to kill both of them, but killing only Arlene would be far from good enough. Jade knew the secret to their downfall; as long as she was alive, their freedom was at risk.

Arlene smirked. "You'd like to know, wouldn't you?" she said softly. She tried to hide her growing fear that Jade would come through that door at any moment, carrying a bucket full of ice.

Jay raised his eyebrows. In disbelief, he kneeled beside the detective's head, next to his partner. "You taunting me, Cop? You fuckin' taunting me?" He shook his head in disgust.

Her stomach started to turn. Maybe saying that wasn't such a good idea, after all. She opened her mouth and started to scream…

Whack! Brett's gloved hand covered her mouth before anything but a peep could leave it. With wide eyes, she silently stared at Jay.

"You think I'm nobody to bargain with?" asked Jay, angrily hunched over her. "You think Feng was the big honcho, and I'm just the weak little guy?"

This wasn't going well, she realized fearfully.

"Surprise, bitch. Surprise."

She screamed out in pain as Jay slapped her cheek hard. Dizzy, she watched as he ordered Brett to get off her. Arlene felt the blond man's weight suddenly lift from her body, and she watched as Jay prepared to mount her.

In a moment of sheer fury, she whipped her knee up and into Jay's groin. He howled in frenzied pain, and she rapidly fired a swift kick into Brett's jaw. With both men stunned, she rolled over and jumped to her feet. She dived across a bed to the telephone, and picked up the receiver.

With a strong leap across the bed, Jay reached for the telephone cord that ran to a wall jack. He grabbed it, and yanked hard. Arlene's heart sank as the ringing tone went dead.

She hopped onto the second bed, and sprung off to the far side of it. "Help!" she screamed with all her strength. She pounded hard onto the wall that divided her room from her neighbor.

Just then, the door opened.

"Arlene...?"

"Jade!" cried the detective. "Get the hell out of here! Get out!"

Jade watched in horror as Brett turned around and faced her. With a sickening grin, he ran towards her.

"What the..." Acting instinctively, Jade thrust the ice bucket at her assailant. The hard plastic bucket whacked him in the eye, and sharp ice shards pelted his face and neck. He shouted out in pain, and momentarily sank to his knees.

Jade looked up to see Jay snarling at her. He was wielding an eight-inch knife, and was standing between her and Arlene.

"Jade," pleaded Arlene, "go! Get out of here! I'll meet you at our ultimate destination! I'll make it! Now go!"

Before she could react, Brett was on his feet again. Enraged, he threw himself towards her.

Screaming, Jade turned and bolted down the hall. She ran towards the elevator. To her horror, she looked back and saw him holding an ice pick. He was sprinting towards her.

"Help!" she screamed, but nobody was around. Suddenly, she did hear the sound of a door whipping open, at the far end of the hall. A man started yelling in Chinese.

She reached the elevator, but with Brett thirty feet behind her, she didn't have time to wait for it! She rushed to the nearby stairwell, flung open the door, and ran in.

Jade flew down the stairs, taking two at a time. She reached out to the handrail near the bottom of each flight, and used her momentum to fling herself into a new flight. Looking back, she saw the man chasing her; he was gaining on her.

Within seconds, she was at the ground floor. She flung open the door, and emerged into the cold night air. She was in a back alley! Damn! she thought. The lobby was on the second floor!

Jade turned left and dashed towards the main street. She glanced back; he was still there. She pushed herself harder. Go! Go!

Suddenly, she quivered in fear as a loud 'clank!' sounded from the chain-link fence, running beside her to the right. In horror, she looked down to see the ice pick spinning on the ground. He had aimed for her head, she realized.

But he had missed.

She dashed forward, sprinting towards the open street. Finally, she emerged onto the concrete sidewalk of a lighted avenue. The neon Hyatt sign welcomed visitors to her left. She spun around.

He was gone.

She looked left, then right, then up, then down. She stared back at the stairwell door. It was closed.

She stumbled towards the chain-link fence, gulping air into her oxygen-starved lungs.

She didn't know where he had gone. But for now, it didn't matter.

For now, he was gone.

28

After catching her breath, Jade trotted towards the Hyatt entrance. She spotted her familiar bellhop, and ran towards him.

"Help! Please help me!"

The red-suited Chinese man looked up. Alarmed, he quickly walked towards her. Another bellhop, a young man with a buzzed haircut, also approached her.

"Help!" she cried, as she drew to a halt before them.

The first man started firing questions in Mandarin. He wore a worried expression, and put a hand on her shoulder to show his support.

"I don't speak Chinese," she said. She stomped her foot in frustration, as he continued to talk in his native tongue. Now would be a wonderful time for that dictionary!

"Jing," said the man with the buzzed cut. "Jing, she only speaks English." He rolled his eyes, and then barked some Chinese words to his fellow bellhop.

"English?" asked Jing. "My English not too good, Nurizar."

"Don't worry about it," said the other bellhop. "I'm fluent. Let me help her. You get back to the cars before we draw too much attention." Jing winced and shook his head. Nurizar repeated himself in Mandarin, and the first man nodded and smiled.

"Oh good. You help her." He bowed, and then returned to the cars.

The young man grinned at Jade. He had a round baby face, which looked somewhat peculiar with his buzzed head. "Sorry, ma'am. How can I help you?"

Jade continued to catch her breath. "There are two men in your hotel who want to kill me and another woman. They have a knife. One chased me down to that back alley, and the other is still upstairs with the other woman. I'm scared for her life."

His baby face suddenly turned stern. "Come on," he said. "Let's go up and find her."

Jade was taken aback. "Shouldn't we tell the authorities? I mean, those guys are dangerous up there."

He shrugged. "I will leave that up to you, ma'am. You can certainly tell the police. But think about it. You are an American woman who comes in here, claiming that two killers are on the loose in the heart of Beijing. That is not something that our 'authorities' will take lightly." He leaned closer to her. "Your rights are a little more…how shall I put it…*restricted* here. Please remember, ma'am, you are in Communist China now. The police will help you, but the interrogations will be long, and you will probably be held by the authorities while they search for answers."

She looked at him. His eyes showed his sincerity, and his tone verified his trustworthiness. She thought about it for a moment. He was essentially telling her that unless she knew that she was in imminent danger, she'd be crazy to tell the cops.

Well, she was in imminent danger. She knew that. But the thought of being held by the Chinese government wasn't too enticing. She had a mission to complete, and that was a very high priority. Still, ensuring Arlene's safety was an even higher priority.

"I don't know," she said. "I appreciate your warning, but I still might tell the officials. But for now, you're right. Let's you and I go up there, and let's see what's going on."

He nodded. He turned, yelled some Chinese words to another bellhop, and proceeded into the hotel. She followed closely behind, her eyes scanning the lobby for any sign of the attackers.

They took the elevator to the fourth floor. Jade's heart started pounding as they approached room 410. With a strong fist, Nurizar knocked on the door.

There was no answer.

He knocked again.

Still, no answer.

He retrieved a keycard from his trousers pocket, and inserted it into the metallic scanner.

"Nurizar, are you sure…"

But he had already swung open the door. He stepped inside. Jade cautiously hung back, holding the door open, but not yet walking in. She saw the bed covers ruffled, and she spotted the disconnected phone cord. Besides that, however, everything looked okay.

The bellhop moved into the bathroom, but he emerged two seconds later shaking his head. "Nothing. Nobody's here, ma'am."

Suddenly, a deep angry voice sounded from behind Jade. Startled, she quickly spun around to face its owner.

A short, elderly Chinese man stormed towards her, waving his finger in the air. She recognized his voice as the man who had cried out from down the hall. The man wore a handsome silk robe; it was blue with golden accents.

He got into her face, and continued yelling angrily in Chinese. Feeling helpless, she turned to Nurizar. He quickly stepped out and faced the elderly man.

With a stern look and a loud voice, the bellhop fired Mandarin words at the man. Angrily, the older individual retorted, using wild hand language to help express his frustrations. Nurizar interrupted, and using his own hand language, got the man to quiet down. Then, in a more composed manner, the bellhop asked some more questions. More calmly, the man pointed in various directions, and then answered those questions.

Nurizar turned towards Jade. "He saw your friend run out of here. She ran right, away from the elevator, down this hallway. She actually passed this gentleman's room, and bolted down a stairwell at the far end of this corridor. He says that a man was chasing her, but upon seeing this gentleman, he stopped. He then turned around, and ran back towards the elevator." The bellhop nudged the older man. "He says he thinks he scared him away."

Jade smiled weakly. Thank God. At least Arlene had escaped the room. Who knows where she went from there.

Jade turned towards the older man. "Thank you," she said.

The bellhop grinned slightly. "He also says he was just getting off to sleep, and 'all your racket' woke him up!"

Jade threw up her hands. Nurizar touched her shoulder. “Don’t worry. I said it was a simple domestic dispute, and that you’re all sorry.”

“Thanks,” she said dryly.

The bellhop said a few more words to the older man. The robed gentleman started chuckling, and then waved his hand, dismissing the entire situation. He then turned, and started walking back towards his room.

She frowned. “Well, thank you, Nurizar. You’ve been an incredible help.”

He shrugged. “Hey, no problem. I’m hoping to someday work as a private detective. I love this kind of stuff.”

She smiled, looking at his young, energetic baby face.

“So do you still want to notify authorities?” he asked.

She thought about it. What would be in the best interest of Arlene? Almost certainly, she soon realized, it would be to tell the Chinese officials about the episode.

She sighed. “I think I have to. I mean, I understand your point, and I thank you for it. But I can’t let my roommate just get chased down by these guys, and not tell anyone about it.”

“Well,” he offered. “You could always leave an anonymous message.”

Her face lit up. “Well, I don’t know Chinese.”

“You don’t have to. Why don’t we just do this. I’ll say that you ran up to me, told me what you really told me, and then took off. I’ll say I tried to stop you, to get more answers, but you just ran away.”

She wrinkled her brow. “You’d make all that up for me?”

He shrugged. “It would be a way for you to notify the authorities, but at the same time not be held up by them. If you’re nowhere to be found, they can’t keep you in their grasp and question you to death. Right?”

She nodded slowly. “Sure. But why would you do that for me? I mean, instead of me, you’d be held for questioning.”

He smiled. “It beats working as a bellhop. I hate this job. I want to be a private detective some day. Or maybe a special agent. You know, like that British fellow, Joe Bond.”

She grinned. “James Bond, you mean?”

"Yeah! That's him. And don't worry," he added, "I'll tell them you have red hair. Just so you're not caught later for questioning."

She stared at his boyish face, and her grin stretched wider. "Thank you, Nurizar." She pecked his cheek with a quick kiss.

He blushed. She chuckled as he saluted her, and he then escaped down the hallway.

She entered her room. She saw that her single carry-on bag had been dropped off. But wait, where was Arlene's bag? She thought about it. Could she have grabbed it on her way out? Would she have had time to do that?

Jade shrugged. There was no way to know. The only thing she knew, at this point, was that she needed to get to Lu Mian. Her place was the ultimate destination, and that was where Arlene had told her to meet during the attack. And now that Chinese officials would soon be up here looking for answers, she decided that it was time to get going.

Before she left, Jade dug into her bag for two crucial items. The first was her pocket Chinese dictionary. The second was a small book of Chinese maps. Thank goodness, Arlene had circled Lu Mian's address on one of the pages; she had done that before they had left America. Jade quickly flipped through the various pages. Good, she thought. The railroad routes were nicely marked in red. She should easily be able to reach Lu Mian.

With that, she grabbed her coat, and shoved the dictionary and the mapbook in the deep pockets. She then closed her bag, flung it over her shoulder, and walked out of the room. She turned left, and proceeded down the hallway.

It was a good thing that medical school and residency had prepared her for long, sleepless nights. Because, she thought as she walked towards the elevator, this would most certainly be one of them.

29

Jade opted to steer clear of the hotel's front entrance. If Nurizar intended to claim that she bolted away, then casually strolling by his co-workers would be suspicious at the very least. She took the elevator to the bottom floor, and then found the side stairwell that led to the back alley. After cautiously checking her surroundings, she exited the building, and headed for the main street.

Part of her wanted to stay at the hotel, and wait for Arlene. After all, maybe the detective was already back in their room. But she forced herself on. Arlene had explicitly said to go to their ultimate destination, and that she would meet her there. Wu was an experienced detective, she reminded herself. She was able to escape from the hotel room; she would very likely be able to flee to Inner Mongolia, as well. No, Jade thought; staying here just wasn't an option—not if the Chinese authorities were about to storm into her room looking for a bunch of Americans stirring things up.

As she began walking down the main strip, away from the Hyatt, a hard truth fell upon her. She was now alone. She was in a strange country, with a strange language, and her security blanket—Arlene Wu—was nowhere to be found. Jade swallowed hard. Well, here it goes.

About a hundred meters ahead of her, Jade saw another towering hotel rising into the night sky. This one wasn't part of any American chain, but still, perhaps the employees knew some English. She picked up her pace, and hurried towards the yellow-clad bellhops.

"Excuse me," she said to one of them. "I need a taxi."

He looked confused, and asked her a question in Mandarin.

She quickly retrieved her dictionary, and flipped through the pages to find the "T's". Finding it, she did her best to pronounce 'taxi' in Chinese.

He smiled, and then asked another question in his native tongue. He was trying to speak slowly, and to enunciate his words, but that didn't help Jade!

Using her dictionary, she did her best to convey that she wanted a taxi to a railroad that would lead her to Hohhot, Inner Mongolia.

He seemed to understand. He led her to the sidewalk, flagged down a red cab, and spoke to its driver in Mandarin. The bellhop then opened the back door for her. She smiled widely and handed him a yuan. "Thank you."

Before long, Jade was thanking the cab driver, and getting out at Beijing's major railroad station. She walked through a set of double doors, and found a large, spacious lobby full of crowds. Jade approached a bench and sat down. She took out both her dictionary and her map, and decided that she would learn a few essential phrases before going to the ticket counter.

It proved to be a very good idea. Her communication with the ticket agent was actually somewhat smooth, and forty minutes later, she was on board a train to Hohhot.

Jade was fortunate enough to be alone in her six-seat compartment of this European-style train. She slid the two window seats forward, thereby creating a makeshift bed. She glanced at her watch. It was three a.m., Beijing time. Well, she thought, maybe she'd be able to get some sleep after all. She curled up against the window, closed her eyes, and within seconds, she was fast asleep.

Jade woke up to warm rays of sunlight streaming in through her window. She yawned, and glanced at her watch. It was already 10:45. She sprung up, startled at having slept so long. She quickly retrieved the English version of the train schedule. She flipped through it, searching for the arrival times. Jade then released a sigh of relief, realizing that her train would arrive in Hohhot at noon. She still had over an hour to go.

She stretched, and then pushed in her makeshift bed to reconstruct two facing chairs. She then plopped down on one of them, and turned to the window.

Wow, Jade slowly realized. She was in Inner Mongolia. And it looked very, very cold out there! But at the same time, it was absolutely beautiful. Pristine blankets of white snow covered miles of empty grasslands. Afar, she could see the rolling edges of small hills rising above the flat earth. The sky was a rich, soothing blue, and not a single cloud was in sight. The giant yellow sun sat in the center of the open air, overseeing the majestic landscape like an emperor over his grand kingdom.

As the train rolled forward, an interesting sight caught Jade's eye. Perhaps five hundred meters in the distance, a large, brown felt-covered tent rose above the snowy ground. The doorway was a rustic wooden frame; the loose flap of felt that acted as its door was pinned to the side. Thick ropes stretched out across the entire tent, like a fishing net holding it all together. Patches of snow covered the wide roof, and thick layers of straw were visible beneath the felt shell near the bottom of the structure. Jade recognized the tent from her readings and conversations with Arlene. It was a yurt, a decorated felt tent that nomadic Mongolian herders called home during much of the year. There was probably a herder in there now, perhaps with his family.

The train pressed on, and the yurt disappeared out of Jade's view. She watched with fascination as more awe-inspiring winter landscapes streamed in and out of her panoramic window. She closed her eyes and smiled for a moment. She was halfway across the world, near the Gobi Desert and the Siberian steppes, and she was alone in this splendid wilderness.

She opened her eyes. On most other occasions, that romantic picture would invigorate her. But the hard truth was all too apparent. She had a difficult task ahead of her: to find Lu Mian Tang, and to tell her about her grandsons and the forged letters asking for more Quazhen. And now, as if that wasn't enough, she had to meet up with Arlene; then together, they had to evade their attackers and return to America. Jade shook her head. Suddenly, dealing with the grandmother was becoming the easy part.

The remaining hour passed quickly. Jade was soon exiting the train, and walking onto the platform of the Hohhot railroad station. Upon feeling the frigid air, she immediately zipped up her wool coat. She then dug into her bag, and retrieved her knit winter hat, wool scarf, and leather gloves. Her hands were almost numb by the time she put everything on. So *this* was what negative degree weather was like!

Jade was thrilled to learn that she could rent a jeep directly from the train station. Using her dictionary, and offering plenty of embarrassed smiles, she made the deal with the Mongolian rental agent. She paid him the money, and he led her outside.

The agent took her around the corner of the station, and pointed to her vehicle. Jade stopped in her tracks. Before her was a snow-covered, rusted gray jeep that belonged in the junkyard decades ago. Its torn canvas top shook in the cold wind, and the passenger side of the windshield was badly cracked. The man used his sweater sleeve to wipe the snow off the windshield, and he then jumped into the driver's seat. He inserted a key, and turned. The jeep whined pathetically, but refused to start. Grinning at Jade, he tried again. Nothing. Then again. On the third attempt, the vehicle rattled to life. She could see him bouncing in the driver's seat; he then got out and smiled at her.

Well, she thought. What other choice did she have?

She grinned meekly, and nodded to him. He said a few friendly Mongolian words to her. She just smiled and waved.

Jade got into the vehicle, and almost got right back out; she could feel the rattling motion throughout her body! But after taking a deep breath, she got out her map. Hoping that her road would be the well-plowed, multi-lane main road to her right, she looked for the circled region that marked Lu Mian's property. No, she realized sadly. The road to Lu Mian's was straight ahead. It was a five-meter-wide path of patted snow, with tire tracks embedded into the white ground. In a few patchy areas, pieces of black pavement were visible underneath the hard, packed snow. But for the most part, the route was a narrow, poorly maintained country road that quickly left the urban comforts of Inner Mongolia's capital city. She sighed. Shaking her head, she thrust the jeep into drive, and pressed down on the gas. After a couple seconds of wild bucking, the vehicle obliged, and she was on her way.

After thirty minutes of driving, Jade's tense muscles began to relax. She gradually was able to sit back, and slowly, she began to enjoy the ride. Not a single vehicle was in sight. The spectacular vistas of the Inner Mongolian wilderness were hers alone to enjoy. She tried to take it all in, but the beauty was far too grand to digest in one sitting.

Eventually, Jade did come to a crossroads. Thank goodness, she thought. At least this wasn't the *only* road between Hohhot and its southern border! Actually, she realized, Lu Mian probably lived close to the southern border, near the neighboring province of Shanxi. If that was the case, she probably wouldn't be too, too far from more developed land.

Before crossing the intersecting road, she glanced both ways. She was comforted to see two vehicles approaching the intersection from her left; one was a small brown truck, and the other was a red jeep. Although she enjoyed being alone in this beautiful region, she did like knowing that if her jeep broke down, other people would be around to help.

She drove through the crossroads, and continued on her way. After another ten minutes of driving, more roads were popping up. Yes, she thought, the southern border was probably near. Looking on her map, she saw that she was close to the Yellow River; most likely, she reasoned, there were some small communities along the riverbanks. Well, she thought, she should be at Lu Mian's place quite soon.

Jade drove on. She looked to her right, and smiled to see a figure on horseback, riding in the open fields. Much of the horse was covered in some kind of heavy fabric. Good, she thought. It needed to stay warm, too!

She pressed on. As she drove, she picked up her map. Knowing that she was getting close, she looked for names of nearby roads. She would need some kind of landmark, she realized, to pinpoint this so-called plantation.

Jade glanced down at her map. The grandmother lived off a dead end side road that should be coming up. As one continued down this road, there was supposed to be a pond to the right, and then shortly thereafter, her road would appear to the left. Jade frowned. The street name, of course, was in Chinese; that wouldn't help her. She continued to look at the map.

Suddenly, Jade's stomach sank as a horn blared loudly. She jerked her head up, and looked directly into the grill of another jeep coming head-on! She gasped as she realized that she had accidentally veered into the middle of the road.

She screamed, and yanked her steering wheel to the right. Every sensation in her body tingled as the other car flew by her, avoiding impact by mere inches.

But within a second, her chest struck the steering wheel as her jeep plunged into a snowbank. Thick chunks of snow pelted her windshield and avalanched over her hood. She yelped as some icy snow poured in through the torn canvas roof, and landed on her bare neck.

Another second later, the jeep slammed to a stop as it collided into a rock-solid hunk of ice. Thud! Jade rocketed forward into the thin windshield, which smashed into a storm of splintered glass. As she flew out, sharp blades of glass cut into her face and slashed through her clothes. A particularly sharp piece pierced her right outer thigh and burrowed deep into her skin. Screaming in horror, Jade smacked facedown onto her hood and slid into the unmoving hunk of ice.

Then, a fraction of a second later, her world went black.

30

Jade awoke to the stinging pain of her right outer thigh being rubbed. The burning sensation shot into her buttock, and her entire right leg throbbed from the forceful rubbing. She grunted in protest, and then opened her eyes to see who was doing this.

Her strange surroundings immediately disoriented her. She was lying on her back, facing a yellow, painted ceiling. Large green branches of various floor plants sprouted up around her; they all curved inward, forming a small canopy above her head. Sunlight illuminated many of the green leafy branches, casting long shadows onto the yellow ceiling. She rolled her eyes upward, and realized that her head was near a wall; cut into that wall was an expansive window that allowed the sun's rays to pour into the room. The wall was painted a soft beige, and a six-inch wallpapered border ran along its uppermost edge. The wallpaper had a distinctly Chinese design, with three straight black lines running parallel and making sharp turns and rectangular shapes.

Jade looked to her left. A beautiful black screen blocked much of her view. The glossy screen had images of pink flowers and golden dragons. She rolled her eyes all the way left, and realized that she was on a mattress of some kind. She was lying on silk sheets, patterned in green and blue swirls, and her head was resting on a wonderfully soft pillow.

Ow! The rubbing of her thigh was becoming harder!

She darted her eyes down and to the right. Stunned, she watched as a woman knelt beside her right leg. The woman's eyes were closed, and she seemed to be concentrating as she rubbed globs of a thick gel onto Jade's thigh. The woman had long, straight gray hair, all pulled back into a golden butterfly-shaped clip. Her bare forehead had several deep wrinkles, as did her thin, brown face. The woman wore a simple red knit sweater; the button-down garment was open in the front, and a white camisole was visible underneath. She wore a plain, brown skirt made of a rough, canvas-like material, and her feet were bare.

"Excuse me," said Jade softly. She tried to move her right arm down to push away the woman's hand. But the arm throbbed in a searing pain as she tried to move it.

Without flinching, the older woman kept rubbing the thigh.

"Please," Jade said louder. "That hurts."

Seeming not to hear her, the woman continued to work.

"Hey!" Jade rolled to her left, drawing her hip away from the woman.

The woman opened her eyes. Frowning, she stared at Jade with large, soft brown eyes. "You must not do that," she said in perfect English. She gently reached over to her hip, and firmly tried to move it back down onto the mattress.

"That hurts," Jade repeated, resisting the other woman.

The woman looked at Jade, and stopped pulling. She gave the slightest grin, and then nodded knowingly. "My child, the ointment can sting when it is first applied. But you have a horrible puncture in that thigh. You need the medicine."

Jade glanced down at her oiled skin. She looked back up at the older woman, and wrinkled her brow. Who was this person?

"What medicine?" she asked skeptically.

"Why, this one, of course." She raised a terra-cotta bowl, and showed Jade the clear, viscous gel inside. "It is a mixture of aloe, comfrey, and tea tree oil."

Jade cringed. "Tea tree oil?" She said the name with poorly hidden sarcasm. "Look. I appreciate you trying to help me. Really, I do. But please don't rub any more tea tree oil into my wound. I don't need it getting infected."

The woman smiled smugly, and lowered her head. "My dear, the oil is used to prevent that very thing. It is used to prevent infections."

Jade closed her eyes and shook her head. Be gracious, she told herself. She should be dead, but instead this nice old lady was trying to help her. "Ma'am," she said softly. "Honestly, I am very grateful for your generous assistance. But please realize, I was in an accident, and I need serious medical care. Is there a hospital nearby?"

The woman sighed. “There’s one in Hohhot, but it is over an hour away. And quite frankly, the care at that hospital is awful at best.”

“Well, ma’am, thank you for your opinion. But as I recall, I was in a very bad accident. I veered off the road, crashed into an icy snowbank, and went flying through the windshield.”

“I know. I saw it all.”

Jade frowned. She didn’t remember seeing this mysterious woman at the time of her crash. But, she realized, it really didn’t matter. What she needed now was a hospital.

“Look,” Jade said, “crashing through a windshield is a very serious thing. I could have a subdural or epidural hematoma. I need to get a CT scan, at the very least. Please, help me to a hospital.” Indeed, such hemorrhaging into the brain would be life-threatening.

The woman gently set down her terra-cotta bowl, and then set her solemn eyes upon the younger American. “My child,” she said, “does your head hurt?”

Surprised by the question, Jade tilted her head and stared at her. But after a moment, she thought about the question. Actually, she admitted to herself, she had no headache whatsoever. “No. It doesn’t. But…”

“Are you dizzy?”

Hmm. No. Actually, not at all. “Well, no…”

“Is your vision blurry?”

Jade started to get frustrated. “No. It’s not. But listen, I could be in a lucid interval, a symptom-free period that precedes catastrophic events, like coma and death, by minutes or hours. My lack of symptoms doesn’t mean I have no hematoma.”

The woman closed her eyes, and nodded slightly. “This is true.” She let a moment of silence pass. And then, she opened her eyes. “But lucid intervals are quite uncommon, are they not, Doctor?”

Doctor? How did she know she was a doctor?

“And besides,” continued the woman, “I understand that the CT scan machine in Hohhot has been broken for some time. The next nearest machine is probably Beijing, and that is many hours away.” She shook her head. “If you did have a bleed, you would be in a coma by then.”

Jade looked at her, speechless. Who was this woman?

"No, my child. You were very lucky. With no headache, no dizziness, and no blurry vision, the chance of serious head injury is slim to none."

With Jade staring in confusion, the woman smiled gently, and turned to her terra-cotta bowl. She reached in, swiped another glob of gel, and plopped it onto Jade's thigh. She began rubbing again.

"Hey!" Jade barked, rolling her hip again. "Please, no more tea tree potion!" She sighed. "Look, even if I don't get a head CT scan, I need antibiotics for that thigh wound…"

The woman nodded. "The tea tree oil is from *Melaleuca alternifolia*, a tree native to Australia. It contains various components, such as *p*-cymene, α-terpinene, and terpinen-4-ol. The latter is most useful as a strong antiseptic; it has excellent bactericidal activity. The Australians used it in World War II to prevent infections, and more recently, it has been shown to kill MRSA quite nicely."

Taken aback, Jade just looked at her. Huh. "Did you say MRSA?" she asked sheepishly.

"Yes, dear. Methicillin-resistant staphylococcus aureus; it's a superbacteria that is resistant to almost every synthetic antibiotic known to man."

Jade nodded slowly, completely stunned. She was well aware of MRSA. Indeed, hospitals throughout America required physicians, nurses, and visitors to wear gloves, gowns, and masks before entering the room of a patient infected with the nasty bacteria. And yes, it was highly resistant to almost every Western antibiotic.

Tea tree oil killed MRSA?

Jade shook her head. She was embarrassed. She realized that her dismissal of the woman's ointment had been arrogant; apparently, it *was* a pretty decent antiseptic. But also, she was confused. She was confused about this gentle Chinese woman's seemingly vast medical knowledge. Who was she? And again, how did she know Jade was a doctor?

Maybe it was time for introductions.

"I'm sorry," she said. "I should introduce myself…"

"You're Dr. Jade Evans, of the United States of America." She beamed. "I hope you don't mind, but I checked your identification before lifting you onto Yangshou."

"Yangshou?"

"Oh yes. Yangshou, my horse." She extended her hand and smiled. "Dr. Evans, my name is Lu Mian Tang."

31

Dumbfounded, Jade slowly sat up and accepted the handshake. Her mouth was open in a baffled expression, and she simply stared at Yu-lan's grandmother with obvious bewilderment.

Lu Mian was unprepared for Jade's astonished reaction. Perplexed, she examined her countenance with open curiosity. "Is something wrong, Dr. Evans?"

Jade tilted her head, but she couldn't yet speak. She just sized up the older woman, and tried to make sense of what was happening.

"Dr. Evans?" She started to get concerned.

"I...I'm sorry, Ms. Tang." She shook her head in amazement. "It's just that...this may sound odd, but..." She shook her head, and lowered her voice to a whisper. "I came to China looking for you. You're the sole reason I'm here."

Lu Mian gazed at her. She didn't smile. She didn't laugh. She just looked into her eyes with a straight expression.

Jade simply gawked at Yu-lan's grandmother with unabashed wide eyes. This was a miracle. Her fateful accident had brought her directly to this ultimate destination!

Lu Mian continued to look at her. She patiently waited for Jade to explain.

Within seconds, the sheer amazement of the situation wore off, and reality began to hit the young doctor.

She had to tell her about Yu-lan. And Feng. And Quazhen.

Jade swallowed hard. She looked down, feeling a sudden rush of apprehension. Lu Mian's gaze began to feel heavier and heavier.

"Look, Ms. Tang..."

"Please," she said softly. "Call me Lu Mian." She then listened attentively.

Jade raised her head. She studied the grandmother's face. She saw a leathery brown complexion with many wrinkles, testifying to a long and active life. She saw two soft and gentle eyes, attesting to a kind and caring spirit. She saw a serious and sober expression, affirming that this peace-loving grandmother was now bracing for some serious news. And with all that, she saw an unmistakable strength in her countenance, promising that any bad news would be accepted with dignity and graciousness.

"Okay. Lu Mian, I have come from America to bring you some difficult news." She paused. "But maybe this isn't the right place. Perhaps you'd be more comfortable in another room, or in…"

"My child, please tell me. Tell me here, and tell me now."

Jade nodded. She met the woman's eyes. "Lu Mian, I was a friend of your grandson, Yu-lan."

She nodded very slightly.

Jade's heart began to race, and she felt a tear begin to form in the corner of her eye. "Lu Mian, I am terribly, terribly sorry to tell you this."

Her expression was strong and unbroken.

Jade closed her eyes. "Yu-lan has died. He…he was actually killed."

The grandmother squinted her eyes. She slightly twisted her lips, curling her face into a look of confusion. "Killed?"

"Yes. And the murderer was your other grandson, Feng Hou Tang."

Jade watched as her pupils enlarged, and she started breathing more heavily. Cringing, she slowly leaned forward. "Feng?" she asked incredulously.

Jade nodded. "Feng learned that Yu-lan was going to America several months before he left China. He begged him to let him tag along. Yu-lan said no, but his brother followed him there, anyway. When he just showed up at Yu-lan's store one day, Yu-lan didn't have the heart to turn him away. He let Feng work temporarily as an employee, until he could find other work."

Lu Mian listened with wide eyes and a steadily growing frown. Jade started to say more, but the grandmother quickly lifted a hand, silencing her. She then closed her eyes, and looked up to the ceiling. Jade watched as the older woman muttered some soft Chinese words aloud. Watching her, Jade became mesmerized by the vision. Lu Mian was saying some kind of Chinese prayer for her beloved grandson; her words were both captivating and soothing, even though Jade could not understand them.

Lu Mian slowly tilted back head back down, and faced the American woman. She nodded. "This is horrible news, indeed." She then sighed. "But it doesn't shock me. Yu-lan would certainly offer shelter to the devil, not out of sympathy for its evil cause; but out of hope that he could show it love, and maybe change its wicked ways." She then shook her head. "And Feng, the devil incarnate, he was only capable of evil. He would rape and murder his entire ancestral line of mothers, if only it would give him money or power."

Jade watched her shake her head, in half-mourning and half-disgust.

She looked up at the doctor. "When did it happen?"

"Over three months ago, Lu Mian."

Suddenly, the grandmother's eyes started to narrow, and her lip began to curl. Her soft facial features quickly hardened. Then, in an accusatory tone, "Who are you, Dr. Jade Evans?"

Jade was stunned. "What do you mean, 'who am I'?"

The grandmother's contempt for Feng seemed to be redirecting towards Jade! "You lie, Dr. Evans."

"What?! Lu Mian…"

"I heard from Yu-lan two weeks ago. He sent me a letter."

Oh boy, thought Jade. Now for the second part of the news. She leaned back, closed her eyes, and nodded. She felt the other woman's angry stare upon her.

"Lu Mian, that letter was a phony." As she reopened her eyes, the older woman opened her mouth to speak. Jade raised a hand. "Please, ma'am, let me finish." She took a deep breath. "Look, you said you found my identification in my bag. So I presume that my bag is here somewhere?"

She slowly nodded.

"May I have it? I have something for you inside."

Still staring skeptically, Lu Mian slowly rose to her feet. She then abruptly turned around, and left the room. Within seconds, she was back with Jade's black rolling duffel bag. She handed it to her, and then knelt back down by the mattress.

Jade took the bag, and unzipped an outer compartment. She retrieved the smoothed out letter from Yu-lan, and silently handed it to her.

Lu Mian took the folded oval sheet, opened it, and read.

Jade watched as she poured over the words. Her eyes repeatedly darted from left to right across the page; she reread the entire letter three times before closely examining Yu-lan's hand drawn symbol at the bottom of the page. She stared at the symbol, and suddenly, a flood of tears cascaded down her cheeks.

Jade rose to her knees. She approached the grandmother, and spread out her arms.

Lu Mian suddenly clutched the letter in one hand, and drew it to her chest. She then embraced Jade with the other arm, and let her tears fall over her shoulder.

Jade held her as she cried. Well, she thought, it looked like Yu-lan's letter had convinced her that she was telling the truth. But actually, Jade was somewhat surprised. How did she know that Yu-lan's letter wasn't a phony? The evidence wasn't all that strong, was it?

After over two minutes, Lu Mian slowly backed away. With wet eyes, she peered down at the oval paper again. She shook her head. "I thought he had forgotten," she whispered.

"Excuse me, Lu Mian?"

The grandmother looked up, and then grinned tenderly. "I had taught Yu-lan how to draw a very special symbol. It's this one here." She pointed to the familiar design that Yu-lan himself had described to Jade. "He promised that he would draw it on all of his letters to me." She wiped a lingering tear away. "I never told him that the symbol was my mother's family crest.

"Anyway, his recent letters had the crest." She shook her head. "But it was always drawn slightly wrong. You see this part?" She pointed to an elaborate cluster of small triangles. "The angles need to change as you go from left to right. It's drawn perfectly on this paper; it's just like I had taught him. But on the recent correspondence, the angles are all the same." She grinned. "I thought he had forgotten how to draw my crest. But no, my angel remembered." She stared at the paper lovingly.

She then set her eyes upon Jade. "This letter is real, Dr. Evans..."

"Jade. Please, Jade."

"Very well. This letter is real, Jade. The others were indeed phonies." She bowed her head. "I am sorry for not believing you."

"Lu Mian," she whispered, "it's okay."

"So," said the grandmother, beginning to compose herself. "In this letter, Yu-lan tells me that my herb may actually harm some Americans." She raised her eyebrows. "Interesting. Difficult to believe, but Yu-lan would never lie to me. He says that he will pull the herb from the store shelves, and he asks me not to ship him any more, until further notice." She looked up at Jade. "This is consistent with the later letters being fake. I have received four letters in the past three months requesting unusually large shipments of my Quazhen." She shook her head. "So it's Feng, isn't it? He killed his brother, and is now writing to me for more of the herb."

"Actually, Feng is dead, too. He was killed by a police officer. But it was his plan to send you phony requests for the Quazhen; he then intended to sell it to an American supplement corporation."

She shook her head. "Well, thank goodness he was killed before that could happen."

"No, Lu Mian, it did happen. Feng was killed, but his plan is being carried out right now by two friends of his. Here, look at this." She dug into her duffel bag, and retrieved the crushed box of Botanicure's Quazhen. She handed it to the grandmother.

Stunned, she took the box. She examined it with unbelieving eyes and a wide open mouth. After a few moments of becoming angry and disgusted, she handed it back to Jade. "I'm getting bits and pieces of the story. But as I can gather, Feng and his so-called friends wanted to get rich off of my Quazhen. Yu-lan, of course, stood in the way. Besides refusing to let outsiders control the family herb, he thought the herb might be dangerous to your population. So clearly, there was a conflict. Feng solved it as I would expect him to; he murdered his brother. And only after he made the deal with a huge American industry, he was killed by your police. Now, my herb is being mass-marketed in America. And Feng's demonic friends are getting rich off the deal." She paused. "Did I get that right?"

Jade grinned dryly. "Every bit of it. However," she sighed, "there are some details missing. Most importantly, those two friends of his want *me* dead. And they're here in China looking for me, right now."

Lu Mian nodded. "But by telling me the truth, you've ensured that I'll never again ship my herb to America. Those friends are out of business."

"Good. Also, I was hoping you could tell me where you've been sending these recent shipments. It's not to Yu-lan's old address, is it?"

She shook her head. "No. A recent letter claimed that he had moved to a neighboring state. Foxboro, Massachusetts?"

Foxboro! So Botanicure was getting the Quazhen directly! She groaned. "Wow. That explains a lot, Lu Mian. A lot."

"Look," said the grandmother, rising to her feet. "This is all happening so fast. I want to slow it down. Why don't we move into the kitchen? I'll make us some tea, and then you can slowly tell me the whole story. From beginning to end. I want to hear everything slowly, as one whole package."

Jade nodded, and rose up. "That's a very good idea."

The women moved into the kitchen. They entered a square room with many windows, several plants, and a simple round table in the center. As Jade sat down at the table, Lu Mian moved to a stove, and began brewing her best herbal tea.

When the red tea was ready, she poured two cups, and then joined Jade at the table. Graciously accepting the tea, Jade then retold the entire story, sparing no detail. She mentioned her early finding of strange symptoms in her patients. She then described how she and John related the odd symptoms to Quazhen. In detail, she talked about her encounters with both Yu-lan and Feng. She mentioned how Feng's friends tried to injure both John and her, and how they did put John into the hospital. She then described the cold-blooded murder, and how she was initially framed for robbery. She discussed her final encounter with Feng, and then told her about the death threats and her temporary move to Rhode Island. Jade went on to describe the time she first found the mass-marketed Quazhen on the shelves.

She also mentioned that nobody could get a hold of Lu Mian by phone. At that point, the grandmother apologized profusely. Her telephone had been broken for several weeks. Since nobody usually ever called her, she had been in no hurry to fix it.

Jade went on to describe the incident at Botanicure's main office. She then described the flight to China, and the terrifying episode in the hotel. Finally, she described her friend Arlene. She said that she hoped to meet her here, as she had shouted out from the hotel room. She also said that the Chinese police had been notified about the incident via a bellhop. But, she confessed, she had no idea whether or not Arlene was even alive.

Lu Mian attentively listened to the incredible story. When Jade was done, she sipped on her tea for a few moments, silently reflecting upon it all. Then, "Well, at least we know you will be safe here."

"We do?"

"Yes. Those two evil men must know where I live; they've been mailing me phony letters from Yu-lan. But, they wouldn't dare disturb me here. After all, I'm the supplier of their precious goldmine." She shook her head. "This is a safe haven for you, Jade. I know it."

She nodded. "Speaking of that, Lu Mian, is it possible that they're getting the Quazhen from somewhere else? I mean, in addition to your shipments?"

She vehemently shook her head no. "Not a chance. It won't even grow in my own greenhouse. I think it needs some peculiar nutrient in the natural soil; and for some strange reason, the only soil that has the required nutrient must be in my backyard." She looked at Jade confidently. "It has been known for generations and generations, my child, that Quazhen only grows here. Be assured about that."

That was that, realized Jade. Chu-too, or whoever Botanicure said their supplier was, simply didn't exist.

"Now," continued Lu Mian, "we'll need a plan. I believe you should wait here, where it's safe, until your friend Arlene arrives. When she does, I will personally escort you back to Beijing. Those men wouldn't touch me; I supply their herb. Therefore, I'd be your perfect bodyguard."

Jade cracked a smile. "Lu Mian, you don't have to do that..."

"I do," she replied sharply. "Jade Evans, Yu-lan's spirit rides on your shoulders. Surely you must see that. You have delivered his message, and you have brought him justice. Jade," she said solemnly, "I am indebted to you."

They exchanged a serious stare, one based upon rapidly growing mutual respect.

"I will accompany you and Arlene to Beijing," continued the woman. "When you get home, go to this Foxboro address, and make your arrests. Bring, once and for all, Feng and his minions to final justice. Quazhen, of course, will never leave China again."

Jade nodded slowly. It was a good, basic plan. But two things bothered her. "Lu Mian, what if Arlene never shows up?"

"She will, Jade. You must believe that she will."

She didn't press that one further, at least not for now. But she raised her second issue. "And Lu Mian, I'm not so sure that we're both safe here. Couldn't those thugs kill us both, and take over your plantation? Then they'd have endless Quazhen to themselves, and they'd never need you to make the shipments."

The grandmother looked at her. Her face drew longer; she obviously hadn't considered this. She lowered her eyes to the table, and began to think about this important point. Then, "Well, Jade Evans, that is conceivable, yes. But remember, we have Yu-lan's spirit riding on your shoulders. We must have faith that he will protect us. We must have faith that he will bring those two evildoers to justice before they can do harm to us."

Not liking the sound of that, Jade began to protest.

"You will stay here until Arlene arrives," repeated the grandmother sharply. "Then we will all go to Beijing, and see you off safely. Then, back in America, you will bring Feng's minions to justice." She nodded in strong confidence. "That will be our plan."

And that, realized Jade, was final.

32

Jade sat in a small, rectangular room with ivory walls and a deep blue carpet. Her cushioned straw chair faced a large window, and she rested her legs upon a wooden ottoman. The warm sun streamed into this small den, and Jade was almost nodding off to sleep when Lu Mian walked in. She smiled as the grandmother presented a tray before her. On the ornate, red and gold tray were several small snacks. Thin, pastry like skins enveloped a mixture of chopped foods, and rising steam warned her about the hot temperature of these delicacies. The snacks appeared to be small, steamed appetizers, something between a spring roll and a dumpling. Jade smiled as a tantalizing spicy aroma emanated from these dainty refreshments.

"Thank you, Lu Mian," she said graciously. She took a pair of chopsticks on the tray, and grabbed one of the pieces.

As she popped it into her mouth, Lu Mian smiled gently. "They're called shaomai. They are quite popular in Hohhot. The filling is made of various raw materials, and I use my special seasoning to make it just right."

She sat down on another straw chair, next to Jade.

The American smiled widely. "They are wonderful!" she said, swallowing her first one. "Thank you!"

"Please, take more."

Jade did. And she washed down the steamed delicacies with Lu Mian's own milk tea, another staple food of Inner Mongolia.

"Lu Mian," she said, settling back in her chair, "how did you know all that medical information? All the stuff about hematomas and about MRSA?"

The woman smiled. She rose from her chair, and walked to a wicker bookcase. She knelt down, and opened a bottom drawer. "I haven't touched this in many, many years," she said. She dug out a magazine. Smiling, she handed it to Jade.

Jade's eyes widened as she looked at the front cover. Written in plain English, at the top of the cover, she read the journal title: 'New England Journal of Medicine'. This medical journal was arguably the most prestigious American resource in biomedical research. Much of Western medicine's sacred evidence-based medicine was rooted in new discoveries first published in the New England Journal. This particular issue was an old one; it was dated July 31, 1962.

"Go to page 94," the grandmother said.

Jade did so. Her heart nearly stopped as she looked at the page. The title was "A Randomized, Double-Blind, Placebo-Controlled Trial Comparing the Efficacy of Four Cardiac Glycosides in the Treatment of Atrial Fibrillation". The primary author—the one who did most of the work—was Lu Mian Tang. Jade quickly scanned down to the corner of the page. A small blurb was written on each of the three authors. Lu Mian Tang was identified as an assistant professor of medicine at University of California, Los Angeles.

Jade shot her head up. She stared at the other woman incredulously. Lu Mian simply smiled, and downed a piece of shaomai.

"This is you?" she blurted out.

Lu Mian glanced at her with mock insult.

Yes, it was her. Jade quickly scanned the abstract of the paper. It was a highly technical paper that detailed some important findings about digitalis and other cardiac glycosides. After skimming it, Jade looked up. "You were an assistant professor at UCLA School of Medicine?"

She nodded. "I was."

"But, I don't get it. Haven't you been in China for many years?"

"Since 1965, yes. My sister had lived in this house, our parents' old house, until she died in late 1965. My husband and I moved back here, to China, in the summer of '65 to be with my family during that troubling time."

Jade wrinkled her brow. "I thought China's borders were closed at that time."

"To outsiders, yes. But my husband and I were born here. We went to America when we first married, at age seventeen, just before the Communist party took over this country. That was in 1949. But since we were born here, we were allowed to come back in 1965, before the borders were open to foreign tourists."

"So you left America to be back with your family?"

"That was part of it, yes."

Jade looked at her. "And the other part?"

Lu Mian smiled. "That's a good question, but it has a long answer. You really want to know?"

The doctor nodded, enthusiastically.

Lu Mian slowly sipped some milk tea, and then turned to the younger woman. "Jade, I have published in five different American and European journals: The New England Journal, the Journal of the American Medical Association, Annals of Internal Medicine, the Lancet, and the British Medical Journal. I loved biomedical research. I was convinced that it was to be my life's work."

"Okay," she replied, shaking her head at these very impressive accomplishments.

"But I also loved clinical medicine. I had taken two years of medical science at the Peking University Health Sciences Center, over in Beijing, before leaving for America. I loved it. But at the time, I realized, I enjoyed research just a bit more." She shrugged. "My plan was quite simple, really. I would go to America, and first get a doctorate degree in the biomedical sciences. Then, after teaching and doing academic research for some time, I would enroll in an American medical school, and get a medical degree. That way, I could fully live out both of my medical passions—research and clinical medicine."

"Fine." Jade continued to stare at her, stunned.

"Well, I got my Ph.D. in California, and I did my research. It was wonderful stuff, while it lasted. But ten years into it, around 1960, I decided that I needed more. The test tubes and the pipettes were getting old. Like I had anticipated, I was beginning to want to work with people. I knew that medical school was calling me."

Jade listened attentively. Apparently this wasn't the traditional Chinese grandmotherly woman whom she had envisioned; somehow, she now had trouble picturing Lu Mian carrying stone jugs of water back and forth from a river!

"I enrolled in medical school at UCSF, the University of California, San Francisco." She shook her head. "It was the most enlightening experience of my life." She smiled. "After my third year of medical school, I was absolutely convinced that I'd never be an allopathic physician."

Jade recognized the term 'allopathic'; it essentially meant 'Western'. She was an example of an allopath; almost all American and European 'regular doctors'—both generalist and specialist—were allopaths.

"I thought UCSF was supposed to be a good school," noted Jade.

"Oh, it was excellent. For allopathic medicine, it was excellent."

Jade leaned closer. "So what happened? What changed your mind about getting your American medical degree?"

She sighed. "Let me tell you a true story; it happened during my third year of medical school. One autumn day, a forty-year-old woman walked into her internist's office. She was complaining of pain in her fingers that radiated up towards her shoulders, and then down into her waist. It was a throbbing, aching pain that did not respond to simple analgesics, and it had been there for over a year. An odd complaint, right?"

Jaded nodded. Such a presentation would be quite unusual. Pinched cervical nerve roots could easily cause pain to radiate *from* the neck and *into* the arms and hands; but the other way around was very strange. And for the pain to then shoot into her waist? That was even tougher to explain.

"Well, her internist took some history, and did a decent physical. But he found nothing to help him. So he decided to do some blood work." She shrugged. "Fine. But the lab tests were completely normal. Normal blood count, normal metabolic profile, normal sed rate, normal thyroids. There you had it: all normal. And those were pretty much the most sophisticated blood tests they had back then."

Jade nodded.

"So, perplexed, he then ordered some x-rays. Decent idea, right?"

Jaded nodded again.

"Well, they were all normal. He then ordered a nerve conduction study; but it was normal. So basically, you had a middle-aged woman with this unusual chronic pain. The internist didn't know what to do. So he sent her to a specialist—a neurologist, I believe. So she sees the neurologist. During the entire visit, he looks at her skeptically, hums and haws a little bit, and then says he doesn't know. So he gives her some mild pain medicine, and then ships her to a rheumatologist. The rheumatologist spends four minutes with her, doesn't look her in the eye once, and diagnoses her with fibromyalgia."

Jade thought about this. "Did she have the trigger points?"

"Not a single one. The diagnosis was wrong; it was painfully obvious. But he wanted to label her with *something*. So he gives her a bunch of exercises to do, and then basically says 'Have a good life.'

"Three months later, she goes back to her internist. The pain is much worse; it's nearly unbearable. She starts to tell him about her suffering, but literally six seconds into it, he interrupts her. He wants to know if she's been taking her pain medicine that the neurologist prescribed. She says that she has. He tells her to double the dosage, and then leaves the room. As far as he's concerned, the visit is over."

Jade frowned. "What a jerk."

Lu Mian grinned dryly. "Yes. Of course, that kind of treatment would *never* occur in American medicine today."

Jade felt the jab, but did not respond.

"Anyway," continued the grandmother, "her pain is so bad in three more weeks, that she desperately calls her internist one more time. She pleads for some better pain medicine. He starts to become angry with her, saying that he's not comfortable carelessly giving out those 'addicting' medicines. When she insists that her pain is real, he retorts that nothing is wrong with her. Maybe she has some fibromyalgia, he says, but otherwise there's nothing wrong. He asserts that her lab tests were normal, the imaging tests were normal, the nerve conduction study was normal, and two excellent specialists found nothing to be seriously wrong. He says that everyone gets aches and pains, and she needs to learn to live with it. Then he hangs up on her."

Jade shook her head. "Pretty awful story. So what happened to the poor woman?"

Lu Mian smiled. "Fortunately, my pain finally responded to acupuncture. I convinced a resident to give me some narcotics in the meantime, but the ultimate cure was the acupuncture."

Jade looked at her, astonished. A few silent moments hung in the air. Then, "Well, I'm happy to hear you're doing better. And I'm sorry you had to go through that awful experience. But, tell me, did you abandon allopathic medicine solely because of that one bad personal experience?"

"No, not at all. That was one of many reasons. But many of the patient encounters that I witnessed throughout medical school did reinforce my own experience. Time and time again, I watched doctors interrupt patients. They rudely fired rehearsed questions, not *listening* to what the patient was really telling them. And time and time again, I watched patients get shuffled from one specialist to the next; 'expert' doctors kept looking for their favorite damaged tissue or obstructed organ, confident that they could explain the patient's symptoms in that way. They never stopped to think that maybe something bigger was going on; maybe the patient was suffering from psychological or social problems, and maybe that was materializing into physical symptoms."

Jade listened. As difficult as it was for her to admit, much of this was ringing true.

"Then comes the whole notion of evidence-based medicine," continued Lu Mian. "Of course, they didn't call it evidence-based medicine in my day, but we certainly had the scientific studies. Hey, I published five of them!"

"What's wrong with good, solid studies?" asked Jade, beginning to feel defensive.

"Nothing. Nothing at all. It's the black-and-white conclusions drawn from those studies that bothered me."

Jade wrinkled her brow. "I don't get it."

"How reliable are statistics, Jade?"

"Extremely reliable, if done correctly. The whole field of statistics consists of mathematical laws and equations; it's all hard facts."

"I see. Tell me, which hard mathematical law draws the line between a statistically significant finding, and a non-statistically significant finding?"

Jade thought about it. "Well, from what I can remember, there's a number called a 'p-value'. The p-value is the cut-off point that says whether or not your result could have occurred by chance alone."

"And what number does the p-value usually have?"

"Um, point zero five, I think."

"That's right. Oftentimes, researchers say that if their statistical result falls below 0.05, or five percent, it is statistically significant."

"Uh-huh." Jade had forgotten much of her statistical training. But Lu Mian, having published in five major medical journals, was obviously very much on top of it.

"So in layman's terms, Jade, what are we saying with this p-value stuff?"

"Well, basically, whenever a scientific finding is deemed acceptable to the scientific community, we must acknowledge a five percent chance—or a one in twenty chance—that the finding is wrong. That is, of course, if the researcher decides that the p-value equals 0.05, which is standard practice."

"That's right. So again," said Lu Mian, "when I ask which hard mathematical law draws the line between statistically significant facts and supposedly untrue facts, the correct answer is this: there is no such law. A human being must decide what number the p-value will be. It's consequently a human decision to accept the idea that many of our medical discoveries have a five percent chance of being wrong."

Jade shook her head defensively. "Fine. But what's the better way to do it? Please tell me, Lu Mian, how could the scientific world better analyze its data?" She looked at the older woman with growing defiance.

Lu Mian smiled. "There is no better way. Science is a beautiful tool. And statistics is an exquisite way to learn from that tool."

"Then why are you challenging our system?"

"I'm not challenging it, Jade. I'm just pointing out a solid fact: even the very best scientific studies can be wrong. It is a truth inherent in statistics."

"Fine. So what?"

Lu Mian leaned into the other woman. "So tell me then, why does allopathic medicine worship the findings of evidence-based medicine as Almighty Truth? Why do allopaths trust the knowledge revealed by randomized, double-blind, placebo-controlled trials *more* than the time-tested knowledge of Asian cultures that has stood for millennia? After all, as we just discussed, the results of any scientific trial with a p-value of 0.05 could be *wrong* one-twentieth of the time. One-twentieth, Jade."

"But," asserted Jade. "these trials are often repeated. After several repetitions, that one-in-twenty goes down considerably."

"Sometimes, yes. But in many of those repeated studies, you'll end up with conflicting results, won't you Doctor? That doesn't exactly reassure me. And remember, we've been discussing the very best, most carefully laid out scientific studies. How many randomized trials out there are badly flawed in design? And yet we still praise their results above the knowledge of other cultures."

Jade was becoming flustered. Practically all of her medical knowledge rested upon the foundation of evidence-based medicine. She was very uncomfortable with somebody challenging that foundation.

"Again, Lu Mian, you're pointing out some flaws in Western Medicine. But what's the better way to go? I mean, herbal medicine and other non-Western medicines have *no* hardcore evidence to back them up. You're saying that's better?"

"Correction, Doctor. They have no or little 'hardcore' *science* to back them up. But they have millennia of a certain evidence that Western medicine just doesn't have: observations."

Jade raised an eyebrow. "What do you mean, observations? Scientific studies are based upon observation…"

"You misheard me. I said *millennia* of observations." She looked at Jade with firm and confident eyes. "Western medicine has been around for a few centuries. Traditional Chinese Medicine has been around for a few millennia. And those millennia of observations have yielded certain tried-and-true philosophies upon which Chinese medicine has become based."

Jade just stared at her, frustrated, but not knowing how to respond.

"Anyway," continued Lu Mian, "you had asked for the whole reason why I left America and came to China. First of all, it was to see my dying sister and to be with my family. But secondly, I had developed a distaste for American medicine. With all due respect, many doctors over there were arrogant, rude, and simply refused to really listen to their patients. And moreover, it bothered me to see a close-minded medical establishment worshipping the so-called evidence-based medicine. After all, evidence-based medicine is *not* perfect. That's a fact."

She sipped her milk tea. "So I came here. I educated myself in the art of Chinese medicine." She turned to the younger doctor. "And I learned more than I ever thought possible."

The women sat together, in a mild state of tension, for several minutes. Jade reflected upon the older woman's points. Lu Mian thought about Jade's responses. Then, the grandmother stood up. "Dinnertime will soon be here. Do you eat duck?"

Jade turned, and nodded softly. She started to get up. "Let me help..."

Lu Mian gently pushed her down. "Please just relax, my child. It is an honor for me to prepare our food."

As the grandmother approached the door, she turned back. "By the way, any headache yet?"

Jade shook her head.

"Good. Any dizziness? Or blurry vision?"

"No."

"Good." With a smile, she left the room.

33

Jade woke up the next morning atop the soft mattress and beneath the silky sheets; she was in the same room in which she had awoken yesterday. Sunlight streamed in overhead, and she looked up at the gorgeous canopy of green branches. Yawning, she sat up. She examined her right thigh; the wound had closed nicely, and pink healing tissue was already beginning to form.

She neatly tucked in her sheets, and folded an overlying quilt. Wearing a sweatshirt and sweatpants, she then sauntered into Lu Mian's kitchen. The delicious aroma of fresh bread filled the room.

"Good morning," smiled the grandmother. She was standing over her stove, stirring a small pot of milk.

"Hello." She stretched. "Something smells wonderful."

Lu Mian beamed. "I'm baking a loaf of buckwheat bread. It should be ready in an hour. Did you sleep well?"

"Yes, thank you. I was completely out." She looked outside. The sun was shining in another cold but cloudless sky. "No Arlene yet, eh?"

"No, dear." She approached the kitchen table, and set down two mugs of the warmed milk. Jade graciously took one, and the women sat down together. Jade put the mug to her lips, and drank.

Ugh! She quickly placed it back down. "Um, Lu Mian?"

She turned to the younger woman.

"Does your milk taste sour?"

"Why, of course. Everyone in this region prefers milk to be slightly soured." She looked at Jade's gagging expression, and then smiled warmly. "Tell you what, how about some tea?"

"Oh, I don't mean to be ungrateful…" She started to get up.

"Sit, sit." The grandmother rose, and retrieved her tea kettle. "I always keep some hot." She poured her a new mug of a fresh brew.

Slightly embarrassed, but much happier with the herbal tea, Jade slowly sipped from the mug. "Delicious."

The two women sat together at the table, drinking their hot beverages, and enjoying each other's company.

"I was thinking more about our conversation yesterday," said Jade. "It actually kept me up last night. I respect your views, but I still don't see Chinese medicine as superior to allopathic medicine."

"I never said it was superior, Jade. I simply reminded you that Western medicine has its faults and limitations. To be sure, Chinese medicine does too. Perhaps it is most wise for us to be open to both of them, yes?"

Jade thought about this. "I suppose," she said skeptically. "But, I was thinking about this as I was trying to fall asleep last night: the whole notion of Chinese medicine seems so haphazard to me. I mean, ancient healers observed that certain herbs had healing properties, and so they used them for medicinal purposes. And people have been using those same herbs for millennia since then, for those same purposes. But where is the structured theory that binds this herbal knowledge together? In allopathic medicine, we have studied the human body down to the most minute molecules. We have collected millions of observations, and have grouped them into larger bodies of knowledge—such as anatomy, physiology, biochemistry, and so on. Our medical knowledge is well organized, and so we are able to make educated clinical judgments, based upon that organized knowledge. But how can you do that with a big collection of isolated observations?"

Lu Mian smiled. "Is that what Chinese medicine is? A big collection of isolated observations?"

Jade shrugged. "I mean no offense by that. But where is the Chinese version of physiology, or the Chinese equivalent of biochemistry? Without those organized fields of knowledge, how can you extrapolate your knowledge to unproven new ideas?" She sipped her tea. The morning was already off to a pretty deep start!

"Jade, dear, you are exemplifying typical allopathic shortsightedness. Of course Chinese medicine is based upon organized fields of knowledge. It is not simply based upon unrelated observations." She smiled warmly. "What may be confusing you, however, is that whereas allopathic medicine is rooted in science; traditional medicine is rooted in philosophy."

Jade looked perplexed.

"Here, let me give you a taste of that philosophy. You've heard of Yin and Yang?"

Jade nodded. "Aren't those the opposite swirls in that circular Chinese symbol thingy?"

The grandmother chuckled. "They're a little more than that; and the 'symbol thingy' is called the Taiji. Yin and Yang, according to Taoist philosophy, are descriptors of the interacting, dynamic, opposite forces that exist in everything in nature. Think of Yin as cold, dark, still, passive, and so on. Think of Yang as hot, light, activity, expression, and so on. *Everything* in the universe contains both Yin and Yang. Think about it. Water is a good example. The Yin form of water is a hard, cold block of ice; the Yang form is hot, flowing steam. Do you follow?"

Jade nodded.

"Well, according to one of the most fundamental laws of Chinese medicine, Yin and Yang should always be in balance. In fact, disharmony of the two forces produces illness in an individual. For example, too much of the hot and active Yang will give you a fever. Too much of the cold and immobile Yin could make you depressed. You still follow?"

Jade nodded again.

"So, the object of Chinese medicine is to restore balance between Yin and Yang when somebody is ill. If you have a fever from an infection, for example, you may need more Yin. Well, certain herbs can invigorate your Yin, or listening to certain music can do it, too. However it's accomplished, the idea is to restore balance, or homeostasis, to the individual."

Jade raised an eyebrow. "Homeostasis? That's a very allopathic word. Restoring homeostasis is the goal of allopathic medicine, isn't it? I mean, so much of disease is due to lack of proper coordination between the heart, lungs, and kidneys, for example."

Lu Mian thunked her mug onto the table, in mock surprise. "Dr. Jade Evans," she said sarcastically, "are you telling me that the almighty allopathic medicine may have a similar fundamental—what did you call it—'structured theory' as that hokey Chinese medicine?"

Jade couldn't suppress a grin.

Lu Mian continued. "Look, I'm not going to try to teach you all of Chinese medicine over milk and tea. I won't get into Qi. I won't get into the Five Elements. I won't even mention how the goal of Chinese medicine is to restore balance to the *whole* person, not just an organ or two. Just realize, Jade, Chinese medicine certainly *is* based upon its own organized system of knowledge. Its tenets go back to ancient philosophy, which rivals the best of your 'Western science' when it comes to discovering Truth in the universe. Therefore, it is perfectly reasonable to base one's medical system upon philosophy, and not in fact, upon science."

Jade thought about this. Philosophy over science? Not a chance.

Lu Mian read her cynical countenance. "You're uncomfortable with a medical system based upon philosophy, aren't you? You believe that science is a better way to understand our universe. Well, tell me this, Doctor: what is the greatest question in the universe? What one piece of Truth would help mankind to finally *really* understand our place in the universe?"

Jade thought about it. She faced the grandmother. "That's easy. It's the question of how we work. Without knowing how we function, we cannot know how to survive."

"Funny answer," said Lu Mian, quite seriously. "And not unsurprising from an allopath. To me," she said solemnly, "the greatest question about our place in nature is this: who are we? And next comes this: why are we here?"

Jade stared at her.

"How does your almighty science, Doctor, answer those questions?"

Jade was silent.

Smiling, the grandmother spoke. "Is doesn't answer those questions. It has no idea where to begin. Philosophy, on the other hand, has addressed those questions for ages. Now tell me, Doctor, which is the better system to understand ourselves, our universe, and the ways in which our universe can heal us? Science—which is powerless to answer the greatest mysteries of the universe? Or philosophy—which in its purest form, is built upon answering those very questions?"

Jade's head was spinning. Her scientific mind was unaccustomed to these philosophical questions. She closed her eyes, and sipped her tea.

"Well," said Lu Mian, more lightheartedly. "How'd we get onto this topic, anyway?" Smiling, she rose. "I'm going to get bathed and dressed. Our bread should be ready in a half hour or so. If I'm still bathing, please help yourself."

Jade grinned, and nodded.

She then made a mental note. Maybe it was time to crack open a textbook of Chinese medicine. Maybe there was more to the whole field than she had realized.

Lu Mian, wearing a simple green dress, emerged from her bedroom to find Jade munching on a chunk of buckwheat bread. The young doctor had changed from sweats to a turquoise blouse and khakis.

"This bread is amazing," praised the younger woman, with her mouth half full.

The grandmother beamed. "It was Yu-lan's favorite."

Jade tightened her lips, and nodded. Then, "By the way, Lu Mian, where do you grow the Quazhen?"

The grandmother shrugged. "You want to see it?"

Jade wrinkled her brow. "Wouldn't it all be covered in snow right now?"

"Sure. But that hardy little critter grows all year long. The snow doesn't even bother it." She shoved a small piece of bread into her mouth. She opened a narrow closet, and retrieved both her coat and Jade's. "Here. Let's take a look."

The two women put on coats, hats, and gloves, and then went outside. They tromped through two inches of snow, and headed for a large, wooded area behind Lu Mian's house. As they walked, Jade glanced back at the house, seeing its outside for the first time. Most of it was a simple, white square structure. But the ornate roof consisted of layered red tiles that extended to upward-bowing points, and gold trim lined the edge of the rooftop. It was a nice mixture of simple charm and elaborate elegance.

"About twenty meters into those woods is a small stream," said Lu Mian. We'll cross it, and then we'll come to a huge clearing. The Quazhen grows like wildfire in that clearing. Seriously, I've never seen any plant grow that fast; I'll harvest a hundred square meters of it in a day, and then two days later, the stuff is back again. It's amazing."

Jade nodded. "Wow. So you pretty much have an endless supply of it, don't you?"

"Yes." She grunted. "Enough to feed an entire American corporation for years and years."

Jade smirked dryly.

"So," asked Lu Mian, "people really got ill from my herb?"

"It wasn't really an illness, no." Jade described the peculiar personality changes and altered sex drives. She mentioned her belief that the limbic system was affected.

Lu Mian shrugged. "Fascinating. Unfortunate, but fascinating. Nobody in my family has ever suffered those consequences." She shook her head. "The limbic system? Perhaps. But to me, it sounds more like a disease of the spirit."

Jade looked at her quizzically. "A disease of the spirit?"

"Sure. There are diseases of the body, and diseases of the mind. Why shouldn't there be diseases of the spirit?"

Jade had no good answer. She was about to say that she had never heard about 'diseases of the spirit' in medical school. But not wanting another long philosophical discussion, she held her tongue.

Soon, the women were brushing through the wooded area. They came to the stream, an offshoot of the Yellow River, and crossed it. Then, they arrived at the clearing.

"Wow," whispered Jade. Before her, several acres of open, snowy ground was encircled by a ring of tall, thick trees. The enormous size of the clearing was impressive, but moreover, the perfectly circular shape of the bare earth gave the scene a very majestic feel. Perhaps most dazzling, however, was the purple sea of flowers emerging through the thin layer of snow. These sturdy plants reached up to the Chinese sky, like a field of purple soldiers looking toward the heavens.

Entranced, Jade slowly stepped forward, trying not to crush the thick flora with her boots. She knelt down, and carefully examined the beautiful Quazhen. Each flower had a lavender-colored central pistil, with six deep purple petals fanning out symmetrically. The petals were short, thick, and pointed, and their rich color gave the flower a regal appearance. The slender green stem of each flower was covered in thick, matted hair, and three or four pointed green leaves sprouted out from the sturdy stalk.

Jade was breathless as her eyes scanned the vast, purple sea of Quazhen. She felt a strange sense of tranquillity amidst the peculiar plants. At the same time, she was enveloped in a strong feeling of respect for these medicinal botanicals. After all, she was aware of their awesome—and frightening—power.

"Impressive, is it not?" whispered Lu Mian, as if they had stepped onto sacred ground.

Jade nodded. "It's one of the most beautiful sights I have ever seen."

Jade rose to her feet, and stood beside the grandmother. Together, they silently admired one of Nature's secret masterpieces.

But suddenly…

Crash!!!

The women jumped. They turned around in horror. That was the sound of breaking glass.

It had come from the house.

34

Her heart pounding, Jade quickly led Lu Mian back towards the house. The snow crunched loudly under their feet, as they quickly retraced their steps.

Jade stared ahead. She couldn't see any broken windows from here, a hundred feet away. With eyes wide open, she broke into a nervous trot. But Lu Mian quickly whispered a protest, and she immediately slowed back down to a brisk walk.

The women slowed down even further as they reached the side of the house. Cautiously, Jade crept along the outer white wall, avoiding any windows as she walked. Lu Mian did her best to stick behind the younger woman.

Soon, they arrived at the back porch. Jade considered going in, but then reconsidered. Perhaps, she reasoned, it would be better to walk around the entire outside perimeter first. Then, she could find which window—if any—had been broken.

She turned to the grandmother, and with a hushed voice, told her to remain put. Lu Mian obliged, and Jade crept forward, towards the next corner of the outside walls.

She rested for a moment against the corner of the house. She glanced back at Lu Mian, who was nervously hunched down near the back porch. She nodded to the older woman, and then slid around the corner.

Jade quickly scanned the windows of the new side. Within seconds, she spotted the smashed glass. A foot-wide jagged hole was punched through the window that led to Jade's temporary bedroom. She frowned. There was very little broken glass below the window, on the snow. Clearly, someone or something had smashed the glass from the outside, causing most of the splintering shards of glass to shatter inwards.

Jade swallowed hard. That hole was too small for someone to fit through. And she knew that both the front door and the back door were locked. That meant, she reasoned, that whoever had broken the window was still outside...

"Aaraugh!" She jumped, as both Jay and Brett suddenly appeared from around the corner, straight ahead.

Jay smiled. Casually strutting toward her, he shook his head and smiled. Brett was two steps behind him, wearing the more traditional 'tough guy' scowl.

"Doctor, Doctor, Doctor," Jay remarked. She instantly began to take backwards steps.

"Oh, come on now, Doc." He paused, and put his hand up to stop his companion. "What, are you afraid of *us*?" His was the same deep voice that had delivered both death threats.

Jade continued to step back. She was now within view of Lu Mian. She tried to inconspicuously flap her hand at the grandmother, motioning for her to run away. "Who are you guys?" she stammered.

Jay's face twisted into mock insult. "Doctor, dear. How can you forget our little fun on those Manchester streets? Surely, you remember my black truck? And Brett's blue Ford? And," he added, "you did just talk to me a few days ago."

She wrinkled her brow, still motioning for Lu Mian to bolt. "What do you mean, I just talked to you…"

"At my company, Doctor." He smiled widely. "You're looking at the new vice president of Botanicure." He raised both arms jovially.

She stared with wide eyes, completely stunned.

"By the way," he continued, "thanks for telling me you're coming here. How else would we know to come all the way here, just to kill you?" He glanced at her signaling hand. "Hey, who are you motioning to, Doc?"

Curious, he briskly walked forward. Brett followed. Gasping, Jade turned on her heels and bolted towards the back porch. Quickly on her tail, the two men charged forward.

"Come on!" she screamed to Lu Mian. "Get the door!" The grandmother jumped up, and after fidgeting with the key for a moment, managed to unlock the back door. With no second to spare, Jade sprinted inside, pulling Lu Mian with her. She quickly locked the door from the inside, a fraction of a second before Jay slammed into it. He violently rattled the doorknob, but it wouldn't give.

"Oh, hi grandma!" he yelled through the door's small glass window. "I should've figured she was talking to you." He continued to rattle the doorknob.

Lu Mian froze in terror.

"Listen, grandma. You know that little bitch you're with? She really isn't your friend. Because of her, we'll have to kill you, too."

Lu Mian started trembling. Jade squeezed her hand.

"You see," he continued, mockingly, "originally we weren't going to kill you for another year or so. I mean, obviously at some point, we needed to come and take over the ol' Quazhen farm. But we had planned to wait at least a year. Moving to China is a pretty big deal, you know; you can't just pack up and do it in a few days. Brett here still has to learn the whole damn language." He shook his head. "Another year would've been really good for you, you know grandma? I mean, chances are, you could've been dead by then anyway, old lady. Then, everybody would've been happy."

Brett muttered something to his companion.

"Good point," Jay said aloud. "Can you even understand me, old lady? Or do you only speak Chinese?"

Jade turned to the grandmother. "Lu Mian," she said softly but sternly. "*This* is why you need a working telephone."

Jade scanned the room for ideas. Quickly, she needed a plan!

Suddenly, another crash sounded from the back door. Brett's fist had fired through the door's small window. He was now grasping for the inside doorknob.

"Quick, follow me!"

Jade led the older woman into her small front foyer. "Lu Mian, where's your horse?"

The grandmother shook her head. "Yangshou is in the stable, a few hundred meters away."

Damn. Suddenly, she heard the back door slam open. She heard footsteps running into the house.

"Let's go!" she exclaimed, and whipped open the front door.

Jay stood at the front entryway, smiling and wielding his eight-inch knife.

"Aaraugh!" The women quickly turned around, but Brett was already standing behind them, in the foyer.

Jay marched in through the front door, shaking his head. "So sad, isn't it? You were so close, and yet—not to sound cliché—just so damn far." He raised his knife into the air.

Jade quickly put her back toward a wall, and sandwiched the shaking Lu Mian between her and the wall. She outstretched her hands.

"Look," she said firmly, as he approached her. "It's in your best interest to spare Lu Mian. Do you hear me? You'd be stupid to kill her!"

"Oh, really?" he asked mockingly.

"Yes!" she spat back. "You don't know how to grow Quazhen, do you?"

He didn't answer. He shot a glance at Brett, who returned a dumb stare.

"Quazhen doesn't exactly grow on trees, you idiot! It takes lots and lots of hard work. You have to cultivate the plant, to make it grow just right. To be honest, it takes years of experience to get the very delicate plant to grow properly. You kill Lu Mian, and you can kiss your little Botanicure supplement good-bye."

He stared at her, snarling. He shot a demonic look at the grandmother. "Is that true, old lady?"

Jade quickly stepped on her toe. "She doesn't speak any English, asshole." She stared at him squarely in the eyes.

He nodded. After a few frustrated moments, he smirked. "Well, old lady, I guess we'll need you around after all." He shot a glance at his partner. "Brett, tie her up in the kitchen, will ya?"

Grunting, the blond man roughly yanked Lu Mian out from behind Jade. The younger woman watched her helpless eyes as Brett took her wrist, and jerked her toward the kitchen.

Jade was alone with Jay. He moved closer to her, pressing her near the wall. Wearing a devil's smirk, he lowered the knife to his side, and looked into her hard eyes.

It was now or never, she thought.

"Listen," she said softly, "I don't even know your name."

He nodded. "Yes. That would be a shame. Could you imagine dying, and never knowing who killed you?" He chuckled. "Doctor, honey, my name is Jay Grose. I'll be your personal murderer today."

With seductive eyes and an open mouth, she suddenly leaned closer to him. "Jay," she whispered, "are you sure there's *nothing* I can do that would make you think twice about killing me?"

She had taken him by surprise. He looked down at her pretty face and shapely figure.

He grinned. "What'd you have in mind, Doc?"

She glanced up at him innocently, and shrugged.

Falling under her spell, he put his lips to her ear. She did all she could to keep from vomiting as he described his pleasures.

"Well," she whispered when he was through, "maybe we can arrange for that."

Grinning like a naughty schoolboy, Jay eagerly nodded at her. Pathetic, she thought! What a miserable, weak, and pathetic creature!

Seductively, she loosely slid her arms around his neck. With a flashy wink, she lowered her hands to his shoulders. He grinned as she then slowly rubbed her hands down his chest. She swung around her long, blond hair as she continued to feel down to his abdomen.

Anticipating his schoolboy fantasy, Jay momentarily looked up at the ceiling, smiled victoriously, and then closed his eyes.

Suddenly, Jade swung her arms outward and grabbed his hands.

"Hey!" Furious, he looked down and tried to writhe away from her grasp. But holding on tightly, she used all her strength to snap his hands back at the wrists.

"Aaaraugh!" He screamed out in pain as his hands were jolted back. Uncontrollably, he dropped the knife. "You bitch!" With a swift motion, he sprung his knee upward, slamming it into her stomach.

"Uh!" Bearing the pain, she pushed her weight into him, and threw him to the ground. As he tried to scamper back up, she quickly jumped forward, and landed her hard boot on his face.

Howling in pain, Jay violently swung his open hand at her leg. He caught her ankle, and with a swift jerk, tripped her to the ground.

"Brett! Brett, you idiot!" he cried. "Get in here!" Jay dived across the small foyer for his knife. But as he reached for it, Jade's hard boot slammed onto his outstretched arm. "Yeow!" She then kicked the knife out of the foyer, and into the connecting hallway.

In a rage, she threw herself toward him, and swung hard at his face; she landed a powerful punch in his left eye. As he cried out, she violently struck his chin with her other fist. In a sheer fury, she thrust another punch into his nose.

"Jay! What the hell!" Brett ran into the hallway. Seeing the struggle, he screamed out. "Die bitch!"

In a moment of terror, Jade looked up to see Brett lift the knife off the floor. He then growled at her with red eyes, and held back the weapon, poised to throw it at her.

In a wild effort to save herself, Jade screamed out in terror, and clutched Jay's hair from behind. In a moment of slow motion, she watched Brett fling the knife into the air, aiming directly at her. The knife spiraled forward, flying towards her chest. With all her strength, Jade yanked hard on Jay's hair, lifting his head into the air. She ducked behind him as she continued lifting.

"Blaaaraugh!!!" Jay spat out, as the knife burrowed itself deeply between his eyes. Like a open spigot, the deep wound spewed out a flood of dark red blood, and Jay's lifeless head fell from her grasp with a thump onto the foyer floor.

"No!" Brett covered his mouth with his hands, and stared at the dead body of his partner. With loathing eyes, he turned his demonic glare toward Jade.

In a mad frenzy, he sprinted into the foyer, his hands outstretched to tackle her neck. Screaming as he dashed forward, he was like a rabid animal pouncing on its prey.

"No!" cried Jade, desperately. She threw her hands up, and braced for his body's impact.

Bang! Bang! Bang!

The foyer window smashed to smithereens as three bullets penetrated Brett's skull. Blood spurting from his wounds, he dropped to the ground with a hard thud. His lifeless head smacked down onto Jay's foot.

Shaking violently with fright, Jade peered out the shattered window. Arlene Wu stood there smugly, her firearm still smoking.

35

Jade and Arlene quickly untied Lu Mian from a kitchen chair, and removed the dishtowel from her mouth. Immediately, the grandmother fell into Jade's arms, and began to sob.

The rest of the day would always be a blur to Jade, as would the subsequent week. Using her cellular phone, Arlene had called both the Chinese authorities, and the police back home in America. The Chinese authorities were less callous than Jade had imagined. After ascertaining the truth from Jade, Arlene, and Lu Mian, they quickly removed the dead bodies, and then provided the women with counselors. After two days, they allowed some American officials to come to the crime scene. Chief Preston, accompanied by several U. S. Marshals, arrived as soon as they were welcome. Preston's familiar face brought comfort to Jade and Arlene, and the U. S. Marshals brought them both security in this foreign country.

A few days after the whole episode, Lu Mian went to the forest clearing with a book of matches. Within minutes, the entire purple sea was burning in flames. Jade had stood beside her, solemnly watching it all burn.

A day after that, Jade and Arlene received word that after thirteen years in business, Botanicure was filing for bankruptcy.

And a week after the episode, Jade was sitting beside Arlene in the first class section of a large airplane. Finally, they were heading home. In the seats behind them, Chief Preston was chatting with a newly-made friend: Lu Mian Tang. Lu Mian decided that she wanted to be with her grandson, Yu-lan. And since Yu-lan's spirit always rode on the shoulders of Jade Evans, she realized that she had no choice but to follow them both back to America.

Epilogue:

Two Years Later

Jade grabbed the empty manila folder from its plastic holder, attached to the examining room door. Ah, a new patient, she realized.

She knocked on the door, and then proceeded inside. Seated before her was an older, heavyset woman, wearing thick make-up and sporting blue hair.

Jade extended her hand and smiled. "Ms. Kerabutski? I'm pleased to meet you. My name is Dr. Jade Harper."

A wide grin spread across the patient's face. She accepted the handshake. "Well, how do you do, Doctor? I'm Marla Kerabutski, and I'm very pleased to meet you."

Jade sat down on her familiar stool, and opened Marla's empty chart. "So, what can I do for you today?"

"Well, I'm looking for a new doctor. After two years with another fellow, I decided to fire him." Her round, blue eyes sparkled as she spoke. "His name was Dr. Zapola. Know him?"

"I do."

"What do you think of him?"

Jade put on an apologetic face. "Oh, Ms. Kerabutski, it's my policy not to comment on another physician—unless of course I'm praising that person."

Marla grinned. "Fine, fine. Well, I thought he was a jerk."

Jade couldn't suppress a slight grin; she had despised Jerome Zapola from the minute she had met him. The arrogant internist had personally insulted her on more than one occasion. He was the kind of old-school physician who insisted that all family doctors were incompetent, and that internists were the only 'real' adult primary care physicians.

"So," continued Jade, "does anything bother you today? Anything we can try to cure today?"

"No, not really; I'm actually feeling quite well. I'd just like a check-up."

"Very well," smiled Jade. "Then let me start by getting to know you." She put down her pen, sat back, and faced her new patient. "Tell me about yourself."

"Gee," she grinned. "Where do I begin?"

"Well, how about giving me some general information about yourself? And then share with me the details of a typical day for you."

Marla smiled, and launched into her life story. She talked about her years as a schoolteacher in the small town of Windham. She mentioned how she and her husband, Theodore, moved to Florida for their retirement. Marla spent some time reflecting upon beautiful Theodore; he had died five years ago next month, she said sadly. She said that she returned to Connecticut roughly two years ago, to be with her family.

Marla then turned to details about her typical day. She got up at six a.m. every day, and went for an hour-long walk outside. If the weather was bad, she would wait a few hours, and then walk around a local mall instead. Her breakfast usually consisted of cereal, toast, fruit, and juice. She would often have lunch with friends from church, and she spent her afternoons either visiting family, chatting with friends, or staying home to read or knit. For dinner, she enjoyed fish or chicken, rice or noodles, and lots of fresh vegetables. She would often watch the television before bed, and she'd then usually call it a day.

Jade listened attentively to her entire story. For the entire four minutes and seventeen seconds, she quietly listened, and did not interrupt.

Then, she smiled. "You sound quite healthy, Mrs. Kerabutski. That's excellent. Any health problems at all?"

Marla beamed. "Not a single one, Doctor. I am extra careful to take care of my body. Besides eating right and exercising regularly, I take my trusty vitamins and herbs."

Jade raised her eyebrows. "Is that right? Tell me, which vitamins and herbs do you take?"

"Uh-oh," she said lightheartedly, shrinking back in her chair. "You're going to tell me to stop taking those supplements, aren't you? Just like Dr. Zapola."

"No," Jade answered, quite firmly. "That's not necessarily true at all."

Marla grinned. "Well, I take a multivitamin, an extra vitamin E tablet, ginseng, ginkgo, and St. John's Wort. Oh, and there's also a new tonic on the shelves; it's called Wuzzoo. I take that, too. Oh, and I used to take this stuff called Quazhen, but that's been off the market for a couple of years."

Jade nodded, and smiled faintly. "How much of each?"

"One of each of them, each day."

"No, I mean what is the dosage of each?"

Marla wrinkled her brow. "Well, I don't really know their exact dosages."

Jade leaned closer. "Mrs. Kerabutski, I have no problem with you taking a dietary supplement, *if* you know exactly what you're taking, what you're taking it for, and how much you're taking. Many of these herbs do have their benefits; there's no question about that. In fact, in the past couple of years, I've started prescribing some herbs to patients."

The patient's make-up-caked face lit up. "Really, Doctor?"

"Yes," she answered matter-of-factly. "I've also referred patients to licensed acupuncturists, licensed naturopaths, and licensed homeopaths."

Marla smiled, delighted.

"*But*," continued Jade, "I always respect the fact that these herbs are drugs. There is no question about that. If the dose is slightly too high, an herb or vitamin can kill you. That is a fact."

Marla looked skeptical.

"Take Vitamin E," pressed Jade. "In high doses, it inhibits proper clotting, and you could bleed out. You could have intestinal bleeding, or even a stroke."

Marla raised her eyebrows.

"Also realize that many of these herbs have nasty side effects. And many of them interact with regular medicines that people take, making them very dangerous to use together. So, Mrs. Kerabutski, if you don't know what you're taking, why you're taking it, and how much you're taking, you are absolutely putting your life in danger."

"Gee," Marla said, alarmed, "I just take what's in the box. That can't hurt me, right?"

"Wrong. First of all, who knows what's 'in the box'? True, the FDA now requires a 'Supplement Facts' label on the packages of most dietary supplements; that gives some information. But I'm a bit skeptical about what those labels *really* tell you. For example, let's say that your so-called Wuzzoo pills each contain five grams of pure Wuzzoo; let's say that's written on the box. Well, who knows what five grams can do to you? Wuzzoo's manufacturer never had to prove to the FDA that it was safe. For all anyone knows, five grams of Wuzzoo could kill you."

Marla shook her head. "Well, how is any patient supposed to choose his or her own herbs? How do we learn how safe these things are?"

Jade smiled. "Get professional help. Some medical doctors are becoming more and more informed about herbal medicines. And there are naturopaths and herbalists who specialize in the stuff. My advice, Mrs. Kerabutski, is to never self-medicate. Don't self-medicate with regular drugs, and don't self-medicate with herbal drugs. I would always talk to a physician or a *licensed* naturopath first."

Marla nodded slowly, taking all of this in.

"In fact," continued Jade, "I happen to know a wonderful herbalist who has a thorough knowledge about these products. I would be happy to refer you to her."

Marla nodded. "I would appreciate that."

"Very well. Her name is Lu Mian Tang. She owns a small herbal boutique on Main Street in Manchester." Jade grabbed a small slip of paper, and scribbled down the address of Lu Mian's store.

Marla nodded. "Gosh. You seem pretty even-handed about these herbs. You're not against them, but you don't want patients to get hurt by them."

"Again, there's a lot that herbal medicine and other ancient healing systems can teach us. It's arrogant and irresponsible for American doctors to simply dismiss non-Western medicine as 'quackery'."

Marla grinned. "I think I'm going to like you, Dr. Harper."

The remainder of the examination went well. Marla got a clean bill of health, but was advised to stop the Wuzzoo, and to call in the dosages of the other pills.

"So I'll see you in six months for another check-up?" asked the blue-haired woman.

Jade smiled. "Actually, in six months I'll be on maternity leave."

Marla's face exploded with delight. "Oh Doctor! Congratulations!"

She beamed. "Thank you. Actually, it's a little more than maternity leave. I'll be out for a year. But you can schedule an appointment with my husband; I assure you he's fantastic."

"Ah, the other Dr. Harper."

"Yes. Last year, we decided to cut our individual patient loads in half. That way, while I'm home with the baby, he can take all of my patients. Then, after a year, he'll stay home for a year and I'll take over both sets of patients. We'll keep swapping time home and at work for a while."

"Sounds like you two have it all figured out."

Jade smiled as she walked Marla to the door. "We try. Yes, Mrs. Kerabutski, we try."

Appendix

A Brief Summary and Discussion of Past and Present Legislation Affecting Dietary Supplements

"It took a tragedy—poisoning caused by the use of an elixir of sulfanilamide—to prompt Congress to pass the Food, Drug, and Cosmetic Act of 1938, and it took reports of birth defects among the children of women who took thalidomide during pregnancy to secure passage of the Kefauver-Harris Amendments to that act in 1962. Congress has shown little interest in protecting consumers from the hazards of dietary supplements, let alone from the fraudulent claims that are made, since its members apparently believe that few of these products place people in real danger."

—Former FDA Commissioner David A. Kessler, MD, JD in a June 2000 editorial in the *New England Journal of Medicine*.[1]

"As for the safety of supplements, an interesting comparison was published last year; 106,000 people die a year from prescription drugs; 42,000 a year from automobile accidents. It is more likely that you will be struck by lightning and die in this country than it is that you will die from using a dietary supplement, with just 16 deaths reported from that last year."

—U. S. Representative Dan Burton, Chairman of the 106th Congress Committee on Government Reform, at a March 1999 hearing on dietary supplements.[2]

The role of dietary supplements in current American culture is unmistakably prominent. These supplements—broadly defined as vitamins, minerals, herbs, and other nutritive and non-nutritive food additives—are growing in popularity among Americans. In 1998, a well-respected research team found that nearly 20% of individuals taking prescription medicines are also consuming herbs, vitamin megadoses, or both.[3] Presumably, much of this heightened interest in dietary supplements is attributable to various scientific reports that suggest certain health benefits may be derived from specific supplements. For example, research has shown that vitamin E may protect against heart disease[4] and that ginkgo biloba may delay symptoms of dementia.[5] Despite these assertions, the precise dosage of a supplement required for a given desired effect is often unclear, and the validity of the scientific findings themselves is often called into question by newer studies. Unfortunately, such flaws in the scientific studies may go ignored by consumers.

Besides using supplements for specific health benefits, the public-at-large may seek a general health benefit from using them. One may believe that multivitamins provide essential nutrients that may be deficient in their diets. Or one may believe that certain herbs globally enhance well-being through as-yet-undefined mechanisms.

In addition to supplements providing both specific and general health benefits, however, their current popularity in America may exemplify a larger modern phenomenon: there is tremendous interest in complementary medicines of all kinds. According to the 1998 study quoted above, over 42% of Americans have recently used some form of alternative medicine for health maintenance or illness treatment[3]; this is increased from the 1993 estimate that 34% of our nation uses unconventional therapies.[6] The reasons for this explosive interest in alternative medicine remain unclear. In one study, a researcher suggested that higher education, poorer health status, a nontraditional worldview, or a specific cultural identity predicted alternative medicine use.[7] But even that study's author acknowledged that the widespread interest in integrative medicine exemplifies a complex human behavioral phenomenon, and therefore his predictors are actually limited in what they can really tell us.

Whatever the reason for the popularity of dietary supplements, one thing is clear: Americans are using them and other forms of unconventional medicine in increasing numbers. But in a time when dietary supplement sales have reached approximately $17 billion a year[8], a disturbing question arises: how safe are these supplements?

To answer that question effectively, one must consider the legislative history that pertains to the regulation of dietary supplements. The story begins with President Lincoln's appointment of a chemist, Charles Wetherill, to the new Department of Agriculture in 1862.[9]

Within the Department of Agriculture, Wetherill established the Bureau of Chemistry, an agency concerned with analyzing food, soil, fertilizer, and other agricultural products. One of the initial projects of this new bureau involved grape juice and winemaking. The bureau was given the charge to determine whether adding sugar to grape juice to increase a wine's alcohol content was legitimate. The issue had arisen from a growing concern over "adulterated" products in the national food supply. Indeed, the bureau found the winemaking practice to be legitimate (though this was later overruled by a court ruling that claimed the contrary).[10] This early federal inquiry is among the earliest examples of a federal investigation into specific foods or drugs.

Food adulteration investigations continued into the late nineteenth century. Members of the food industry were becoming increasingly concerned about the competition of their food products with new substances, such as oleomargarine's threat to butter. Because of this, Congress began to feel pressure to pass a Federal law against adulteration of foods.[11] At this same time, concerns were growing over fraud within the drug industry; specifically, the misbranding and adulteration of drugs was rampant.[12] Despite these concerns over food and drugs, however, strong opposition against federal regulation came from wealthy whiskey distillers and patent medicine firms. These groups argued that such regulation would put them out of business.[10] For many years, such opposition had the winning hand and the politicians' ears; bills that would regulate food and drugs were repeatedly defeated.

The appointment of an Indiana chemistry professor, Dr. Harvey W. Wiley, to chief chemist of the Bureau of Chemistry in 1883 turned the tides. Wiley became known as the "Crusading Chemist" in his passionate effort to urge Congress to pass legislation that would legislate food and drugs. His hard work paid off in 1906, when the Food and Drugs Act was passed, and then signed into law by President Theodore Roosevelt. The law prohibited interstate commerce of misbranded and adulterated food and drugs.[10]

Although the 1906 law was a victory for the regulation of food and drugs, it was a relatively weak piece of legislation. It required foods and drugs to be "pure", but it did not address the safety of those foods and drugs. Indeed, lawmakers seemed to ignore such safety issues for about thirty years.[12] In that time, however, a historic development occurred: the Bureau of Chemistry was divided into the nonregulatory Bureau of Chemistry and Soils, and the regulatory Food, Drug, and Insecticide Administration (soon thereafter shortened to the Food and Drug Administration).[9]

Unfortunately, after thirty years of paying little attention to the safety of food and drugs, a tragedy struck.

In 1937, an elixir was developed for the drug sulfanilamide; this was primarily for Southerners who preferred to drink their medicines. The product, which was sulfanilamide dissolved in diethylene glycol, underwent no animal toxicity testing prior to its marketing. In a tragic consequence, some 105 people died from acute kidney failure due to the poisonous diethylene glycol.[13] Albeit too late for those 105 victims, the elixir of sulfanilamide was recalled, and an enraged public cried for better drug regulation to ensure safer medicines.[12]

The result of the public outcry was the passage of the 1938 Federal Food, Drug, and Cosmetic Act, which was signed into law by President Franklin D. Roosevelt. The law required drug manufacturers to provide scientific proof about the safety of their products *before* those products reached the market.[14] After a few amendments were added in the subsequent years, the United States finally had solid legislation that regulated food and drugs: the burden of proving the safety of food and drugs rested with the manufacturers of those products. As such, many of the ill effects of unsafe medicines would be prevented; if a product was unsafe, it would not reach the market.[15]

The regulation of food and drugs became even stronger in 1962; unfortunately, however, it was another tragedy that precipitated more legislation. Thalidomide, a German sedative widely used in Europe, was found to be a very powerful teratogen. When thalidomide was taken during a critical phase of pregnancy, 30 to 40 percent of pregnant women gave birth to physically deformed babies. Although the drug was never marketed in the United States, further concerns regarding drug safety exploded in this country.[12] Such concerns paved the way for the Kefauver-Harris Drug Amendments in 1962. This legislation required manufacturers to prove the effectiveness of their drug products before they could market them in this country.[16, 17].

Legislation was now in place that required the drug industry to prove safety and efficacy of their products—including over-the-counter drugs, such as herbs—before they could sell them. Unfortunately, the Food and Drug Administration was left in the position to evaluate the industry's claims of safety and efficacy—a monstrous task. Evaluating all of the herbal medicines alone was daunting, let alone all of the non-herbal drugs. But the FDA made its attempt. In an arguably bold move, they attacked the labeling of herbal products across-the-board. They declared that if an herb's labeling claims were not in accordance with the FDA's research findings, that herb could simply be yanked from the market. As a result of such a threat, many herbal product manufacturers simply removed much of the information on their products' labels, and then claimed that their herbs were food, nutritional supplements, or food additives. In so doing, the herbs would not be subject to the FDA's declaration.[12] Of course, the herbal product manufacturers knew that consumers were often aware of the medicinal purpose of the herb; plenty of "outside literature" was available to guide the consumer in buying herbs for medicinal uses.

Unfortunately, then, the vagueness of many herbal products' identities—and the vagueness of their labels—arose, at least in part, from the FDA's attempt to regulate the herbal medicines. The notion of whether or not herbs were drugs consequently became much less clear, and the marketing of herbs as supplements or food additives became quite common.

After the 1906 Food and Drugs Act, the 1938 Federal Food, Drug, and Cosmetic Act, and the 1962 Kefauver-Harris Drug Amendments, the next most important piece of legislation affecting dietary supplements probably came about in 1990. The Nutrition Labeling and Education Act of 1990 was enacted to control questionable health claims made on food labels and in advertising. The act regulated food labels and brought some scientific validity to label claims.[18] Of note, the law did not directly affect the labeling of dietary supplements. Because of that, however, a Dietary Supplement Task Force was established by the FDA in 1991 to study possible label regulations on herbs.[12]

At the same time that the Dietary Supplement Task Force was established, Congress began considering two bills that would enhance the food and drug regulations already in place. They were the Food, Drug, Cosmetic, and Device Enforcement Amendments of 1991 and the Nutrition Coordinating Act of 1991.[19, 20] The passage of these bills would have meant, among other things, that tougher guidelines would have been implemented for advertising health claims for various dietary supplements.[21]

The herbal medicine industry became alarmed at the establishment of the task force and the consideration of the 1991 bills. They feared that their industry would become subjected to extensive government regulation, or worse, that the sales of dietary supplements could be stopped all together.[12] As a result, industry leaders led an intense campaign to express their frustrations over the issue to Congress. With large amounts of propaganda, health food retailers and consumers were urged to write to their representatives. Retailers were warned that they could be put out of business; consumers were told that the FDA might strip them of their right to buy vitamins.[21] As a result, members of Congress received more protest mail on this topic than any other issue since the Vietnam War.[12]

The result of the intense protests was a major victory for the dietary supplement industry: the passage of the Dietary Supplement Health and Education Act of 1994 (DSHEA). This act—the most important U. S. legislation regarding dietary supplements ever—defined dietary supplements, provided a presumption of their safety (unless proven otherwise by the FDA), provided guidelines for supplement labeling, mandated the development of good manufacturing practices, and established the Office of Dietary Supplements within the National Institutes of Health.[22] Of particular note for the manufacturers of herbal products, herbs were formally defined as dietary supplements under DSHEA. That meant that all of the protections given to vitamins, minerals, and other supplements under the new law were also extended to herbs.

It is a fact that under DSHEA, herbal medicines are not regulated as drugs. Indeed, they are categorized as supplements. The implications are impressive. For example, unlike non-herbal medicines, herbal medicines are presumed safe under DSHEA. As discussed above, non-herbal drug manufacturers must prove that their products are safe and effective before the federal government allows those products to reach the market. Manufacturers of herbal medicines, however, do not have to prove the safety or efficacy of their herbs before selling them. Furthermore, if an herb is suspected of being unsafe, the FDA must prove the lack of safety before it can remove that herb from the market.[22] The FDA must rely upon adverse event reporting, product sampling, and scientific literature to learn about potentially unsafe herbs and other supplements. The fact that thousands of herbs are on the market (and new products are continually arising) makes effective surveillance for unsafe herbs very difficult, if not impossible.[21] To worsen matters, the FDA staffs under two dozen people to monitor these supplements, which is an enormous task for such a light crew.[23] As a result, unsafe herbs are certainly on the market today. One small example of that fact is the recent finding that aristolochic acid—a known component of an herbal medicine currently marketed in the United States—is strongly associated with the development of urothelial (or urinary tract) cancer.[24]

Of note, the Secretary of Health and Human Services does has the authority to ban any dietary supplement if there is compelling evidence that it may cause an "imminent hazard" to public health or safety.[25] But this is an emergency power for cases of obvious harm. And like the FDA's regulatory power, this is a postmarketing measure; that is, serious harm would likely have occurred in consumers *before* the Secretary banned the product. Again, such power would be rarely used by the Secretary, as the FDA is by far the main watchdog against unsafe health products.

Of particular interest to this novel is the notion of "new dietary ingredients", as the fictional Quazhen would supposedly fit into that sub-category of dietary supplements. DSHEA defines "new dietary ingredients" as dietary ingredients (consumed products) that were "not marketed in the

United States before October 15, 1994 and does not include any dietary ingredient which was marketed in the United States before October 15, 1994".[22] Section 8 of DSHEA does state that dietary supplements with these so-called new dietary ingredients are considered adulterated unless one of two criteria are met: 1) those ingredients "have been present in the food supply as an article used for food in a form in which the food has not been chemically altered"[22], or 2) evidence of the supplements' safety has been provided to the federal government.[22] At first glance, this appears to provide strong regulation that would prevent a product like Quazhen from ever reaching consumers.

However, potential loopholes abound. As seen in the story, one could theoretically argue (in this author's opinion) that although Quazhen is a new dietary ingredient, it has been present in the food supply, and therefore is not subject to FDA approval under the first clause of DSHEA Section 8. The character Feng claimed that Quazhen was indeed used as a spice for years before its introduction as an herbal remedy. Therefore, one could argue that Quazhen's manufacturer (eg. Yu-lan Tang) would not need to notify the FDA before marketing the product. Indeed, in the September 23, 1997 Federal Register (the daily publication of various federal agencies, including the FDA), the Deputy Commissioner for Policy of the FDA reaffirmed the notion that if a supplement was once used in the food supply—and if it did not chemically alter that food supply—then the FDA did not need to be notified before the supplement was marketed.[26] The ultimate outcome of this hypothetical scenario involving Quazhen's legality in the American market would lie with the courts.

In *The Herb*, the lawyer Phil Santiago dismisses the above possibility, claiming that the courts would almost certainly rule that "food supply" means "U.S. food supply". If that was true, then to be legally marketed as a new dietary ingredient in the United States, the Tangs would need to register Quazhen with the FDA. They would need to provide evidence, according to DSHEA, of why they believe their product to be safe. They could submit virtually any information—including tests that *they* have performed (which could bias the tests), material documenting the history of Quazhen's use in China, or virtually any other evidence that they could muster. Then, they would have to wait at least 75 days before introducing Quazhen to the American market. However, after those 75 days, *whether or not the FDA has responded to their submission*, they could legally market Quazhen in this country. They would not have to wait for the administration to approve the product before marketing it, as long as the required 75 days had passed.[25, 27] It is evident, then, that the "safety" measures for new dietary supplements are much less stringent than those mandated for other pharmaceutical products. So even the most regulated dietary supplements—the newest ones—are very unregulated relative to regular medicines.

The quotation by Congressman Dan Burton that begins this appendix is worth considering. Burton pointed out that only sixteen deaths had been reportedly caused by dietary supplements in a recent year.[2] That figure is probably accurate. However, the key word is "reportedly". Between 1993 and 1999, approximately one hundred American deaths were reportedly associated with dietary supplements.[23] But how many more supplement-induced deaths went unreported? In a society in which much of the public construes supplements to be safe, how many times did a link between a supplement and a death go unnoticed? Furthermore, most harmful supplements presumably do not cause death. But they still cause injury. Quazhen, for example, never killed anyone in *The Herb*; however, it was clearly a harmful product in the American population. If the mark of a safe medicine was non-lethality, then the FDA would probably approve thousands of pharmaceutical products that are currently being denied due to safety concerns!

As discussed above, legislation in the middle of the twentieth century protected consumers from unsafe drugs by *preventing* unsafe drugs from ever entering the market. Legislation at the end of the twentieth century did the exact opposite with herbal medicines and other dietary supplements. Unsafe herbs are *not* prevented from entering the market; in fact, the main way to get unsafe herbs off the market is for the FDA to prove that they are unsafe. This could mean that the herbs have already hurt many consumers by the time they are declared unsafe. The rare exception to this rule is the small subset of so-called new dietary ingredients. But as discussed above, even new dietary supplements enjoy much less regulation than prescription and over-the-counter medicines in America.

As a final note, the purpose of *The Herb* is not to tear down the dietary supplement industry, nor is it to attack the enormous field of complementary medicine. In Part Four of the novel, the character Lu Mian offers many compelling reasons to be open-minded to non-Western medical therapies. To truly support complementary medicine, however, one must acknowledge the fact that herbal medicines are poorly regulated in America, and because of this, many unsafe herbs are on the market. Before America can fully embrace herbs into our medical armamentarium, we must embrace our moral and professional duty to monitor the safety and effectiveness of *any* medicine: natural, synthetic, or combined.

References

1. Kessler DA. Cancer and Herbs. New England Journal of Medicine 2000;342:1742-43.
2. Burton D. 106th Congress. Opening Statement; Committee on Government Reform; March 25, 1998.
3. Eisenberg DM, Davis RB, Ettner SL, et al. Trends in Alternative Medicine Use in the United States, 1990-1997. Journal of the American Medical Association1998;280:1569-75.
4. Stephens NG, Parsons A, Schofield PM, et al. Randomised Controlled Trial of Vitamin E in Patients with Coronary Disease: Cambridge Heart Antioxidant Study (CHAOS). The Lancent 1996;347:781-86.
5. Oken BS, Storzbach DM, Kaye JA. The Efficacy of Ginkgo biloba on Cognitive Function in Alzheimer Disease. Archives of Neurology 1998;55:1409-15.
6. Eisenberg DM, Kessler RC, Foster C, et al. Unconventional Medicine in the United States. New England Journal of Medicine 1993;328:246-52.
7. Astin JA. Why Patients Use Alternative Medicine: Results of a National Study. Journal of the American Medical Association 1998;279:1548-53.
8. U.S. Dietary Supplements Market Size Expressed as Dollar Sales by Top Six Product Categories for 1994 to 1998 and Forecast for 1999 and 2000. National Business Journal 2000; Dialog file No. 93, San Francisco: The Dialog Corporation, 2000.
9. Milestones in U.S. Food and Drug Law history. FDA Backgrounder. U.S. Food and Drug Administration Center for Food Safety and Applied Nutrition, May 1999.
10. Janssen WF. The Story of the Laws Behind the Labels, Part One: 1906 Food and Drugs Act. FDA Consumer. Food and Drug Administration, 1981.

11. Young JH. The Long Struggle for the 1906 Law. FDA Consumer. Food and Drug Administration, 1981.
12. Robbers JE, Tyler VE. Tyler's Herbs of Choice: the Therapeutic Use of Phytomedicinals. New York: The Haworth Herbal Press, 1999.
13. Leech PN, ed. Journal of the American Medical Association 1937;109:1531-39.
14. Federal Food, Drug, and Cosmetic Act of 1938. Pub. Law. 1938.
15. Janssen WF. The Story of the Laws Behind the Labels, Part Two: 1938—The Federal Food, Drug, and Cosmetic Act. FDA Consumer. Food and Drug Administration, 1981.
16. Kefauver-Harris Drug Amendments. Pub. Law. 1962.
17. Janssen WF. The Story of the Laws Behind the Labels, Part Three: 1962 Drug Amendments. FDA Consumer. Food and Drug Administration, 1981.
18. 101st Congress. Nutrition Labeling and Education Act of 1990. Pub. Law 101-535. 1990.
19. 102nd Congress. Food, Drug, Cosmetic, and Device Enforcement Amendments of 1991. H.R. 2597 SC. 1991.
20. 102nd Congress. Nutrition Advertising Coordination Act of 1991. H.R. 1662 SC2. 1991.
21. Barrett S. How the Dietary Supplement Health and Education Act of 1994 Weakened the FDA. http://www.quackwatch.com/02ConsumerProtection/dshea.html.
22. 103rd Congress. Dietary Supplement Health and Education Act of 1994. Pub. Law 103-417. 108 Stat. 4325. 1994.
23. Moore TJ. Big Trouble in the Health Store. http://www.thomasjmoore.com/pages/dietary_main.shtml.
24. Nortier JL, Muniz M-C, Schmeiser HH, et al. Urothelial Carcinoma Associated with the use of a Chinese Herb (*Aristolochia fangchi*). New England Journal of Medicine 2000:342:1686-92.
25. Henney JE. Statement by Jane E. Henney, M.D., Commissioner of Food and Drug Administration, before the Committee on

Government Reform, U.S. House of Representatives, March 25, 1999.

26. Schultz WB. Premarket Notification for a New Dietary Ingredient. Federal Register, Sept 23 1997;62:49886-892.
27. Levitt JA. Statement by Joseph A. Levitt, Esq., Director of Center for Food Safety and Applied Nutrition, Food and Drug Administration, before the Committee on Government Reform, U.S. House of Representatives, March 20, 2001.

This book is a work of fiction, although it is based upon fact. Except for certain historical information; people, events, and situations are purely fictional. Companies, agencies, and organizations in this work are largely fictional, but if real, are described in fictitious scenarios without intention to describe actual events. The herb Quazhen is entirely a product of the author's imagination.

Printed in the United States
745000001B